THE EYE OF GOD

JAMES ROLLINS

First published in Great Britain in 2013 by Orion Books,
an imprint of The Orion Publishing Group Ltd
Orion House, 5 Upper Saint Martin's Lane
London WC2H 9EA

An Hachette UK Company

1 3 5 7 9 10 8 6 4 2

A CIP catalogue record for this book is
available from the British Library.

ISBN (Hardback) 978 1 4091 1390 4
ISBN (Export Trade Paperback) 978 1 4091 1391 1
ISBN (Ebook) 978 1 4091 1392 8

Printed in Great Britain by Clays Ltd, St Ives plc

The Orion Publishing Group's policy is to use papers that are natural,
renewable and recyclable products and made from wood grown in
sustainable forests. The logging and manufacturing processes are expected
to conform to the environmental regulations of the country of origin.

www.orionbooks.co.uk

To Dad

Who gave us the wings . . . and all the sky to fly high

The distinction between the past, present and future is only a stubbornly persistent illusion.

—ALBERT EINSTEIN

ACKNOWLEDGMENTS

I could spend countless pages trying to list all the ways that the people below have helped in the creation of this book. Each name deserves a trumpet of praise of its own—if not the blast of a full brass section. But here we go. First, I must thank my first readers, my first editors, and some of my best friends: Sally Barnes, Chris Crowe, Lee Garrett, Jane O'Riva, Denny Grayson, Leonard Little, Scott Smith, Judy Prey, Will Murray, Caroline Williams, John Keese, Christian Riley, and Amy Rogers. And as always, a special thanks to Steve Prey for the handsome maps (now and in the past) . . . and to Cherei McCarter for all the cool tidbits that pop in my e-mail box! To Carolyn McCray, who inspires as much as she is a firm taskmaster when it comes to details . . . and David Sylvian for accomplishing everything and anything asked of him and for making sure I put my best digital foot forward at all times! To Avery and Josie Lim for helping with all things linguistic. To Shawna Coronado and everyone at the Fermi National Accelerator Lab (Fermilab) for arranging and allowing me to tour your amazing facility, where I was inspired and allowed to ask stupid questions. To everyone at HarperCollins for always having my back: Michael Morrison, Liate Stehlik, Danielle Bartlett, Kaitlyn Kennedy, Josh Marwell, Lynn Grady, Richard Aquan, Tom Egner, Shawn Nicholls, and Ana Maria Allessi. Last, of course, a special acknowledgment to the people instrumental to all levels of production: my editor, Lyssa Keusch, and her colleague Amanda Bergeron; Laurie McGee for her sharp copyediting eye; and my agents, Russ Galen and Danny Baror (and his daughter Heather Baror). And as always, I must stress that any and all errors of fact or detail in this book fall squarely on my own shoulders, of which hopefully there are not too many.

EURASIA

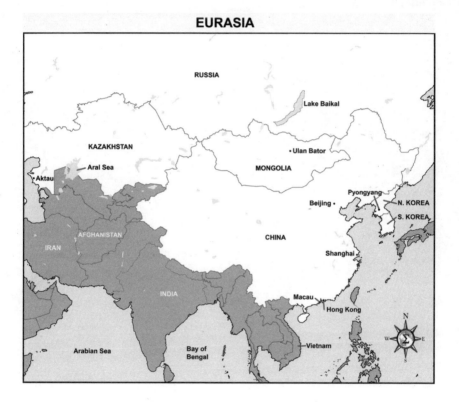

NOTES FROM THE
HISTORICAL RECORD

WHAT IS THE TRUTH? When it comes to the *past,* that's a difficult question to answer. Winston Churchill once stated that *History is written by the victors.* If he's right, then what historical document can truly be trusted? What has been written down only goes back some six thousand years, tracking only the briefest steps of humans on this planet. And even that record is full of gaps turning history into a frayed and moth-eaten tapestry. Most remarkable of all, down those ragged holes many of history's greatest mysteries have been lost, waiting to be rediscovered—including events that mark pivotal shifts in history, those rare moments that change civilizations.

One such moment occurred in AD 452, when the ravaging forces of Attila the Hun swept through northern Italy, destroying all in their wake. Ahead of his barbarian horde, Rome was all but defenseless, sure to fall. Pope Leo I rode out of Rome and met Attila along the banks of Lake Garda. They spoke in private, in secret, with no written record of what transpired. After that meeting, Attila turned away from certain victory, from the very sacking of Rome by his barbarians, and promptly left Italy.

• • •

Why? What had transpired at that conclave to turn Attila away from certain victory? History holds no answer.

Turn this page to discover how close we came to destroying ourselves, a lost moment in time when Western civilization itself came close to shattering upon the point of a sword—a blade known as the Sword of God.

NOTES FROM THE SCIENTIFIC RECORD

WHAT IS REALITY? It's both the simplest question to answer—and the hardest. Over the ages, it has baffled both philosophers and physicists. In *The Republic,* Plato described the *true* world as nothing more than a flickering shadow on a cave wall. Oddly enough, millennia later, scientists have come full circle to a similar conclusion.

The very page this is written upon (or the e-reader in hand) is made mostly of *nothing.* Stare more deeply at what appears solid, and you discover a reality made up of masses of atoms. Tease apart those atoms, and you find a tiny hard nucleus of protons and neutrons, encircled by empty shells that hold a few orbiting electrons. But even those fundamental particles can be split tinier: into quarks, neutrinos, bosons, and so on. Venture deeper yet, and you enter a bizarre world occupied only by vibrating strings of energy, which perhaps may be the true source of the *fire* that casts Plato's shivering shadows.

The same strangeness occurs if you stare *outward,* into the night sky, into a vastness beyond comprehension, a boundless void dotted by billions of galaxies. And even that enormity may just be *one* universe among many, expanding ever outward into a multiverse. And what of our own universe? The newest conjecture is that all that we experience—from the tiniest vibrating string of energy to that massive galaxy spinning around a maelstrom of reality-ripping black holes—may be nothing more than a *hologram,* a three-dimensional illusion that, in fact, we may all be living in a created simulation.

Could that be possible? Could Plato have been right all along: *that we are blind to the true reality around us, that all we know is nothing more than the flickering shadow on a cave wall?*

Turn this page (if it is a *page*) and discover the frightening truth.

THE EYE OF
GOD

PROLOGUE

Summer, AD 453
Central Hungary

The king died too slowly atop his wedding bed.

The assassin knelt over him. The daughter of a Burgundy prince, she was the king's seventh wife, newly wed the night prior, bound to this barbarian lord by force of marriage and intrigue. Her name, Ildiko, meant *fierce warrior* in her native tongue. But she did not feel fierce as she quailed beside the dying man, a bloody tyrant who had earned the name *Flagellum Dei,* the *Scourge of God,* a living legend who was said to wield the very sword borne by the Scythian god of war.

His name alone—*Attila*—could open city gates and break sieges, so mightily was he feared. But now, naked and dying, he seemed no more fearsome than any other man. He stood little taller than her, though he was weighted down with thick muscle and the heavy bones of his nomadic people. His eyes—wide parted and deep set—reminded her of a pig's, especially as he had stared blearily upon her, rutting into her during the night, his eyes stitched red from the many cups of wine he had consumed at their wedding feast.

Now it was her turn to stare down upon him, measuring each gurgling gasp, trying to judge how long until death claimed him. She knew now she had been too sparing with the poison given to her by the bishop of Valence, passed through him by the archbishop of Vienne, all with the approval of King Gondioc de Burgondie. Fearing the tyrant might taste the bitterness of the poison in his bridal cup, she had been too timid.

She clutched the glass vial, half empty now, sensing other hands, higher even than King Gondioc, in this plot. She cursed that such a burden should come to rest in her small palms. How could the very fate of the world—both now and in the future—fall to her, a woman of only fourteen summers?

Still, she had been told of the necessity for this dark action by a cloaked figure who had appeared at her father's door a half-moon ago. She had already been pledged to the barbarian king, but that night, she was brought before this stranger. She caught the glimpse of a cardinal's gold ring on his left hand before it was hidden away. He had told her the story then—only a year past—of Attila's barbarian horde routing the northern Italian cities of Padua and Milan, slaughtering all in their path. Men, women, children. Only those who fled into the mountains or coastal swamps survived to tell the tale of his brutality.

"Rome was doomed to fall under his ungodly sword," the cardinal had explained to her beside her family's cold hearth. "Knowing this sure fate as the barbarians approached, His Holiness Pope Leo rode out from his earthly throne to meet the tyrant on the banks of Lake Garda. And upon the strength of his ecclesiastical might, the pontiff drove the merciless Hun away."

But Ildiko knew it wasn't *ecclesiastical might* alone that had turned the barbarians aside—but also the superstitious terror of their king.

Full of fear herself now, she glanced over to the box resting atop a dais at the foot of the bed. The small chest was both a gift and a threat from the pontiff that day. It stretched no longer than her forearm and no higher, but she knew it held the fate of the world inside. She feared touching it, opening it—but she would, once her new husband was truly dead.

She could handle only one terror at a time.

Fearful, her gaze flickered over to the closed door to the royal wedding chamber. Through a window, the skies to the east paled with the promise of a new day. With dawn, his men would soon arrive at the bedchamber. Their king must be dead before then.

She watched the blood bubbling out of his nostrils with each labored breath. She listened to the harsh gurgle in his chest as he lay on his back. A weak cough brought more blood to his lips, where it flowed through his forked beard and pooled into the hollow of his throat. The beating of his heart could be seen there, shimmering that dark pool with each fading thud.

She prayed for him to die—and quickly.

Burn in the flames of hell where you belong . . .

As if heaven heard her plea, one last rough breath escaped the man's flooded throat, pushing more blood to his lips—then his rib cage sagged a final time and rose no more.

Ildiko cried softly in relief, tears springing to her eyes. The deed was done. The Scourge of God was at last gone, unable to wreak more ruin upon the world. And not a moment too soon.

Back at her father's house, the cardinal had related Attila's plan to turn his forces once again toward Italy. She had heard similar rumblings at the wedding feast, raucous claims of the coming sack of Rome, of their plans to raze the city to the ground and slaughter all. The bright beacon of civilization risked going forever dark under the barbarians' swords.

But with her one bloody act, the *present* was saved.

Still, she was not done.

The *future* remained at risk.

She shimmied on her bare knees off the bed and moved to its foot. She approached the small chest with more fear than she had when she slipped the poison into her husband's drink.

The outer box was made of black iron, flat on all sides with a hinged top. It was unadorned, except for an inscribed pair of symbols on its surface. The writing was unknown to her, but the cardinal had told her what to expect. It was said to be the language of Attila's distant ancestors, those nomadic tribes far to the east.

She touched one of the inscriptions, made of simple straight lines.

"Tree," she whispered to herself, trying to gain strength. The symbol even looked somewhat like a tree. She touched its matching neighbor—a *second* tree—with great reverence.

Only then did she find the strength to bring her fingers to the chest's lid and swing it open. Inside, she discovered a second box, this one of the brightest silver. The inscription on top was similarly crude, but clearly done with great purpose.

The simple strokes meant *command* or *instruction*.

Sensing the press of time, she steadied her shaking fingers and lifted the silver box's lid to reveal a *third* coffer inside, this one of gold. Its surface shimmered, appearing fluid in the torchlight. The symbol carved here looked like a union of the earlier characters found inscribed in iron and silver, one stacked atop the other, forming a new word.

The cardinal had warned her of the meaning of this last mark.

"*Forbidden,*" she repeated breathlessly.

With great care, she opened the innermost box. She knew what she would find, but the sight still shivered the small hairs along her arms.

From the heart of the gold box, the yellowed bone of a skull glowed out at her. It was missing its lower jaw, its empty eye staring blindly upward, as if to heaven. But like the boxes themselves, the bone was also adorned with script. Lines of writing descended down from the crown of the skull in a tight spiral. The language was not the same as atop the triple boxes, but instead it was the ancient script of the Jews—or so the cardinal had told her. Likewise, he had instructed her on the purpose of such a relic.

The skull was an ancient object of Jewish incantation, an invocation to God for mercy and salvation.

Pope Leo had offered up this treasure to Attila with a plea for *Rome's* salvation. Additionally, the pontiff had warned Attila that this potent talisman was but one of many that were secured in Rome and protected by God's wrath, that any who dared breach its walls were doomed to die. To press his point, the pope offered up the story of the leader of the Visigoths, King Alaric I, who had sacked Rome forty years prior and died upon leaving the city.

Leery of this curse, Attila took heed and fled out of Italy with this precious treasure. But as in all things, it seemed time had finally tempered those fears, stoking the Hun's desire to once again lay siege to Rome, to test his legend against God's wrath.

Ildiko stared across his prostrate body.

It appeared he had already failed that trial.

Ultimately, even the mighty could not escape death.

Knowing what she had to do, she reached for the skull. Still, her eyes fell upon the scratches at the center of the spiral. The skull's invocation was a plea for salvation against what was written there.

It marked the date of the end of the world.

The key to that fate lay beneath the skull—hidden by iron, silver, gold, and bone. Its significance only came to light a moon ago, following the arrival of a Nestorian priest from Persia to the gates of Rome. He had heard of the gift given to Attila from the treasure vaults of the Church, a gift once passed to Rome by Nestorius himself, the patriarch of Constantinople. The priest told Pope Leo the truth behind the nest of boxes and bone, how it had come from much farther east than Constantinople, sent forward to the Eternal City for safekeeping.

In the end, he had informed the pope of the box's *true* treasure—along with sharing the name of the man who had once borne this skull in life.

Ildiko's fingers touched that relic now and trembled anew. The empty eyes seemed to stare into her, judging her worth, the same eyes that, if the Nestorian spoke truthfully, had once looked upon her Lord in life, upon Jesus Christ.

She hesitated at moving the holy relic—only to be punished for her reluctance with a knock on the chamber door. A guttural call followed. She did not understand the tongue of the Huns, but she knew that Attila's men, failing to gain a response from their king, would soon be inside.

She had delayed too long.

Spurred now, she lifted the skull to reveal what lay below—but found *nothing*. The bottom of the box held only a golden imprint, in the shape of what had once rested here, an ancient cross—a relic said to have fallen from the very heavens.

But it was gone, stolen away.

Ildiko stared over at her dead husband, a man known as much for his keen strategies as for his brutalities. It was also said he had ears under every table. Had the king of the Huns learned of the mysteries shared by the Nestorian priest in Rome? Had he taken the celestial cross for his own and hidden it away? Was that the true source of his sudden renewed confidence in sacking Rome?

The shouting grew louder outside, the pounding more urgent.

Despairing, Ildiko returned the skull to its cradle and closed the boxes. Only then did she sink to her knees and cover her face. Sobs shook through her as the planks of the doors shattered behind her.

Tears choked her throat as thoroughly as blood had her husband's.

Men shoved into the room. Their cries grew sharper upon seeing their king upon his deathbed. Wailing soon followed.

But none dared touch her, the grieving new wife, as she rocked on her knees beside the bed. They believed her tears were for her fallen husband, for her dead king, but they were wrong.

She wept for the world.

A world now doomed to burn.

Present Day
November 17, 4:33 P.M. CET
Rome, Italy

It seemed even the stars were aligned against him.

Bundled against the winter's bite, Monsignor Vigor Verona crossed through the shadows of Piazza della Pilotta. Despite his heavy woolen sweater and coat, he shivered—not from the cold but from a growing sense of dread as he stared across the city.

A blazing comet shone in the twilight sky, hovering above the dome of St. Peter's, the highest point in all of Rome. The celestial visitor—the brightest in centuries—outshone the newly risen moon, casting a long, scintillating tail across the stars. Such sights were often historically viewed as harbingers of misfortune.

He prayed that wasn't the case here.

Vigor clutched the package more tightly in his arms. He had rewrapped it clumsily in its original parcel paper, but his destination was not far. The towering façade of the Pontifical Gregorian University rose before him, flanked by wings and outbuildings. Though Vigor was still a member of the Pontifical Institute of Christian Archaeology, he only taught the occasional class as a guest lecturer. He now served the Holy See as the prefect of the Archivio Segretto Vaticano, the Vatican's secret archives. But the burden he carried now came to him not in his role as professor or prefect, but as friend.

A gift from a dead colleague.

He reached the main door to the university and marched across the white marble atrium. He still kept an office at the school, as was his right.

In fact, he often came here to catalog and cross-reference the university's vast book depository. Rivaling even the city's National Library, it held over a million volumes, housed in the adjacent six-story tower, including a large reserve of ancient texts and rare editions.

But nothing here or at the Vatican's Archives compared to the volume Vigor carried now—nor what had accompanied it in the parcel. It was why he had sought the counsel of the only person he truly trusted in Rome.

As Vigor maneuvered stairs and narrow halls, his knees began to complain. In his midsixties, he was still fit from decades of archaeological fieldwork, but over the past few years, he had been too long buried in the archives, imprisoned behind desks and stacks of books, shackled by papal responsibility.

Am I up for this task, my Lord?

He must be.

At last, Vigor reached the university's faculty wing and spotted a familiar figure leaning against his office door. His niece had beaten him here. She must have come straight from work. She still wore her Carabinieri uniform of dark navy slacks and jacket, both piped in scarlet, with silver epaulettes on her shoulders. Not yet thirty, she was already a lieutenant for the Comando Carabinieri Tutela Patrimonio Culturale, the Cultural Heritage Police, who oversaw the trafficking of stolen art and relics.

Pride swelled through him at the sight of her. He had summoned her as much out of love as for her expertise in such matters. He trusted no one more than her.

"Uncle Vigor." Rachel gave him a quick hug. She then leaned back, finger-combing her dark hair back over one ear and appraising him with those sharp caramel eyes. "What was so urgent?"

He glanced up and down the hall, but at this hour on a Sunday, no one was about, and all of the offices appeared dark. "Come inside and I'll explain."

Unlocking the door, he ushered her across the threshold. Despite his esteemed position, his office was little more than a cramped cell, lined by towering cases overflowing with books and stacks of magazines. His small desk rested against the wall under a window as thin as a castle's arrow slit. The newly risen moon cast a silver shaft into the chaos found here.

Only after they were both inside and the door closed did he risk clicking on a lamp. He let out a small sigh of relief, reassured and comforted by the familiar.

"Help me clear a space on my desk."

Once that was done, Vigor placed his burden down and folded back the brown parcel wrap, revealing a small wooden crate.

"This arrived for me earlier today. With no return address, only the name of the sender."

He turned back a corner of the wrapping to show her.

Fr. Josip Tarasco

"Father Josip Tarasco," Rachel read aloud. "Am I supposed to know who that is?"

"No, nor should you." He stared over at her. "He was declared dead over a decade ago."

Her brows pinched, and her posture stiffened. "But the package is too pristine to have been lost in the mail for that long." She turned that discerning gaze back on him. "Could someone have forged his name as some cruel hoax?"

"I don't see why. In fact, I think that's why the sender addressed this package by hand. So I could verify it came from Father Tarasco. We were dear friends. I compared the writing on the parcel to a smattering of old letters still in my possession. The handwriting matched."

"So if he's still alive, why was he declared dead?"

Vigor sighed. "Father Tarasco vanished during a research trip to Hungary. He was preparing a comprehensive paper on the witch hunts there during the early eighteenth century."

"Witch hunts?"

Vigor nodded. "Back in the early 1700s, Hungary was beset by a decade-long drought, accompanied by famine and plague. A scapegoat was needed, someone to blame. Over four hundred accused witches were killed in a span of five years."

"And what about your friend? What became of him?"

"You must understand, when Josip left for Hungary, the country had only recently shaken free of Soviet control. It was still a volatile time there, a dangerous place to be asking too many questions, especially in rural areas. The last I heard from him was a message left on my machine. He said he was on to something disturbing concerning a group of twelve witches—six women and six men—burned in a small town in southern Hungary. He sounded both scared and excited. Then nothing after that. He was never heard from again. Police and Interpol investigated for a full year. After an additional four years of silence, he was finally declared dead."

"So then he must have gone into hiding. But why do that? And more important, *why* surface a decade later, why now?"

With his back to his niece, Vigor hid a smile of pride, appreciating Rachel's ability to get to the heart of the matter so quickly.

"The answer to your last question seems evident from what he sent," he said. "Come see."

Vigor took a deep breath and opened the hinged lid of the crate. He carefully removed the first of the package's two objects and placed it in the shaft of moonlight atop his desk.

Rachel took an involuntary step backward. "Is that a skull? A *human* skull?"

"It is."

She moved past her initial surprise to step closer. She quickly noted the hen-scratched inscription across the bone of the cranium, following the spiral of its course with a fingertip without touching.

"And this writing?" she asked.

"Jewish Aramaic. I believe this relic is an example of early Talmudic magic practiced by Babylonian Jews."

"Magic? Like witchcraft?"

"In a way. Such spells were wards against demons or entreaties for help. Over the years, archaeologists have unearthed thousands of such artifacts—mostly incantation bowls, but also a handful of skulls like this. The Berlin museum holds two such relics. Others are in private hands."

"And this one? You said Father Tarasco had an interest in witches, which I assume extended to an interest in occult objects."

"Perhaps. But I don't think this one is *authentic*. The practice of Talmudic magic started in the third century and died out by the seventh." Vigor waved his hand over the skull as if casting his own spell. "I suspect this artifact is not that old. Maybe thirteenth or fourteenth century at best. I've sent a tooth to the university lab to confirm my estimate."

She slowly nodded, contemplating in silence.

"But I also studied the writing here," he continued. "I'm well familiar with this form of Aramaic. I found many blatant mistakes in the transcription—reversed diacritics, wrong or missing accent marks—as if someone made a poor copy of the original inscription, someone who had no true understanding of this ancient language."

"So the skull is a forgery then?"

"In truth, I suspect there was no foul intent in its crafting. I think its forging was less about *deception* than it was about *preservation*. Someone feared the knowledge found here might be lost, so he or she hand made copies, trying to preserve something more ancient."

"What knowledge?"

"I'll get to that in a moment."

He reached into the crate and removed the second object and placed it beside the skull on the table. It was an ancient book, as wide as his outstretched hand and twice as tall. It was bound in rough leather, the pages secured by crude stitches of thick cord.

"This is an example of *anthropodermic bibliopegy*," he explained.

Rachel screwed up her face. "And that means . . . ?"

"The book is bound in *human* skin and sewn with sinew of the same."

Rachel took a step away again, only this time she didn't return to the desk. "How can you know that?"

"I can't. But I forwarded a sample of the leather to the same lab as the skull, both to test its age and its DNA." Vigor picked up the macabre volume. "But I'm sure I'm correct. I examined this under a dissection microscope. Human pores are distinctly different in size and even shape from that found in pigskin or calfskin. And if you look closer, in the center of the cover—"

He drew a fingernail along what appeared to be a deep crease in the center of the cover.

"Under proper magnification, you can still make out the follicles of eyelashes."

Rachel paled. "Lashes?"

"On the cover is a human *eye,* sewn shut with finer threads of sinew."

Visibly swallowing, his niece asked, "So what is this? Some text of the occult?"

"I thought as much, especially considering Josip's interest in the witches of Hungary. But no, it's not some demonic manuscript. Though in some circles, the text is considered blasphemous."

He carefully parted the cover, cautious not to overly stress the binding. He revealed pages written in Latin. "It's actually a Gnostic book of the Bible."

Rachel tilted her head, well versed in Latin, and translated the opening words " '*These are the secret sayings which the living Jesus spoke . . .*' " She glanced over at him, recognizing those words. "It's the Gospel of Thomas."

He nodded. "The saint who doubted Christ's resurrection."

"But why is it wrapped in human skin?" she said with disgust. "Why would your missing colleague send you such ghoulish items?"

"As a warning."

"A warning against what?"

Vigor returned his attention to the skull. "The incantation written here is a plea to God to keep the world from ending."

"While I certainly appreciate that plea, what does—?"

He cut his niece off. "The prophetic date for that coming apocalypse is also written atop the skull, in the center of the spiraling inscription. I converted that figure from the ancient Jewish calendar to today's modern accounting." He touched the center of the spiral. "This is why Father Josip came out of hiding and sent these items to me."

Rachel waited for him to explain.

Vigor glanced out the window to the comet glowing in the night sky, bright enough to shame the moon. With that portent of doom hanging there, a shiver of certainty rang through him. "The date for the end of the world . . . *it's in four days.*"

FIRST

CRASH & BURN

1

Panic had already begun to set in.

From the observation deck above the control room, Painter Crowe read the distress in the sudden cessation of idle chatter among the technicians in the room. Nervous glances spread up the chain of command and across the floor of the Space and Missile Systems Center. Only the base's top brass were in attendance at this early hour, along with a few heads of the Defense Department's research divisions.

The floor below them looked like a scaled-down version of NASA's flight control room. Rows of computer consoles and satellite control desks spread outward from a trio of giant LCD screens affixed to the back wall. The centermost screen showed a map of the world, traced with glowing lines that tracked the trajectories of a pair of military satellites and the path of the neighboring comet.

The two flanking screens showed live feed from the satellites' cameras. To the *left,* a curve of the earth slowly churned against the backdrop of space. To the *right,* the glowing blaze of the comet's tail filled the screen, casting a veil over the stars beyond it.

"Something's gone wrong," Painter whispered.

"What do you mean?" His boss stood beside him atop the observation deck.

General Gregory Metcalf was the head of DARPA, the Defense Department's research-and-development agency. Dressed in full uniform, Metcalf was in his fifties, African-American, and a West Point grad.

In contrast, Painter simply sported a black suit, made more casual with a pair of cowboy boots. They were a gift from Lisa, who was on a research trip in New Mexico. Half Native American, he probably should have balked at wearing the boots, but he liked them, especially as they reminded him of his fiancée, gone now a full month.

"Something's got the OSO spooked," Painter explained, pointing to the operations support officer in the second row of consoles down below.

The lead mission specialist moved over to join his colleague at that station.

Metcalf waved dismissively. "They'll handle it. It's their job. They know what they're doing."

The general promptly returned to his conversation with the commander of the 50th Space Wing out of Colorado Springs.

Still concerned, Painter kept a keen eye on the growing anxiety below. He had been invited here to observe this code-black military mission not only because he was the director of Sigma, which operated under the aegis of DARPA, but also because he had personally engineered a piece of hardware aboard one of the two military satellites.

The pair of satellites—*IoG-1* and *IoG-2*—had been sent into space four months ago. The acronym for the satellites—*IoG*—stood for Interpolation of the Geodetic Effect, a name originally coined by the military physicist who had engineered this project for a gravitational study. He had intended to do a complete analysis of the space-time curvature around the earth to aid in satellite and missile trajectory.

While already an ambitious undertaking, the discovery of the comet by a pair of amateur astronomers two years ago quickly shifted the project's focus—especially after an anomalous energy signature had been detected out there.

Painter glanced sidelong to his neighbor on his left, noting the lithe form of the researcher from the Smithsonian Astrophysical Observatory.

Only twenty-three, Dr. Jada Shaw was tall, with a runner's lean physique. Her skin was a flawless dark mocha, her black hair trimmed short, highlighting the long curve of her neck. She stood in a white lab coat and jeans, with her arms crossed, nervously chewing the edge of her thumbnail.

The young astrophysicist had been whisked from Harvard seventeen months ago and ensconced in this code-black military venture. Clearly she still felt out of her league, though she was doing her best to hide it.

It was unfortunate. She had no reason to be so nervous. She had already won international recognition for her work. Using quantum equations—calculations well above Painter's intellectual pay grade—she had crafted an unusual theory concerning *dark energy,* the mysterious force that made up three-quarters of the universe and was responsible for its accelerating cosmic expansion.

Further proving her prowess, she had been the only physicist to note the small anomalies in the approach of this celestial visitor blazing in the night sky—a comet designated as IKON.

A year and a half ago, Dr. Shaw had tapped into the digital feed of the new Dark Energy Camera, a 570-megapixel array engineered by the Fermilab here in the States and installed at a mountaintop observatory in Chile. Using that camera, Dr. Shaw had tracked the comet's passage. It was there that she had discovered anomalies that she believed might be proof that the comet was shedding or disturbing dark energy in its wake.

Her work quickly became cloaked under the guise of national security. A new energy source such as this had vast and untapped potential—both economically and militarily.

From that moment forward, the ultrasecret *IoG* project was repurposed for one goal only: to study the potential dark energy of the comet. The plan was to fly *IoG-2* across the comet's blazing tail, where it would attempt to absorb that anomalous energy detected by Dr. Shaw and transmit it back to its sister craft orbiting the earth.

Luckily, to accomplish this task, engineers had to only slightly modify the earlier mission satellite. A part of its original design included a perfect sphere of quartz buried in its heart. The plan had been to set that sphere to spinning once the satellite was in orbit, creating a gyroscopic effect that could be used to map the curve of space-time around the mass of Earth. If the experiment was successful, the beam of dark energy from one spacecraft to the other should cause a minute disturbance in that curve of space-time.

It was a bold experiment. Even the acronym *IoG* was now jokingly referred to as the *Eye of God*. Painter appreciated the new nickname, picturing that whirling perfect sphere as it waited to peer into the mysteries of the universe.

The lead specialist called out. "Spacecraft will be entering the tail in *ten*!"

As the final countdown began, Dr. Shaw's eyes remained fixed to the flow of data on the giant screen.

"I hope you were mistaken earlier, Director Crowe," she said. "About something going wrong here. Now is not the time for mistakes, not when we're tapping into energy connected to the birth of our universe."

Either way, Painter thought, *there was no turning back now.*

7:55 A.M.

Over the course of six painstaking minutes, the flight path of *IoG-2* slowly vanished deeper into the ionizing stream of gas and dust. The screen to the right—running live feed from the satellite's camera—was a complete whiteout. They were now flying blind, entirely reliant on telemetry data.

Painter tried taking in everything at once, catching the room's excitement, sensing the historical significance of this moment.

"I'm registering an energy spike in *IoG-2*!" the EECOM tech called from his station.

A smatter of small cheers broke out, but the pressure of the moment quickly quashed them. The reading could be an error.

All eyes swung to another console, to the aerospace engineer monitoring *IoG-1*. He shook his head. There seemed to be no evidence that the energy picked up by the first satellite had been transmitted to its Earth-orbiting twin—then suddenly the engineer jerked to his feet.

"Got something!" he yelled.

The SMC control officer hurried over to his side.

As everyone waited for confirmation, Dr. Shaw pointed to the world map, to the scroll of telemetry data. "So far it looks promising."

If you say so . . .

The crawl of incoming data was incomprehensible to him. And it only continued to flow faster. After another tense minute, the flood of data grew to a blur.

The EECOM tech popped to his feet. Warnings and error messages flashed on his screens as he continued to monitor *IoG-2*'s passage through the comet's tail. "Sir, energy levels here are off the map now, redlining across the board! What do you want me to do?"

"Shut it down!" the control officer commanded.

Still standing, the EECOM tech typed rapidly. "No can do, sir! Satellite navigation and control are not responding."

To the right, the giant screen suddenly went black.

"Lost camera feed now, too," the tech added.

Painter pictured *IoG-2* sailing from here out into space, a cold and dark chunk of space debris.

"Sir!" The engineer assigned to *IoG-1* waved the control officer to his side. "I've got new readings here. You'd better see this."

Dr. Shaw shifted to the rail of the observation deck, plainly wanting to catch a glimpse. Painter joined her, along with most of the brass gathered on the deck.

"The geodetic effect is altering," the engineer explained, pointing to a monitor. "A point two percent deviation."

"That shouldn't be possible," Dr. Shaw mumbled at Painter's side. "Not unless space-time around the earth is starting to ripple."

"And look!" the engineer continued. "The Eye's gyroscopic momentum is growing stronger, far stronger than prelaunch estimates. I'm even getting a propulsive signature!"

Dr. Shaw gripped the rail harder, looking ready to leap below. "That can't happen without an external source powering the Eye."

Painter could tell she wanted to declare it *dark energy*, but she restrained herself from jumping to premature conclusions.

Another voice called out—this time from a station marked CONTROL. "We're losing orbital stability of *IoG-1*!"

Painter turned to the big board in the center, the one showing the world map and the flight paths of the satellites. The sine wave of *IoG-1's* trajectory was visibly flattening.

"The gyroscopic forces inside the satellite must be pushing it out of orbit," Dr. Shaw explained, sounding both panicked and thrilled.

The screen to the left showed the profile of the earth growing larger, filling up the monitor, eclipsing the dark void of space. The satellite was falling out of orbit, starting its slow crash back into the gravity well from which it came.

The transmitted image quickly lost clarity as the satellite entered the upper atmosphere, showing streaks of data artifacts and ghost shadows, drunkenly doubling and tripling the picture.

Continents flashed by, swirls of clouds, bright blue expanses of ocean.

A moment later, the screen went dark like the other.

Silence settled heavily over the room.

On the world map, the satellite's path split into a frayed end as the mission computer attempted to extrapolate various crash trajectories, taking into account a slew of variables: the roil of Earth's upper atmosphere, the angle of entry, the rate at which the craft broke apart.

"Looks like debris will strike along the eastern border of Mongolia!" the telemetry specialist said. "Maybe even spilling into China."

The commander of the 50th Space Wing groused under his breath. "You can bet Beijing will pick this up."

Painter agreed. China would not miss a flaming piece of space garbage hurling toward them.

General Metcalf glanced hard at Painter. He understood that look.

The advanced military technology aboard that satellite was classified. It couldn't fall into foreign hands.

For a fraction of a second, the screen to the left flickered, then died again—a last hiccup of the dying satellite.

"Bird is gone!" the control officer finally declared. "All transmissions ceased. It's a falling rock now."

The telemetry data slowed to a crawl across the world map—then finally stopped.

Dr. Shaw's hand suddenly clutched Painter's forearm. "They need to bring up that last image," she said. "The one before the satellite died."

She must have noted something anomalous in the data, something that clearly had her scared.

Metcalf heard her, too.

Painter stared hard at his boss. "Do it. Make it happen."

The order passed along the chain of command to the floor. Engineers and technicians worked their magic. After several long minutes to re-digitize, sharpen, and clean up that brief flicker, that final image bloomed again on the large screen.

Gasps spread across the room.

Metcalf leaned to Painter's ear. "If even a *sliver* of that satellite survived, it must be found. It must never reach our enemies."

Painter didn't argue, fully understanding. "I've got field operatives already in the region."

Metcalf gave him a quizzical stare, silently asking how that could be.

Just dumb luck.

Still, he would take that bit of good fortune and mobilize a recovery team immediately. But for the moment, he gaped at the screen, unable to look away.

It displayed a satellite view of the Eastern Seaboard of the United States, the photo taken as the satellite blazed a trail across the sky. It was detailed enough to make out the major coastal metropolises.

Boston, New York City, Washington, D.C.

Every city lay in smoldering ruin.

2

They had crossed half the world to hunt a ghost.

Commander Gray Pierce followed the midnight crowd off the boat and into the ferry terminal. The high-speed catamaran had made the passage from Hong Kong to the peninsula of Macau in a little over an hour. He stretched a kink from his back as he waited to clear passport control in the crowded terminal building.

People were pouring into the peninsula to celebrate a special Water Lantern Festival in honor of the comet in the sky. A large party was under way this night, where floating lanterns were set adrift in the lakes and rivers as offerings to the spirits of the deceased. Hundreds of lights even bobbed in the waters around the terminal, like a scatter of luminous flowers.

Ahead of him in line, a wizened old man cradled a reed cage with a live goose inside. Both looked equally sullen, matching Gray's mood after the seventeen-hour journey here.

"Why does that duck keep looking at me?" Kowalski asked.

"I don't think it's just the duck," Gray said.

The big man, wearing jeans and a long duster, stood a head taller than Gray, which meant he towered over everyone in the terminal. Several people took pictures of the American giant, as if some craggy-faced Godzilla with a crew cut had wandered into their midst.

Gray turned to his other traveling companion. "It's a long shot that we'll learn anything from our contact here. You understand that, right?"

Seichan shrugged, seemingly unperturbed, but he read the tension in the single crease between her eyebrows. They had traveled this far to question this man in person. The meeting was Seichan's last hope to discover the fate of her mother, a woman who had vanished twenty-two years ago, ripped from her home in Vietnam by armed men, leaving behind a nine-year-old daughter. Seichan had believed her mother was long dead—until new information had come to light four months ago, suggesting she might still be alive. It had taken all of Sigma's resources and connections in the intelligence communities to get them this far.

It was likely a dead end, but they had to pursue it.

Ahead, the line finally cleared, and Seichan stepped forward to the bored customs officer. She wore black jeans, hiking boots, and a loose emerald silk blouse that matched her eyes, along with a cashmere vest to hold back the night's chill.

At least she fit in here, where ninety-nine percent of the patronage was of Asian descent. In her case, with her mix of European blood, she struck a slightly more exotic pose. Her slim face and high cheekbones looked carved out of pale marble. Her almond-shaped eyes glinted like polished jade. The only softness to her was the loose cascade of her hair, the color of a raven's wing.

All this was not missed by the border agent.

The round man, his belly straining the buttons of his uniform, sat straighter as she stepped forward. She matched eyes with him, moving with a leonine grace that was equal parts power and threat. She handed over her passport. Her documents were false, as were Gray's and Kowalski's, but the papers had already passed muster at the stricter entry point back in Hong Kong after their flight from D.C.

None of them wanted their real identities known by the Chinese government. Gray and Kowalski were field operatives for Sigma Force, a covert wing of DARPA, made up of former Special Forces soldiers who had been retrained in various scientific disciplines to protect against global threats. Seichan was a former assassin for an international criminal organization, until recruited by force of circumstance to ally with Sigma. Though she wasn't officially part of Sigma, she remained its dark shadow.

At least for now.

After Gray and Kowalski also cleared customs, they hailed a taxi outside. As they waited for it to pull to the curb amid the milling crowds, Gray stared across the breadth of the Macau peninsula and its connected islands. A sea of neon beckoned, along with the blare of music and the echoing muffle of humanity.

Macau, a former Portuguese colony, had become the Sin City of the South China coast, a gambling mecca that had already surpassed Las Vegas in gaming revenues. Only steps away from the ferry terminal rose the gold tower of one of the city's largest casinos, the Sands Macau. It was said that the three-hundred-million-dollar complex had recouped its costs of construction in less than a year. Other gaming powerhouses continued to pour in, with new casinos popping up regularly. The total count stood at thirty-three, all in a city one-sixth the size of D.C.

But the appeal of Macau did not stop at gambling. The hedonistic pleasures of the city—some legal, most not—went well beyond slot machines and poker tables. The old adage of Vegas applied equally here.

What happens in Macau, stays in Macau.

Gray intended to keep it that way. He maintained a close watch on the crowd as their taxi pulled up. Someone tried to shoulder past him to steal their ride, but Gray stiff-armed him away. Kowalski bowed his way into the front seat, while Gray and Seichan ducked into the backseat of the cab.

Leaning forward, she spoke to the driver in rapid-fire Cantonese.

Moments later, they were quickly headed toward their destination.

Seichan settled back in her seat and handed Gray back his wallet.

He stared down at the billfold in surprise. "Where did you—?"

"You were targeted by a pickpocket. You have to watch yourself out here."

Kowalski barked out a sharp laugh from the front seat.

Gray craned around, remembering the man who tried to shove past him. It had been a ruse to distract him, while another relieved him of his wallet, apparently stealing his dignity also. Luckily, Seichan had skills of her own, learned on streets not unlike these.

After her mother had vanished, Seichan spent her childhood in a series of squalid orphanages across Southeast Asia, until eventually she was recruited off the streets and trained to kill. In fact, the first time the two had met, she had shot Gray in the chest, not exactly the warmest of meetings. Now, after the destruction of her previous employer's cartel, she found herself orphaned once again, left adrift, still unsure of her footing in the new world.

She was a trained killer with no roots.

Even Gray expected her to vanish at any moment and never be seen again. While they had grown closer over these past four months, working side by side to hunt for clues to her mother's fate, she still kept a wall between them, accepting his companionship, his support, and once even his bed. Not that anything had happened that night. They had simply been working late, and it was a matter of convenience, nothing more. Still, he had gotten no sleep, lying next to her, listening to her breathe, noting small twitches as she dreamed.

She was like some wild beast, skittish, feral, wary.

If he moved too fast, she would likely spook and bolt.

Even now she sat stiffly in the taxi, wound as tightly as the strings of a cello. He reached over to her, slid a palm along her back, and pulled her closer. He felt the steel in her slowly soften. She allowed herself to sag against him. One hand fiddled with the small pendant at her neck, in the shape of a tiny silver dragon. Her other hand found his, one finger tracing a scar across the back of his thumb.

Until she found her place in this new world, this was the best he could hope for. He also sensed what fueled the intensity of this four-month-long search for her mother. It was a chance for her to rediscover herself, to reconnect to the one person who had loved and sheltered her, to rebuild the family she had lost. Only then, he suspected, could she turn from the past and look to the future.

Gray shared that goal with her, wanted that for her, and would do anything to make that happen.

"If this guy knows anything," he promised aloud, "we'll get it out of him."

12:32 A.M.

"They're en route," the caller said. "They should reach their destination in another few minutes."

"And you've confirmed their identity, Tomaz?"

Ju-long Delgado paced the length of his desk, constructed of solid Ceylon satinwood. The wood was as rare as it was expensive, which defined his interests. The remainder of his office was shelved with antiques, a mix of Portuguese and Chinese, like himself.

"We attempted to steal the smaller man's papers," Tomaz said, "but the woman intervened. She somehow got his wallet back from us."

She was certainly skilled.

Ju-long stopped and touched one of a trio of photos on his desk. The woman was Eurasian, a mix of cultures like him, but in her case, she appeared to be French Vietnamese.

He caught his own reflection in the dark computer monitor. He carried his father's surname, marking their family's Portuguese presence in Macau going back to the opium wars of the early nineteenth century. His given name came from his mother's side of the family. Likewise, he also shared his father's round eyes and heavy facial hair, trimmed tight to his face, and his mother's refined features and smooth skin. Though he was in his forties, most considered him much younger. Others made the mistake of assuming him inexperienced from his youthful demeanor—and made the worst mistake of trying to take advantage of that.

It was an error that was never repeated.

He returned his attention to the woman in the photo. As an assassin of some distinction, she had a steep price on her head. The Israeli Mossad had placed the highest bounty so far, for some past crime of hers, with the promise that she would be killed, silenced before anyone learned of his involvement.

That was Ju-long's best talent: to move unseen, to manipulate from afar, to find profit in opportunity.

He stared at the picture of the soldier, a former army ranger. His face was deeply tanned, his gray-blue eyes sun-crinkled at the corners, his strong jaw shadowed with dark stubble. The bidding for this one still continued to grow, especially over the past twelve hours. It seemed this man had made many enemies—or knew secrets of considerable value. It was of no matter. Ju-long dealt merely in commodity. So far, the anonymous buyer from Syria held the highest bid for him.

The third man—with a face like a gorilla—seemed to be nothing more than a bodyguard. Someone to sweep out of the way to reach the true prizes here.

But first Ju-long had to secure them.

It would have been easy enough to grab them both from the ferry building, but such a kidnapping in the open would have drawn too much attention. After the Chinese took over control of Macau in 1999, he had to operate with more stealth. On the positive side, though, the crackdown by the new government had rid the peninsula of most of the warring Chinese Triad gangs, eliminating his competition and allowing him to assume greater control of his organization. Now, as the Boss of Macau, as some called him, he had a thumb in everything, and the Chinese government turned mostly a blind eye as long as he kept a firm rein on matters, and the officials here got their weekly cut.

As Macau grew richer, so did he.

"Your men are in position at Casino Lisboa?" Ju-long asked Tomaz, wanting no mistakes. "They are ready to receive them?"

"*Sim, senhor.*"

"Good. And what resistance do you expect?"

"They carry no firearms. Yet we suspect they all have knives on their persons. But that should not matter."

He nodded, satisfied.

As he ended the call, he glanced over to a plasma screen resting atop an antique Portuguese naval chest. Earlier, he'd had Tomaz bribe one of the security guards at Casino Lisboa to gain access to their internal video surveillance, specifically the feed into one of their VIP rooms off the main gaming floor. Such rooms were plentiful throughout Macau, servicing high-stakes gamblers who wanted a private table or some exclusive time with one of Macau's elite prostitutes.

This room held a lone occupant, seated on a red-silk sofa, awaiting his guests. The man had been too loose with his tongue over the past few days, telling of this midnight rendezvous, sharing the story of his upcoming good fortune. And when it came to reports of newfound money of this size, especially windfalls from foreign lands, word eventually reached Ju-long Delgado. He quickly learned the identity of the newcomers.

Where money flowed, there was always a way to turn a profit.

Ju-long stepped behind his desk. His family's mansion overlooked Leal Senado Square, the historic colonial heart of Macau, where for centuries Portuguese troops had paraded in force and where now Chinese dragons danced during holidays. Even this night, lanterns hung in the neighboring trees, amid cages holding songbirds. Across the plaza, small shrines to the dead held floating candles in small earthenware bowls, all to light the way for the departed spirits.

But the biggest flame of them all hung in the sky, shimmering and bright: the silvery fire of a comet.

Content, he settled into his seat and swung his attention to the plasma screen, ready to enjoy the night's entertainment from Casino Lisboa.

12:55 A.M.

This was not the Macau she remembered.

Seichan climbed out of the cab and stared around. It had been over fifteen years since she had last set foot here. On the dark ride from the harbor, she could barely pick out the sleepier Portuguese town of the past, a place of narrow alleys, colonial mansions, and baroque plazas.

It was now hidden behind towering walls of neon and glitz. Back then, even Casino Lisboa had been a seedier affair, nothing like the remodeled neon birthday cake of today, not to mention its newest edition, the Grand Lisboa, a thousand-foot-tall golden tower in the shape of a lotus flower.

Definitely *not* the Macau she remembered.

The only semblance of those sleepier times was the thousands of glowing lanterns floating in the neighboring Nam Van Lake. Incense burned on the shores, too, and perfumed the gentle sea breeze with the scents of cloves, star anise, and sandalwood. It was a tradition that went back millennia to honor the dead.

Over the years, Seichan had cast afloat many such lanterns in memory of her mother.

But maybe no longer.

Gray checked his watch and urged her onward. "We've only got five minutes. We're going to be late."

He led the way with Kowalski, while she trailed back a step behind—not like some subservient wife, but to watch their backs. Macau may have hidden its face behind the glare of neon and flashing lights, but she knew that whenever so much wealth flowed into such a small space, especially a region of the world not known for such riches, crime and corruption took deep root. She knew old Macau—a place of gangland wars, human trafficking, and murder—still thrived in its shadows.

She spotted a clutch of Thai prostitutes idling near the entrance, an example of the web of corruption stretching from Macau across the entire region. One of them moved toward Gray, likely drawn by his rugged handsomeness and the promise of American wealth—but Seichan caught her painted eyes, and she retreated quickly.

Unmolested, they crossed under the flashing neon ribbons of Casino Lisboa and through its front doors. The overpowering reek of cigarette smoke struck her immediately, stinging her eyes and throat. A pall hung in the air, adding to the dark, sinister quality of the main casino floor ahead.

She continued to follow Gray into that heart of darkness.

Here was none of the over-the-top dazzle of a big Las Vegas casino.

This was old-school gaming, a throwback to the Rat Pack era. The ceilings were low, the lighting dim. Slots rang and flashed, but the machines were restricted to a neighboring separate hall. Only tables occupied the central floor: baccarat, pai gow, sic bo, fan tan. Crowds of pockmarked men and sullen-looking women filled the tables, chain-smoking, rubbing talismans of good luck, trapped here as much by addiction as hope. Twelve stylized dragons hung overhead, clutching glowing balls of changing colors. Sadly, two globes had gone dark, speaking to the lack of maintenance.

Still, Seichan found herself relaxing, enjoying the cutthroat nature of the place, appreciating the lack of pretense. She felt a black camaraderie with this space.

"The elevators are over there," Gray said and pointed to a bank of cages along the wall to the left.

Their destination lay above this floor, deeper into the shadowy fringes of the complex, into its maze of VIP rooms, where the *true* wealth flowed through Macau. The quantity of tables hidden away in those private spaces outnumbered those on the main floor.

Inside the elevator cage, Gray hit the button for the fourth floor. The upper-level VIP rooms were run exclusively by junket operators, private companies who would fly in high rollers from mainland China or elsewhere and lavish their customers with every extravagance, meeting any desire. Even the basement shopping arcade of the casino doubled as a prostitutes' mall, where a young woman could be ordered on a whim.

Twenty different companies did business among those rooms, including several run by organized crime syndicates, where money laundering was commonplace. Such anonymity and discretion suited Gray and Seichan's objective. They had come here posing as two high-stakes gamblers. The payment to their informant would be washed away by the junket operator, keeping their hands clean. Their goal was a simple one: get the information, pay the man, and leave.

The elevator cage opened into a hallway decorated in a faded attempt at opulence, all in reds and golds. Doors lined the halls, many with burly men standing guard.

Kowalski eyed them like a testy bull.

"This way," Seichan said, taking the lead.

With the end in sight, she hurried now. This was her last chance to discover her mother's fate; all other leads—one after the other—had dried up. Seichan struggled to keep her anxiety at bay. For the past four months, she had leaned on her training, staying hypervigilant, keeping her focus away from that knot in her gut, that tangle of hope, despair, and fear. It was why she had held Gray off at arm's length, despite his plain desire to explore something deeper with her.

She dared not lose control.

Their VIP room lay at the end of the hall. A pair of large men with bulges under their jackets flanked its door, bodyguards supplied by the company who had booked this space.

Reaching them, she showed her false I.D.

Gray and Kowalski did the same.

Only then did one of the guards knock on the door and open it for them. Seichan stepped through first and quickly sized up the space. The walls had been painted gold, and the carpet was woven in a pattern of crimson and black. A lone green baize baccarat table stood to her left, a nest of red-silk chairs and lounges to her right. The room was empty, except for a single occupant.

Dr. Hwan Pak.

His presence was the reason for so much precaution and subterfuge. He served as the lead scientist at the Yongbyon Nuclear Scientific Research Center in North Korea—a facility known for enriching uranium used by the country's atomic program. He also had a severe gambling addiction, though that was known only to a few intelligence agencies.

Stubbing out a cigarette, Hwan Pak rose from a couch, standing only a few inches over five feet and thin as a cane. He bowed slightly in greeting, his eyes on Gray, as if sensing the one in charge, already dismissing her, a mere woman.

"You are late," he said politely but firmly, his accent barely evident. He reached to a pocket and removed a cell phone. "You have purchased one hour of my time. For eight hundred thousand as agreed."

Seichan folded her arms, letting Gray type in the transfer code arranged by the junket organizer.

"Four hundred thousand now," Gray said. "The rest only if I'm satisfied with your information."

The price was in Hong Kong dollars, which exchanged to about eighty thousand in U.S. currency. Seichan would have gladly paid ten times that amount if the man truly had any knowledge of her mother. And from the tinge of desperation in Pak's eyes, the scientist would likely have settled for far less than they'd offered. He had large debts to settle with unsavory sorts, debts that even this transaction would not settle completely.

"You will not be disappointed," Pak said.

1:14 A.M.

From his offices halfway across Macau, Ju-long Delgado smiled as he watched Hwan Pak wave his new guests to the nest of red-silk lounges. The brutish one hung back, moving instead to the baccarat table, leaning his rear against it, absently picking at the felt surface.

The two high-value targets—the assassin and the former soldier—followed Pak and sat down.

Ju-long wished he could have eavesdropped on their conversation, but the security feed from the Lisboa was video only.

A shame.

But it was a minor quibble compared to the rewards to come.

And as he well knew: *All good things come to those who wait.*

1:17 A.M.

Seichan let Gray take the lead on the interrogation of Hwan Pak, sensing the North Korean scientist would respond more fully to another man.

Chauvinist bastard . . .

"So you know the woman we seek?" Gray started.

"*Ye,*" Pak answered with a swift nod. He had lit a fresh cigarette and puffed out a stream of smoke, plainly nervous. "Her name is Guan-yin. Though I doubt that is her real name."

It isn't, Seichan thought. *Or at least it wasn't.*

Her mother's real name had been Mai Phuong Ly.

A flash of memory suddenly struck her, unbidden, unwelcome at the moment. As a girl, Seichan had been on her belly beside a small garden pond, tracing a finger in the water, trying to lure up a golden carp—then her mother's face reflected next to her, wavering in the rippled surface, surrounded by a floating scatter of fallen cherry blossoms.

They were her mother's namesake.

Cherry blossoms.

Seichan blinked, drawing herself fully back to the moment at hand. She was not surprised that her mother had adopted a new name. She had been on the run, needing to keep hidden. And a new name allowed a new life.

Utilizing all of Sigma's resources, Seichan had discovered the identity of the armed men who had taken her mother. They had been members of the Vietnamese secret police, euphemistically called the Ministry of Public Security. They had learned of her mother's dalliance with an American diplomat, her father, and of the love that grew from there. They had sought to pry U.S. secrets out of her.

Her mother had been held at a prison outside Ho Chi Minh City—until she escaped during a prison riot a year later. For a short period of time, due to a clerical error, she had been declared dead, killed during that uprising. It was that lucky mistake that gave her enough of a head start to flee Vietnam and vanish into the world.

Had she looked for me? Seichan wondered. *Or did she think I was already dead?*

Seichan had a thousand unanswered questions.

"Guan-yin," Pak continued. A faint smile traced his lips, mocking and bitter. "Such a beautiful name certainly did not fit her . . . certainly not when I met her eight years ago."

"What do you mean?" Gray asked.

"*Guan-yin* means *goddess of mercy.*" Pak lifted his left hand, revealing only four fingers. "This is the quality of her mercy."

Seichan shifted closer, speaking for the first time. "How did you know her?" she asked coldly.

Pak initially looked ready to ignore her, but then his eyes slightly crinkled. He stared harder at Seichan, possibly truly seeing her for the first time. Suspicion trickled into his gaze.

"You sound . . ." he stammered. "Just then . . . but that's not possible."

Gray leaned forward, catching the man's eye. "This is an expensive hour, Dr. Pak. Like the lady asked . . . how did you know Guan-yin? In what capacity?"

He flattened the lapels of his suit coat, visibly collecting himself. Only then did he speak. "She once ran this very room," he said with a small nod to indicate the VIP lounge. "As the dragonhead of a gang out of Kowloon, the *Duàn zhī* Triad."

Seichan flinched at that name, unable to stop herself.

Gray made a scoffing noise. "So you're saying Guan-yin was a *boss* of this Chinese Triad?"

"*Ye,*" he said sharply. "She is the only woman to ever become a dragonhead. To accomplish this, she had to be extremely ruthless. I should have known better than to take a loan from her."

Pak rubbed the stump of his missing finger.

Gray noted the motion. "She had your finger cut off?"

"*Aniyo,*" he disagreed. "*She* did it herself. She came from Kowloon with a hammer and a chisel. The name of her Triad means *Broken Twig*. It is also her signature means of encouraging the prompt payment of a debt."

Gray grimaced, clearly picturing that brutal handiwork.

Seichan was having no easier time of it. Her breathing grew harder, trying to balance this act with the mother who had once nursed a broken-winged dove back to health. But she knew the man wasn't lying.

Gray was less convinced. "And how are we to know that this Triad boss is the woman we came looking for? What proof do you offer? Do you have a photograph of you with her?"

Inside the intelligence inquiry sent out broadly, Sigma had included a picture of her mother, one taken from the records of the Vietnamese

prison where she had been incarcerated. They'd also posted possible locations, which unfortunately covered a large swath of Southeast Asia, along
with a computer-enhanced image of how she might look now, twenty
years later.

Dr. Pak had been the only promising fish to bite on that line.

"A photograph?" The North Korean scientist shook his head. He lit
another cigarette, plainly a chain-smoker. "She keeps herself covered in
public. Only those high in her Triad have seen her face. If anyone else sees
her, they don't live long enough to speak of it."

"Then how do you—?"

Pak touched his throat. "The dragon. I saw it when she wielded the
hammer . . . dangling from her neck, the silver shining, as merciless as its
owner."

"Like this?" Seichan slipped a finger to her collar and pulled out
her own coiled dragon pendant. The intelligence dossier had included a
picture of it. Seichan's charm was a copy of another. The memory of the
original remained etched in her bones, often rising up in dreams

. . . *of being curled in her mother's arms on the small cot under an open
window, night birds singing, moonlight reflecting off the silver dragon resting
at her mother's throat, shimmering like water with each breath . . .*

Hwan Pak had a different memory. He cringed back from her pendant, as if trying to escape the sight.

"There must be many dragon pendants of a similar design," Gray said.
"What you offer is *no* proof. Only your word about a piece of jewelry you
saw eight years ago."

"If you want real proof—"

Seichan cut him off, standing and tucking the silver dragon away. She
motioned for Gray to move aside for a private conversation.

Once they retreated to beyond the baccarat table, she spoke in his ear.
Kowalski's bulk helped shield them further.

"He's telling the truth," Seichan said. "We must move beyond this line
of questioning and find out *where* my mother is in Kowloon."

"Seichan, I know you want to believe him, but let me—"

She gripped his bicep to shut him up. "The name of the Triad. *Duàn zhī*."

He went silent, letting her speak, plainly seeing something in her face.

She felt tears rising, coming from a place of happiness and grief, a place where night birds still sang in the jungle.

"The name . . . Broken Twig," she said. Even speaking it, she felt something break inside her.

He waited, not understanding, but he allowed her the space to explain at her own pace.

"My name," she said haltingly, feeling suddenly exposed, "the one given to me by my mother . . . the one I abandoned, a necessity to bury my childhood behind me . . . it was *Chi*."

A new name allowed a new life.

Gray's eyes widened. "Your real name is Chi."

"*Was*," she still insisted.

That girl had died long ago.

Seichan took a steadying breath. "In Vietnamese, *Chi* means *twig*."

She read the understanding in Gray's face.

Her mother had named the Triad after her lost daughter.

Before Gray could respond, a sharp coughing sounded from beyond the door—but the noise came from no human throat. Bodies thudded out in the hallway, felled by the barrage of noise-suppressed gunfire.

Gray was already swinging to face that threat, drawing Kowalski with him.

Pak called from across the room. "You asked for proof!" He pointed his smoldering cigarette at the door. "Here it comes!"

Seichan immediately realized what Pak had done. She should have suspected it sooner, considering what they had just learned. She cursed herself. In the past, she never would have been blindsided like this. Her time with Sigma had softened her.

Pak backed away from the door, but he did not look scared. This was his play, a path to a far bigger payoff than Gray had offered, a possible way to clear *all* his debts. In a clever act of betrayal, the bastard had turned the

tables on them, sold them out to her mother's Triad, passing on a warning to a woman who had gone to great lengths to keep her face hidden
from the world.

Such a woman would destroy anyone who got too close to the truth.

Seichan understood that.

She would have done the same.

You did what you must to survive.

1:44 A.M.

Ju-long Delgado was not as understanding about the sudden turn of
events at Casino Lisboa. He stood up and grabbed his cell phone.

On the plasma screen, he watched the three foreigners react to some
commotion beyond the VIP room door. The two men flipped the baccarat
table on its side, placing it between them and the door to act as a shield.
On the other side of the room, the North Korean scientist seemed less
perturbed, but even he retreated into a far corner, placing himself out of
harm's way.

With one thumb, Ju-long speed-dialed Tomaz out at the Lisboa. Earlier, Ju-long had specifically ordered his team *not* to pursue the targets
until Dr. Pak left. He didn't want any trouble with the North Koreans.
He had many lucrative ties with their government, helping shuttle prominent members, like Hwan Pak, to and from Macau. In fact, he had visited
Pyongyang himself, grooming and securing those connections.

As soon as the line was picked up, Tomaz reported in, panting heavily
as if running. "We saw it, too, on the security feed, *senhor*. A firefight. I'm
heading up there now. Someone is assaulting the same VIP room."

A lance of righteous indignation stabbed through Ju-long. Was someone trying to steal his merchandise? Had a disgruntled bidder decided to
circumvent the auction and take a direct approach?

Tomaz corrected him. "We believe it's one of the Triads."

He balled a fist.

Damned Chinese dogs . . .

His plan must have leaked to the wrong ears.

"How do you wish us to proceed, *senhor*? Back off or continue as planned?"

Ju-long had no choice. If he didn't retaliate in full force, the Triads would take it as a sign of weakness, and he'd be fighting turf wars for years. The cost to his organization, along with the weakening of his position in the eyes of the Chinese officials who ran Macau, could not be tolerated.

Extreme measures were needed.

"Lock down the Lisboa," he ordered, intending to make an example of the trespassers. "Bring in more men. Any known Triad on the property, whether involved or not, I want killed on sight. Any *suspected* ally, anyone who might have helped facilitate or knew about this strike, I want dead."

"And the targets?"

He weighed the advantages and disadvantages. While the profits to be gained by the pair were considerable, their deaths could also serve as an important lesson. It would demonstrate Ju-long's willingness to sacrifice profit in order to maintain his authority and position. Among the Chinese, honor and saving face were as important as breathing.

He allowed the anger to drain out of him, reconciling himself to the reality of the situation. What's done is done.

Besides, in the end, their bodies could still fetch a tidy sum.

And a little profit was better than none.

"Kill them," he ordered. "Kill them all."

3

Chaos still ruled the floor of the Space and Missile Systems Center.

It had been almost two hours since the satellite image of the smoldering Eastern Seaboard had glowed on its giant monitor. Base personnel had immediately confirmed that New York, Boston, and D.C. were all safe and unharmed. Life continued on out there without mishap.

The relief in the room had been palpable. Painter's reaction was no exception. He had friends and colleagues across the Northeast. Still, he was glad his fiancée was in New Mexico. He pictured Lisa's face, framed in a fall of blond hair, grinning at him with a trace of mischief that always set his heart pounding harder. If anything had happened to her . . .

But in the end, nothing was amiss out east.

So what the hell had the satellite transmitted as it crashed?

That had been the critical question of the past two hours. Theories had flashed across the floor of the control room. *Was the picture some extrapolation? Some computer simulation of a nuclear strike?* But all the engineers claimed such calculations were beyond the scope of the spacecraft's original programming.

So what had happened?

Painter stood with Dr. Jada Shaw in front of the giant screens, along with a handful of engineers and military brass.

A satellite image of the island of Manhattan glowed before them. A young technician stood with a laser pointer in hand. He passed its glowing red dot across the breadth of the island.

"This is an image obtained from an NRO satellite at the exact same time that *IoG-1* burned past the Eastern Seaboard. Here you can make out the grid of streets, the lakes dotting Central Park. Now here is the same fractional picture taken by *IoG-1.*"

He clicked a handheld button, and another image appeared beside the first. The new picture was a blown-up section of the photo snapped by the satellite as it crashed, featuring the identical chunk of Manhattan.

"If we overlay, one atop the other . . ."

The technician worked his magic to superimpose the second over the first. Through the smoke and the flames, the grid of streets lined up perfectly. Even the lakes of Central Park matched in every dimension.

Murmurs spread through the crowd.

Dr. Shaw took a step forward to look more closely. She wore a frown of distaste.

"As you can see," the tech continued, "this *is* New York City, not some facsimile. The destruction depicted is not some digital noise that inadvertently *looks* like the East Coast is burning. Not at this level of detail."

To prove his point, the tech zoomed upon key locations of the island. Though the resolution became grainy, it appeared Manhattan was correct down to its tiniest details. Except now, the Empire State Building was a blazing torch, the financial district a cratered ruin, and the Queensboro Bridge a shattered twist of steel girders. It looked like some exquisite digital matte painting for a disaster film.

Boston and D.C. fared no better.

Questions flared among the audience, but Dr. Shaw simply moved closer, resting a hand on her chin, staring between the two images as they were split apart again.

General Metcalf called to Painter from a few yards away, irritation piquing in his voice. "Director Crowe, a moment of your time."

Painter moved to join his boss in front of the world map.

"This is the latest and most refined telemetry data," Metcalf said, pointing to the crash path of the falling satellite on the map. "The impact site is likely here, in a remote region of northern Mongolia. As you can see, it's not far from the borders of both Russia and China. So far, there have been no rumblings from either country about this crash."

"What about eyes on the ground out there?"

Metcalf shook his head. "This region of Mongolia is mountainous and remote. Populated only by nomadic tribesmen."

Painter understood. "In that case, we've got a small window to get out there and find that burned piece of military space hardware before either Russia or China catches wind of it."

"Precisely."

Painter glanced over to the other screen. No one understood what had happened to generate that disturbing image, but they all knew any answers lay amid the crashed ruins of the *Eye of God*. Secondarily, it was vital that the satellite's advanced technology not be lost to a foreign nation.

"I've already got Captain Kat Bryant over at Sigma command working on the logistics for a search team."

"Very good. I want you on the first plane back to D.C. There's a jet being fueled for you. That's your top priority. Find and secure that wreckage."

Metcalf turned his back, dismissing him.

Off to the side, Dr. Shaw had her head bowed next to the technician. The man kept nodding his head, glancing at the screen, then finished with a scared look on his face.

What's that all about?

The technician stepped away from Dr. Shaw and crossed to an engineering station, waving others to join him.

Curious, Painter stepped to the young astrophysicist's side as she continued to study the screen.

She noted his attention. "I still say it's the comet."

Painter had heard her earlier theories. "Dr. Shaw, you still believe all this is a consequence of dark energy?"

"Call me Jada. And, yes, from the last spool of data from the satellite, the geodetic effect registered a misalignment of 5.4 degrees."

From the ardent look in her eyes as she glanced at him, he saw she expected this to strike him as significant.

It didn't.

"That means precisely what?" he asked.

She sighed with frustration. She had spent the last two hours arguing with the brass at the base, trying to get them to listen to her, and clearly she was losing patience with them all.

"Picture a bowling ball resting on a thin stretch of trampoline," she said. "The mass of the ball would create a depression in the surface. That's what the earth does to the geography around it. It curves space and time. This is proven by both theory and experiment, and the geodetic effect is a measuring rod for that curvature. So when the data reports a misalignment, it's registering a *wrinkle* in that space-time. Something my theory posited could happen if *IoG-1* collected an influx of dark energy. But I never expected such a *deep* wrinkle."

A worried crinkle of her own formed between her brows.

"So what has you looking so concerned?" he asked.

"At best, I had hoped to see merely a twitch in the geodetic effect. Something less than 0.1 percent, and something brief, on the nano-scale level of time. A twist of alignment of over five percent and sustained for almost a full minute . . ." She gave her head a slight shake.

"Earlier, you theorized that the massive burst of dark energy might have torn a small hole in space-time, possibly opening a brief window into an alternate universe, one parallel to our own, one where the Eastern Seaboard was destroyed."

She studied the screen. "Or it may be a peek into our own future."

That was a disturbing possibility she hadn't previously voiced.

"Time is not a linear function," she continued, almost as if she were working something out in her head. "Time is just another dimension. Like up-down or left-right. The flow of time can also be affected by gravity or by velocity. So when space-time got ripped or wrinkled, it could have made time skip a beat, like the needle of a record player hitting a scratch in the vinyl."

The fear in her eyes brightened.

Painter tried to stave off that panic. "Since when do you kids still listen to vinyl?"

She turned to him, the anxiety pushed back by indignation. "I'll have you know I have a vintage jazz collection that rivals the best in the world. B.B. King, John Lee Hooker, Miles Davis, Hans Koller."

"Okay." He held up a placating palm.

"Nothing compares to old vinyl," she finished with a righteous huff.

He didn't disagree with her.

He was saved from any further diatribe by the return of the technician.

"You were right," he said to her, looking even more scared.

"Right about what?" Painter asked.

"Show me," she said, ignoring him.

The technician crossed back to the giant screen and once again brought up the NRO satellite image and superimposed it over the photo taken by *IoG-1*. He flickered them back and forth, one atop the other.

"The shadows don't match, like you thought. Not just here, but we tested some spots in Boston, with the same anomaly registering." He pointed to the clutch of engineers and techs by his workstation. "We're zeroing in on different points along the Eastern Seaboard and calculating the degree of variance."

She nodded. "We need the time differential calculated."

"We're on it."

Painter didn't follow. "What's wrong?"

She pointed to the giant screen. "The shadows don't match between the two images. They are fractionally off from one another."

"Which means what?"

"The two images were taken at the same time, so the shadows *should* match. Like two pictures of the same sundial taken at the same moment."

She stared hard at them. "But they don't. The shadows don't line up, which means—"

"The sun's position in the sky is different between the two photos."

A sense of dread drew his spine straighter.

She took a worried breath. "The *Eye of God* snapped a picture of Manhattan at a different time, *not* the one registered by our clocks as it crashed."

Painter pictured that needle skipping over a scratch in a vinyl record.

Jada continued, "The technicians are trying to figure out what *date and time* correspond to the position of the sun captured in the satellite image. They're triangulating spots up and down the Eastern Seaboard to pinpoint that exact time."

By now the growing commotion at the engineering console had drawn others.

The lead tech straightened and stared at Jada.

"The variance is eighty-eight . . . !" Someone tugged his sleeve. He ducked to the screen, then back up again. "Make that *ninety* hours from now."

That was less than four days.

General Metcalf joined him. "What's this all about?"

Painter's gaze fell upon Jada's face, where he found certainty shining.

"That image." Painter nodded to the destruction. "That's not a glitch. That's how the world will look in four days."

6:54 P.M. CET
Rome, Italy

Rachel Verona woke out of a dream of drowning to the ringing of the phone. She struggled up, gasping a breath, taking a moment to realize she was not in her bed, but on the overstuffed sofa in Uncle Vigor's office. She had dozed off while reading a text about St. Thomas.

The smell of garlic and pesto still hung in the air from the take-out meal she had fetched earlier for them both. The cartons still rested on her uncle's desk, by his elbow.

"Can you get the phone?" Vigor asked.

With his reading glasses perched on the bridge of his nose, he was bent studiously over the old skull. He held a measuring compass open and poised across the length of the nasal bone. He scribbled a note on a sheet of graph paper.

As the phone rang loudly, Rachel rolled to her feet and stepped to his desk. She stared at the sliver of moon through the arrow-slit of a window accented by the arc of the comet's long tail.

"It's getting late, Uncle. We can finish this in the morning."

He waved the compass dismissively. "I only sleep a few hours. And when it's quiet like this, I get my best work done."

She picked up the ringing phone on his desk. *"Pronto?"*

A tired masculine voice answered, *"Sono Bruno Conti, dottore di recerco da Centro Studi Microcitemia."*

Rachel covered the receiver. "Uncle, it's Dr. Conti from the DNA lab."

He waved for the phone. "Took them long enough."

Rachel stared over at the skull as Vigor spoke rapidly with the research geneticist. She recognized the source of her uncle's impatience, noting the faint writing on the crown of the skull, marking a fateful date. She felt no misgivings at the prediction etched in bone. People had been predicting the end of the world since the beginning of time—from the ancient Maya with their prophetic calendar to the turn-of-the-millennial doomsayers back in 2000.

How is this any different?

Vigor's conversation became more heated—then he promptly hung up.

Rachel noted the dark circles under her uncle's eyes. "What's the news from the lab?" she asked.

"They've confirmed my estimates of the age of the skull and the book."

He gestured to the copy of the Gospel of Thomas bound in human skin. For the hundredth time, she wondered why anyone would do that. Yes, the book was considered heretical during its time. It dismissed religious orthodoxy as the only way to salvation, claiming instead that the path to God lay inside anyone, if they'd only open their eyes and follow it.

Seek and you shall find.

Still, heresy or not, why bind such a copy in human skin?

"So how old are the book and skull?" she asked.

"The lab has dated them to the thirteenth century."

"So not the *third* century as the Aramaic writing suggested? That means it can't be an authentic Jewish magical talisman, like those found by archaeologists in the past."

"No. It's just as I surmised. It's likely a *copy* of an original. In fact, the skull itself is not even *Jewish*."

"How do you know that?"

He motioned for her to join him. "While you were napping, I was studying the cranial structures and conformational anatomy. First of all, this skull is mesocranic."

"Which means?"

"That the skull is broad and of intermediate height. Additionally note how these cheekbones are thick, the eye sockets rounded, and the nasal bones are flat and wide." He picked up the skull and flipped it over. "And look at the teeth. The incisors are shovel shaped, very different from Mediterranean stock."

"Then where did this skull come from?"

He turned to her, tapping his measuring compass on his notepad. "From my calculations of the various cranial dimensions—eye width, the depth of the prenasal fossa, the degree of prognathism—I'd say this skull is East Asian in origin, what used to be called Mongoloid."

A measure of respect flashed through her as she was reminded yet again that her uncle was far more than a man of the cloth. "So the skull came from somewhere out in the Far East?"

"As did the book," he added.

"The book?"

He looked over the edge of his reading glasses at her. "I thought you heard, when I was speaking to Dr. Conti."

She shook her head.

He hovered a palm over the wrinkled leather binding with the macabre eye sewn on the cover. "According to Dr. Conti's analysis, the skin of the book and the skull share identical DNA. They're from the *same* source."

As the implication struck her, Rachel swallowed back bile.

Whoever had made these talismans, they'd crafted them from a single body. They used some man's skin to bind the book, then his skull to make this relic.

Vigor continued, "I'm having the lab continue to build a racial profile using both autosomal and mitochondrial DNA to see if we can narrow down the origin of these relics. When Father Josip sent them to me, he must have done so for a reason. Time was running out. He knew I could help and that I had access to resources he didn't."

"Like the DNA lab."

He nodded.

"So why didn't Father Josip simply write you a note?"

Vigor offered a coy wink. "Who says he didn't?"

Rachel scowled at this revelation. "Then why didn't you tell—?"

"I only discovered it a quarter hour ago. While I was examining the skull. I wanted to finish my measurements, and you needed your sleep. Then the phone rang, and I got distracted with the news from the DNA lab."

Rachel stared at the skull. "Show me."

Vigor flipped the relic over and pointed to the hole where the spinal cord enters the skull. He lifted a penlight and shone it inside. "Where else would someone hide secret knowledge?"

Rachel leaned closer and peered into the cranium's interior. A dollop of crimson wax had been affixed to the inner surface of the skull, like the seal on a papal letter. Tiny letters, written in Latin, had been meticulously carved into the wax. She pictured Josip inscribing each letter with some sharp, long-handled instrument through the skull's narrow fossa.

Why such a degree of secrecy? How paranoid was this man?

She stared at the message.

Adjuva.
Veni In
Aral Mare

46 7'41.78" N
60 28' 8. 59" E

She translated the Latin aloud. *"Help. Come to the Aral Sea."*

She frowned. The Aral Sea straddled the border between Kazakhstan and Uzbekistan in Central Asia. It was a desolate area. She also remembered her uncle's morphological determination of the skull's origin as *East Asian*. Had Father Josip determined the same? Had the racial heritage of the relic drawn him from Hungary out east to continue his search? But if so, what was he searching for and why such secrecy?

Squinting, she also made out a faint series of Arabic numbers inscribed under the Latin inscription.

Vigor guessed what had drawn her attention. "Longitude and latitude markings."

"To a key specific location." Rachel could not hold back the distrust in her voice. "That's where Father Josip wants you to meet him?"

"So it would appear."

Rachel frowned. She didn't want her uncle traipsing to parts unknown based on some cryptic note of an errant priest who had vanished nearly a decade ago.

Vigor set the skull back down. "I'm going to set out at daybreak. Catch the earliest flight out to Kazakhstan."

Rachel balked at this, but she knew from long experience that she'd never convince him otherwise. She settled on a compromise. "Not without me, you're not. And I've got plenty of vacation time accrued. So you have no excuse."

He smiled. "I had hoped you'd say that. In fact, I wonder if we shouldn't contact Director Crowe to see if he could offer us additional field support."

"You want to involve Sigma Force? All because of something written on a skull back in the thirteenth century, some ancient prophecy of doom."

She rolled her eyes at such a thought. She and her uncle had dealings in the past with Sigma, and she certainly would not object to an excuse to see Commander Gray Pierce again. The two had an off-again, on-again relationship over the years that had settled into a mutual friendship. Sometimes with benefits. But both knew such a long-distance relationship would never last. Still . . . she gave it a moment's more thought, then dismissed it. Sigma's team of scientific and military experts didn't need to be bothered with a minor matter such as this.

"I think we could benefit from their expertise," Vigor pressed. "Besides, I sense we're running short on time."

As if proving this, a shatter of glass sounded. Glass cascaded into the office. An object ricocheted off the stone edge of the narrow window and rebounded to the room's far side.

Vigor flinched from the sudden noise. Rachel's training had her already moving. She scooped her uncle around the waist and rolled him away from the window, toward the opposite side of the room.

She drove her uncle to the floor, sheltering him behind the desk with her body—as the grenade exploded with a concussive blast of fire and smoke.

10:18 A.M. PST
Airborne over California

The sprawl of Los Angeles vanished below the wings of the jet as it began its cross-country flight to D.C. Painter had asked the pilot to spare no fuel, to push the Bombardier Global 5000 to its severe limits. The luxury of the richly appointed interior, with its full bar and leather seating groups, belied the jet's state-of-the-art engines, which could reach an upper speed of 590 mph.

Painter intended to test the manufacturer's claims during this flight, especially with the Eastern Seaboard set to burn in less than four days.

Whether true or not, General Metcalf had requested he set aside such mysteries for now and tasked him with a more practical concern: the crashed *IoG-1* satellite. Those orders still rang in his ears.

Find the wreckage of the satellite. That remains your primary objective. The technicians will deal with the image taken by the satellite. And as a precaution, I'll begin a risk assessment in regards to pending threats to the East Coast.

They each had their roles to play.

The plane banked as it headed out of Los Angeles airspace. The comet shone in the blue sky, luminous enough to see during the day. At night, the tail stretched far across the stars, so bright that one could discern the wavering scintillation of its tail, making it appear a living thing. It was expected to blaze up there for almost a month as the comet made a slow pass by the earth.

Slipping into the leather seat next to him, she noted his attention. The only other passenger aboard the jet, she tinkled a glass of cola in one hand.

Jada had shared with Metcalf her theories of time skipping a beat due to a wrinkle in space-time. Her theory offered an explanation for the errant shadows discovered in the photo, shadows that suggested the image might be a glimpse of ninety hours into the future.

"I don't think we convinced the general," Painter said, turning to her.

"And I'm not sure I'm convinced either," Jada added.

This surprised him—and it must have shown on his face.

"There are so many variables in play here," she explained, shifting uncomfortably in the seat. "As I mentioned before, the image could be a peek into an *alternate* future, not necessarily ours. I refuse to believe that the future is written in stone. In fact, quantum physics defies such linear paths to time. Just the act of observation can change fate, like with Schrödinger's cat."

"And that applies how?"

"Well, take that cat. It's a classic example of the spookiness of quantum mechanics. In that thought experiment, a cat is put in a box with a poison pellet, one that has an equal chance of killing the cat or not. While the box is closed, the cat is considered to be in a suspended state—both alive and dead. It's only after you open the box and check on the cat that its fate is truly settled one way or the other. Some theorize that when the box is opened, the universe splits into two. In one universe, the cat's alive. In the other, he's dead."

"Okay."

"And the same situation may be involved with the photo taken by the satellite as space-time wrinkled around it. In one universe, the world burns. In the other, it doesn't."

"So we have a fifty-fifty chance of surviving. For some reason, with the fate of mankind hanging in the balance, I'm not particularly happy with those odds."

"Yet the flow of time gets even murkier from there. Just the fact that the satellite took the picture and we all saw it is an act of *observation*. What we do from here can change fate—but we don't know if our actions will make that doomsday more likely to happen or less."

"It sounds as if—for the next four days—we're all like Schrödinger's cat in the box, trapped in that suspended state between survival and death."

She nodded, not looking any happier than he did.

"So we're damned if we do and damned if we don't."

She shrugged. "That pretty much sums up quantum physics."

"So then what do you suggest we do?"

"We find that satellite. That's the most important agenda."

"You sound like General Metcalf."

"He's right. All my theories are just conjecture. But by analyzing the wreckage, I may have something more concrete to offer." She shifted in her seat to more fully face him. "I know you were not keen on me joining the team headed to Mongolia to search for the wreckage, but no one knows more about that satellite than I do. Without someone intimately knowledgeable on hand, valuable data could be lost—or worse."

"What do you mean by *worse?*"

She sighed heavily. "I told you how that influx of dark energy likely *wrinkled* space-time, a wrinkle much deeper than any estimates projected. But my preliminary calculations warn of a larger danger."

"What danger?"

"There is a slim possibility that we might've created a *kink* in space-time, something semipermanent, capable of lasting for a period of time— and that the kink could still be entangled at the quantum level with the remains of that satellite."

"Entangled?"

"Such an event occurs when two objects interact for a period of time, come to share quantum states, then become separated. In certain instances, their quantum states can remain linked, where a change in the quantum status in one changes in the other instantly. Even over vast distances."

"That seems to defy logic."

"And violates the speed of light. In fact, it kind of freaked Einstein out. He called this effect *spukhafte Fernwirkung,* or *spooky action at a distance.* Yet, not only has this phenomenon been demonstrated in labs at the subatomic level, but a group of Chinese researchers recently accomplished the same with a pair of diamonds visible to the naked eye. All it takes is enough energy."

"Something like a blast of dark energy."

"Exactly. If there is a *kink* in the curvature of space-time around the earth, and if its quantum state became entangled with the satellite, any mishandling of the crash debris could result in that kink ripping a hole from space to the ground."

"And that would not be good."

"Not if you like life on this planet."

"You make a compelling case, Dr. Shaw."

Before he could make a final comment, his satellite phone rang.

Checking the screen, he saw the incoming call was from Sigma command in D.C. It was Captain Kathryn Bryant, his second-in-command. Kat's specialty was in intelligence-gathering services for Sigma, but he had tasked her with the preliminary logistics in putting a search team together.

Painter had spoken to her briefly earlier. The tentative plan had been to have Commander Pierce's group proceed directly from China to Ulan Bator, the capital of Mongolia, where his group would rendezvous with a two-man team sent from Washington.

Kat had suggested keeping the expedition small, as the region where the satellite crashed was in Mongolia's Khan Khentii Strictly Protected Area, a region of the country where access was highly restricted, especially to foreigners, due to preservation efforts—both natural and historical. The region was also considered to be sacred to the people of Mongolia. Any misstep and the team could be booted out of there.

As a consequence, logistical details were still being worked out.

Painter hoped for better news from Kat as he answered the phone.

Her first words quickly quashed that hope.

"Director, we have another problem."

Of course, we do . . .

Kat continued, "I just heard word through the intelligence channels of an attack in Italy. Details are still sketchy, but apparently someone shot a rocket-propelled grenade into the university offices of Monsignor Verona."

"Vigor? Is he okay?"

"He is. In fact, I've got him queued up on the line for a conference call with you. He's still a little shaken up, but his niece was present during the attack and got them both out safely. He insisted on talking to you—and I think you might want to hear him out."

Painter had plenty on his plate, but he owed the monsignor this courtesy. "Put him on."

Kat made the connections and the familiar tenor voice of Monsignor Verona came onto the line.

"Director Crowe, *grazie*." Vigor sounded surprisingly calm considering what had just transpired, but he was a resilient old bird. "I know you are busy, but I have a grave concern that I wanted to bring to your attention."

"What's wrong?"

"To be blunt, I believe the world is coming to a major crisis point."

Painter felt an icy chill begin to develop. "Why do you say that?"

The monsignor went on to explain about a mysterious package from a dead archaeological colleague: a skull and a book bound in human skin. Vigor talked about Hungarian witches, Talmudic magical relics, and an inscription begging for salvation.

As the story continued, the chill slowly seeped away. Relief set in. This had *nothing* to do with what Painter had witnessed at the space center.

Vigor continued, "After the attack, I suspect now why my colleague, Father Josip, went into hiding. Whatever he is pursuing has clearly drawn the attention of a violent group, someone who seeks to keep his knowledge from reaching the world. He has asked for me to join him in Central Asia, near the Aral Sea. I was hoping you'd be able to offer some field support— especially as time is running short."

Painter wished he had the resources to help, but considering what he faced, he couldn't justify such a diversion of manpower. "I'm sorry—"

Kat interrupted, still on the conference call. "Monsignor Vigor, I think you should tell Director Crowe *why* you believe time is running short."

"*Mi dispiace,*" he apologized. "I thought I already had, but I realize now I only told you, Captain Bryant, not the director."

"Tell me what?" Painter asked.

"The inscription on the skull, the one asking for salvation . . . it was a plea against the world ending."

"You mentioned that already."

"Yes, but I failed to mention *when* the world was prophesied to end."

Painter felt that chill creep back up his spine. "Let me guess," he said. "In four days."

"*Sì,*" Vigor replied, surprised. "But how did you know that?"

For the moment, Painter refrained from explaining. He had Kat put

Vigor back on hold, while he and his second-in-command talked in private.

"What do you think?" he asked Kat.

"I find it intriguing that such a relic should match the doomsday time frame reported by the Space and Missile Systems Center."

Apparently Kat had already learned about that strange bit of news from out west. He shouldn't have been surprised. That was her field of expertise, gathering intelligence. Nothing escaped her notice.

"But is it a mere coincidence?" Painter asked. "Do we divert resources toward what may be just an archaeological wild-goose chase?"

"In this case, I'm interested enough to say yes. First, it wouldn't necessarily be that much of a diversion. The coordinates supplied by Monsignor Verona are in Central Asia and happen to be along the route from D.C. to Mongolia. It would be easy enough for our U.S.-based team to make a short stop at the Aral Sea to investigate this mystery. It wouldn't set the timetable back significantly. Besides, I still need to get resources airdropped out to Mongolia. In the meantime, we can send a second team, one that's already closer, in advance for an initial reconnaissance of the area."

"You mean Gray, Kowalski, and Seichan."

She nodded. "It's only a few hours from Hong Kong to Ulan Bator, the capital city of Mongolia."

"It sounds like you've thought this all out. But I should let you know, there may be a *third* member of the U.S. team." He glanced over to Jada. "A civilian who has convinced me her expertise may be needed."

"Not a problem. I value Dr. Shaw's help."

He smiled. As usual, Kat had read his mind.

"Also," she said, "there is another advantage in making this detour. By working with the monsignor and his mysterious colleague, it offers us the perfect cover story for our search into the restricted Khan Khentii Strictly Protected Area."

"Of course," Painter said, nodding, pleased at her resourcefulness. "They can pose as an archaeological team."

"Exactly. Especially if the monsignor would be willing to venture to Mongolia with us—as it seems we have a common goal."

Saving the world . . .

"Then let's get things rolling," Painter said. "Put a call in to Gray and get his team moving."

Kat sighed, her irritation plain. "I would if I could reach him . . ."

4

The Casino Lisboa had become ground zero for World War III. Or at least it sounded that way to Gray from inside the barricaded VIP room. The initial spats of suppressed gunfire had escalated into a full-out firefight in the hallway.

More blasts echoed in the distance.

Inside the room, Gray crouched behind their makeshift barricade in front of the door. With Kowalski's help, he'd manhandled the upended baccarat table and blocked the only way inside. Seichan had slid one of the red-silk sofas to further brace their fortification. The only other way out was the narrow window, but it was a straight four-story drop through the dark to the asphalt pavement below.

Across the room, Dr. Hwan Pak huddled in the far corner. His self-satisfied elation at his betrayal had turned to terror. Plainly something had gone wrong with his plan. The *Duàn zhī* Triad's attempted ambush had run into a snag. Gray had initially hoped it was hotel security thwarting the attack, but as the fighting grew in volume and severity, including spats of assault rifles and the chugging rattle of machine guns, he suspected this was a gangland turf war.

And apparently we're the prize.

Gray knew their barricade would not last forever. Someone would get the upper hand. Proving this assumption, a shotgun blast tore a fist-sized hole through the door.

"Now or never, Kowalski!" Gray yelled.

"You try doing this when your pants keep falling down!"

The large man crouched on his knees in the middle of the floor as Gray and Seichan kept their backs to the sofa, using its bulk as shelter.

Kowalski had stripped off his belt and positioned it in a circle on the floor, cinching the buckle in place and affixing a radio receiver to it. Kowalski was Sigma's demolitions expert. While they couldn't risk bringing weapons to China, Kowalski had traveled with an ace up his sleeve. Or in this case, laced through his belt.

The high-yield detonation cord had been developed by DARPA. It was sealed in a tube of carbon graphene, making the explosive inside undetectable to airport screening processes.

"All set," Kowalski said and rolled back to join them, dragging a chair behind him.

"What are you doing?" Pak called over to them.

The three of them crowded behind the chair.

"Fire in the hole!" the big man yelled and pressed the transmitter in his hand.

The blast rocked the room, ringing Gray's head like a struck bell. Smoke billowed. For a moment, the firefight outside halted as all parties froze at the sudden explosion.

"Go!" Gray yelled, shoving the chair aside.

He prayed the detonation cord had done its job. Otherwise, they were out of luck, as they'd blown Kowalski's only supply of explosives.

Ahead, the fiery smoldering of burned carpeting glowed through the smoke. A crater had been blasted in the floor—or rather, *through* the floor. The larger steel trusses were intact, but the explosion had ripped a hole between them.

Gray stared down through the wreckage. He knew the third floor below had an almost identical layout as the fourth. Luckily the VIP room under them was empty.

As the gunfire resumed out in the hallway, sounding even more furious, Gray waved Seichan through first. She slipped between the trusses and smoothly leaped to the floor below.

Gray and Kowalski started to follow, but Hwan Pak tried to interfere, begging for them to take him with them. Kowalski punched out with a fist, as if swatting at a fly. Bone crunched, and Pak flew backward, landing on his backside, blood pouring from his nose.

A moment later, Gray stood next to Seichan by the third-floor door. Kowalski landed heavily behind them.

"Sounds clear out there," Seichan said, her ear to the door. "But we'll have to move fast. That ruse won't last long."

"We need a way out of this war zone," Gray warned. "But all the exits from the hotel will be guarded."

"I may know a way."

Seichan opened the door, stuck her head out, then bolted into the hallway.

"So how about telling us," Kowalski groused as he and Gray followed.

Seichan ran for the fire stairs and pounded through the door—only to be faced with a gunman running down from above, leaping steps.

Seichan ducked and hit him low, flipping the assailant over her back.

Gray, a few steps behind, spun on one toe and snap-kicked out with his other leg, catching the flying man in the jaw, cracking his head back. He landed in a crumpled pile.

"Remind me never to get on your bad sides," Kowalski said.

Gray relieved the Triad member of his weapon, an AK-47 assault rifle. A search quickly revealed a holstered Chinese army Red Star pistol. He tossed the handgun to Kowalski.

"It's Christmas already?" he mumbled, efficiently checking it over.

"Let's go!" Seichan urged, poised at the steps leading down, checking the stairwell below.

Gray joined her with the rifle, and they hurried together down the steps, leaping from landing to landing. The firefight above faded slightly. But when they reached the first floor, the exit door began to swing open ahead of them. Whether it was someone seeking refuge or new reinforcements, Gray didn't care. He fired a spat of rounds, peppering the door.

It quickly closed.

A pistol cracked behind him as Kowalski angled a shot up the stairwell, discouraging anyone from following.

Seichan ignored the first-floor door and continued down toward the basement level. From Gray's study of the Lisboa, he knew an extensive shopping market tunneled beneath the casino floor. The place was also notorious for its parade of prostitutes, earning the level its nickname, Hooker Mall.

Seichan reached the basement door and cracked it open enough to peek through. It was eerily quiet out there compared to the ruckus above.

She spoke softly. "As I thought, all the shops are barricaded closed."

Likely the owners had locked down their gates as the firefight began, battening down their hatches.

Gray began to get an inkling of Seichan's plan. While the public entrances were surely under armed guard, no one was likely to be watching the market's warehouse ramps and doors. Like Seichan, the Triads knew the shops would bottle themselves up to protect their wares from looting.

So how did she expect—?

Seichan wiggled out of her sweater vest and tossed it aside. She then ripped open her silk blouse, popping buttons across the floor, exposing a black bra, revealing the flat curve of her stomach. She pulled a tail of her shirt out of her jeans and disheveled her hair.

"How do I look?" she asked.

Gray was speechless—and for once, so was Kowalski.

She rolled her eyes at them, turned, and slipped out the door. "Hang back until I get someone to unlock a security gate."

Gray took her place at the door.

Kowalski clapped him on the shoulder. "You are one lucky bastard, Pierce."

He wasn't about to argue.

2:14 A.M.

Ju-long Delgado cursed his bad luck.

He stood before the plasma screen in his office, staring at the smoking hole blasted through the floor of the VIP room. He wanted to blame such misfortunes on the comet in the sky, but he was not a clinger to such superstitions. He knew the true source of his grief.

He had simply underestimated his quarry.

That would not happen twice.

A few moments ago, he had watched the larger of the two men detonate the explosive device—then he could only stand idly by as the trio made their escape, like rats down a hole.

The room's only remaining occupant huddled in a corner.

Dr. Hwan Pak.

As he stared at the North Korean scientist, Ju-long tapped a finger on the edge of the Portuguese naval chest under the television, running various scenarios through his head, weighing each option for its best advantage.

He settled upon one course.

Earlier, Ju-long had tried to raise Tomaz at the Lisboa, to warn of their targets' pending flight, but he had failed to reach anyone. He pictured the firefight being waged across the floors of the casino. It was a war being fought at his own behest, so he could not fault that it demanded Tomaz's full attention at the moment.

So be it.

He pressed a button on his phone. As it was answered, he passed on a terse order. "Bring my car around."

As he waited, someone knocked softly on his door. He turned to see it open, and a small figure slipped inside wearing a short silk robe and slippers. She was a vision in tanned skin, draped with a flow of honey-colored hair. As she crossed toward him, she cradled her swollen belly with one hand.

"Natalia, my sweet, you should be in bed."

"Your son won't let me," she said with a tender smile, her eyes glancing invitingly toward him. "Perhaps if his father were lying beside me . . ."

"How I wish I could, but first I must attend to some business."

She pouted.

He crossed to her, dropped to his knees, and kissed her belly where his son slumbered. "I'll be back soon," he promised them both, adding a kiss to her cheek as he ushered her out.

He truly wished he could join her—but at his father's knee, he had learned that whether in war or business, sometimes one simply had to get one's hands dirty.

2:16 A.M.

Seichan sensed the walls closing in on her.

The longer they remained trapped inside Casino Lisboa, the slimmer were their chances of escaping.

She drew upon that desperation as she rushed from the stairwell door and out into the open of the basement shopping mall. Feigning a slight limp, she put on a great show of distress, pretending to be one of the mall's prostitutes caught amid the firefight.

She spun around in a circle, pulling at her hair, crying for help in Cantonese. Tears streamed down her face as she ran from one gate to another, pounding to be let inside, for someone to rescue her.

As with many such places, she understood there was an unspoken relationship between the storeowners and the prostitutes who prowled this lower level, defined by the mutually beneficial flow of commerce.

The shops drew prospective clients, while the prostitutes lured potential shoppers.

The great circle of life.

She counted on that relationship extending to the two sides protecting each other. When she reached a farmers' market, she sank to her knees against its steel fence. She rocked and moaned, looking lost and frightened.

As she had hoped, her plaintive cries finally drew someone out of hiding. A tiny white-haired man with a dirty apron came timidly to the gate. He made a motion to shoo her away, scolding her.

Instead, she clung to his gate, hanging from it in an operatic display of despair and fear, pleading with him.

Realizing she wasn't going to leave, he dropped to a knee. He searched over her shoulder to make sure she was alone, and only then did he risk unlocking the gate.

As soon as he began to lift the steel fence, Seichan secretly motioned to Gray and Kowalski.

The stairwell door creaked open behind her, accompanied by the pounding of boots coming toward her.

The proprietor's eyes grew huge. He tried to push the gate back down. Before he could, Seichan skirted under it and elbowed him back with one arm and yanked the fence higher with the other.

Gray ran up and skidded on his knees under the gate.

Kowalski barrel-rolled after him, slamming into a stand of oranges.

Gray pointed his rifle at the man.

"Lock it," Seichan ordered, straightening her back and shedding her act like a snakeskin.

The storeowner obeyed in a rush, resecuring his gate.

"Tell him we mean him no harm," Gray said.

Seichan translated, but from the cold look in her eyes and her stony countenance, he did not seem soothed. She questioned him briefly, then turned to Gray.

"The warehouse exit is back this way," she said and led them in that direction.

Moving deeper into the market, they passed along a long counter supporting boxes of locally grown fruits and vegetables. On the other side, rows of watery tanks held live fish, turtles, frogs, and shellfish.

Upon reaching the far side, she found a concrete ramp headed up, ending at a large roll-up door used by delivery trucks. A smaller service entrance beckoned to the left.

Glad to be rid of them, the proprietor keyed the side door open and angrily waved them out into the night.

Gray led the way with his rifle.

Seichan followed, pushing into a narrow service alley.

Sirens echoed from all directions as emergency vehicles closed in on the Lisboa, but the press of the festival's crowds around Nam Van Lake and its surrounding streets continued to stymie a fast response.

In fact, out here, most of the drunken revelers seemed unaware of the neighboring turf war. Fireworks rang out from the crowd around the lake, exploding over the waters, reflecting among the thousands of candlelit lanterns floating on the lake. Closer at hand, the neighboring Wynn casino danced with flumes of water, rising from an acre-sized fountain, the jets set to the tunes of the Beatles.

"What now?" Kowalski asked, having to yell somewhat.

"We need a fast way out of here," Gray said, heading down the alley toward the crowds around the lake. "But it'll be hard to hail a cab, and it's not like we can blend into the crowd."

"I can," Seichan said.

She closed her ripped blouse by crossing one side over the other like a sarong and tucking the ends into her jeans to hold everything in place.

"You stay here," she ordered. "Stick to the shadows until I return."

2:28 A.M.

Gray kept to the mouth of the alley, his eyes never leaving the festival crowd. Kowalski hung back deeper in the alley, making sure no one snuck up behind them.

A moment ago, he had traded weapons with Kowalski. The big man's long duster made it easier to hide the length of the AK-47 rifle. Gray kept the pistol at his thigh, turning his body to keep it out of direct sight.

Sirens grew louder and louder.

To his right, the grounds around the neighboring lake were still packed with revelers, but to his left, the throngs on the streets were already beginning to stream away, heading to bed or into one of the many casinos or bars.

As he stared down the street, the flow of pedestrians began to scatter, like startled pigeons.

The sharper timbre of a two-stroke engine cut through the cacophony of music and voices. A motorcycle burst into view, carrying a familiar rider. Seichan artlessly plowed through the straggling crowd, trusting them to jump out of her way.

As the people cleared, Gray saw it wasn't a cycle but more of a rickshaw. The front end was a motorbike, the back end a small-wheeled buggy. Such vehicles were called *trishaws*. He had seen them whizzing about the streets on their way here. In Macau, a city with one of the densest populations, trishaws were much more practical than cars.

But maybe not when one was being hunted by warring Triads.

Seichan skidded to a stop next to them. "Get in! Stay low!"

With no choice, Gray and Kowalski climbed into the buggy in back. Gray felt exposed in the open like this, especially as one of the rare white faces amid a sea of Asian countenances.

Kowalski tried to sink into the depths of his long coat, clearly mindful of his conspicuous bulk. "This is a bad idea."

Once they were seated, Seichan sped the vehicle around and headed away from Casino Lisboa, skirting the edge of Nam Van Lake.

"It's the best I could commandeer," she yelled back to them. "Roads are blocked all over the city. No way I could get something larger through in time."

She continued around the lake.

Gray realized they were heading *away* from the Macau ferry terminal.

"Where are you going?"

"Over the causeway." She pointed across to the neighboring island of Taipa. A brightly lit bridge crossed to it from here. "A smaller ferry terminal lies on that side, not far from the Venetian hotel. It's less likely anyone will be looking for us over there. I learned the last boat of the night leaves in twenty minutes."

And we need to be on it.

With targets painted on their backs, Macau had become too hot.

Gray hunkered low in the buggy seat as Seichan hit the main drag and raced toward the causeway. She wound in and out of traffic, even flying through slower-moving bicycles and pedestrians when necessary.

As they hit the bridge, it was a straight three-kilometer shot to the other island. Congestion bottlenecked on the bridge, but it barely slowed Seichan. They whisked along at a heady pace, weaving and dodging their way across. To either side, the moonlit waters of the Pearl River Delta glowed with thousands upon thousands of floating lanterns, spreading far out to sea, mirroring the stars in the sky.

Ahead, Taipa Island blazed with neon, a cheap spectacle to the quieter beauty found here.

In less than ten minutes, they had cleared the causeway and turned for the narrow streets that fronted the Taipa ferry terminal.

Before they had gone twenty yards, the massive grill of a Cadillac Escalade careened out of an alley to the right and T-boned their trishaw, sending it spinning and slamming it hard into a waist-high beach wall.

Gray got tossed, flying, tangled with Kowalski.

They hit the rocky sand and rolled. Gray managed to keep hold of his pistol as he came to a skidding stop. Still on his back, he swung the weapon up toward the road, where the Cadillac sat askew, blocking traffic.

Men—a mix of Chinese and Portuguese—burst out of its doors, but they kept low, the wall blocking a clear shot. They swarmed to the left as a group.

Only then did Gray realize Seichan wasn't there.

With his heart pounding in his throat, he rolled to his knees for a better vantage and began firing. He struck one assailant in the arm; the next three shots went wide. Then he saw Seichan hauled up among them. She was dragged toward the Cadillac, dazed, her face half covered in blood.

Cursing, Gray lowered his pistol, fearful of shooting into the cluster of men who held Seichan.

The enemy was not so reticent.

Sand blasted around Gray's knees.

Steps away, Kowalski finally freed his AK-47. Holding it with one arm, he strafed the wall, driving back the pair of shooters. His other arm pointed toward the shelter of the causeway.

They were open targets on the beach.

With no other choice, they sprinted for its shelter. Gray fired a few potshots back toward the Cadillac. A tall, bearded man stood beside the SUV, unfazed by the rounds ricocheting off its bulletproof windows. The figure scooped Seichan's limp form from the men and rolled her into the back.

Doors slammed, and with a squeal of tires, the Cadillac careened away. A few gunmen remained, shooting toward them, but Gray reached the causeway and ducked under the bridge, Kowalski at his heels.

"I told you this was a bad idea," Kowalski said.

"Keep moving."

Ducking his head, Gray passed beneath the causeway. He needed to shake the gunmen left behind. Reaching the far side, he crossed back to the beach wall next to the bridge and clambered over it. The snarl of traffic was slowly clearing.

Taking advantage of the bedlam of honking horns and bumper-to-bumper vehicles, Gray kept low and maneuvered across the street. To his left, a gunman searched the beach. Another one hopped over the wall to get an angle of fire under the bridge.

Gray rushed across the road and into the densely packed maze of streets and alleyways. Kowalski followed, huffing heavily next to him.

"Seichan?" Kowalski asked.

"They didn't immediately shoot her," he answered.

Thank God for that.

They continued for another quarter mile, mostly paralleling the beachfront, heading away from the causeway. The streets were still crowded, but not as thickly as earlier in the night. Still, in a sea of Asian faces, the two Americans stuck out too prominently. It would not be hard for the hunters to track them.

Knowing that, they dared not stop moving.

"What's the plan?" Kowalski asked.

Until now, Gray had been running on pure adrenaline, but Kowalski was right. They needed to think strategically.

Whoever had staged this attack had cleverly assumed they might make a break for the other ferry terminal. With the causeway being the closest access to the other island, it was easy enough to set up the ambush at this choke point and wait for their targets to come to them.

"They'll certainly be watching the ferry terminal," Gray said, planning aloud. "That means we'll have to find another means to reach Hong Kong."

"What about Seichan? Are we just going to leave her?"

"We have no choice. If the gangs have her, we don't have the firepower to go after her, even if we knew where she was being taken. And it's not as if we can move about Macau inconspicuously."

"So we run?"

For now.

Gray had slowly sidled back toward the waterfront. He nodded to a marina a few blocks away. "We need a boat."

He shifted into the flow of carousing partiers still cruising along the beachfront, Kowalski in tow. Once they reached the marina, he turned into it. Lanterns decorated the waters around the moored yachts and motorboats. They marched along the docks until they found a sleek midnight-blue speedboat being prepped by a middle-aged couple, who from their accents appeared to be British expats, a husband and wife, likely on their way home after the festival.

Gray stepped over to them. "Excuse me."

The two stopped in midargument.

Gray grinned sheepishly as they looked over. He ran fingers through his hair as if his next words pained him to admit.

"I was wondering if you were heading back to Hong Kong and might be willing to help out a pair of guys who lost their shirts playing pai gow. We don't even have enough left over for a ferry ticket back to Kowloon."

The man straightened, clearly suspicious, but also a little drunk. "You're Yanks," he said, with no less surprise than if they'd been Lilliputians. "Normally I would say yes, my good chaps, but you see—"

Gray showed them his pistol, while Kowalski parted his duster to reveal his AK-47.

"How about now?" Gray asked.

The man sagged as if the air had been let out of him. "You know my wife will never let me live this down."

She crossed her arms. "I told you we should have left sooner."

The husband shrugged.

After tying and gagging them aboard a neighboring dark yacht, Gray chugged their craft out of the marina. Once clear, he opened the throttle and set off across the dark waters toward Hong Kong.

As the lights of Macau receded behind them, Gray stepped away from the helm. "Take the wheel."

Kowalski, a former seaman, gladly took his place, rubbing his palms in anticipation. "Let's see what this baby can do."

That normally would have worried Gray, but he had greater concerns.

With this brief respite, he unbuttoned his satellite phone from his jacket pocket. He saw he had multiple voice mails from Sigma command. Earlier, he had turned the ringer off before taking that meeting back at the Lisboa. Since then he'd never had a safe moment to turn it back on.

Rather than listening to the recordings, he simply called up Sigma command in D.C. The phone had DARPA's latest encryption software to discourage unwanted eavesdropping.

Kat Bryant immediately picked up. "About time you checked in."

"Been a little busy."

From the tone of his voice, she picked out something was wrong. "What happened?"

He gave her a thumbnail version of the night's events.

Kat asked a few probing questions, quickly assessing the depth of the quicksand. "Gray, I can't get you help. Certainly not in time to do any good, not with her already in their hands."

"Understood. That's not why I was calling. I just wanted to give Sigma a situation report."

In case things went south from here.

"We're having our own crisis out here," Kat said. "That's why I was trying to reach you. Director Crowe wanted you and your team to travel to Mongolia."

Mongolia?

She told him a sketchy story of a downed satellite and a last image that showed the East Coast burning.

"I can't head there," he said as she finished. "At least not now."

"Of course. The circumstances have changed." Her next words were laced with worry. "But what *are* you going to do out there, Gray? You have no resources. And the criminal organizations in Macau are notoriously ruthless and well funded."

"I have a plan."

"To do what?"

Gray stared across the waters ahead toward the distant glow on the horizon.

"To fight fire with fire."

5

Jada held her breath.

What am I doing here?

It felt like she had fallen through Alice's looking glass.

To her side, Painter Crowe placed his hand on a security pad inside the elevator. A blue line scanned his palm, and the elevator cage began to drop into the earth.

Their jet had made the cross-country trip in less than five hours. After landing, they had been whisked by private car to the National Mall, stopping at the majestic Smithsonian Castle, a flag waving from its highest tower. As she had stepped out of the car, she had looked with new eyes at the historic building with its jumble of redbrick parapets, turrets, and spires. Completed in 1855, the structure was considered one of the finest examples of Gothic Revival in the United States and now served as the heart of the many museums that made up the nation's Smithsonian Institution.

Having grown up in Congress Heights, a poorer area southeast of D.C., she had visited the Castle countless times as a girl. Admission to the museums had been free, and her mother, a single parent, encouraged her daughter's education in every way she could.

"I never knew this was under here," Jada said in a hushed voice as the elevator dropped into the subterranean world beneath the Castle.

"These levels were once bunkers and fallout shelters. Back in World

War II, it even served as home to a scientific think tank. After that, it was abandoned and forgotten."

"Such a prime piece of Washington real estate as this?" She offered Painter a crooked grin.

He smiled back. For someone two decades older than her, he was a fine-looking man, with his dark hair laced by a single snowy lock and those blue eyes. After their long conversation during the flight here, she also found him remarkably smart, with a wide swath of knowledge on many subjects—with the exception of the history of jazz. But she could forgive him that lapse, especially when those blue eyes danced in sunlight.

"Once I discovered these dusty levels," he said, "it struck me as a perfect haunt for Sigma to set up shop, what with its easy access both to the labs of the Smithsonian and to the halls of power in D.C."

She heard the flicker of fatherly pride in his voice; he was plainly happy to show it off to newcomers, which she suspected must be a rare event.

The elevator doors whooshed open into a long central hallway.

"This is the command level," he said, leading the way. "Ahead is our central communications nest, the nerve center of Sigma."

As they approached, a slim woman in the dress blues of the navy stepped out of the room to greet them. She was handsome in a hard way, perhaps made more severe by the short bob of her auburn hair. Jada also thought she noted a trace of faint scars across her cheeks, but she refrained from staring.

"Director Crowe," the woman said. "Good to have you back, sir."

"This is Captain Kathryn Bryant," Painter introduced. "My second-in-command."

"Kat is fine." She shook Jada's hand with an overly firm grip, but the warmth of her small smile softened the greeting. "Welcome, Dr. Shaw."

Jada licked her lips, anxious to see more of this world, but she knew their timetable was short.

"How are preparations going?" Painter asked. "I'd like to have this team moving in less than an hour."

"You heard about Commander Pierce?" she asked and led them into the communications room. The oval space was small, dominated by a curved bank of monitors and computer interfaces.

"I did. We'll work around him if need be. I assume you're offering him whatever support he needs."

Kat cast him a withering glance, suggesting she'd do nothing less. She settled into a chair before the monitors, like a pilot taking the helm. "As to the itinerary for this mission, Monsignor Verona and his niece will be taking the first morning flight out of Rome headed to Kazakhstan. It's a five-hour flight for them. If we stay on schedule here and get wheels up in an hour, our team should touch down about the same time as the Veronas . . . midafternoon local Kazakhstan time."

Jada frowned. This was one part of the expedition that made no sense to her. "So as I understand it," she said, wanting clarification, "we'll be collecting these others to substantiate our claims that our search of Mongolia's remote mountains is archaeological in origin."

"That's right," Kat said. "But we'll also be using the remainder of that day in Kazakhstan to investigate a mystery that may or may not be connected to the current threat. If nothing pans out, you move on."

Painter had briefly explained about a skull and book. But she had hardly listened, not giving his story much credence. But this wasn't her call.

"And who else will be on this expedition?" Jada asked.

The answer came from behind her. "That would be me, for one."

She turned to find a man standing a few inches shorter than her, but beefy as a pit bull. He wore sweatpants, a T-shirt, and a Washington Redskins baseball cap that did little to hide his perfectly smooth head. Her first instinct was to dismiss the man, but she noted the sharp glint of intelligence in his dark eyes—and amusement.

Though she couldn't put a finger on why, she felt an instant fondness for him, like for a goofy older brother.

It seemed she wasn't the only one.

Kat Bryant leaned back in her chair. The stranger crossed over and kissed the woman on the lips.

Okay, maybe not a *brother*.

As the man straightened, Kat glanced back to Jada. "He'll take good care of you."

"She has to say that because she's my wife." He kept one hand lovingly on her shoulder.

Jada finally noted the other hand was prosthetic, attached at his wrist by a thicker cuff of electronics. It was so real she almost missed it.

Painter nodded to him. "Monk Kokkalis is one of Sigma's best."

"One of?" he asked, looking wounded.

Painter ignored him. "You'll also be accompanied by another, one of our newest members. His specialty is electrical engineering and physics. He also knows a fair amount about astronomy and has some, shall we say, *unique* talents. I think you'll find him a great asset."

"That would be Duncan Wren," Kat explained.

"Speaking of which, where is he?" Painter asked. "I thought I asked everyone to attend this mission briefing."

Kat shared a glance with her husband, then swung around to face her monitors. She mumbled under her breath. "I've already briefed him. He had a medical matter he had to attend to before leaving."

Painter frowned. "What medical matter?"

6:18 P.M.

"Don't move," he was warned.

Duncan balanced his six-foot-two bulk on a tiny folding chair with a wobbly leg. "It would be easier, Clyde, if you took into account that *not* all your clients are emaciated meth addicts."

Across from him, his friend wore a surgical mask and a set of magnifying eyeglasses affixed to his face. Clyde looked like he might break ninety pounds when wet, most of which was hair, which trailed in a long ponytail down his back.

Clyde grasped Duncan's large hand atop the table, as if about to read his palm. Instead, he reached with a scalpel and nicked the edge of Duncan's left index finger near its tip. Fire lanced up his wrist, but he kept his hand steady on the metal table.

Clyde plunked the scalpel down. "This next part may hurt."

Ya think . . .

Picking up a sterilized pair of tweezers, his friend probed the new wound. As steel scraped nerves, pain set Duncan's teeth to grinding. He closed his eyes, controlling his breathing.

"Got it!" his torturer said.

Duncan opened his eyes to see a tiny black pellet, the size of a grain of rice, extracted from the cut, clutched in the jaws of the tweezing forceps.

It was a sliver of rare-earth magnet.

"Now to replace this old worn one with a new one . . ."

Using the same tweezers, Clyde lifted a fresh magnet from the cache Duncan had supplied. The magnets were courtesy of a DARPA lab in New Brunswick, though their current use was definitely off-label.

The rice-sized pellet—coated by Duncan in Parylene C to prevent infection—was slipped through the wound. Once in place, a few drops of surgical glue closed the cut, sealing the magnet beneath his skin, where it rested beside the somatosensory nerves responsible for a fingertip's percep-tion of pressure, temperature, and pain.

This last sensation was certainly responding strongly.

"Thanks, Clyde."

Duncan opened and closed his fist, squeezing away the worst of the postsurgical throbbing. This wasn't his first time to the rodeo. Each of his ten fingers had similar slivers of magnet in place, and every now and then, they had to be replaced.

"How does it feel?" Clyde yanked down his mask, revealing a nasal stud through his septum and a thick steel ring through his lower lip.

Not your typical doctor.

In fact, the man had been a dental hygienist in a former life. In his new profession, operating out of a warehouse near the Ronald Reagan air-port, he was the local biohacking community's best *grinder,* someone who designed and installed body enhancements.

Clyde preferred the term *evolutionary artist.*

Myriad other professions shared the industrial space, each separated by opaque plastic curtains: a tattoo artist who had developed a luminescent ink, a piercer who inserted tiny bits of jewelry into the whites of a client's eye, another who implanted RFID chips into bodies as wearable storage devices.

Although most patrons came here for the novelty or the thrill, a handful had turned biohacking into a new religion, and this was their church. For Duncan, it was simply a matter of professional need. As an electrical engineer, he found this particular biohack a useful tool, a new way of perceiving the world.

"Want to take the new magnet out for a spin?" Clyde asked.

"Probably too sore, but let me see what you've sculpted."

He knew that's what Clyde really wanted to show him.

His surgeon waved him over to a neighboring table wired with circuit boards, spools of exposed wires, and stacked series of hard drives of varying heights.

"I'm still fine-tuning my latest bit of art."

"Power it up."

Clyde flipped the toggle. "It'll take a few seconds to fully generate the field I created."

"I think I can wait that long."

Despite misconceptions, the magnets at his fingertips couldn't pick up coins or even demagnetize credit cards. Even airport screening machines failed to pick them up. But what they did do was *vibrate* in the presence of an electromagnetic field. The minuscule oscillations were enough to excite the nerve endings in his fingertips to create a unique sensation very distinct from touch, almost a sixth sense.

With practice, he had discovered that EM fields triggered a variety of sensations, each uniquely different in size, shape, and strength. Palpable bubbles surrounded power transformers. Microwave ovens cast off rhythmic waves that pushed against his hands. High-tension wires pulsated with a silky energy, as if running his fingertips over the smooth skin of an undulating snake.

He also used the magnets for more practical purposes as an electrical engineer. His sixth sense could discern the level of power running along cables or judge if a hard drive was spinning properly inside a laptop. He'd even once used it to diagnose a problem with the distributor cap in his 1995 Mustang Cobra R.

After discovering the rich complexity of this hidden electromagnetic world, he never wanted to go back. He'd be blind without his magnets.

"Should be ready," Clyde said, waving his arm over the table of carefully manipulated electrical appliances.

Duncan lifted his hands over the table. The energy generated by Clyde's assembly seemed to *push* back against his fingers, giving a haptic sensation of form. He ran his magnetic fingers over that surface, discovering the unique shape artfully sculpted by Clyde through the judicious placement of hardware and flow of current.

He felt upswept wings of energy spreading wide to either side. Beneath the wings, his fingertips grew warmer the deeper he probed, even turning hot as he neared the table's surface.

As he probed, his fingertips gave form and substance to the invisible. An image grew in his mind's eye, as real as any sculpture.

"Incredible," Duncan said.

"I call this piece *Phoenix Rising from the Ashes of the Digital Age*."

"Ever the poet, Clyde."

"Thanks, Dunk."

He paid the man for his services, checked his watch, and headed across the warehouse floor.

He could have had someone at Sigma perform this for him. Monk Kokkalis, with his background in medical forensics, was certainly skilled enough. But he'd known Clyde and his friends from his prior life, back when he thought he was going to rule the world as a college basketball star with La Salle. His muscular arms still bore sleeves of tattoos from the elbow up—and he still wore a silver stud through his upper left ear, in the shape of a tiny eagle, a memorial to friends lost in Afghanistan during a firefight in Takur. He'd ended up in the U.S. Marines after his rising basketball career imploded following a series of injuries that sidelined him, forcing him to forfeit his scholarship.

By the time he was twenty-four, he had served six tours of duty in Afghanistan, the last two with Marine Force Recon, but after Takur, after he failed to reenlist, Painter Crowe ended up at his doorstep. In his prior life, he had been studying engineering in college and must have shown enough aptitude to be approached by Sigma. Now, after a fast-tracked education, he had a dual degree in both physics and electrical engineering—and was about to go on his first official mission with Sigma.

To find a crashed satellite.

Wanting to be fully prepared, he had come here.

He opened and closed his fist. The pain was already receding.

As he stepped through the warehouse door, he noted a pair of shadowy figures crouched by his parked Mustang. The black Cobra R was family, a muscular piece of his past, as much a memorial as the stud through his ear. He had originally bought the used car for his kid brother, back when Duncan believed his future was a spinning orange ball. Cancer finally caught up with Billy at eighteen, taking away forever that shit-eating grin. But the car remained, full of happy memories of two brothers ruling the world, along with grimmer recollections of loss, pain, and good-byes said too soon.

He stalked toward the men by the Mustang, anger building inside of him. Up on his toes, keeping to deeper shadows, he crept until he stood behind them, both clearly stymied by the locking mechanism he had specially engineered for the car.

They remained unaware of his presence—until he cleared his throat.

Surprised, one swung around with a tire iron.

Really?

A moment later, the two were fleeing, bloodied and limping.

Duncan reached to the door's handle. It unlocked before he touched it, triggered by the tiny glass-encased RFID chip implanted in his upper arm, another bodily addition like his magnets.

While he chalked up all these modifications to *professional need,* he knew down deep it was something more basic. Even before being approached by Sigma, he had already begun altering his body with tattoos.

He knew these changes had more to do with Billy, with the way he died, his body ravaged by cells gone mad. These modifications were Duncan's way of taking control, of defying cancer. It was his armor against the vagaries of fate, where a body could suddenly turn against itself.

His first tattoo had been a copy of Billy's palm print. He inked it over his heart and later added the date of his brother's death. Duncan often found his own hand covering that mark, wondering what twist of genetic fate had allowed him to live while his brother had to die.

The same could be said of his friends who had never returned from Afghanistan, those few who had caught a stray bullet or who were the first to step on a hidden IED.

I lived. They died.

It defined a fundamental constant of the universe.

Fate was a cruel, heartless bitch.

Fired by equal parts adrenaline and guilt, he yanked open the car door, hopped in, and took off. He raced through the outskirts of D.C., zipping through gears, punching past stop signs.

Still, he could not outrun the ghosts of his past—of his fellow teammates, of a kid brother who had laughed in the face of death.

Having survived, he must now live for all of them.

That truth, that burden of responsibility, grew heavier with every passing mile, every passing year. It was becoming too much to bear.

Still, he did the only thing he could.

He pressed harder on the gas.

6:34 P.M.

"You look a bit overwhelmed," Painter said.

And why wouldn't I?

Jada stared down at the thick mission dossier on her lap. She sat in Director Crowe's subterranean office. She felt suddenly claustrophobic, not so much because of the mass of the Smithsonian Castle above her head, but because of the weight of the packet resting on her knee.

And all it signified.

She was about to travel halfway around the world, to search for a crashed military satellite that might hold the fate of the world, or at the very least make or break her career as an astrophysicist.

So, yeah, as the once nappy-headed girl out of Congress Heights who ran home from school every day to keep from being beaten up because she was an honor student and liked books . . . I'm feeling a little pressure.

"You'll have a good team with you," Painter promised her. "It's not all on your shoulders—nor should you let it be. Trust your team."

"If you say so."

"I do."

She took a deep steadying breath. Painter's office was spartan, limited to a desk, a filing cabinet, and a computer, but the space as a whole had a worn-around-the-edges warmth to it, like a comfortable pair of tattered sneakers. She noted the personal touches. On the cabinet rose a swirling chunk of black glass that looked like a sculpture but was more likely a memento. On the wall, suspended in a shadow box, was a curved fang from some jungle beast, but it seemed impossibly long. And on his desk stood a cluster of framed photos of a woman.

Must be his fiancée.

He had mentioned her often on the flight here and clearly loved her.

Lucky lady.

The room also plainly served as the hub for Sigma command. Three large video monitors had been mounted on the walls around his desk, like windows upon the world. Or in this case, the *universe*.

On one screen was a real-time view of Comet IKON; on another, the final image taken by the falling satellite; the last showed a live feed from the Space and Missile Systems Center out west.

The scuff of shoes and low voices drew her attention to the door. Kat Bryant appeared with someone in tow.

"Look who I found," Kat said.

Painter stood and shook the tall man's hand. "About time, Sergeant Wren."

Jada found herself also on her feet.

This had to be her other teammate. Duncan Wren. He was surprisingly young, likely only a couple years older than her. She sized him up. His physique was bulky and hard, filling out his marine T-shirt, with tattoos peeking down from the sleeves. But he didn't seem muscle-bound, far from it. She imagined he could match her stride for stride in a sprint—and she was fast.

She shook his hand, noting the scraped knuckles. "Jada Shaw."

"The astrophysicist?" he asked.

Surprise sparked in his green eyes, irking her somewhat. Over her short career, she had seen that look plenty of times. Physics was still a man's world.

As if to look her over better, he brushed back a few stray locks of dark blond hair, laced with lighter streaks that didn't come out of any bottle.

"Great," he said with no hint of condescending sarcasm. He placed his fists on his hips. "So then let's go find us a satellite."

"Jet is fueled and waiting," Kat said. "I'll take you there."

Jada's heart climbed higher in her throat. This was all happening so fast.

Duncan touched her elbow, as if sensing her growing panic.

She remembered Painter's earlier advice.

Trust your team.

But what about trusting herself?

Duncan leaned toward her, his eyes crinkling with concern but also shining with damnable enthusiasm. "You ready?"

"I guess I'd better be."

"That's all anyone can ask."

Before they left, Kat stepped around them and placed a folder on Painter's desk, keeping a finger on top of it. "The latest report on Gray's plan of operation in Hong Kong."

He nodded, sighing a bit. "I skimmed it earlier on the computer. That's a dangerous path he's about to tread."

"It seems he's willing to walk it for Seichan."

6

Gray prepared to enter the lion's den.

Or *lioness,* in this particular case.

He stood on the street amid the crush of the morning rush hour in the Mong Kok district of the Kowloon peninsula. People raced through the morning drizzle, heads low, some with umbrellas, others with wide bamboo hats. Everywhere his eye settled, there was movement. Cars crept down the narrow streets between towering skyscrapers. Laundry flapped from balconies like the flags of a thousand nationalities. Crowds milled and flowed.

Even the smells changed with every breeze: the sizzle of pork fat, the burn of Thai spices, the pungent stink rising from the overflowing trash bins, the stale whiff of perfume from a woman passing close by. Calls echoed all around him, mostly the pleas of commerce, drawn by his white face.

Hey, boss, guess how much for a suit . . .

You want copy watch, yes . . .

Food is very good, very fresh . . . you try . . .

The cacophony of Kowloon deafened the senses. New York City considered itself crowded, but it was a ghost town compared to the squash of humanity found here. The Kowloon peninsula was half of what was considered Hong Kong. The other half across Victoria Harbor—Hong Kong Island—was a place of mansions, glittering skyscrapers, and green parks, all surrounding the majesty of Victoria Peak.

Earlier this morning, with the sun not yet up, Gray and Kowalski had chugged into the local waters aboard their stolen speedboat. The skyline of Hong Kong Island beckoned, looking like a modern-day Oz, an Emerald City that promised magic, where every wish could be granted for the right price—which, in fact, might be true of the decadent place.

Instead, Gray had directed Kowalski to pull into a derelict dock on the darker, urban side of Hong Kong, here in Kowloon. They took a short two-hour nap in a nondescript hotel as they waited for intel from D.C. Once the information came through, Gray led Kowalski to the red-light district of Mong Kok with its chaotic array of karaoke bars, brothels, saunas, and restaurants.

"This way," Gray said after checking a map.

He headed away from the clamor of the main drag and down a maze of tight alleys. The earlier pleas for attention dwindled with every new twist, the invitations transforming into sullen glares of suspicion at their pale faces.

"I think that's the building up ahead," Gray said.

Passing a final turn in the narrow street, he reached a trio of seventeen-story apartment complexes, all connected by bridges and ramshackle construction into a single massive structure. It looked like a rusted mountain held together by the accretion of corrugated tin, patches of wood, and refuse. Even the balconies, unlike those on the nearby buildings, had been sealed shut behind gates. But even here, laundry hung from the bars or streamed on strung ropes, flapping in the wind.

"Looks like a prison," Kowalski said.

In many ways, it probably was. Gray imagined the inhabitants here were trapped as much by economic reality as by iron bars—with the exception of those rumored to be occupying its highest floors, those levels closest to the sun and fresh breezes. According to Sigma's intelligence report, it was home to the *Duàn zhī* Triad.

Gray had traveled here to meet the Triad's infamous dragonhead.

Back in Macau, Dr. Hwan Pak had sold Gray's group out to the Triad, luring them into that ambush. Their leader, who wished her face never to be seen, plainly did not take kindly to anyone looking too closely in her direction. It was a gamble for him to come to her doorstep.

But he had no choice.

Seichan had been nabbed by some criminal element. He doubted it was the *Duàn zhī* Triad. He had spotted European faces—likely local Portuguese—among those who hauled her into the black Cadillac, and the Chinese Triads notoriously disdained Westerners.

So who took her . . . and where?

He had to assume she was still alive. They could have shot her in the streets of Macau, but they hadn't. It was a slim hope, but he grasped it with both hands.

Gray could think of only one option for information on her kidnappers. In the past, the *Duàn zhī* Triad had operated out of Macau, so its leader likely knew the major players and still had contacts out there. More important, she also had the manpower and resources Gray would need to mount a rescue—a rescue to save her own daughter.

But can I get her to listen before she kills us?

Gray turned to Kowalski. "Last chance to back out. I can go in alone. Might even be better."

Gray had made the same offer back at the hotel.

He got the same response.

"Fuck you." Kowalski headed for the closest door.

Gray joined him, matching him stride for stride. Together, they entered through a set of steel security gates that were open during the day but sealed at night. Faces watched their every step: some with suspicion, others with hatred, most with disinterest.

The gates led to a central courtyard between the three original apartment complexes. The bridges and rickety erections blocked most of the meager daylight overhead, though the steady drizzle found its way down, weeping off every surface. Makeshift shops lined the lower level of the courtyard, including a butcher with plucked geese hanging from hooks, a liquor and tobacco store, even a candy shop full of goods too bright and cheerful for this dreary place.

"Stairs are over there," Kowalski said.

The only way up appeared to be the open staircases that climbed the sides of each of the buildings. Gray had no idea which of the original towers housed the *Duàn zhī* Triad, or if it even mattered.

So they set off for the closest and began climbing. The plan was to keep scaling the complex until someone tried to stop them—preferably not someone prone to shooting first and asking questions later.

As they crossed landing after landing, leaving the commercial district below for the residential levels, Gray glanced through several open doors. Inside the apartments was a strange sight. Large wire-mesh cages were stacked floor to ceiling, like rabbit hutches. Men lounged or slept inside them. Clearly it was all they could afford as housing, but the residents did their best to make them tiny homes, decorating them with bamboo liners or privacy screens made of tarpaulin. Even a few televisions glowed. From all of them, cigarette smoke wafted in thick clouds, but it only faintly blocked the smell of human waste.

A fat, brown rat ran down the steps between them.

"Smart rat," Kowalski said.

Crossing the tenth floor, Gray began to note the glass eyes of closed-circuit television cameras pointed at the stairs.

The handiwork of the Triad.

"This is probably high enough," Gray finally said. "They're clearly already watching us."

Reaching the next landing, Gray moved off the stairs and into the open-air hallway that overlooked the courtyard. He positioned himself in front of one of the CCTV cameras. He carefully and slowly reached to his belt. Using two fingers, he slipped out his Red Star pistol and placed it at his feet. Kowalski performed the same ritual with his AK-47 rifle.

"I wish to speak to Guan-yin, the dragonhead of *Duàn zhī*!" he called out to the camera and anyone listening nearby.

The response was immediate.

Doors slammed open in front and behind. Four men came at them with bats and machetes.

So much for conversation.

Gray dropped low and kicked the closest man in the knee. As the attacker fell forward, Gray punched him hard in the throat, leaving him writhing and gasping. He retrieved his pistol, while ducking under the swing of a machete as it shaved through his hair. Inside the man's guard now, Gray trapped the assailant's arm, swung him around, and got his own arm around the man's neck.

He placed the muzzle of the pistol into his captive's ear.

Behind Gray, Kowalski had coldcocked the first of his two assailants, snatching the steel bat out of the man's limp fingers as he fell. In a round-house swing, he struck the second in the shoulder. His machete clattered to the ground.

Kowalski kept his bat pointed, warning, as the man stumbled back in pain, cradling his bruised arm.

Gray turned his attention to the camera.

"I only wish to talk!" he called out.

Proving this, he let his captive go and pushed him away. Again, Gray bent down and placed his pistol on the floor. He lifted his hands high, showing his palms to the camera.

He hoped this sudden attack had been a test.

He waited, feeling a trickle of sweat run down his back. A hush seemed to have fallen over the entire complex. Even the chatter of televisions and echoing music was subdued.

Suddenly Kowalski bellowed behind him. "Don't any of you speak goddamned English?"

A door opened at the end of the hall.

"I do."

A figure stepped out of the shadows and into the hallway. He was a tall man, with his white hair pulled back in a knot of a ponytail. Though in his sixties, he moved with a silky power in each step. He carried a long, curved sword in one hand, an ancient Chinese Dao saber. His other palm rested on the butt of a holstered SIG Sauer.

"What do you wish to tell our esteemed dragonhead?" he asked.

Gray knew the wrong answer would get them killed.

"Tell her I carry a message concerning Mai Phuong Ly's daughter."

From the swordsman's blank expression, the name meant nothing to him. As answer, he simply turned and walked calmly back into the shadows.

Again they were left to wait. One of the guards barked in Cantonese and forced Gray and Kowalski to retreat a few steps, so another could grab their weapons.

"This gets better and better," Kowalski said.

The tension stretched to the tautness of a piano wire.

Finally, the swordsman returned, stepping again out of the shadowy doorway to confront them.

"With graciousness, she has agreed to see you," he said.

Gray let the knot between his shoulders relax slightly.

"But if she doesn't like what she hears," the swordsman warned, "her face will be the last thing you ever see."

Gray didn't doubt that.

8:44 A.M.

Seichan woke to darkness.

She remained motionless, a survival instinct going back to her feral years on the streets of Bangkok and Phnom Penh. She waited for her muzzy-headedness to clear. Memory slowly seeped out of a black well. She'd been grabbed, drugged, and blindfolded. From the bite of restraints, her wrists and ankles must also be bound. She still wore the blindfold, but enough light seeped through the edges to tell it was day.

But was it the same day she'd been grabbed?

She pictured the crash, Gray and Kowalski flying.

Had they survived?

She didn't want to think otherwise.

Despair weakened one's resolve—and she would need every bit of tenacity to survive.

She cast out her addled senses to gain her bearing. She lay on something hard, metal, smelling of motor oil. Vibrations and the occasional
jarring bump revealed she was in some sort of vehicle.

Perhaps a van, maybe a truck.

But where were they taking her?

Why not just kill me?

She could guess the answer to that easily enough. Someone must have
learned about the bounties placed on her head, someone who aimed to
sell her.

"You may now stop pretending to sleep." The voice came from a foot
or two away.

She inwardly cringed. Her senses had been honed sharp by the coarse
streets and back alleys of her youth. Still, she'd been totally unaware that
someone sat so close. It unnerved her. It wasn't just his silence, but his
complete blankness. Like he didn't exist.

"First, you may relax," the man continued, his Cantonese formal and
flawless but tinged with a European patois. Considering it was Macau, the
accent was likely Portuguese. "We do not intend to kill you, or even harm
you. At least, not me personally. It's merely a business transaction."

So she had been correct about someone selling her for profit. But it
was little consolation.

"Second, in regard to your friends . . ."

This time she did flinch, imagining Gray's face, Kowalski's bluster.
Were they still alive?

A soft scolding chuckle rose from the man.

"They are alive," he said, reading her like a book. "But simply for
the moment, I'm afraid. It took us a while to track them down—only
to discover they had turned up in a most unexpected place, the home of
a competitor. Which left me baffled, wondering *why*? Then I realized it
didn't matter. There is the old Chinese saying: *yi jian shuang diao.* I think
it applies to this circumstance."

Seichan translated in her head.

One arrow, double vultures.

She went cold at the implication. The Chinese phrase was the equivalent of a more common idiom.

Killing two birds with one stone.

8:58 A.M.

The elevators opened, delivering them from hell to heaven.

Gray followed the swordsman into what must have once been the apartment building's penthouse. Here there was none of the stifling cramp and grime of the lower complex. The entire space was open, decorated in white furniture with simple, clean lines. The floor was polished bamboo. Potted orchids of every shade and shape dotted the room. A fish tank curved in the shape of a standing wave held myriad snow-white fish. It acted as a divider from a kitchen of stainless European appliances.

But the biggest difference from the hellish landscape below was the amount of light. Even the drizzling overcast day did little to dampen the brightness. Huge windows looked out over Kowloon, high enough to view the shining towers of Hong Kong City. In the center of the penthouse stood a glass-walled atrium open to the sky above, holding a fountain, along with a riotous spread of plants and flowers, all surrounding a fish-pond with floating lilies.

A single lantern also gently rocked atop the water.

A slim shape in a belted robe bent over it. With a long taper in hand, she lit a fresh candle in the lotus-shaped lantern.

Gray pictured the festival at Macau, with its thousands of lights, each glow marking the memory of a past loved one.

Gray was marched out of the elevator and toward the atrium.

Kowalski looked darkly back at the elevator. "So why did we climb fourteen flights when they have a frickin' elevator?"

Its use was likely restricted to the Triad, but Gray didn't bother explaining, keeping his full attention on the figure behind the glass.

The swordsman led them to a few yards from the atrium door. "Remain standing."

The woman—and it was plain from her petite bare feet and the curve of her hip that this was a *woman*—remained bowed before the lantern, hands now folded around the burning incense taper.

For a full two minutes, no one spoke. Kowalski fidgeted, but he had the good sense for once to keep his mouth shut.

Finally the woman gave a deeper bow toward the pond, straightened, and turned. Her robe was hooded against the drizzle, its edges long, folding around her face as she stood. She crossed to the atrium door and slowly slid it open.

With great grace, she stepped into the penthouse.

"Guan-yin," the swordsman intoned, bowing his head.

"*M`h' gōi*, Zhuang." A pale hand slipped from a sleeve and touched the swordsman's forearm, an oddly intimate gesture.

The dragonhead of the *Duàn zhī* turned next to Gray.

"You speak of Mai Phuong Ly," she said, her voice low and calm but laced with the steel edge of a threat. "You come speaking of someone long dead."

"Not in the memories of her daughter."

The woman showed no reaction, a demonstration of her degree of control. After a long pause, her voice came back quieter.

"Again you speak of the dead."

"She was not hours ago when she came to Macau looking for her mother."

The only reaction was the slight lowering of her chin, perhaps realizing how close she had come to killing her own daughter. Now she was likely wondering if he spoke the truth.

"It was you at the Casino Lisboa."

Gray motioned to Kowalski. "The three of us. Dr. Hwan Pak recognized your dragon pendant, said he knew you. So we came to Macau to discover the truth."

A small sniff of derision. "But what is the truth?" she asked.

Doubt and disbelief rang in her voice.

"If I may . . ." Gray pointed to the pocket of his jacket, where they'd left his phone after the Triad members below had frisked him.

"With care," Zhuang warned.

Gray removed his phone and pulled up the photo log. He scrolled until he reached a folder labeled SEICHAN. He flipped through photos until he came to one that showed a clear picture of her face. Seeing her now, an ache of fear for her safety struck him deeply, but he kept his arm steady as he held out the phone as proof.

Guan-yin leaned forward, her features still shadowed, making it impossible to read her expression. But in the stumble of her step as she moved closer, Gray read the recognition, the barely restrained hope. Even after twenty years, a mother would know her daughter.

Gray motioned for her to take the phone. "There are other pictures. You can swipe to view them."

Guan-yin reached out, but her fingers hesitated as if a part of her feared the truth. If her daughter was still alive, what did that say about a mother who failed her?

Finally, fingers slipped the phone from his hand. She turned her back to Gray as she searched the folder. A long stretch of silence—then the woman trembled and slipped to her knees on the bamboo floor.

Zhuang moved so swiftly Gray hardly noted it. One moment the swordsman was at his side . . . the next, he was on one knee beside his mistress, with his Dao saber pointed back at them, cautioning them to remain where they were.

"It is her," Guan-yin whispered. "How could this be?"

Gray could not imagine the emotions that must be warring inside her: guilt, shame, hope, joy, fear, anger.

The last two won out as the woman quickly composed herself, standing and turning to them. Zhuang joined her, protective—but from the depth of concern in his eyes, it was clear his need to shield her went beyond professional duty.

Guan-yin shook back her hood, revealing a long cascade of black hair with a single streak of gray along one edge of her face, the same edge that bore the curve of a deep purplish scar. It curled from her cheek to across her left brow, sparing her eye. It was too purposefully twisted to be a wound received in a knife fight. Someone had intently and painfully carved into her face, a memento of old torture. But as if to turn such a scar into a badge of honor—to perhaps wrest control from that old pain—she had her face tattooed, incorporating the scar, transforming it into the tail of the dragon now inked across cheek and brow.

It was an uncanny match to the silver serpent at her throat.

"Where is she now?" Guan-yin asked, her voice rising in volume, showing again that steel. "Where is my daughter?"

Gray swallowed back the awe at the sight of her face and quickly explained about the attack, its aftermath, and the abduction on the street.

"Tell me about the man you saw standing beside the car," Guan-yin demanded.

Gray described the tall powerful-looking man with the trimmed beard. "He looked Portuguese, with maybe some Chinese blood."

She nodded. "I know him well. Ju-long Delgado, the boss of all Macau."

A shadow of concern swept her features.

If this hard woman was worried, that was a bad sign.

9:18 A.M.

With a complaint of brakes, the vehicle came to a stop.

Seichan heard the stranger speak in low tones to the driver in Portuguese, but she didn't understand the language. Doors opened and slammed.

A hand reached to her face. She thrashed back, but fingers merely removed her blindfold. She blinked against the sudden glare.

"Calm yourself," her captor said. "We still have a long way to go."

The man was dressed meticulously in a finely tailored silk suit and jacket. His dark brown eyes matched his shaggy hair and manicured beard, the latter shorn tight to his cheeks and square chin. His eyes, pinched slightly at the corners, revealed his mixed-blood heritage.

A glance around revealed she was on the floor of a panel van.

The rear door popped open, stabbing her eyes again with brighter light. Another man stood outside: he was younger, a smooth-faced brute with cropped black hair and massive shoulders that strained his suit jacket. He had striking ice-blue eyes.

"Tomaz," her captor said. "Are we ready for the flight?"

A nod. "*Sim,* Senhor Delgado. The plane is ready."

The man called Delgado turned to her. "I'll be accompanying you on this flight," he said. "To ensure I receive full compensation, but also I believe it would be a good time for me *not* to be in Macau. Not after what is about to transpire in Hong Kong. The aftermath will be bloody for some time."

"Where are you taking me?"

Ignoring her, he scrambled out of the van and stretched his back. "It looks to be a beautiful day."

His underling, Tomaz, grabbed her bound ankles and yanked her into the morning sunlight. A dagger appeared in his hands and sliced the plastic ties. Her wrists remained bound behind her back.

Placed roughly on her feet, she realized she was on the tarmac of some remote airstrip. A sleek jet waited thirty yards away. Its stairs were down, ready to receive its passengers. A figure appeared in the open doorway and stepped into the light.

A large splinted bandage covered his broken nose.

Dr. Hwan Pak.

"Ah, our benefactor." Delgado headed toward the jet, checking the Rolex on his wrist. "Come. We don't want to be anywhere near Hong Kong after the next few minutes."

9:22 A.M.

"That's all you know?"

A mother's love for her daughter ached in Guan-yin's voice. She had questioned Gray intently for the past several minutes, probing Seichan's past, trying to understand how she could still be alive.

They had retreated to one of the sofas.

Zhuang stood guard beside her. Kowalski had wandered over to the fish tank, tapping at the glass, his nose close to its surface.

Gray wished he could fill in more blanks for Guan-yin, but even he did not know the full extent of Seichan's history, only fragments: a series of orphanages, a rough time on the streets, a recruitment into a criminal organization. As Gray recounted this past, Guan-yin seemed to understand. In some ways, both mother and daughter had taken parallel paths, hardened by circumstances but still able to rise above it, to survive and flourish.

In the end, Gray could not paint a full enough picture to satisfy a mother who missed so much of her daughter's life. He doubted any number of words could fill that void.

"I will find her," Guan-yin swore to herself.

She had already passed down a command through her organization to discover where Ju-long Delgado might have taken her daughter. They still awaited word.

"In the past, I failed her," Guan-yin said, as one finger rose to wipe a tear from the edge of her dragon scar. "My Vietnamese interrogators were cruel, crueler than I suspected even back then. They told me my daughter was dead."

"To make you despair. To make it easier to break you."

"It only made me *angry*, more determined than ever to escape and get vengeance, which eventually I did." A glint of fire burned through her haunted look. "Still, I did not give up. I searched for her, but it was made difficult in those early years, as I dared not set foot again in Vietnam after escaping. Eventually I had to give up."

"It hurt too much to keep looking," he said.

"Hope is sometimes its own curse." Guan-yin looked to her folded hands in her lap. "It was easier to bury her in my heart."

Several long moments of silence stretched, marked by the tinkling of the fountain in the atrium.

"And you?" Guan-yin asked, her voice faint. "You have risked much to bring her here, to come to me now."

Gray did not need to acknowledge that aloud.

She lifted her face to stare him in the eye. "Is it because you love her?"

Gray met those eyes, knew he could not lie—when the first explosion shook the complex.

The blast rocked the entire apartment tower. Water sloshed in the fish tank. The long-stemmed orchids swayed.

"What the hell!" Kowalski yelled.

Guan-yin was on her feet.

Her shadow, Zhuang, already had a phone at his ear, talking swiftly, moving to the wall of windows. Smoke rose up through the rain from below.

Another explosion erupted, sounding farther away.

Guan-yin followed her lieutenant to the window, towing Gray and Kowalski with her. She translated what she overheard from Zhuang.

"Cement trucks have pulled up to all the entrances, coming from all directions at once."

Gray pictured the large vehicles squeezing down the narrow canyons surrounding this mountain, converging here in a coordinated assault. But they were not *cement trucks* . . .

Another blast from another direction.

. . . *but bombs on wheels.*

Someone intended to bring this entire place down around their ears. Gray could guess who: Ju-long Delgado. He must have discovered Gray and Kowalski had come here. The passage of their pale faces through here would be hard to miss.

"We need to get out!" Gray warned. "Now!"

Zhuang heard him and agreed, turning to his mistress. "We must get you to safety."

Guan-yin stood her ground, back straight, the dragon shining more prominently on her angry face. "Mobilize the Triad," she ordered. "Get as many residents to safety as possible."

Gray pictured the mass of humanity below.

"Use our underground tunnels," she said.

Of course, the Triad would have secret ways into and out of their stronghold.

"You must first go yourself," Zhuang pressed.

"After you pass on that order."

It seemed this captain was willing to go down with her ship—and it was coming down. Loud splintering crashes echoed as parts of the complex collapsed. The pall of black smoke now covered the entire wall of windows, as if driven upward by the muffled screams from below.

Zhuang returned to his phone, shouting now to be heard. Moments later, loudspeakers blared throughout the complex, echoing across its many levels, as the command of the dragonhead was spread to all.

Only then did Guan-yin relent.

Zhuang wisely led her away from the elevators. He ushered her through a double set of doors to the same stairs they had climbed earlier.

"Hurry now! We must reach the tunnels!"

As they descended at a run, pandemonium overtook the central courtyard. Multiple fires glowed below. Several floors down, a section of bridge that had spanned the space suddenly broke, spilling a handful of flailing people into the fiery depths. The apartment building across from them began to fold in on itself, imploding floor by floor, falling crookedly away, slowly ripping itself free from the other towers.

Gray ran faster now, leaping from landing to landing. Guan-yin kept pace with him, Zhuang at her side, Kowalski trailing.

A thunderous crack shook the stairs, sending them all to their knees.

The entire stairwell began to peel from the side of the tower.

"This way!" Gray hollered.

He leaped from the stairs, across the growing gap, and reached the tower's exterior hallway that faced the courtyard. The others followed. Guan-yin tripped, slipping out of her lieutenant's arms as he jumped. Left behind, she teetered at the edge—but Kowalski scooped her up and vaulted with a bellow to join Gray.

"Thank you," Guan-yin said as he set her down.

"We'll never make it to the tunnels," Gray said.

No one argued, accepting his grim assessment. Fires raged fiercely below, roiling with smoke, continually fueled by whatever tumbled into them from above.

"Then where do we go?" Kowalski asked. "We're still a good ten stories up, and I forgot my wings."

Gray clapped him on the shoulder, appreciating the suggestion. "Then we'll have to make our own." He faced Zhuang. "Take us to the closest corner apartment."

Ever the lieutenant, the swordsman obeyed without question. He rushed them into the inner labyrinth of the tower. In a few short turns, he reached a door and pointed.

Gray tested and found it locked. He backed a step and kicked his heel into the deadbolt. The aged wood frame offered little resistance, and the door ripped open.

"Inside!" he yelled. "I need bedsheets, clothing, laundry, anything we can tie together to make a rope."

He left this chore to Kowalski and Guan-yin.

With Zhuang in tow, he hurried through the sliding doors to the outside. Like all the other balconies he had spotted from the street, this one had been turned into a steel cage, sealed from the outside with chain-link fencing.

"Help me," Gray said and set about freeing a section from the balcony rails.

As they worked furiously, the tower rumbled and shook, slowly coming apart as it was eaten below by fire.

At last, Gray kicked a piece of fencing loose and sent it tumbling through the smoke to the street below.

"How's it going with the rope?" he yelled into the apartment.

"We'll never make something long enough to reach the ground!" Kowalski called back.

That wasn't the plan.

Gray moved inside to check on their handiwork. He found the two had managed to knot together a length of about twenty yards. The tower gave a massive shake, helping him make his final decision.

"Good enough!"

Gray hauled one end outside and tied it to the balcony's top rail. He tossed the rest of its length over the edge.

"What are you doing?" Kowalski asked.

Gray pointed to the open balconies of the building across the narrow street.

"You are stupid mad," Kowalski said.

No one argued.

Looking down, Gray again wondered how the cement trucks had made it through such a tight squeeze of alleys to reach here. But at the moment, he silently thanked the Hong Kong city planners who allowed such dense construction in Kowloon.

Gray mounted the balcony rail and grabbed their makeshift rope. Holding his breath, he lowered himself down hand by hand. A few slips made his heart pound harder, but as he climbed, he silently eyeballed the distance to the neighboring building, judging the length of free rope he would need.

Once satisfied, he began to shift his weight, setting the rope to swinging. He ran his boots along the caged balconies, passing through thick smoke, burning his eyes. Within a few passes back and forth, his arc began to swing clear of the building, stretching toward its neighbor.

Not far enough.

Needing more distance, he ran faster across the balconies, extending the arc of each swing wider and wider. Smoke continued to choke his throat, growing ever thicker, making it harder to catch his breath.

But he dared not stop.

Finally, sweeping out over the street, the tips of his toes struck the far balcony. It was not enough to gain purchase, but the contact fired his determination. Swinging back again into the smoke, his feet sped across the rain-slick balconies.

C'mon . . .

"Pierce!" Kowalski yelled from the balcony. "Look below you!"

Gray searched under his legs as he ran. The end of his rope must have brushed through a hot patch at some point and caught fire. Flames chased up the rope toward him, trailing fiery cinders of cloth.

Oh, no . . .

This time, when he felt his momentum ebbing, he kicked hard off the last rail he could touch, trying to eke out a few more yards of swing, knowing this was his last chance.

Then back he fell.

Gravity dragged him across the surface of the fiery tower and out over the street. Bending at the waist, he kicked his legs up and stared through them. The balcony swooped toward him. Timing it as well as he could, he lifted his feet to clear the rail—then clamped his knees down and successfully hooked the top bar.

Relief swept through him.

In that moment of inattentiveness, he slipped and lost his hold. His legs slid along the bar until only his heels remained hooked to the rail. He hung there, knowing it couldn't last.

Under him, flames swept up the rope.

Then hands suddenly grabbed his ankles.

He stared past his toes to see a man and woman, husband and wife, the owners of the apartment, gripping him, coming to his aid. They pulled him over the balcony's rail to safety. Back on his feet, he stamped and slapped out the flames from the rope and tied its end to the top bar. All the while, the pair chattered to him in Cantonese, clearly scolding him at such a rash action, as if he had done it on some lark.

Once the rope bridge was secure—or as secure as he could make it—he called over to the others.

"One at a time! Hands and legs! Climb over!"

Guan-yin came first, moving swiftly like a gymnast, barely disturbing the bridge. She bowed her thanks to the couple, as Zhuang came next, his sword slung over his chest and hanging under him.

Kowalski followed last, fueled by a string of curses.

Apparently the gods were not happy with his profanity. Halfway across, the far end of the bridge frayed away and snapped, sending him plummeting toward the street.

Gray gulped, his belly pressed hard against the rail, not knowing what to do.

Luckily, Kowalski kept his massive meat hooks on the rope. As the slack ran out, the rope flung his bulk toward the façade below. He crashed headlong into a balcony three stories down, bowling into a group of on-lookers gathered there.

Cries of shock echoed up.

"Are you okay?" Gray hollered, bending over the rail.

"Next time, *you* go last!" Kowalski bellowed back.

Gray turned to find Zhuang gently wrapping his mistress's face in a crimson silk scarf, hiding her again from the world.

Once covered, she turned to Gray. "I owe you my life."

"But many others lost theirs."

She nodded at this, and they both soberly observed the aftermath of the attack. Across the way, the rusted mountain slowly succumbed to the fires, crumbling and crashing to ruin.

Behind them, Zhuang conversed rapidly on his phone, likely assessing the damage.

After a minute, he returned to his mistress's side. They spoke with their heads bowed. Once her lieutenant stepped back, Guan-yin faced Gray.

"Zhuang has heard news from Macau," she said.

Gray tensed for the worst.

"My daughter still lives."

Thank God.

"But Ju-long has whisked her off the peninsula, out of China."

"Where—?"

Her scarf failed to muffle the dread in her voice. "To North Korea."

Gray pictured that reclusive country, an isolated no-man's-land of macabre desolation and dictatorial madness, a place of strict control and impenetrable borders.

"It'll take an army to get her out," he mumbled to the smoke and fire.

Guan-yin clearly heard him, but instead said, "You never answered my earlier question."

He faced her, finding only a terrified mother staring back.

"Do you love my daughter?"

Gray could not lie, but fear choked him silent. Still, she read the answer in his eyes and turned away.

"Then I will give you that army."

SECOND

SAINTS & SINNERS

7

"It looks like the ocean."

Monsignor Vigor Verona stirred at the words of his niece. He lifted his nose from a DNA report. He kept returning to the papers over and over again, sensing he was missing something important. The results had been faxed from the genetics lab just before the early-morning flight to this westernmost port city of Kazakhstan.

He took a deep breath and pulled himself back to the present, needing a break anyway. *Maybe if I clear my head, I'll figure out what is nagging me.*

He and Rachel were seated at a small restaurant overlooking the Caspian Sea. Beyond the windows, its wintry waters crashed against the neighboring white cliffs for which the small town of Aktau had been named. The team from Sigma was scheduled to meet them here in less than an hour. Together, they'd take a chartered helicopter from here to the coordinates Father Josip had hidden inside the inscribed skull.

"Once upon a time, the Caspian was indeed an ocean," Vigor said. "That was five million years ago. It's why the Caspian still has salt in it, though only about a third of the salinity of today's oceans. Then that ancient ocean became landlocked, eventually drying out to become the Caspian Sea, the Black Sea . . . and where we're headed next, the Aral Sea."

"Not that there's much *sea* left in the Aral Sea," Rachel said with a smile. She had traded her Carabinieri uniform for a red turtleneck sweater, jeans, and hiking boots.

"Ah, but that's not the fault of geology, but the hand of man. The Aral Sea used to be the fourth-largest lake in the world, about the size of Ireland. But then the Soviets diverted its two main rivers for irrigation back in the sixties, and the sea dried up, losing ninety percent of its water, becoming a salty, toxic wasteland, dotted by the rusting hulks of old fishing boats."

"You're not selling this upcoming tour very well."

"But Father Josip must believe the place is important. Why else summon us there?"

"Besides the fact that he might be crazy? He's vanished for almost a decade."

"Perhaps, but Director Crowe has enough confidence in this venture to supply us with field support."

She leaned back and crossed her arms, scowling her dissatisfaction. After the attack at the university, she had been against this venture entirely, even threatening to lock him up in order to keep him in Rome. He knew the only reason they were seated at the edge of the Caspian Sea was because of Sigma's conditional support.

Yet Director Crowe hadn't explained *why* he had agreed to supply this help—not to Vigor or Rachel—which was troubling to both of them. The director had only expressed that he might need their help afterward as a cover story for a mission in a restricted area of Mongolia.

Mongolia . . .

That fact intrigued him.

His eyes drifted again to the DNA report concerning the relics—the skull and the book—but Rachel reached across and shifted the papers to the side.

"Not this time, Uncle. You've been looking at those for hours, and only growing more frustrated. I need you to focus on what's ahead."

"Fine, but then let me talk it out. I'm sensing I'm missing something critical to all this."

She shrugged, conceding.

"According to the initial report compiled by the lab, the DNA is consistent with an East Asian ethnicity."

"You mentioned that already. The skin and the skull came from the same guy, someone from out in the Far East."

"Right, but from the autosomal study that was faxed overnight, the lab compared our sample to various known ethnicities. From that, they were able to compile a rank of the top possibilities of race." He ticked them off on his fingers. "Han Chinese, Buryats, Daur, Kazakhs—"

Rachel interrupted, "As in the people of Kazakhstan."

"Right. But at the top of the ranking was *Mongolian.*"

She sat straighter. "Where Painter's team wants us to go."

"That's what has got me so obsessed. I know there's a connection I'm missing."

"Then let's start there," she said. "Did Director Crowe say exactly *where* his team was planning to head in Mongolia?"

"Somewhere in the mountains northeast of their capital . . . the Khan Khentii Mountains."

"And that's a restricted area."

He nodded.

"Why?"

"It's both a nature preserve and historically significant."

"Why *historically?*"

Vigor opened his mouth to answer—then went cold as a frightening possibility struck him. For a moment, the insight blinded him to his surroundings, so filling his brain he could not see.

"Uncle . . ."

His vision snapped back, as he recognized the mistake he'd made. "I've been looking at the trees and missed the forest . . ."

He reached into his pocket and took out his phone. He dialed the DNA lab and demanded to speak to Dr. Conti. Once the researcher came on the line, he told him what he needed done to confirm his fear. It took some convincing, but Conti finally relented.

"Check those Y chromosome markers," Vigor finished. "And get back to me as soon as you can at this number."

"What's wrong?" Rachel asked as he hung up.

"The Khan Khentii Mountains. They are sacred to the Mongolian people because those peaks are said to hide the lost tomb of their greatest hero."

Rachel was versed enough to guess the identity of that hero. "Genghis Khan?"

Vigor nodded. "The Mongolian warlord who forged an empire under the might of sword and will . . . an empire that extended from the Pacific Ocean to the waters outside this window."

Rachel glanced out and back. "You don't think the skull is—?"

"That's what I've asked Dr. Conti to confirm."

"But how can he even do that?"

"A few years back, a well-documented genetics study showed that *one out of two hundred* men in the world carry the same unique Y chromosome, a chromosome with a set of distinct markers that trace their roots to Mongolia. That number climbed to *one out of ten* in regions that were once part of the ancient Mongol Empire. The report concluded that this Super-Y chromosome came down from *one* individual, someone who lived approximately a thousand years ago in Mongolia."

"Genghis Khan?"

Vigor nodded. "Who else? Genghis and his close male relatives took multiple wives, had even more offspring through rape and conquest. They conquered half the known world."

"And spread their genetic stamp."

"A stamp we can verify. Those Y-chromosome markers are well known to geneticists and easy enough to compare to our sample."

"That's what Dr. Conti is doing right now?"

"He said he could have the results almost immediately, as the DNA sequencing on our samples had already been completed."

"But if you're right and the markers match, what does that tell us? Like you said, many men carry this Y-chromosome."

"Yes, but Genghis died in 1227."

"The thirteenth century . . ." Her brows knit together. "The same age as the skull."

He lifted an eyebrow. "How many men back then carried that specific chromosome?"

Rachel did not look convinced.

Vigor pressed his case. "After Genghis died, his followers slaughtered his entire funeral procession. Those who constructed his tomb were also killed. So were the soldiers who oversaw its construction. And apparently such bloody efforts were effective in keeping it secret. Despite centuries of searching, the location of his tomb remains a mystery to this day. A tomb said to hold all the riches from his conquered lands."

"The discovery of which might be worth killing someone over," Rachel said, plainly referring to the grenade attack.

"We're talking about a treasure that would put Tutankhamen to shame. The world's greatest treasures flowed into Mongolia and were never seen again, the vast spoils of war from China, India, Persia, Russia. The royal tomb was even said to hold the crowns of the seventy-eight rulers he conquered. Not to mention the priceless religious artifacts pillaged from countless churches, mostly those of the Russian Orthodox."

"And nothing was ever found?"

"More important to us, his *body* was never found."

Before Rachel could respond, Vigor's phone rang. He snatched it up to find Dr. Conti on the line.

"I did as you asked, Monsignor Verona. We compared the twenty-five genetic markers that make up the Genghis Khan haplotype to your sample."

"And how many match?"

"*All* twenty-five."

Blood drained from Vigor's face. He stared down at the rolling case at his feet, realizing what it might hold. He understood now why someone might kill to possess what it contained, how the contents inside might hold clues to the world's greatest treasure. Inside his suitcase, he perhaps held the skull and skin of the world's greatest warlord, a man revered as a semigod by his people.

The relics of Genghis Khan.

2:10 P.M.

"You were right," Duncan said. "Our Italian friends picked up a tail."

He stood with Monk Kokkalis at a beachside barbecue stand. Cold sunlight shone off the neighboring sea. The day was chilly, but the wood and charcoal grill—where skewers of meat, fat, and vegetables sizzled—cast off enough heat to make even Duncan's light jacket feel too warm. The burn of Persian spices and oils also wafted over him, stinging his eyes with every gust off the sea.

After landing at the Aktau International Airport, they had shuttled Dr. Jada Shaw to their chartered helicopter at a neighboring private air-field. Once she was secure, Monk and Duncan had headed to the central district of the small port town to retrieve the final additions to their team. Duncan had been informed about the attack on the pair, and Monk had suggested caution in approaching them, to make sure the two weren't be-ing tracked from Rome.

If they're dragging a tail, Monk had said, *let's cut it off now.*

It proved to be a smart precaution.

Duncan recognized that he could learn a thing or two from this more seasoned Sigma operative.

"How do you want to play this?" he asked.

During their twenty-minute vigil on the restaurant, they spotted a pair of people showing an inordinate amount of interest in the couple seated at the window. The restaurant bordered the beach's pedestrian thoroughfare, where joggers and bikers vied for space on the narrow strip of asphalt. Though it was November and the off-season, this central dis-trict of the town still bustled with activity. So it was easy to spot anyone suspiciously lingering by the restaurant.

A dark-haired man, clearly Asian, had settled onto a bench on the far side of the restaurant, at the edge of the beach. He wore a knee-length coat, his hands stuffed deep in his pockets, his back to the view, seldom taking his eyes off the restaurant.

Not exactly sophisticated.

The other, a woman, matched her partner's hair and features. She wore a black woolen cap, and a shorter version of the man's brown coat. She was slim and not unattractive with high cheekbones and smoldering eyes. She leaned against a light pole on this side of the restaurant.

"I'll go along the beach," Monk said. "Approach the man from behind. You get close to the woman. Wait until I'm in position. Upon my signal, we'll grab them both."

"Got it."

"And keep your weapon hidden, march them over to our SUV. Be discreet. We'll secure them there and question them en route back to the airfield. I want to know who the hell they are and why they tried to blow up my friends."

"Why do you think they're watching now versus attacking?"

Monk shook his head. "Might be too public to act in broad daylight. Or maybe they've been ordered to follow them, to discover why the pair traveled from Rome to Kazakhstan? Either way, it ends here for them."

Monk set off, moving onto the sand and casually strolling down the beach. He never looked once toward the seated man. Once his partner was halfway toward his target, Duncan pushed away from the counter and headed toward the woman. He did his best to match Monk's pace, to time his approach so that they'd reach their respective targets at the same time.

That was the plan—until the ring of a bell drew Duncan's attention to the asphalt path. He glanced back to find a bicyclist signaling him out of the way. Only steps away, the woman also stirred.

As the bicycle swept past, she followed, as if drawn in its wake, heading toward her partner. In an unfortunate set of circumstances, Monk chose that moment to shift from the beach toward the bench.

The woman's shoulders stiffened. She stopped, clearly sensing something amiss. She swung around, her eyes immediately locking onto Duncan's. Whether it was some telltale giveaway in his face or the fact that he was clearly American, like the other closing in on her friend, she reacted instantly.

She bolted straight for the restaurant.

Damn it . . .

Duncan lunged after her, his arm outstretched, his hand grabbing for the tail of her coat. Waterproof fabric slipped through his fingertips. A jogger got in her way, bouncing her to the side like a startled deer. The brief stumble gave Duncan the extra moment to catch and grab a firmer hold. He yanked her back to him, hugging his other arm around her chest.

From the corner of his eye, he spotted Monk slamming his target back down onto the bench as the man tried to stand.

So much for being discreet.

The flow of pedestrians slowed, stirring away from the commotion.

Duncan shifted his arm, getting a better grip. But where he should have felt soft breasts, he found only stiff, rigid contours. Worse still, his fingertips buzzed as the tiny rare-earth magnets registered a strong electrical current hidden under the coat.

He immediately knew *why* the woman was running headlong toward the restaurant. Lifting her off her feet and twisting at the waist, he flung her bodily back toward the sand. Her small form flew high and far.

"Bomb!" he hollered to all around him, especially his partner.

As people scattered or froze, he sprinted toward the restaurant window. Monk vaulted the bench, throwing an elbow into the man's face, knocking him backward—then followed.

Duncan had his pistol out. He shot two rounds into the plate glass, aiming away from any diners. With the glass weakened, he leaped and hit the window with his shoulder, shattering through it.

Glass scattered in a tinkling rain around him as he landed inside. With his next bound, he bowled into the two Italians, clotheslining them both to the ground.

He turned to see Monk dive headlong through the same hole— followed on his heels by a thunderous blast.

The entire wall of windows blew out, accompanied by a rain of rock, sand, and smoke. Monk shoulder-rolled amid the carnage across the restaurant floor. Duncan sheltered the two civilians.

Before the glass even stopped bouncing across tabletops and floor tiles, Duncan got his two charges up on their feet.

"Move it! Out the rear!"

The old man resisted, his arm reaching for a roller bag.

Duncan grabbed it versus arguing. Feeling like the most overpaid bellhop, he rushed the pair through the smoke toward the kitchen. He collected Monk along the way. The man bled from several lacerations, an imbedded shard of glass still poking out of his coat.

With Duncan's ears ringing, his head pounding, he swore Monk said, "That could've gone better."

They sped through the kitchen, dodging cooks crouched beside their stations, and out the back door. Once in the open, none of them slowed. They all knew where there were two suicide bombers, there might be more.

Fleeing the column of smoke at the beachfront, they reached a main drag through the business district. Duncan stopped a cab by stepping in front of it.

They all piled in. In the front seat, Monk, whose face was still dripping blood, ordered them to be taken to the airfield. The driver looked pale but nodded rapidly when Monk shoved a fistful of bills at him.

Only after they were speeding out of town did they relax. Duncan turned to the woman in the center of the backseat and discovered pretty caramel eyes—of course, they would have been even prettier if she wasn't glaring at him.

"I knew we never should have left Rome."

2:22 P.M.

She didn't know what she was doing here.

Jada sat in the large cabin of the blue-gray Eurocopter EC175. Though she might not like this detour to Kazakhstan, she could not complain about the legroom. She had her legs up and sprawled across the neighboring seats. The cabin could easily hold a dozen or more passengers versus the five that would be making the overland flight to the Aral Sea. Duncan had explained earlier that they needed such a large bird in order to haul the long distance, as there was no convenient airfield for a plane to land out there.

It was *that* remote.

But at least I'm not totally disconnected from the world.

She sat with her laptop open, reviewing the latest data on Comet IKON. A glance out the tinted windows showed the tiny blaze of its tail, like a shining comma in the daytime sky. Apparently it was putting on quite a show on the opposite side of the world, where it was the middle of the night.

She stared at the video footage on the screen from Alaska.

A large meteor shower blazed through the aurora borealis, in winking streaks and silvery trails, flashing every few seconds, if not more. All of it was overseen by the sweep of the comet's tail; the footage was distinct enough to see the split between its dust tail and gas tail. One huge meteor shot across the screen, accompanied by a shout of surprise by the amateur videographer. It looked like a lance of fire that shattered into a ball of fireworks.

She had also been in touch with the Space and Missile Systems Center via the encrypted satellite phone supplied to her by Director Crowe. She had the phone at her ear now—though there was no need for encryption on this call.

"Yes, Mom, I'm fine," she said. "It's very exciting here in California."

She hated to lie to her mother, but Painter had been adamant.

"Are you watching the light show in the night sky?"

"Of course, I am."

At least that wasn't entirely a lie.

"I wish I could be there watching it with you, honey," her mother said. "Like we used to do back when you were a little girl."

Jada smiled at the memory of lying sprawled in the grass of the National Mall, shivering under a blanket, watching the Leonid or Perseid showers. It was her mother who had instilled in her a love of the stars, who had taught her that the annual meteor shows were named after the constellations that seemed to birth them: Leo and Perseus. Growing up in a world where life seemed small and hand-to-mouth, Jada was reminded by the stars of a greater universe, of larger possibilities.

Like a girl from Congress Heights becoming an astrophysicist.

"I wish I could be with you, too, Mom." She checked the time. "Hey, you'd better get going if you're going to make your morning shift at the Holiday Mart."

"You're right, you're right . . . I should be going."

Pride rang through the line, traveling halfway around the world to reach her.

"I love you, Mom."

"I love you, too, honey."

As the connection ended, Jada felt a twinge of sorrow, feeling suddenly selfish and guilty that she got to live this life.

Blinking back tears, she returned to her work. She rewound the meteor shower footage once again. Over at the SMC, they were still trying to determine if this showy display was simply a coincidence or if it had something to do with the passage of Comet IKON through the solar system.

She had texted with a tech buddy, learning the latest conjectures. The current belief was that the passage of the comet might have disturbed the *Kuiper belt,* a region of icy asteroids past the orbit of Neptune, drawing an entourage of rocks in its wake and splashing them across the earth. The Kuiper belt contained over thirty thousand asteroids larger than a hundred kilometers in diameter, along with being the home to many short-period comets like the famous Halley's comet.

The most exciting news, though, was the growing belief that IKON came from the much more distant *Oort cloud,* a spherical cloud of debris that circled one-fifth of the way toward our closest star. It was home to long-period comets, those rare visitors, like Hale-Bopp, that traipsed by only once every forty-two hundred years.

The latest calculations suggested that the last time IKON passed through the inner solar system was twenty-eight hundred years ago, definitely an ancient visitor. If true, it was an exciting proposition, as objects out in the Oort cloud were untouched remnants of the original nebula from which the entire solar system formed, making IKON a blazing herald from that most distant time, potentially carrying with it the keys to the universe.

Including perhaps the mystery of dark energy.

A loud rumble shook the helicopter's cabin, followed by a low roar. The rotors overhead began a slow sweep.

What . . . ?

She sat up straighter.

The copilot hopped out, came around, and opened the side door. The noise grew deafening.

The pilot leaned back, yelling to her, "Strap in! Just heard word! Got an order to prep for a fast takeoff!"

Her heart thudded harder as she snapped closed her laptop. She glanced out the open hatch as the copilot dashed about performing a final preflight check. In the distance, an angry column of black smoke climbed into the blue sky above the center of town.

Moments later, a taxi came racing into view, coming straight at them. She spotted Monk's face in the front seat. But he and Duncan had left here in a black Mercedes SUV.

She clutched the edge of the door.

What is going on?

The taxi braked with a squeal, and doors popped open all around. She spotted Duncan climbing out the back. Out the other rear door came an older man in a light jacket and a black V-neck sweater, revealing the Roman collar of a priest. He was helped out by a young, petite woman with a pixie-bob of a haircut.

Vigor and Rachel Verona.

Neither looked happy.

Duncan had crossed to the trunk and retrieved their luggage: a single roller bag suitcase. Was that all their gear?

Monk was bent half through the passenger door, settling with the driver. When he straightened, she saw the blood covering his face and gasped. Her gaze flicked to that rising smoke signal above the town, knowing the two were connected.

The group hurried to the waiting helicopter.

Rachel's scowl deepened with every step, as if reluctant to climb aboard. At the hatch, she finally stopped.

"We should stay here!" she yelled, clutching the priest's arm. "Head back to Rome!"

Jada hoped that would be their decision. It would mean they could leave Kazakhstan immediately and head straight to the mountains of Mongolia to start their hunt for the crashed satellite.

Monk shook his head. "Rachel, you've already got a target on your back. Whoever planned this is more resourceful than we first imagined. They'll try again."

Duncan agreed with his partner. "That Father Josip got you all into this mess. He's the best chance to get you out."

Rachel clearly recognized the practical wisdom of that. She freed her uncle's arm, and they both climbed in. Jada made room, nodding to the pair as they strapped in across from her, delaying any formal introduction until they were in the air.

Duncan found a spot next to Jada. She appreciated his physical presence, his solidity, even the warmth of his body as he breathed deeply, still running high on adrenaline.

As Monk strapped in, he leaned over and touched Jada's knee. "Sorry for the rush. We didn't want to be trapped on the ground if Kazakh law enforcement shuts down airspace because of the bombing."

Jada stared around the cabin.

What the hell have I got myself into?

3:07 P.M.

As the Eurocopter reached its cruising altitude, Duncan looked below at the passing scenery. With a roar of its rotors, the chopper rushed away from the expanse of blue sea and out over a desert landscape of rust-colored sand, patches of scrub, salt-white mesas, and wind-carved rock. The territory below could pass for sections of New Mexico, except for the scatter of camels and the occasional lone yurt, the white tent standing out starkly against the darker terrain.

A tug on his sleeve drew his attention back to the cabin.

Monsignor Verona pointed to the suitcase on the seat next to Duncan. "*Scusa*, Sergeant Wren, could you open my bag? I'd like to make sure everything is still intact after the commotion."

Only a priest would describe what happened as a *commotion*.

"Monsignor, you can call me Duncan."

"Only if you call me Vigor."

"Done."

Duncan bent and hauled the case up with one arm and dropped it across his knees. He unzipped it and folded back the top. He found some clothing packed around two objects insulated in black foam.

"I'm mostly concerned about the larger of the two," Vigor said. "It's the most fragile."

The monsignor waved for Duncan to strip back the foam to expose what was inside.

Duncan could guess what concerned the older man, so he knew what to expect. As he removed the top half of the padding, the crown of a skull appeared, its empty eye sockets staring up at him.

"Can you remove it and pass it over so I can examine it for damage, please?"

Duncan had seen plenty of death in Afghanistan, but a part of him still cringed inwardly. Next to him, Jada's face wavered between professional interest and disgust.

Ignoring his own aversion, Duncan reached in with both hands, prepared to grab the skull, but even before touching bone, the nerve endings in his fingertips registered a tingling pressure, stimulated by the stirring of his tiny magnets.

Surprised, he pulled his hands away, shaking his fingers.

"There's nothing to fear," Vigor said, misreading his reaction.

Ignoring the monsignor, Duncan hovered his fingers over the dome of the cranium. It was nothing like he'd ever felt before, like slipping his fingers into cold gel, both electric and oily.

"What are you doing?" Jada asked.

He realized how this must look. "The skull is giving off some sort of strange electromagnetic signature. Very faint, but there."

Jada drew her brows together. "How . . . why do you say that?"

He had never told her about the magnets, but he explained to everyone now. Finishing, he said, "My fingertips are definitely picking up something off this skull."

"Then you should examine the old book, too," Rachel said. She reached over and tugged back its protective foam.

The leather of the tome was worn and deeply wrinkled.

He slowly ran his fingers along the surface. This time, he had to touch the leathery skin to feel the tiniest buzz. Still, the *feel* was the same. Goose bumps pebbled his flesh.

"Even fainter . . . but it's identical."

"Could it be some form of residual radiation?" Rachel asked. "We don't know where these relics have been kept until now. Perhaps it was near a radioactive source."

Jada frowned, not buying that explanation. "In my suitcases, I have equipment to examine the crashed—"

She stopped abruptly and glanced over to Monk, plainly realizing how close she'd come to mentioning their mission objective, which so far had been kept from the Veronas.

Clearing her throat, she continued. "I have tools to check for various energy signatures. Geiger counters, multimeters, et cetera. Once we land, I can verify Duncan's claims."

He shrugged. "It's there. I can't explain *why,* but it's there."

Vigor settled back into his seat. "Then the sooner we reach the coordinates supplied by Father Josip, the happier we'll all be."

Duncan placed little faith in the monsignor's assessment. He zipped the case back up and returned his attention to the desolate landscape. After a moment, he realized he had been rubbing his fingers together, as if to erase that oily sensation. He had a hard time expressing in words what his sixth sense had perceived.

For lack of a better term, it felt *wrong*.

8

Steam hissed from the hot pipes lining the subterranean chamber deep beneath the streets of Ulan Bator. Oil lanterns illuminated the clan's meeting place with a fiery glow. The Master of the Blue Wolves stood before his lieutenant and the clan's innermost circle. He adjusted the wolf mask to better hide his features.

Only his lieutenant knew his true name.

Batukhan, meaning *firm ruler.*

"And they survived the attack in Aktau?" he asked his lieutenant.

Arslan gave a fast nod of his head. The young lieutenant, not yet thirty years old, was barefaced, lean and tall, his hair as black as the shadows. He wore typical Western clothes jeans and a thick wool sweater, but from his high cheekbones and his ruddy face, shining with steamy dampness, he was of pure Mongolian stock—not tainted by the blood of the Chinese or Soviets, his people's former oppressors.

His lieutenant was like many of the younger generation of Mongolians, stoked with pride, exalted by the freedoms hard won by Batukhan's generation. Here were the true descendants of the great Genghis Khan, the man who had conquered most of the known world on the back of a horse.

Batukhan remembered, during the decades of Soviet rule, how Moscow had forbidden mentioning the name of Genghis, lest it stoke nationalistic pride in its oppressed subjects. Soviet tanks even blocked the roads up in the Khentii Mountains to keep people from visiting or revering the great khan's birthplace.

But all that had changed with the institution of democratic rule.

Genghis Khan was rising again from those ashes to inspire a generation of young people. He was their new demigod. Countless children and young people bore the name *Temujin,* which was the conqueror's original name before he took the title Genghis Khan, meaning *Universal Ruler.* Across Mongolia, streets, candy, cigarettes, and beer all carried that title now. His face decorated their money and their buildings. A 250-ton shimmering steel statue of Genghis astride a horse greeted visitors to the capital city of Ulan Bator.

Newfound pride flowed through the veins of the country's people.

Staring into his lieutenant's face now, Batukhan saw none of that pride, only the shame of failure. He hardened his words, seeking to stir that shame to greater duty.

"Then we must move forward, never relenting. We will wait for the Italians to reach the priest in the desert. It is where they will travel next, if not frightened back to Rome."

"I will go there myself."

"Do so. Yet are you sure the priest does not suspect we have enfolded members of our clan among his workforce?"

"Father Josip sees only the sand and his purpose."

"Then join them."

"And if the Italians come?"

"Kill them. Take what they carry and bring it to me."

"And what of Father Josip?"

Batukhan stared around the room. The clan had existed for three generations, formed as a resistance group by his grandfather during the time of Soviet oppression. Each leader took the title *Borjigin,* meaning *Master of the Blue Wolf,* the ancient clan name of Genghis Khan.

But the world had since changed. Mongolia now had the world's fastest-growing economy, fueled by its mining operations. The true wealth of the country lay buried not in the lost tomb of Genghis Khan, but in the deposits of coal, copper, uranium, and gold, a treasure trove valued at over a trillion dollars.

Batukhan already had a major stake in several mines—but he could not let go of the stories told to him by his grandfather and father, tales of Genghis Khan, of the vast wealth hidden in his tomb.

He kept tabs on anyone searching for that sacred grave site.

That included the reclusive and odd Father Josip Tarasco.

Batukhan had heard rumors six years ago about a man appearing out of nowhere in Kazakhstan, hiding under many different names, digging holes in sand and salt, chasing the receding waters of the dying sea. The stranger had already been doing that for two years before word finally reached Ulan Bator about his intent: that he was seeking clues to Genghis Khan's burial site. It was such a strange place to be looking that Batukhan hadn't given these excavations much thought—other than infiltrating a handful of clan members to keep track of the elusive man.

Then, three days ago, word came of a strange sight, of ancient relics said to be the source of the man's quest. No one had ever viewed them before, as they had been hidden away from sight all these years by the man's paranoia. But according to his spies, the man had become increasingly agitated over the past month, desperate and frantic, and let slip the existence of these relics.

Word spread among the workers. Many fled in fear, speaking of a skull and a book bound in human skin. Then suddenly the man crated them and sent them off, perhaps fearing that word of the relics might reach the wrong ears—which, in fact, it did.

Batukhan's ears.

Intrigued, he tried to intercept the package before it was mailed to Rome. But he had acted too slowly, letting it escape his fingertips. Still, he finally learned the man's true name, written on the package.

Father Josip Tarasco.

Batukhan also learned *where* the package was to be delivered.

And still the relics escaped him.

But not for long.

Arslan stirred, awaiting his decision concerning the strange priest.

Batukhan lifted his face. "If possible, take Father Josip also. Bring him here for me to question."

"And if it's not possible?"

"Then put him in the grave with the others."

With matters settled, he headed back through the maze of steam tunnels, climbing toward the early evening. The other clan members dispersed in various directions along the way.

Batukhan kept his wolf mask on as he passed through areas where many of Ulan Bator's homeless sought shelter from the cold. Derided as the *ant tribes,* they were mostly alcoholics and the unemployable. He ignored them, dismissing them. These were not the hope of a new Mongolia, but something best kept out of sight.

Men, women, and a few children scattered like vermin from his path, turning away fearfully from the mask he wore.

Finally, he reached a ladder and climbed through a secret exit into an alleyway. A clan member closed the manhole cover as he exited.

Only after that man left did Batukhan remove his wolf mask and tuck it away. Straightening his suit, he headed out into the main street. The night was brisk, but still unseasonably warm. Ulan Bator was considered the coldest capital city in the world, but true winter seemed to be holding its hoary breath, as if anticipating something great about to happen.

Across Sükhbaatar Square rose the country's parliament house. At the top of its marble stairs, a giant bronze figure of a seated Genghis Khan, lit brightly by spotlights, looked out across the city.

Or perhaps he was staring at the comet's fiery show in the sky.

It was said that Halley's Comet had appeared during Genghis's lifetime. The khan came to consider it his personal star. He took its westward trajectory as a sign to launch his forces toward Europe.

Could this new comet also be a sign of great things to come?

As Batukhan headed into the square, he spotted the brief flashes of two falling stars in the sky, as if acknowledging this thought.

With a surge of renewed vigor, he headed toward the parliament building. A figure crossed toward him, noted his approach, and bowed his head as Batukhan passed. While he wished to believe the gesture was some acknowledgment of his being the rightful keeper of Genghis Khan's legacy, he knew it was simply recognition of his station with the government—as the Mongolian minister of justice.

Batukhan glanced back to the comet.

Like Genghis, maybe that is my own personal star . . . guiding me to conquest, power, and wealth.

9

It was a strange way to invade a country.

Gray sat near the back of the rattling bus. Behind him, Kowalski sprawled his big bulk across the large seat at the rear, snoring. The rest of the vehicle was full of Chinese men and women, drowsing or talking in low voices, some with cameras around their shoulders, others wearing baseball caps emblazoned with the same Cheshire-grinning yellow cat that was painted on the side of the gray bus, the official symbol of a Beijing-based tour company.

Near the front of the bus, Zhuang kept vigil by the driver, who was also a member of the *Duàn zhī* Triad, like the rest of their fellow travelers.

This morning, the group had flown in private jets from Hong Kong to a small airfield not far from the China–North Korea border. There, they found the two tour buses waiting. Unlike the heavily fortified demilitarized zone between North and South Korea, the border to the north was a cursory affair, mainly meant to restrict the flow of refugees from fleeing into China from the Democratic People's Republic of Korea.

That proved to be the case.

Gray and Kowalski had been hidden in a secret compartment that also held a major cache of weapons during the border crossing, but not a single member of the North Korean military even stepped aboard. Such buses were commonplace as the more affluent Chinese flocked to tour the natural, rugged beauty of the forested green mountains between the border and Pyongyang. Plus the impoverished North Korea did nothing to discourage visitors, a major source of needed tourism dollars.

Once across the border, the pair of buses had slowly trundled the winding mountain roads, working their way south toward the capital city. Four hours later, Pyongyang came into view, sprawled in the flatlands beyond the hills. After the bustle and dazzling lights of Hong Kong, the city ahead looked deserted and dark. Shadows of skyscrapers stood silhouetted against the night sky. A few monuments glowed in the darkness, along with a handful of streetlamps and windows, but little else. Nothing seemed to be moving, like a city frozen in time.

A figure stirred in the seat ahead of Gray, straightening and noting his attention. "It is a sad testament," Guan-yin said, looking as though she'd not slept at all, worry for her daughter shining in her eyes. "The residents of Pyongyang are only allowed three hours of electricity a day. So it must be used sparingly."

As they headed toward the city, traveling along a four-lane highway, not a single vehicle was seen. Even as they reached the outskirts, they found no other cars on the streets; even the traffic lights were dark. A hush fell over the bus, as if they were all afraid to disturb the ghosts of this seemingly deserted town.

The first sign of life was a lone military vehicle circling slowly in the front of a massive well-lit building.

"That's the Kumsusan Palace of the Sun," Guan-yin whispered. "It was once the official residence of President Kim Il-Sung. After his death, it now serves as his mausoleum, where his embalmed body lies in state inside a glass sarcophagus."

Just one example, Gray thought, of the elaborate cult of personality promoted by the state, where Kim Il-Sung and his descendants were worshipped as gods.

As the tomb vanished behind them, Guan-yin scowled darkly. "Some estimates put the mausoleum's construction at close to a billion dollars . . . all while the people of North Korea starved."

Gray knew the death of Kim Il-Sung in the midnineties coincided with a nationwide famine, where almost 10 percent of the population died. It became so bad at the end that cannibalism broke out in rural areas. Children were warned not to sleep in the open.

And life here had grown little better for the people of North Korea.

Under strict sanctions, the country still could not feed itself. The entire infrastructure of North Korea continued to operate on a shoestring budget. Even its factories had a hard time running due to a lack of spare parts and a scarcity of electricity.

The only industry still going strong was political theater.

Outside the bus window, canyons of dark apartment buildings spread far and wide. The only bits of brightness to break up the monotony were tall billboards and murals. But none of them advertised colas, beers, or the latest electronics. Instead, they all featured various versions of their Supreme Leader's beneficent countenance.

As the pair of buses turned onto an empty six-lane road, their goal loomed into view: the Ryugyong Hotel. It was the tallest building in all Pyongyang. It looked like a glass rocket ship rising up on three wings. It towered a hundred stories over the city. But like the rest of the city, it was also dark. Only the lobby level and a scatter of lit windows indicated any sign of life.

The plan was to use the nearly deserted hotel as a staging ground. Through Guan-yin's resources and heavy-handed use of bribes, they had discovered that a woman matching Seichan's description had been taken to a military *kyohwaso,* a reformatory prison, a few miles outside of the capital city.

In a poor country where corruption ran rampant, money talked.

Here at the hotel, they would all change into North Korean military uniforms and arm themselves. At two in the morning, an empty military transport truck would be abandoned near a service exit of the hotel, courtesy of Guan-yin's largest bribe. They would then use the truck and the uniforms to lead an assault on the camp in the dead of night.

Reaching the hotel, the lead bus rolled around the circular entrance and passed under the massive porte cochere.

Gray's vehicle followed.

The hotel had partially opened a few months ago after a plague of problems and delays. Its construction had stretched over twenty years, the building standing empty and dark for all that time, a bitter metaphor for the capital city itself. It was why the place had earned its nickname in the press.

The Hotel of Doom.

Gray prayed that name did not prove true in the coming hours ahead.

Unfortunately, he didn't have to wait even an hour.

As the first bus braked to a stop, a surge of men in military uniforms poured out of the lobby, weapons bristling, shouting angrily. Behind them, lights flared as military jeeps raced out of hiding to close off the driveway behind them.

They had rolled straight into a trap.

7:33 P.M.

Ju-long Delgado stood before a window looking into the next room. He studied the assassin strapped to the interrogation chair, a device straight out of the Spanish Inquisition. She had been stripped to bra and panties as a psychological ploy to make her feel vulnerable. Each limb was secured separately in thick cuffs, allowing the hinged chair to twist the victim's body in countless painful stress positions.

Currently she was bent backward, straining her spine, pulling on her hip and shoulder joints. She'd been in that position for the past three hours.

To make her more pliant, Hwan Pak had said, *willing to bend.*

The scientist had laughed much too loudly at his feeble joke, snorting through his bandaged broken nose. He plainly wanted revenge, to soothe his wounded pride. To that end, he intended to hurt her as he had been hurt.

The position must certainly be agonizing. The room was frigid, but sweat glowed across her bare skin, a shining testament to the pain. Delgado imagined her grimacing, teeth grinding, but her head was covered in a tight hood, with sound-dampening earphones in place, limiting her senses, making her focus only on the pain.

The North Koreans knew what they were doing.

And from the gaunt half-starved souls he'd seen moving listlessly about the packed camp, they were no kinder to their own people. Prisoners were crammed forty to a room, each space no larger than a double-car garage. He had watched a pair of men fighting over a dead body, to see who would win the right to bury it, all in order to earn an extra supplement of food.

It was a North Korean version of Auschwitz.

Ju-long's phone chimed in his pocket. He removed it, guessing it was an update from the Ryugyong Hotel. Tomaz had traveled there with the strike team.

Instead, a softer voice answered, "Ju-long . . ."

He smiled, some of the tension ebbing. "Natalia, my love, why are you calling? Is everything all right?"

He pictured her full belly, holding his son.

"I just wanted to hear your voice before I fell asleep," she said, her voice muffled at the edge of slumber. "I miss your warm body next to me."

"This will be the last night your bed will be empty. I promise I'll be home by tomorrow afternoon at the latest."

"Mmm," she mumbled sleepily. "Don't break your promise."

"I won't."

They said their good nights and good-byes.

As he pocketed his phone, he stared at the tortured woman in the neighboring room, feeling a twinge of guilt. But he had been paid well to soothe such pangs. With the deal done, he would return to Macau tomorrow morning.

He would have left that very night, but he had gotten word earlier of Guan-yin's escape from the fiery destruction of her Triad's stronghold. He had also learned that the Americans had survived, hearing of their high-flying trapeze work to escape the flames. Then just half an hour ago, further intelligence filtered in from various sources suggesting that not only was Guan-yin in North Korea, but she intended to attack this base.

After he informed Hwan Pak, they were able to scramble a strike team to ambush the others at the Ryugyong Hotel, to quash their attempted rescue of this woman before it even began.

He stared into the room, bothered by a question.

Why are you so valuable?

Ju-long believed now that he had settled on too low of a price for her, but Pak was not to be dissuaded. With his honor as wounded as his nose, the highly placed North Korean nuclear scientist had left Ju-long with little choice but to accept his offer. Pak wanted revenge and would not be denied it.

As if eavesdropping on his thoughts, Pak appeared, smiling broadly as he entered the room. "They arrived as you described, Delgado-*ssi*. We have them in hand."

He pictured Guan-yin joining the young woman here. Perhaps that was enough of a bonus for Ju-long's troubles. With her gone, it would strengthen his position in Macau.

"But now we have business we must finish here," Pak said, eyeing the room with raw lust. "You say she is an assassin with many criminal connections. We must know who they are, how they might benefit us, and, more important, what her connection is with the two Americans."

"Were those two with Guan-yin?"

So far, Ju-long had not heard a definitive answer one way or the other from his contacts. Some said yes, others no.

"I do not know yet, but I'll have answers within the hour."

The door opened behind Pak. Another man entered, tall, skeletal, his head shaved bald, wearing a long white lab coat and carrying a stainless-steel tray of wicked-looking surgical tools and pliers. His face was impassive as he gave a small bow.

"Nam Kwon," Pak introduced. "There are no answers he cannot extract with his tools."

The interrogator headed into the next room, drawing Pak with him.

Pak paused in the doorway. "Do you care to join us? You are welcome. This is your merchandise."

"No longer *mine*," he corrected. "You have paid in full. What you do with the merchandise from here is no longer my concern."

Or my fault, he added silently.

Dr. Pak shrugged and left.

Ju-long looked one last time into the neighboring room.

All this time, bent on a modern rack, the woman hadn't cried out once—but she would soon.

7:39 P.M.

"Throw the bus in reverse!" Gray hollered to the front. "Don't slow down!"

He was instantly on his feet as the military police surrounded the first bus and swarmed from the hotel lobby toward their vehicle. They had moments to react before being permanently trapped in this vise.

Zhuang was enough of a tactician with the Triad to recognize the same. He repeated the instruction to the driver in Cantonese, and the bus lurched heavily backward.

As its speed picked up, Gray dropped to his knees beside the hidden trapdoor in the floorboards and yanked it open.

Gunshots peppered the side of the retreating bus, shattering windows. The front took the brunt of the assault. The driver suddenly fell to the side with a cry of pain. The bus listed crookedly. Zhuang rolled the driver aside, tossing his body roughly into the stairwell and taking the seat himself.

The bus immediately straightened and sped faster.

Gray grabbed the assault rifle strapped to the underside of the trapdoor. It had been readied there in case there was any trouble at the border. He had noted it earlier when he and Kowalski had hidden down there.

"Pass the weapons out," he ordered Kowalski, pointing to the remainder of the cache below.

If they were to survive this, he needed this bus to become an urban assault vehicle—one with a smiling yellow cat on its side.

But first they had to break free of this closing trap.

He leaped atop the backseat, switching places with Kowalski, and popped open the emergency exit in the roof of the bus. Jumping, he pulled himself halfway through the hatch and braced himself there. He hauled up the assault rifle and aimed it at the pair of jeeps swinging up the circular driveway to cut off their retreat.

He strafed the windshield of the first, sending the vehicle careening off the driveway and into the manicured lawn. The second veered but kept on the road—until the bus, barreling in reverse, struck it a glancing blow.

The jeep crashed to the side, going up on two wheels.

The impact came close to throwing Gray out of the hatch, but at least they had broken free of the closing snare.

The bus reached the end of the driveway and did a 180-degree skid into the six-lane highway, turning the face of the bus away from the hotel. Gears cranked, the engine roared, then they were rolling forward again, gaining speed on the empty road.

Back at the hotel, the remaining military jeeps gave chase.

More vehicles with sirens flashing appeared ahead, racing toward them along the wide street. In the distance, the spearing lights of a helicopter rose into the sky over the darkened city.

So far, the North Korean ambush, though a surprise, had a rushed feel to it. Whoever had planned this attack must have had little time to fully mobilize the Pyongyang police force. But now the city was waking up, preparing to bring all force to bear.

Throughout the bus, weapons were handed out, windows pulled down. Assault rifles poked out on all sides. Still, how long could they hope to hold off the might of the North Korean armed forces?

The answer: *not long at all.*

Gray ducked back down and called over to Guan-yin. "Can you reach the man scheduled to bring the military transport truck? Get him to abandon it elsewhere for us."

She nodded, slung her rifle over her shoulder, and took out her phone.

Their only hope of surviving, of reaching Seichan, was to stick to the old adage: *If you can't fight them, join them.*

They had to create enough confusion and obfuscation to create a small window to offload the bus and get everyone into that transport truck. With all the military vehicles about to flood the streets of Pyongyang, they might be able to blend in with them during the chaos.

"There's an underpass near the highway that heads south out of town," Gray said. "Tell him to leave it there . . . and do it now!"

Leaving the details to her, he shoved up through the hatch again.

The military jeeps from the hotel were closing in on them, firing over the top of their windshields toward the fleeing bus. But the shots mostly went wide, a few pelting into the rear. One lucky round sparked near his elbow.

Gray ducked lower, aimed his assault rifle, and shot back. A windshield shattered on one jeep, and it swerved into its neighbor, bumping and rebounding away. The collision slowed the jeeps enough for the bus to stretch its lead substantially.

At the same time, flashing lights drew down upon the bus from up ahead. A barrage of gunfire erupted from both sides of the bus. Police vehicles scattered to either side. A few tried to barricade the way, but the six-lane thoroughfare proved too wide. The bus careened through them, delivering a merciless salvo of gunfire as punishment as they passed.

Then they were momentarily free of ground pursuit.

Unfortunately, the same couldn't be said for the *air*.

A helicopter swept into view along the road ahead. It banked in a turn and dove toward them. A chain-gun under the nose blazed with fire, chugged heavy rounds, drilling across the asphalt straight toward their vehicle.

The heavier bus could never outmaneuver that deadly bird.

Gray twisted around and fired at the helicopter, but it was too thickly armored to have any effect. He might as well have been firing spitballs.

Then the side door opened at the front of the bus. A large form leaned out—Kowalski—shouldering a Russian RPG-29 grenade launcher. It was meant as a weapon against tanks, but anything with armor was fair game.

Kowalski whooped loudly as he fired at nearly point-blank range. The rocket-propelled grenade shot skyward in a trail of smoke and struck the bird just below its rotors.

Gray dropped back through the hatch and flattened to the floor. Through the exit door in the roof, he saw the helicopter explode above the bus as the vehicle shot under it, trying to escape both the blast and the rain of carnage.

It failed.

The explosion rocked the bus. A piece of rotor speared through the rear, slicing the air a foot above Gray's sprawled body, close enough to feel the heat of its blasted steel on his face.

But they were still moving, limping now on a blown tire.

Using the rotor as a step-up, Gray climbed back through the hatch. The fiery wreckage of the helicopter smoked and receded behind them. But more birds lit up the skies across the city, converging toward them.

As if sensing the need for cover, Zhuang swung the bus off the wide thoroughfare and into a mazelike canyon of apartment buildings. He kept the headlamps off to keep their passage as hidden as possible.

Gray hoped the burning helicopter on the ground would draw the others toward it, like moths to a flame, allowing their bus to gain some further distance. They continued in a circuitous path southward through the city, avoiding main thoroughfares where they could.

Sirens rang throughout Pyongyang.

Still, the streets remained empty, the windows dark. The residents knew better than to show their faces.

After several tense minutes, the highway underpass appeared ahead down a narrow alley of closed shops and garages. Zhuang slowed as they crept toward that well of deeper darkness. The underpass was so low that Gray had to duck down through the hatch or risk getting decapitated.

He hurried to the front of the bus, where Kowalski still held the tube of the grenade launcher. They slid under the highway. The space appeared empty, but it was too dark to say for sure.

If the transport isn't here . . .

With his heart in his throat, Gray whispered to Zhuang, "Try the lights."

The swordsman flicked on the headlamps. Light exploded throughout the underpass, exposing every hidden corner.

Nothing.

Gray glanced back to Guan-yin, who had followed him forward.

She shook her head. "He said he'd be here."

Kowalski slammed his palm against the door. "Motherfu—"

A set of headlamps suddenly blazed a few streets up. A large truck shot into view, skidded around a corner at a fast clip, and sped toward them.

Gray pulled the door release of the bus and hopped out.

He raised his weapon toward the racing vehicle.

Guan-yin joined him, urging him to lower his weapon. "It's our truck."

She was proven correct as the dark green vehicle braked hard next to theirs. It was a Chinese model with a tall driver's compartment and an enclosed rear bed. It wasn't armored, but Gray was not complaining.

The driver hopped out, collected a satchel of money from Guan-yin, then sprinted away.

"Guess he's not big on small talk," Kowalski said.

They quickly offloaded all their gear from the bus, both uniforms and weapons. Likewise, three military motorcycles were rolled out of the truck bed and onto the asphalt. The bikes would act as an entourage for the personnel carrier.

Five men—those who looked the most Korean and spoke the language fluently—dressed immediately. Three of them mounted the motorcycles, and two climbed into the truck's cab. The rest of the crew ducked immediately into the rear bed.

Except for one plucky volunteer who agreed to stay with the bus.

The transfer was done in less than five minutes. The bus took off in one direction, the truck and motorcycles in the other. The hope was for the bus to lure the hunters away, to give them as hard and long a chase as possible. Then the driver would ditch the bus and vanish into the vastness of the dark city.

Gray stared out the back flap of the bed, watching the bus disappear. Once it was gone, he dropped the flap and stared around the dark, tight space as everyone switched into North Korean uniforms.

He caught one face, shadowed by a tattoo, staring back at him.

They both shared the same worry.

Once word reached Seichan's captors of their escape, how would they react? Would they move her to a new location or kill her immediately?

And the more important question, *How much time do we have left to save her?*

8:02 P.M.

Seichan writhed in her restraints as a steel needle was slowly driven under her fingernail. Four others already poked from the same hand. Pain shot all the way to her shoulders. She breathed heavily through her nose, refusing to scream.

Her torturer sat on a stool, bent over her arm, expressionless but intently focused, as if he were giving her a manicure.

Other tools of black interrogation were spread in plain view behind him, shining coldly under the fluorescent lights. She knew this was as much psychological as anything, a warning of what was to come if she continued to refuse to talk.

The room's only other occupant paced to her other side, wringing his small hands. "Tell us who the Americans are," Pak repeated, his voice high and nasal through his splinted bandage. "And this will stop."

Like hell it would.

She knew they intended to wring everything and anything they could out of her. Her coming days promised endless suffering. Her worst fear was not the shining drill bits or threats of rape, but that she would eventually break. In time, she would tell them anything; whether true or false, it wouldn't matter then.

Still, she took comfort where she could.

If they were questioning her about Gray and Kowalski, then likely the pair had survived the ambush in Macau and the fiery attack in Hong Kong. If he was breathing, Seichan knew, Gray would not stop trying to reach her.

But can I last that long?

Does he even know where I am?

She held back hope, knowing that path only led to weakness. In the end, it would be better if Gray never tried freeing her, because to do so would only get him killed.

Her interrogator—who had been introduced to her as Nam Kwon— gently attached tiny electrical clips to each of the five imbedded needles. He spoke softly, never looking up, his voice a whisper, almost apologetic.

"The jolt of electricity will feel as if your fingernails are being ripped out all at the same time. The pain will be beyond imagining."

She ignored his words, knowing that he *wanted* her to imagine that pain. Often the anticipation of pain was worse than enduring it.

Pak came forward, leaning his face close to hers. "Tell us who these Americans are."

She stared up at him and smiled coldly. "They're the ones who are going to rip off your balls and feed them to pigs."

As his eyes narrowed in anger, she slammed her head forward and butted him square in the face.

He bellowed, falling backward, fresh blood spurting from his nose.

Pak waved to Kwon. "Do it! Make her scream!"

Kwon remained calm. Unhurried, he reached and twisted a dial. "This is the lowest voltage," he said—then flipped a switch.

Pak got what he asked for.

Pain ripped through her. Surprise more than agony squeezed a cry from her throat. Her arm turned to fire as electricity contorted her body. Rigid muscles fought the restraints in convulsive trembles.

Through the red fire, she saw the door open behind Kwon and Pak.

The interruption drew their attention. Kwon flipped the switch back, and she sagged into the chair, her body still quaking with aftershocks, her hand burning.

Delgado stared toward her, his face ashen but doing his best not to show any reaction. He finally had to look away.

Clearing his throat, Delgado said, "I've just heard word from my man Tomaz at the Ryugyong. Half of the *Duàn zhī* Triad have been captured or killed at the hotel. But another half escaped in a second bus. All Pyongyang is out searching for them."

Confused, Seichan focused through the residual pain. The *Duàn zhī* was her mother's gang. But what were they doing here in North Korea? She struggled to understand. Was her mother simply seeking revenge from the attack on her stronghold in Hong Kong? Or was it something more personal?

She swallowed back hope but failed to completely stanch it.

Pak glowered at Delgado. "And Guan-yin?"

Her mother . . .

Seichan held her breath.

Delgado did not look any happier than the North Korean. "She was not among those captured. Neither was Zhuang, her lieutenant."

Pak stamped back and forth, balling a fist. "But she remains on our soil. She will not escape for long."

Delgado made a noncommittal noise, plainly less convinced. Guan-yin had survived his fiery assault on her stronghold. He was not going to underestimate his opponent.

"I have more news," Delgado said. "It appears the Americans came with Guan-yin."

"They are here!" Pak's face flushed darkly.

Seichan also felt a surge of emotion—hope rising inside her despite her efforts to rein it back.

"What about the prisoner?" Delgado asked, returning his attention to Seichan. "It would not be prudent to leave her here."

Pak nodded. "There's a prison camp near my lab. It's in the remote northern mountains, known to only a handful of those in power, and well guarded. I had planned on transferring her tomorrow anyway. We will do that now."

So he meant to keep her close to him, clearly intending to enjoy her every scream. Not good. Seichan knew that if she reached that camp, all was lost.

"It would be better to kill her now," Delgado suggested and nodded to Pak's holstered pistol. "A bullet to the head."

Seichan sensed this proposition was expressed more as a concern for her than for Pak. A quick death would be better than months of torture that ended in the same grave.

Pak wasn't having any of it, puffing out his chest with nationalistic pride. "That would be a cowardly response to a minor threat."

Delgado shrugged.

Pak glanced at her, blood still dripping from his nose. She read his expression. His decision against killing her was less about honor and more about his fondness for torture. He had a small taste of it a moment ago. He wanted more.

Pak called to the guard outside the door, while slipping his own pistol free. Once the soldier stepped inside, he pointed to Seichan. "Free her, and take her to my jeep. Make sure she is securely bound."

"It is very cold, *seon-saeng-nim*," the guard said formally. "Should I find her clothes for travel?"

Pak eyed her up and down.

"*Aniyo*," he finally declined. "If she wants warmth, she must beg for it."

With the matter settled, the guard pointed his rifle at her. Kwon undid the padded cuffs that held her to the steel chair.

First her ankles, then her wrists.

As soon as her last arm was freed, she lashed out, stabbing the ends of the needles still poking from her fingertips into Kwon's eyes. He stumbled back, partially blocking the guard's angle of fire as she had planned.

She sprang up, grabbed Kwon, and rolled him fully between her and the soldier as the man opened fire. Rounds skewered through the interrogator but did not find her. She shoved his bulk at the guard, tangling them up long enough for Seichan to spin around and snatch the pistol from Pak's stunned fingers.

She whipped back and planted a single shot into the soldier's skull.

Running for the door, she snatched up his rifle with her free hand and fled the room—leaving Delgado and Pak unharmed. Not knowing what she might face, she dared not waste a bullet on them.

Once outside, she dead-bolted the door to the interrogation room. She then painfully pulled out each of the steel needles. Through the small window, she watched Pak rage impotently inside. Insulated against the screams of the tortured, not a sound escaped the room.

Behind Pak, Delgado caught her eyes, his arms folded over his chest. He smiled at her, offering her a small nod of respect.

Turning heel, she ran for the exit to the interrogation building. Luckily it was deserted at this late hour. She slowed only long enough to search a bank of lockers near the front door, hoping to find a North Korean uniform.

Failing that, she at least found a crumpled set of inmate clothing at the bottom of one locker. She slipped into the dark Communist tunic and pulled on a set of loose pants. The only decoration to its drabness was a red badge featuring Kim Il-Sung's face on the left breast.

With regret, she placed the stolen assault rifle in the locker. It was too large to hide, and wearing the clothes of a prisoner, she would have a hard time explaining the presence of a rifle.

With the pistol hidden against her leg, she slipped out into the night. Off in the distance, she heard a faint echo of alarm sirens coming from the direction of Pyongyang.

Even with a pistol in hand, she would never make it through the heavily guarded front gates on her own. And even if she did, where could she go? She had to trust that Gray and her mother knew where to find her, that they'd come for her.

She ran for the rows of barracks, intending to hide herself among the prisoners, to keep out of sight until help could arrive.

For the first time in her life, Seichan put her trust in hope.

10

The Eurocopter sped over an endless landscape of blowing sand and crusted salt. Jada stared listlessly below, finding it hard to believe this blighted region was once a beautiful blue sea, teeming with fish, the shores dotted with canneries and villages, all full of vigorous life.

It seemed unimaginable.

She had read the mission dossier concerning the Aral Sea, how the Soviets had diverted its two major rivers to irrigate cotton fields back in the sixties. As the decades passed, the sea quickly dried up, dwindling to only 10 percent of its original size, draining a volume equal to Lake Erie and Lake Ontario combined. Now all that remained of the sea were a few salty pools to the north and south.

Between them, this wasteland was born.

"They call this the Aralkum Desert," the monsignor whispered as the others slept, noting her attention. "Its toxic salt fields are so large they can be seen from space."

"Toxic?" she asked.

"As the sea vanished, it left behind pollutants and pesticides. Strong winds regularly stir up that sand and dust into dark storms called *black blizzards.*"

As Jada stared, she watched a swirling zephyr spin across the salt flats as if chasing them.

"People began to get sick. Respiratory infections, strange anemias, spikes in cancer rates. The average life expectancy dropped from sixty-five to fifty-one."

She glanced at him, surprised by those numbers.

"And its effect was not just local. These fierce winds continue to blow the desert's poison around the globe. Aral dust can be found in the glaciers of Greenland, in the forests of Norway, even in the blood of penguins in Antarctica."

Jada shook her head, wondering for the thousandth time why they had detoured to this desolate place. If given a choice, she would have preferred to visit another location in Kazakhstan: the Baikonur Cosmodrome, Russia's premier space center. It lay only two hundred miles east of their coordinates.

At least there, I could collect more data on the crash.

That is, if everything weren't so top secret.

Still, she looked sidelong at Duncan, at his fingertips. He said he had noted some energy signature emanating from the archaeological relics. As much as she was in a hurry, a part of her was intrigued by his assessment.

But was it all nonsense?

Jada studied Duncan's features as he lightly drowsed beside his stocky partner. The man did not strike her as someone prone to flights of fantasy. He seemed too well grounded.

The pilot came over the intercom. "We're ten minutes out from the coordinates."

Everyone stirred.

She returned her full attention to the window. The sun sat low on the horizon. Hillocks and the rusting remains of old ships cast long shadows across the flat desert.

As the coordinates grew closer, the Eurocopter began to descend, sweeping lower, speeding over the salt flats.

"Dead ahead," the pilot said.

Everyone pressed their noses to their respective windows.

The helicopter rushed toward the only feature for miles: the rusted hulk of a massive ship. It sat upright, its keel sunk deep into the sand, a ghost ship riding this dusty sea. Oxidation and corrosion had worn away most details, eating away its forecastle, staining the bulkhead a deep orange-red, a sharp contrast to the white salt flats.

"Is this the place?" Rachel asked.

"It matches the coordinates," the pilot confirmed.

Duncan spoke by his window. "I see lots of tire tracks in the salt around the beached ship."

"This must be right," the monsignor insisted.

Monk touched his radio to communicate better with the pilot. "Take us down. Land fifty or so yards away from the ship."

The bird immediately banked to the side, hovered for a breath, then lowered until its wheels touched down, blowing up a whirlwind of sand and salt.

Monk pulled off his earphones and yelled to the pilot. "Keep the rotors turning until I give you the all-clear."

He pulled open the hatch. With an arm raised against the sting of whipping sand, he cautioned everyone to remain inside, except Duncan. "Let us check this out first."

Jada was happy to let them take the lead. From the shadows of the cabin, she watched Monk and Duncan head out across the dusty sand. The winter day was cool, but not bitterly. The air smelled of salt, motor oil, and decay.

Across the way, a dark door in the ship's port-side hull beckoned. It lay even with the sands and open to the elements. Before the two men had crossed half the distance toward it, a desert-camouflaged Land Rover burst out of a hidden hatch in the vessel's stern. It sped on wide, paddle-treaded tires built for the sand and swept in an intercepting arc to reach Monk and Duncan.

The two men had their weapons raised and pointed toward it.

The Land Rover drew abreast of them, keeping a distance away.

An exchange of words followed, with much gesticulation on Monk's part. The monsignor's name was mentioned. After another full minute of discussion, Monk stomped back to the helicopter.

"They say Father Josip is inside the ship," he said. "I tried to convince them to have the priest come out and greet us, to make sure we're not being set up. But they refused."

"I imagine by now the level of Father Josip's paranoia is quite high," Vigor said.

Jada heard a slight catch in the monsignor's voice, as if he were holding something back about the man.

"I'll go meet him alone," Vigor said, hopping out.

"No, you won't," Rachel said. She leaped down to join her uncle. "We stick together."

"We'll all go," Monk said, but he turned to Jada. "Maybe you'd best stay with the helicopter."

She considered it for a few seconds, then shook her head, forcing as much bravado as she could muster. "I've not come all this way to stay in the helicopter."

Monk nodded, then popped his head into the cabin and yelled to the pilot. "I'll be on radio. Lock this bird up tight, but keep her warmed and ready in case we need a fast takeoff."

The pilot gave Monk a thumbs-up. "Wouldn't have it any other way."

With the matter settled, they all took off across the sand to rejoin Duncan. Jada moved into the larger man's shadow. He gave her a wink of reassurance—which surprisingly worked to calm her.

That, and perhaps the assault rifle in his hands.

A lone stranger hopped out of the passenger seat of the Land Rover to greet them. He was her height with shaggy dark hair, likely about her same age, too, dressed in traditional-looking Kazakh attire, consisting of wide trousers, a long shirt, and a sleeveless sheepskin jacket. He came to them empty-handed, but he lifted his arm, exposing a leather cuff around his left wrist.

A sharp whistle from him drew a screeched response.

A dark shape swooped into view overhead and plummeted into a steep dive. Just before striking the Kazakh man, a bird with huge wings swooped wide, braking to a stop. Sharp talons found the leather cuff, and the tall falcon came to a fluttering rest, tucking its wings. Tiny dark eyes stared at the newcomers with suspicion—until the man placed a small leather hood over the bird's head.

The stranger faced them, offering the monsignor a respectful nod of greeting. "Father Josip has shown me pictures of his dear friend, the monsignor Verona. Please be welcome." He spoke flawless English, with a prominent British accent. "I am Sanjar, and my feathered companion of foul temper is Heru."

Vigor smiled. "The Egyptian variant on the Greek name Horus."

"Indeed. The falcon-headed god of the sky." Sanjar headed toward the ship. "Please follow me. Father Josip will be very happy to see you."

He led the group toward the door cut through the ship's hull. To the left, the Land Rover sped away, swinging around the stern and vanishing out of view.

Vigor craned his neck to look up at the tall derelict ship. "Father Josip has been living in here all this time?"

"Not *in* here, but *under* here."

Sanjar ducked into the dark interior of the ship.

Jada followed Duncan, finding herself in the cavernous hold of the ship. The vessel's interior had fared no better than its outside. Over the passing decades, the elements had worked deep into the ship, wreaking great damage, turning the hold into a rotted-out cathedral of rust and ruin.

To the far right, she spotted the Land Rover parked in its makeshift garage, sheltered from the elements.

"This way." Sanjar motioned to the left, to an open staircase, its rails dripping with rivulets of corrosion. He clicked on a flashlight and led the way down.

As they progressed deeper, the steel treads underfoot abruptly changed to rock. Through a rent in the ship's bottom, a steep passage delved downward, dug through the sandstone, leading to a vast maze burrowed beneath the decaying behemoth. Dark tunnels branched off from the main passageway, revealing a warren of rooms and additional passageways and crawlways.

It looked like an entire village could have been housed down here.

"Who built all this?" Duncan asked Sanjar.

"First, drug smugglers back in the early seventies, then it was expanded by militant forces during the late eighties, and it was mostly abandoned after Kazakhstan declared independence in the nineties. Once discovered, Father Josip made it his base camp, where he could work undisturbed and out of the public eye."

A glow rose up from below. As they neared it, Sanjar clicked off his flashlight and returned it to his pocket. The falcon on his wrist stirred with a ruffle of feathers.

Moments later, they reached what appeared to be the lowest level. The stairs emptied into a large man-made cavern, as big as a basketball court. Other halls burrowed out from here, but there was no need to go any farther.

The main room looked like a cross between a medieval library and the mad nest of a hoarder. Rows of bookcases strained under the weight of their volumes. Desks lay buried under mounds of papers and notebooks, along with bits of broken pottery, even a few dusty bones. Additionally, charts and maps had been nailed to the wall, some torn in half, others marked over so heavily with a thick scrawl as to be indiscernible. Then there were the chalked diagrams spanning another section of the walls, with arrows connecting and dividing, as if someone were engineering a giant Rube Goldberg machine.

In the center of the chaos stood the clear master of this domain.

He was dressed similarly to Sanjar, but with the addition of a Roman collar. Over the years, the sun and wind had weathered the priest's skin to a burnished brown, while also bleaching his hair white. His cheeks and chin were scruffy with several days' worth of beard.

He looked much older than Vigor—though Jada knew the man was actually a decade younger.

Still, despite his aged countenance, a pair of eyes blazed brightly as he turned toward them. But Jada wondered: *Was that shine brilliance or madness?*

5:58 P.M.

Vigor could not hide his shock at the state of his colleague.

"Josip?"

"Vigor, my friend!" Josip waded through stacked books on the floor, his thin arms raised in greeting, tears beginning to brim. "You came!"

"How could I not?"

When Josip reached him, they hugged. His friend clung to him, repeatedly squeezing his shoulders as if to test that he was real. In turn, Vigor felt the thinness of his colleague's frame, thinking Josip's years in this harsh desert had almost mummified him. But Vigor suspected it was *obsession* more than anything that had burned his friend to skin and bone.

Sadly, such had been the case in the past, too.

Early in his seminary years, Josip Tarasco had suffered his first psychotic break. He had been found naked atop the roof of the school, claiming he could hear the voice of God in the stars, explaining he needed to remove his clothes so the starlight could bathe him more fully, drawing him closer to the Lord.

Shortly after that, he had been diagnosed with bipolar disorder, a manic condition of deep lows and blazing highs. Lithium and other antidepressants helped stabilize the severity of those emotional swings, but never entirely. On the positive side, that same condition seemed to stoke a fire of genius in the man, a brilliance born out of that streak of madness.

Still, lapses of his mental status did occur, expressed as bouts of obsessive compulsion, tics of behavior, and, in rare moments, full psychotic breaks. So Vigor was not entirely surprised when Josip suddenly vanished off the face of the earth ten years ago.

But what about now . . . ?

As they ended their embrace, Vigor searched Josip's face.

His friend noted the attention. "I know what you're thinking, Vigor, but I am in my right mind." He glanced around the chamber, running a hand through his hair. "Perhaps a bit compulsive at the moment, I will admit that, but stress was always my enemy. And considering the time-table we're all under, I must accept and utilize every unique gift God has given me."

Upon hearing all this, Rachel looked sternly at him. Vigor had failed to mention Josip's mental condition to her, fearing it would dissuade her from allowing him to travel here. He also worried such a revelation might cast doubts on the validity of the man's concerns.

Vigor had no such prejudices.

He respected Josip's genius, regardless of his diagnosis.

"And speaking of that rushed timetable," Vigor said, "perhaps you can explain why you summoned me here in such a strange manner. What you sent brought a great deal of trouble along with it."

"They found you?"

"Who found us?" Vigor pictured the attack at the university and the deadly bombing in Aktau.

Josip shook his head, his gaze turning flighty, edgy with paranoia. Vigor could see the man struggling against it.

He licked his lips. "I don't know. Someone killed the courier I sent overland to mail the crate. On his way back he was waylaid, tortured, his dead body dumped in the desert. I thought . . . I was hoping it was just bandits. But now . . . ?"

Josip was losing his battle. Raw suspicion shone in his face, his gaze glancing off everyone now. It seemed *compulsion* was not the only symptom manifesting during this stressful time.

In order to stem that growing paranoia, Vigor made fast introductions, ending with, "And you must remember Rachel, my niece."

Josip's face brightened with sudden recognition and relief. "Of course! How wonderful!" This slice of the familiar seemed to immediately drain the tension out of Vigor's colleague, to reassure him that he was among friends. "Come, I have much to show you and so very little time."

He marched them over to a long wooden table with bench seating. Sanjar helped him clear the surface. Once that was done, they all settled down.

"The skull and the book?" Josip started, his desire plain to read.

"Yes, I have them with me. On the helicopter."

"Can someone fetch them?"

Duncan stood up and volunteered to retrieve them.

"Thank you, young man," Josip said. He then turned to Vigor. "I assume you've already identified the skull's owner, the same man who once wore that skin."

"Genghis Khan. The relics were crafted from his body."

"Very good. With your resources, I knew you'd solve that mystery."

"But where did you find such macabre items?"

"In the grave of a witch."

The young woman, Dr. Shaw, made a scoffing noise. She had not been won over to their cause during the flight here, even after Vigor had revealed the history of the relics. She clearly suffered from her own single-mindedness and was anxious to continue onward with Sigma's secret mission in Mongolia.

Ignoring her, Vigor encouraged Josip. "I remember you were on a research trip to Hungary, investigating the witch hunts of the eighteenth century."

"Indeed. I was in Szeged, a small town along the *Tisza* River in southern Hungary."

Josip stressed the name of the river, staring harder at Vigor, as if offering a hidden clue. Something about the name did trigger a flicker of recognition. He just couldn't say why.

Josip continued, "In July of 1728, during the height of that witch hunt, a group of twelve local townspeople were burned at the stake on a small island in the river called *Boszorkánysziget*. Which means *Island of the Witches*, named after the great number of innocents torched there."

"Such superstitious nonsense," Rachel muttered with a scowl.

Jada nodded next to her.

"Actually, *superstitions* had very little to do with these particular murders. Hungary was at the end of a decade-long drought. Rivers dwindled to trickles, farmlands turned to dust, famine was rampant."

"The people needed a scapegoat," Vigor said.

"And someone to sacrifice. Over four hundred people were killed during that time, but not all those deaths were born of fearful superstitions. Many public officials used that bloody period to rid themselves of threats or for petty revenge."

"And the twelve in Szeged?" Rachel asked, ready to hear more about this cold case.

"I found a copy of the original trial transcript in a monastery outside of town. Their inquisition was less concerned about witchcraft and more about rumors of the twelve discovering a buried treasure. Whether true or not, they refused to speak. Others took the stand to say they heard some of the twelve talking about finding a skull and a book bound in human skin. Such accusations of the occult eventually led them to be burned at the stake."

Monk tapped one of his prosthetic fingers on the table. "So you're saying that these twelve were tortured to death to find the location of some lost treasure."

"Not just *any* lost treasure." Josip looked hard again at Vigor, as if expecting him to understand this cryptic response.

He didn't. He remained mystified and was about to say so—when suddenly he knew, putting the clues together in a sudden flash of insight.

"The Tisza River!"

Josip smiled.

"What about it?" Jada asked.

Vigor sat up straighter. "It wasn't just the tomb of Genghis Khan that vanished into the mists of time. But also the grave of another conquering warrior, a local Hungarian hero."

Rachel caught on. "You're talking about Attila the Hun."

Vigor nodded. "Attila died from a nosebleed during his wedding night in AD 453. Like Genghis, his soldiers buried him in secret with all his pillaged treasures, slaughtering anyone who knew the tomb's location. The story goes that Attila was entombed inside a set of three coffins. One of iron, another of silver, and the innermost one of gold."

Monk's finger stopped tapping. "And no one ever discovered where he was buried?"

"Over the centuries, rumors abounded. But most historians believe his soldiers diverted the flow of the Tisza River, buried him in a secret vault beneath its mud, then returned the river to its original course."

"That would certainly make it hard to find," Monk admitted.

Struck by another insight, Vigor swung to Josip. "But wait, you mentioned that *drought* during the eighteenth century, the one that triggered the witch hunts."

"When rivers dwindled to trickles," Josip agreed, still smiling.

"It could've exposed that secret vault!" Vigor imagined the receding waters revealing Attila's secret. "Are you saying someone actually found it?"

"And tried to keep it secret," Josip added.

"The twelve conspirators . . . the twelve accused witches."

"Yes." Josip leaned his elbows on the table. "But unknown to the people of Szeged, there was a *thirteenth* witch."

6:07 P.M.

Duncan returned to the subterranean library to find everyone seated in stunned silence. Sensing he had missed something important, he carried the two archaeological relics to the table, the pair still wrapped in their insulating foam. He preferred not to handle them directly with his sensitive fingertips.

He leaned toward Jada and whispered, "What happened?"

She shushed him, waving him to the bench.

As he sat, the monsignor asked Josip, "What thirteenth witch?"

Duncan frowned at the odd question.

Yep, I definitely missed something.

6:09 P.M.

Vigor waited for Josip to explain.

"From the records," his friend said, "I discovered that the bishop of Szeged had failed to attend that particular witch trial, a rarity for the pious man. That struck me as odd."

It would be odd, Vigor thought.

"So I sought out his personal diaries and found them stored at the Franciscan Church in town, a church that dates back to the early fifteen hundreds. Many of the books were water damaged or destroyed by mold. But in one of his journals, I found a hand-drawn picture of a skull resting atop a book. It reminded me of the accusations from the trial. Written in Latin below it were the words: *God, forgive me for the trespass, for my silence, and for what I must take to my grave.*"

Vigor could guess Josip's next move. "So you sought out his grave."

"His remains were stored in a mausoleum under the church." From the reddening of his friend's face, it was clear Josip's next words clearly shamed him. "I did not ask permission. I was too impatient, too sure of myself, deep in a manic phase where every action seemed right."

Vigor reached across and touched his arm, reassuring him.

Looking at the tabletop, Josip admitted his crime. "In the dead of night, I took a sledge to the marble front and broke inside."

"It was there you found the skull and the book."

"Among other items."

"What items?"

"I discovered a final note from the bishop, his written confession sealed in a bronze tube. In it, he explained about the discovery of Attila's grave site. How a farmer stumbled upon it in the dry riverbed—only to find the vault empty, ransacked long ago. Except for an iron box resting on a pedestal, preserving a few precious items."

"The skull and the book."

"Superstitious fear drove the farmer to the town bishop. He believed he'd stumbled upon the meeting place for a coven of witches. Upon hearing this, the bishop commissioned twelve of his most trusted allies to accompany him to the site."

"The twelve who were burned at the stake," Vigor said.

"Correct. At the river, the group discovered who had ransacked the vault. They found a calling card left behind by the thieves, a wrist cuff of gold sculpted with the images of a phoenix fighting demons, with the name Genghis Khan inscribed on it."

So Genghis Khan found Attila's tomb . . . ?

It was not beyond the realm of possibilities, Vigor realized. Their two empires—though centuries apart—overlapped geographically. Genghis must have heard the stories of Attila's burial and sought the treasures hidden within. Mongol forces never fully subjugated Hungary, but there were skirmishes back and forth for decades. During one of those campaigns, some prisoner must have talked, likely under torture, and the tomb was discovered and ransacked.

None of this, of course, answered the larger question.

Vigor stared at Josip. "But how did Genghis Khan's skull and a book bound in his skin end up *back* in Attila's old vault?"

"Because of a warning of doom."

Josip nodded to Sanjar, who had been obviously waiting for this signal. The man carried forward a sheaf of pages, each protectively sealed in Mylar plastic sleeves.

"These pages were also found inside Attila's vault."

They were placed before Vigor. He glanced at the ancient pages, where faint handwriting could be discerned. Squinting, he saw words written in Latin.

He translated the opening lines. *"This is the last testament of Ildiko, descended blood of King Gondioc de Burgondie. These are my dying words from the past to the future . . ."*

Vigor glanced up, recognizing the name. "Ildiko was Attila's last wife. Some believed she murdered the Hun with poison on their wedding night."

"So she admits here." Josip touched the stack of paper. "Read the pages at your leisure. She wrote them while buried alive in that vault with Attila's body, a murder she committed at the behest of the Church."

"What?" Shock rang in Vigor's voice.

"Through intermediaries, Pope Leo the Great enlisted her to recover what had been given to Attila the year prior, an ominous gift to frighten the superstitious king of the Huns away from the gates of Rome."

Vigor knew about that fateful meeting—except for one detail. "What did the pontiff give him?"

"A box. Or rather *three* boxes, one inside the other. The outer of iron, then silver, then gold."

The same as the rumored coffins of Attila.

Was this papal gift the source of that story? Or did Attila copy it for his own grave?

"What was inside the box?" Rachel asked, striking for the heart of the matter.

"First, there was a skull, inscribed in ancient Aramaic."

Vigor pictured the writing he had examined in Rome. "So the box held the *original* relic, the one that was used as a template for Genghis's skull."

Monk cocked a thumb toward the foam-wrapped objects. "So Genghis's skull was just a Xerox copy of this older one. Why do that?"

Rachel explained, "Someone wanted what was written on that first skull—a plea against the end of the world and its date—to survive the march of history."

"But why?" Jada interrupted, sounding offended. "Why go to all this effort to preserve this information, when nothing can be done about this doomsday prediction?"

"Who said *nothing* can be done about it?" Josip quipped. "I said the skull was the *first* of the objects hidden in those triple boxes."

"What else was there?" Vigor asked.

"According to Ildiko, the boxes and their contents came from east of Persia, from the Nestorian sect of the Christian church. The treasure was sent west to Rome for safekeeping in the Eternal City, where it was hoped its contents might be preserved until the end of time."

"Or at least until the date marked on the skull," Vigor added.

Josip bowed his head in agreement. "Pope Leo gave this gift away without full knowledge of what it held. Only after a Nestorian emissary came from Persia and warned the pontiff of the contents' true history did he realize his grave error."

Monk snorted. "So he sent a girl to get it back."

"It may have been the only way to get close to Attila," Josip countered. "But in the end, she failed. Attila must have grown wise to what had been given to him and hid it away."

"What was it?" Vigor asked.

"In Ildiko's own words, a *celestial cross,* one sculpted from a star that had fallen to the earth far to the east."

"A meteorite," Jada said, sitting up.

"Most likely," Josip agreed. "From that fallen star, a cross was carved and given as a gift to a holy visitor, one who came to their eastern shores, spreading word of a new god, one with a risen son."

Vigor glanced again to the wrapped relics, picturing the gospel bound in human skin. "You're talking about St. Thomas," he said with awe. "The Chinese emperor of that time gave St. Thomas that newly sculpted cross."

Historians readily accepted that the apostle Thomas traveled as far as India, where he was eventually martyred. But a few scholars believed he might have made it as far as China, maybe even Japan.

Vigor could not keep the wonder out of his voice. "Are you saying the box held the cross of St. Thomas?"

"Not just his cross," Josip intoned.

Vigor matched his friend's tearful gaze and knew the truth.

It held his skull, too.

Vigor was struck momentarily dumb. Had this same knowledge pushed Josip over the edge? By his own admission, he had already begun to act irrationally. Had this driven him into a full psychotic break?

"According to Ildiko's testament," Josip continued, "St. Thomas had a vision of the fiery destruction of the world, including when it would happen, while holding this cross. This knowledge was preserved by Christian mystics after his death."

"By inscribing it upon the saint's skull."

Josip nodded. "According to St. Thomas, this celestial cross is the only weapon to prevent the world from ending on that date. If it remains lost, the world is doomed."

"And this cross was buried with Attila?" Vigor asked.

Josip glanced to the pages. "Ildiko claims as much. While locked in that tomb, she found the boxes again—only now with the cross returned to its proper place inside. She wrote down her last testament in the hopes someone would find it."

"Which Genghis did," Vigor finished.

Silence hung over the room for several breaths.

Finally, Monk cleared his throat. "So let me get this straight. The pope mistakenly gave Attila this treasure. A plot to retrieve it failed. Centuries later, Genghis ransacked Attila's tomb, read Ildiko's note, found the cross there, and upon his death, he used his own body to preserve this knowledge."

"Not only preserve it," Josip said, "but I believe he was leaving behind a road map for a future generation, offering us a way to find where he hid this cross, turning his own body into a guide."

Vigor acknowledged that possibility. "Genghis Khan always believed the *future* belonged to him. And considering that one out of every two hundred men living today is his descendant, he might have been right. He would want to protect that legacy."

Josip agreed. "Despite his image as a bloody tyrant, Genghis was also forward thinking. His empire had the first international postal system, invented the concept of diplomatic immunity, and even allowed women in its councils. But more important, the Mongols were also unprecedented in their religious tolerance. In their capital city, there was even a Nestorian church. It might have been those priests who helped sway Genghis to this path."

"I think you may be right about that last part," Vigor agreed. "Historically the Nestorians were a huge influence on Genghis. Just the fact that Genghis used his own skin to preserve a copy of the Gospel of Thomas speaks to their influence even in this endeavor."

Rachel, ever the detective, wanted more proof. "This is all fine, but can any of this be substantiated? Is there any piece of tangible evidence that Genghis possessed this cross, this talisman meant to save the world?"

Josip pointed to Vigor. "He has it."

Vigor felt like a victim falsely accused. "What do you mean? Where do I have it?"

"In the Vatican's Secret Archives. You are now the prefect of that library, are you not?"

Vigor racked his brain as to what Josip was implying—then he remembered one of the archive's prize possessions. "The letter from Genghis Khan's grandson!"

Josip crossed his arms, the victorious prosecutor.

Vigor explained to the others. "In 1246, the *grandson* of Genghis, the Grand Khan Guyuk, sent a note to the pope. He demanded the pontiff travel to Mongolia in person to pay homage to him. He warned that if the pope didn't do this, there would be grave consequences for the world."

Rachel stared at him. "It's not definitive proof, but I'll admit it does sound like the grandson knew he had the fate of the world in his possession, or at least in his grandfather's tomb."

Vigor gave a small shrug. "He may have even been offering to return it to the pope, if the pontiff were willing to travel there . . . which unfortunately he refused."

Duncan sighed. "If he had, that would've made things lots easier."

Monk shrugged heavily. "That's all well and good. I appreciate the history lesson. But let's cut to the chase, people. Can anyone tell me *how* finding this cross is supposed to save the world?"

Vigor looked to Josip, hoping for a solution. His friend gave a small, defeated shake of his head. Instead, the answer came from a most unlikely source, from someone who had been as doubtful as St. Thomas all along.

Dr. Jada Shaw raised her hand. "I know."

11

The squeal of truck brakes announced their arrival at the prison gates.

Hidden in the vehicle's enclosed bed, Gray allowed himself a measure of relief. The strike team had made it safely out of downtown Pyongyang and into the swampy outskirts that bordered the Taedong River. En route here, they had run across a few search patrols, but the Triad members on the motorcycles had put on a good front, clearing a path through. With everyone still looking for a bus, their military truck raised no suspicions.

But Gray knew such luck could not last forever. They'd lost half their force back at the hotel. One of those captured would eventually break and reveal their assault plans to the enemy.

Gray listened to the loud voices as the driver shouted to the gate guards. The plan was to pose as reinforcements, sent from Pyongyang to beef up security here. The distant sirens of the city certainly added validity to that claim.

Footfalls and voices flanked the side of the truck, working their way toward the rear. It seemed the guards here were on edge, likely still being kept in the dark in regard to the situation downtown.

Suddenly the rear flap was tossed back. The beam of a flashlight speared inside, blinding them, giving them all a good excuse to shield their faces or turn away. Gray and Kowalski hunkered down closest to the cab, their pale faces blocked by the bodies of the others.

The guard splashed his light around, but after discovering only men and women wearing North Korean uniforms, he let the flap drop and headed back to his gatehouse.

With a grind of gears, the truck began moving again. It rolled slowly forward. Gray risked widening a rip in the bed's tent fabric so he could peek out. The prison covered a hundred acres, all surrounded by high fencing topped with coils of razor wire. Guard towers rose every fifty yards. The facilities inside were a mix of squat cement-block buildings and row after row of wooden barracks.

Gray fingered the map in his hands. He had studied it with a penlight while traveling here. The interrogation center was not far from the main gate. Seichan was likely being held at that location.

But was she still there?

Their vehicle slipped through the outer gate and rolled across a no-man's-land covered in hidden mines before reaching the second fence. This inner gate also trundled open to receive them.

The motorcycles led the way, followed by the truck, a Trojan horse on wheels. As they passed inside, the gates closed behind them.

There was no turning back now.

And getting *in* was the easy part.

Tarps were stripped from the floor, revealing their heavier armaments: machine guns, grenade launchers, even a 60 mm lightweight mortar.

Kowalski picked up one of the rocket launchers. He slung its long tube over his shoulder and gripped his assault rifle with his free hand.

"Now I feel properly dressed," Kowalski said, his voice covered by the rumble of the truck.

The vehicle angled toward the interrogation center and parked in front of its entrance. The driver kept the engine running. With any luck, they could grab Seichan with a minimum of fuss or noise and leave the same way they had come, explaining they'd been recalled back to the city.

Zhuang poked his head out the rear flap, making sure everything looked clear. Apparently satisfied, he waved Gray and Guan-yin forward. They huddled together at the flap.

Gray studied the façade of the interrogation center. The cement-block building was one story and looked mostly dark at this late hour. They should be able to swiftly sweep it.

"Let's go," he said and hopped out.

With the truck blocking the view to the front door, they ran for the entrance. Other Triad members took up defensive positions around and even under the truck.

Gray reached the door and found it open. He slipped inside, did a fast sweep with his rifle, but spotted no one. He strained for any voices, but he heard nothing.

Guan-yin joined him. She looked pale, her jaw tense. Only then did he remember Seichan's mother had spent a brutal year in a camp such as this in Vietnam. He noted the curled scar across her cheek and brow. From the way she jumped when Zhuang touched her elbow as he entered, that physical scarring was probably the least of her damage.

"According to my map," Gray said, drawing her attention to the task at hand, "the holding cells and interrogation rooms are in the back."

Guan-yin gave him a shaky nod.

The three of them set off in that direction, sweeping room by room. At the end of the corridor, a pool of light spilled from an open doorway.

Gray aimed for there, still straining for any noises.

The silence was beginning to unnerve him.

He reached the open door and peeked his head around to search the next room. It was a small space with chairs facing a large window that viewed into a neighboring chamber.

With care, Gray slipped inside and stared through the glass, likely a one-way mirror. The well-lit room beyond revealed a strange sight. Two men lay sprawled on the floor in matching pools of blood. One was a North Korean guard. Gray surmised the other was a lab tech based on the long white coat he was wearing.

Two others shared the space with the dead men and appeared to be locked inside. The pair strained to open the only door. Gray also noted the toppled metal stool on the floor below the window. They must have tried to shatter through the mirrored glass only to find it bulletproof.

Gray recognized one of the trapped men immediately, even with the bandage over his nose.

Hwan Pak.

The other stood taller, with a dark beard and Eurasian features. Gray remembered him from the streets of Macau, hauling Seichan into the Cadillac.

"Ju-long Delgado," Guan-yin said as she stepped beside him.

Gray stared again at the dead men, recognizing Seichan's handiwork.

"I think we have a problem," he said, picturing the hundred-acre prison. "Your daughter escaped."

To make matters worse, sirens suddenly sounded all around the camp, blaring loudly, accompanied by a loudspeaker barking orders.

Gray turned to Guan-yin.

They'd been discovered.

9:16 P.M.

Seichan lay in filth, despairing as the sirens erupted all around.

Earlier, she had crawled under one of the raised barracks to hide. The prison had been built in the swampy marshlands bordering the Taedong River, which regularly flooded its banks, requiring this stilt construction.

Unfortunately, that was as far as the planning went to keep the prisoners comfortable. There was no heat, little ventilation, and from the stink of ammonia and other rank smells, toilet facilities must be lacking above, too.

As she lay there for the past half hour, she listened to the muffled stir of humanity packed above: whispers, sobs, angrier outbursts, even the soft words of a mother comforting a child. Entire families were imprisoned here, condemned for reeducation, but mostly used as slave labor.

Anger burned through her. It was the only thing that kept her warm as the night had turned ever colder. She had chosen this spot so she would have a clear view of the main gate, hoping for some sign of Gray.

Moments ago, she had watched a dark green transport truck roll through the fence flanked by uniformed guards on motorcycles. They were bringing in reinforcements. Worse still, as the truck trundled into camp, it stopped in the shadow of the interrogation center with a wheeze of its brakes.

She cursed her luck.

Shortly after that, the sirens blew. She pictured the new arrivals discovering Pak and Ju-long locked in the torture chamber. Her escape was now known.

As the alarms continued to ring out, spotlights flared all along the fencing. The entire camp was being roused to find her.

She clutched her pistol, wondering where she could hide. She considered mixing with the general population, but surely someone would talk, point a finger at her in order to gain a small favor from the guards.

She began to sidle backward, away from the main gates, away from the brighter lights. Shadows were still her best defense.

Glancing toward the heart of the prison, she spotted the heavy tracks of a tank grinding through the muck. It was crossing from the depths of the camp toward the main gate, intending to close off any hope of escape that way.

She ran low for the next row of barracks and the shadows it afforded.

Moments ago, she had prayed for Gray to come.

Now she hoped he would stay far away.

9:18 P.M.

Gray ran with Guan-yin back toward the entrance to the interrogation building. Zhuang rushed ahead of them, leading the way.

"Someone must have talked back at the hotel," Gray said.

"Or someone saw through our ruse here," Guan-yin offered. From her stern expression, she plainly refused to believe any of her captured men at the hotel would break so soon.

Reaching the door, Zhuang looked out and waved them to his side. Looking past the swordsman's shoulder, Gray saw the dark camp now blazing with lights. Off to the right, the North Korean guards at the gate milled around in momentary confusion. No one seemed to be paying attention to their truck or the fake guards around it.

"Our cover remains intact," Gray said, relieved. "Still, one of your men must have let them know this was our target."

"But not the exact details of our plan," Guan-yin countered, defending the man who was likely being severely tortured.

"At least not yet. Still, that leaves us a small window to take advantage of the element of surprise." Gray eyed the confusion at the prison entrance, knowing it wouldn't last. "We need to gain control of that main gate now."

Guan-yin understood. "And hold it long enough until my daughter can be found."

Gray nodded. Once they acted, all hell would break loose. But they had no choice. The time for stealth was over.

He turned to Guan-yin and her lieutenant. "I need you both to rally your crew—then attack and hold that gate. The firefight should draw all eyes to you, allowing for a small team to make a fast canvass of the remainder of the camp."

In agreement, Zhuang silently slid his sword from the scabbard over his back.

Gray pointed to the motorcycles.

"I'll take Kowalski and two of the bikes. We'll split up and cover as much ground as we can. Seichan is surely watching what's happening. Hopefully, she'll recognize our faces if we can get close enough."

Guan-yin consulted briefly with Zhuang, who then ran out to ready his strike team. She turned back to Gray and gripped his forearm.

"Find my daughter."

"I will," he promised.

Or die trying.

9:22 P.M.

Seichan rolled out from under another barrack and straightened. She'd made it a third of the way across the camp, moving row by row, sticking to shadows, which grew thicker the farther she got away from the fences.

As she turned, ready to bolt for the next barrack, a huge explosion rocked the camp. She twisted around to see a column of black smoke curl through the flare of spotlights off by the main gate.

What the hell . . . ?

A rattle of distant gunfire reached her.

Could that be Gray?

Cursing him for a fool while undeniably relieved, she headed along the length of the barracks. She wanted to reach the end of the row, which offered a clear view back toward the gate.

Lights suddenly flared behind her. With the sirens blaring and her focus elsewhere, she had failed to register the threat until too late. A North Korean jeep raced around the corner of the last barrack, spearing her with its headlamps. Behind the vehicle trotted twin lines of soldiers.

Momentarily frozen in the light, she realized she was holding her pistol in plain sight.

A prisoner with a gun.

9:23 P.M.

Gray rode alongside Kowalski. Their two bikes raced away from the firefight at the gate and headed for the deeper camp.

Through his rearview mirror, Gray had watched the mortar blast take out the inner gate. Black smoke clouded the view as Guan-yin's team ran forward to dispatch the remaining stunned troops. Zhuang's steel blade flashed momentarily through the pall of smoke, like lightning in a thundercloud—then was gone.

Twin fiery explosions from rocket-propelled grenades took out the two guard towers that flanked the gate, turning them into blazing torches, adding to the thick smoke. Spats of additional rifle fire doused the spotlights farther along the fencing to either side, sinking the lower gate into deeper darkness.

As gunfire continued to rattle behind them, Gray waved his arm, signaling for Kowalski to split off. The big man was going to canvass the acres of barracks to the right, Gray to the left.

As his partner took off, Gray hunched over his bike and angled into the shadowy depths of the rows of barracks. He knew the attack at the gate had succeeded only because of the element of surprise. Once the camp fully rallied, their small force could not hold that spot for long.

He searched the dark rows to either side, sensing the press of time.

Where are you, Seichan?

9:24 P.M.

Seichan leaped headlong toward the cover of the closest barrack, taking advantage of the momentary shock of the North Korean troops. She twisted in midair and aimed her pistol back at the jeep. She squeezed the trigger over and over again, taking out one headlamp and driving the troops to cover.

As she hit the ground, momentum rolled her between the stilts of the closest barrack and into darkness. Gunfire peppered the dirt behind her.

She kept going, spinning under the planks and through the muck to the other side. Without pausing, she dove for the next row, rolling again under the barrack.

All the while, she tracked the troops. The jeep sped past her original position, fishtailing around the end of the row, intending to circle around and trap her. Closer at hand, the twin rows of soldiers split apart, running between the barracks, flanking wide to prevent her escape.

Her flight had bought her only a minute or two of freedom at best.

The wave of soldiers would eventually overwhelm her. And with only *one* bullet left in her pistol, she could never fight her way to freedom.

She needed another way.

9:25 P.M.

Over the rumble of his motorcycle, Gray heard gunfire erupt to his left, along with shouts and hollered orders. He headed for the commotion, hoping for the best.

As he raced between a narrow squeeze of barracks, a figure popped into view ahead of him, wearing a muddy set of prison garb. It took him an extra breath to recognize Seichan.

Thank God . . .

Relief flooded through him, along with something deeper that warmed his heart.

She lifted her arm toward him, as if beckoning him to her side.

Only then did he see the pistol in her hand.

She centered her aim and fired.

9:26 P.M.

Seichan needed that motorcycle.

A second ago, she had heard the throaty whine of its engine and headed toward it, knowing it could be her only means of escape. With one bullet left in her pistol, she dared not fail. As she stepped into the open, she aimed for a center-mass shot and pulled the trigger.

The rider flew backward with the impact, spinning off the bike.

The motorcycle twisted and crashed into the side of a barrack. Tossing her pistol aside, she sprinted to the bike. She hauled it off the ground, mounted it, and kicked the stalled engine into roaring glory. With a goose of power, she spun the bike around.

The rider rose to an elbow and reached for his assault rifle.

I could use that, too, she realized.

She gunned forward, leaning her arm out, ready to scoop the weapon off the ground.

The rider lifted his pained face toward her.

She gasped with recognition, blinded to everything but those storm-blue eyes.

Gray . . .

She braked hard as she reached him, skidding sideways.

He stood, with a hand pressed to his bloody shoulder. "You really have to stop shooting me," he mumbled, retrieving the rifle with his good arm. "A simple hello will do next time."

She pulled him to her and kissed his lips.

"Okay, that's a little better . . . but we'll have to practice it some more."

She heard the growl of the jeep stalking along a neighboring row.

Shouts closed in behind her.

"Hop on!" she urged.

Despite the pain, Gray quickly swung a leg over. He circled her waist with one arm, while firing behind her with the other.

In the rearview mirror, she watched soldiers scatter out of view.

"Go!" he said.

She gunned the engine, and the bike took off like a jackrabbit.

Gray tightened his arm around her.

She didn't know if they would make it to freedom, but she knew one thing for sure. She never wanted him to let go.

9:28 P.M.

Gray's shoulder burned with each bump. Blood flowed in hot streams across his chest. If he hadn't shifted to the side at the last moment after seeing Seichan's pistol, she would have struck him square in the chest.

He clung to her with his bad arm, twisted half around, his rifle gripped one-handed. He took potshots whenever he spotted anyone in a North Korean uniform.

Then thirty yards back, a jeep skidded into view, its one remaining headlamp shining toward them. A soldier on the passenger side was on his feet, leveling a rifle on the frame of the windshield.

Gray strafed the front of the jeep, taking out the other headlamp.

The impact swerved the vehicle, ruining the soldier's aim. Rounds tore into the wooden stairs of a barrack to the left. Screams of panic echoed from inside.

"Veer right!" he hollered to Seichan.

She juked the bike in that direction, so fast that he almost lost his grip on her. With his thighs clenched to the seat, he leaned out and returned fire, concentrating on the jeep's right front tire, unloading a full spray, tearing apart the rubber.

"Left!" he yelled.

The bike swung to the other side, as rounds blasted past his ear. Aiming at the left front tire, he fired another burst, shredding it to black confetti.

The trajectory of the jeep, already shaky after losing the first tire, became unruly as the rims drilled into the mud, miring the front end.

As the jeep slowed to a crawl behind them, Seichan sped away, aiming for the gates a hundred yards ahead. Gray kept his rifle pointed back, plinking a few shots to discourage any retaliation.

Suddenly Seichan hit the brakes hard, nosing the bike up on one wheel.

Gray swung around in time to see a tank burst into view ahead of them, treads churning mud in a fast turn toward the prison entrance. It was a forty-ton Chonma-ho battle tank. The behemoth filled the road ahead of them, trundling between a row of barracks and a line of cement-block administration buildings.

The monster ignored them or maybe assumed they were allies. Either way, its long 115 mm gun was pointed toward the gate, ready to put an end to their brief insurgency.

"Get around it!" Gray yelled in Seichan's ear.

Their only hope of escape was to outrace that beast of steel and fire, to reach that main gate ahead of the tank and get everyone moving.

Seichan bent low over the bike's handles and took the first left turn into the narrow space between the barracks. With a scream of the engine, she slipped past the first barrack and skidded into the smaller lane that paralleled the main road. Opening the throttle, they flew down this new track.

Gray stared to the right as barracks flashed past, catching glimpses of the tank churning up the neighboring road.

We'll never make it.

Even if the tank didn't fire its big gun, they would be hard-pressed to clear the gate ahead of that trundling Goliath.

That is, until David appeared.

A smaller shape shot out of the smoke by the gate and raced toward the tank. It was Kowalski on his bike. Gray had radioed his partner earlier to pull back after he found Seichan. The big man must have reached the gates ahead of them—and plainly had his own solution to the problem of the battle tank.

Letting go of his motorcycle's handlebars, Kowalski lifted his RPG-29 launcher to his shoulder and fired. The rocket flew the remaining distance and struck the tank head-on.

The explosion sounded like the earth cracking, accompanied by fire, smoke, and a rain of scorched steel.

Kowalski lost control of his bike, dropped it on its side, and skidded toward the burning tank, which continued to roll forward on its own, about to crush him.

Pushing the bike harder, Seichan got ahead of the slowing tank, turned at the next barrack, and swept to the main road. She plainly meant to go to Kowalski's aid, but as their bike shot through a wall of smoke, they found the big man already on his feet, sprinting for the gate.

The guy was indestructible.

A glance back showed the front of the tank, blast charred and smoking. It was no longer a threat, but they were far from safe.

They reached the gates only slightly ahead of Kowalski.

He huffed and puffed, pointing to Gray, then to Seichan, catching his breath. "Next time . . . don't be so goddamned late."

The rest of the strike team prepped to leave, ready to scramble.

And for good reason.

Out across the prison, the headlights of jeeps and armored personnel carriers converged toward them.

"Time to go," Gray said, staying seated on the bike with Seichan.

One of the Triad members rolled a new motorcycle up to Kowalski and patted his broad shoulder in appreciation.

From here, the plan was for the truck to make a run for Pyongyang, where the vehicle would be ditched and the team would scatter into the city, reaching various prestaged safe houses where new Chinese papers would get them back across the border.

Gray and company would be going a different route on the bikes, away from Pyongyang.

But they wouldn't be going alone.

Guan-yin limped forward, favoring her right leg. Zhuang had an arm around her waist, his sword in the other.

Seichan tensed upon seeing her mother, but now was not the time for a happy family reunion. A resurgence of gunfire made this plain. Still, daughter and mother shared a glance through the smoke, awkward and uncomfortable, obviously needing time to process it all.

Even before the pair could reach them, a bike was brought before the Triad's leaders. Zhuang slipped his sword into the sheath across his back and took the front. Guan-yin climbed behind him, never taking her eyes off Seichan.

The remaining members of the strike team gathered back at the truck.

With a final shout, the heavy vehicle trundled through the blasted gates, drawing the three bikes in its wake. Once beyond the prison, the group quickly picked up speed. A quarter mile later, a small river road branched off from the main highway.

Seichan swung the bike onto it, followed by the other two.

As the truck continued on toward Pyongyang, the three motorcycles swept through the marshlands bordering the Taedong River. Lit by bright stars and the blaze of a comet, the river flowed all the way to the Yellow Sea, only thirty miles away.

As they sped along, Gray noted Seichan glancing frequently into the rearview mirror. He knew she was studying her mother, but Seichan never slowed, keeping her bike ahead of the others, as if being chased by a ghost through the marshes.

And maybe she was.

The ghost of her mother . . . an apparition now given flesh and form.

But any reconciliation of past and present must come later.

Gray kept his gaze ahead, knowing what they still faced, and it was no simple task. Though they had escaped the prison . . . they still had to escape North Korea.

12

"I want to test something," Jada said.

For the first time, she wondered if this side excursion to this desolate landscape of blowing sand and landlocked rusted ships might be of value. Normally history held little interest for her, especially all this talk of Attila the Hun and the relics of Genghis Khan. But this mention of an ancient cross carved out of meteoric metal—*that* piqued her interest.

"According to everything you've told us," she said, waving a hand to Father Josip, "the cross is the key to averting a disaster that is supposed to occur on the date inscribed on the skull."

He nodded, glancing at a faded celestial calendar on the wall. It looked like it might have come from the time of Copernicus, with stylized constellations and astronomical notations.

"Roughly three days from now," he confirmed.

"Right." She glanced to Monk. "And we have confirmation from another source that also suggests a disaster on that date. One connected to the comet in the sky."

Vigor and Rachel turned to Monk, clearly wanting to know what that confirmation was, but he simply crossed his arms.

The monsignor sighed, obviously irked at the secrecy. "Go on," he encouraged her. "You said you might know how this cross could save the world."

"Only a conjecture," she warned. "But first I want to try something."

She turned to Duncan.

All other eyes swung toward him too. He straightened from a slouch, his expression wary with surprise and confusion. "What?"

"Could you please unwrap the skull and the book?" she asked. "Place them on the table."

She waited until he had done so, noting the distaste in his pinched lips as he handled the relics.

"You still feel an energy signature emanating from the objects, yes?"

"It's there." He rubbed his fingertips on his pants, as if trying to remove the sensation.

She faced the two priests. "If Genghis found this cross in Attila's tomb, might he have carried it on his person? Kept it as some talisman on his body."

Vigor shrugged. "After he read Ildiko's account of its importance, I think that's highly likely."

"Genghis would consider it his duty," Josip agreed, "to protect it during his life."

"And maybe afterward," Vigor added, motioning to the skull and book. He eyed her more closely. "Are you suggesting the cross somehow contaminated his bodily tissues, as if it were radioactive?"

"I don't think it's radioactive," she said, though her hands itched to confirm that by examining the skull with the instruments she had left aboard the helicopter. "But I think the cross was giving off some sort of energy that left its trace on his body, altering his tissues perhaps at the quantum level."

"What sort of energy would do that?" Rachel asked.

"*Dark* energy," she said, happy to turn the discourse from history to science. "An energy tied to the birth of our universe. And although it makes up seventy percent of all energy left after the Big Bang, we still don't know what it is, where it comes from, only that it's a fundamental property of existence. It explains why the universe is expanding at an accelerating pace versus slowing down."

Vigor lifted an eyebrow. "And you think the cross carries this energy? What, like a battery?"

"Very crudely put, but yes. Possibly. I can't know for sure without examining it. But such matters are my field of expertise. My theoretical calculations suggest dark energy is the result of virtual particles annihilating one another in the quantum foam that fills all space and time in the universe."

She read their blank expressions and simplified it. "It is the very fabric of space-time. Dark energy *is* the driving force behind quantum mechanics, an energy tied to *all* the fundamental forces in the universe. Electromagnetic, weak and strong nuclear forces, anything that causes an attraction between objects."

"Like gravity?" Duncan asked.

She touched his shoulder, silently thanking him. "Exactly. Dark energy and gravity are intimately entwined concepts."

Rachel frowned at Monk, then turned to Jada. With the mind of a true investigator, she went straight for the secret being kept from them. "Again," she pressed, "not to belabor the point, *why* do you believe this cross might be giving off dark energy?"

"Because the comet in the sky is doing exactly that."

As everyone stirred at her answer, Jada glanced at Monk, knowing she had crossed a line. But she thought Rachel deserved an answer. The woman had an analytical mind that she was growing to respect. It was foolish to keep her in the dark.

Monk returned a small shrug, giving Jada some leeway.

She took it and explained. "Or at least the comet's path was showing tiny gravitational abnormalities in its course that exactly matched my theoretical calculations."

"And the cross?" Josip asked.

"From your story, you said the cross was sculpted from a falling star. A meteorite." She pictured the rain of meteors from the video footage in Alaska. "I wonder if that meteorite could have been a *piece* of that comet, a fragment that fell to the earth when it last passed."

Rachel considered that possibility, then asked, "When did this comet make its last appearance?"

"Approximately twenty-eight hundred years ago."

"So about 800 BC." Rachel turned to Josip. "Does that correlate with anything you've learned about the cross?"

He rubbed the scruff on his chin, looking crestfallen. "Ildiko only says the cross came from a star that fell long before St. Thomas arrived in the East."

That was disappointing. It would have been nice to have definitive confirmation.

Then Josip suddenly sat straighter. "Wait!" He reached and stirred through the parchments left by Ildiko. "Look here!"

7:38 P.M.

As Josip shifted a page to the center of the table, Vigor stood up to get a better view.

His friend tapped an image found in the middle of the parchment.

duas arbores   impero   prohibitum

"According to Ildiko, these three symbols were carved into the boxes holding the skull and the cross."

Vigor adjusted his reading glasses. Very faintly inscribed, he could make out what appeared to be Chinese writing: a set of three symbols with Latin written below them.

Vigor leaned closer to examine the images and read the Latin aloud. "The first symbol is labeled as *two trees*." It did, in fact, look like a pair of trees. "The next is *command*. And the last, *forbidden*."

Josip touched the last character. "Notice how the first two symbols combine to form this third one. The one meaning forbidden."

Vigor saw that, but he didn't understand the significance.

"Read this," Josip said. "Read what Ildiko wrote under the symbols."

Those lines were even fainter, but he recognized two Latin verses from the Old Testament, both from the book of Genesis.

He translated the first one aloud. "*'And the Lord God commanded man, saying, Of every tree of the garden thou may freely eat. But of the tree of the knowledge of good and evil, you shall not eat, for in the day that you eat of it you shall surely die.'*"

Vigor read the next line. Similarly, it was a condemnation against eating from another tree—in this second case, the Tree of Life found in the Garden of Eden. "*'Behold, man is become as one of us, to know good and evil: and now, lest he put forth his hand, and take also of the tree of life, and eat, and live forever . . .'*"

Before he could finish, Josip pulled the page back possessively. "The earliest Chinese writing used pictures to represent words or ideas, and it often combined simple symbols to form more complex concepts."

Vigor glanced over to what Ildiko wrote. "But this seems to imply that the early Chinese knew about the book of Genesis. About the story of *two trees* that God *commanded* were *forbidden* to man."

"I have other examples of the same." Josip stood up, rushed to a neighboring desk, and began shifting through the stacks there.

Vigor studied the pages left on the table, wondering at the implication. Could the ancient Chinese have had knowledge of the events described in the book of Genesis? Was this confirmation of these biblical stories? The Chinese language was the oldest continuously written language, going back four millennia or so.

Josip returned. "I only found two, but I have many more examples."

He placed down his first sheet.

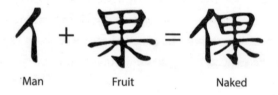

Man   Fruit   Naked

The Chinese symbol for *man* combined with the character for *fruit* became the sign for *naked*. Even Vigor could guess the reference illustrated here.

From Genesis 3:6–7.

He quoted it aloud. "'. . . *she took of its fruit and ate, and she also gave some to her husband who was with her, and he ate. Then the eyes of both were opened, and they knew that they were naked.*'"

Josip nodded vigorously and slid this page aside and replaced it with another. "And here is one more."

Alive   Dust   Man   First

His friend ran a finger along the illustration. "Here we have early Chinese symbols for *alive, dust,* and another variant of *man*. And together they form the character for *first*." He looked expectantly toward Vigor.

"From Genesis again," Vigor said. "A reference to Adam, the first living man God created."

"Out of dust," Josip added, tapping the corresponding symbol. "I can show you more."

He looked ready to do so, the obsession shining in his eyes, but Vigor held up a hand, keeping him on task. "I don't know if we're reading too much into this or not, but what does this have to do with Dr. Shaw's earlier question? About the date that meteorite fell, the one that became St. Thomas's cross?"

"Ah," he nodded. "Sorry. You see, the reliquaries of St. Thomas—the boxes, the skull, the cross—were crafted by Nestorian priests out of the East. They were the ones who inscribed those symbols on the boxes."

"Nestorian?" Jada asked. "I'm not all that familiar with ancient Christian sects."

Vigor smiled at her. "Nestorianism started in the early fifth century, shortly before the rise of Attila the Hun. It was founded by Nestorius, the patriarch at the time of Constantinople. He created a division in the Church by expressing a simple view that the human and divine persons of Christ were separate. Such a thought was deemed heretical, leading to a schism in the Church. Not that the details are important. But the Nestorian Church spread east after that. Persia, India, Central Asia, even as far as China by the seventh century."

"Which brings me to my point," Josip said. "I think the Chinese inscriptions on the reliquary by the Nestorian priests served multiple purposes."

Vigor eyed him, waiting for him to continue. He seemed momentarily lost, staring off into space for several breaths.

Then Josip resumed as if there had been no pause. He counted off on his fingers. "First, I believe they were confirming that St. Thomas did indeed reach China. Second, I think it's plain they were trying to imply that the Chinese writing they discovered out in the Far East held some clues to the veracity of the Old Testament, a truth buried in their ancient script. And third, I think they were sharing some hint as to the extreme age of the cross."

He looked significantly at Jada.

"How so?" she asked.

"Because they paired the cross with a reference to the book of Genesis. I think these Nestorian priests had heard stories of this falling star from the Chinese. They were told about how this meteorite fell in ancient times. And this was their way of venerating the cross's ancient origin."

Jada's lips thinned in thought. "Still, it doesn't confirm a *date* that coincides with the last appearance of the comet. I accept that these Nestorian priests believed it was old. *Biblically* old. But all this is based on conjecture. Until I can examine the cross, I can't substantiate its connection to the comet."

Vigor nodded. "Which leaves us with the big question: *Where is this cross now?*"

7:55 P.M.

Duncan listened to the discussions with half an ear. Instead, as the others talked, he fiddled with the relics sitting on the table. Like picking at a scab, he couldn't stop testing the strange electrical field emanating from the objects.

"The cross must be in Genghis Khan's tomb," Josip insisted. "If we find his tomb, we'll find the cross."

"You're probably right," the monsignor agreed. "If his bones and bits of his body were laid down like bread crumbs, they were most likely meant to lead to his tomb."

Duncan ran his hands over the dome of the old skull, his fingertips registering the slippery field. Goose bumps rose along his arms as he considered Jada's belief that this was *dark energy*. Since he had a background in physics and electrical engineering, he had viewed Jada's calculations that had been included in the mission dossier supplied to him. They'd been as elegant and as sexy as the woman who crafted them.

With a chill, he moved the skull aside and shifted his hands to the book.

Vigor paced around the table. "And that's what you've been looking for, Josip. All these years."

"After finding the relics, I wasn't in the best state of mind. Shame, fear, paranoia sent me in a spiral. I needed somewhere quiet to think, to find my bearings."

Duncan didn't have to be a psychiatrist to sense the priest suffered from some form of chronic mental illness. He was a sack of emotional tics.

"And after dropping off the earth, it was easier to stay here," he explained. "So I could work in peace. This became my self-imposed exile, my monastery where I could be in seclusion."

"If you wanted to be alone," Monk said, "you picked a helluva good spot for it. This is as close to the middle of nowhere as you can get."

"It wasn't just the isolation that drew me to the Aral Sea. Maybe at first, but later I realized somewhere in the back of my fevered brain, something was making connections that didn't fully reach my consciousness until later. Like many times in the past, I've found the manic phases of my disease are not without their benefits."

Ah, he's bipolar, Duncan realized. He should have picked up on the signs. He had a college friend with the same condition. Not an easy cross to bear.

"What connections did you make?" Vigor asked.

Josip motioned to the relics. "Here we have Genghis's skull. And from the eye on the gospel's cover, we know it was bound from the skin of his face and head."

Reminded of what his fingertips were hovering over, Duncan inwardly cringed. Still, macabre curiosity drew him closer, searching for that eye.

The priest continued, "In other words, the relics came from the neck *up* on Genghis Khan."

Vigor mumbled, "You're right. I didn't even make that correlation."

"Sometimes a little bit of madness is a good thing. In my manic phase, I ended up here. Only later did I realize *why*. That I was supposed to be *here*."

"Why?" Vigor pressed.

"I think there are *more* relics. Not just these two."

"Like more bread crumbs," Rachel said.

"In Hungary, Genghis's son left the relics from his father's *head*, marking the westernmost reach of his son's empire, an empire he had inherited from his father. But why just those objects there? It didn't feel right. Over time, I came to a different theory, one I think is right. I believe Genghis had instructed his son to turn the entire known *world* into his grave, to spread his spiritual reach from one end of the Mongol Empire to the other."

"That sounds like Genghis," Vigor agreed. "So he had his head set at one end . . ."

"In Hungary, in the tomb of Attila," Josip said with a nod. "But where next?"

"Here?" Jada asked.

The priest nodded. "The region around the Aral Sea was the west-ernmost reach of the Mongol Empire *during Genghis's reign*. A place of significance. So it seemed a natural place to begin searching."

Vigor turned, looking around the chamber. "You've been exploring for these lost relics all this time?"

"It's a huge expanse. And the terrain was drastically altered after the seas dried up." Josip stepped away and returned with a chart that he unfurled across the tabletop. "This is a map of how the Aral Sea once looked."

Duncan shifted straighter and stared at the huge body of water—then returned his attention to the book, noting something odd.

"The Aral Sea means *Sea of Islands*," the priest explained. "At one time, there were over fifteen hundred islands dotting the water. I assumed Genghis's next relic would have been on one of them."

"So you've been searching one by one?" Vigor asked.

"With help." Josip nodded to Sanjar.

"And how have you paid for all this?" Monk asked.

It was a good question.

The priest looked down at his toes. Plainly it wasn't a *question* he wanted to answer.

He was saved by the monsignor, who had figured it out. "You men-tioned the Hungarian bishop had found a calling card left behind at Attila's tomb, one with the name Genghis Khan written on it. A gold wrist cuff with images of a phoenix and demons."

Josip slumped in on himself. "I sold it. To a buyer in Mongolia. Some-one with a great deal of wealth who bought it for his personal collection. At the very least, I know that piece of history will be preserved."

Rachel frowned deeply. Her work with the Italian police dealt spe-cifically with the black market sale of antiquities. "Whom did you sell it to?"

The priest balked at answering.

Vigor didn't press him. "Right now it doesn't matter."

Still, Josip explained, "Please, do not hold this buyer at fault. It was my choice to sell it, and he only bought it to preserve his own country's history."

Monk returned the discussion back to the problem at hand. "If you're right that the next bread crumb is *here,* I don't see us discovering it in time to do any good. It'll be like trying to find a needle in a very dry haystack."

"I waited too long," Josip conceded.

"Then maybe we should just continue on to Mongolia," Jada said, sounding not overly displeased at the prospect.

As the banter waned toward defeat, Duncan ran his hands over the surface of the book one more time, just to be sure, before speaking.

Satisfied, he hovered a finger over a spot on the surface. "Monsignor Verona ... I mean Vigor ... is this the location of the eye you mentioned?"

Vigor stepped closer and looked over his shoulder. "It is indeed. I know it's hard to see. I only found it myself with the aid of a magnifying loupe."

Duncan ran his fingertip over the book, tracing the surface of the energy field. As he reached the spot near the eye, his finger raised up, then down again after he passed it. "I don't know if this is significant, but the energy is stronger over the eye. I can feel the upwelling of its field. It's very distinct."

Vigor crinkled his brow. "Why would that be?"

Jada moved to his other shoulder, bringing with her a waft of apple blossoms. "Duncan, you said the skull had a significantly stronger field than the skin. Which I assumed was a reflection of mass. More mass, more energy."

Duncan nodded, loving when she talked science. "That must mean this spot on the cover has more *mass* than the rest of the surface."

Vigor frowned. "What are you both saying?"

Duncan turned to the monsignor. "There's something *else* hidden under this eye."

Father Josip gasped. "I never thought to look. I had the book X-rayed, but nothing abnormal showed up."

Jada shrugged. "If it's soft tissue, like the skin, it could easily have been missed by X-rays."

Monk pointed. "We have to open that eye."

Vigor turned to Father Josip.

"I'll get my tools," he said and dashed off.

Vigor shook his head. "I should have considered that. The essential core message of St. Thomas's gospel is that the path to God is open to anyone who looks. Seek and you shall find."

"All you have to do is open your eyes," Rachel added.

Josip ran back with a pointed X-Acto knife, tweezers, and forceps, ready to do some ophthalmological surgery.

Duncan moved aside to make room for Vigor and Josip. The two archaeologists set to work snipping tiny cords that bound the eye closed ages ago. The lids were too dried to peel open, so with great care they excised a circle around the eye and teased the leather up and to the side.

Awe filled Vigor's voice. "Get me a—"

Josip passed him a magnifying lens.

"Thank you."

The monsignor leaned closer to the hole they'd created in the cover. "I see what appears to be the desiccated remains of papillae on the surface. I think the hidden tissue is a thin slice of mummified tongue."

"Oh, great," Jada groaned, moving back. It seemed there were limits to her scientific curiosity.

"They tattooed the surface," Josip commented. "Come see."

Duncan leaned closer, while Vigor held the lens. On the surface of the leathery tissue was a distinct picture inked in black.

"It's a *map*," Duncan realized aloud, recognizing the resemblance to Josip's earlier chart. "A map of the Aral Sea."

Rachel looked no happier than Jada. "Preserved on his tongue?"

Josip glanced at her, feverish excitement shining from his face. "Genghis is *telling* us where to go."

Vigor confirmed this. "One of the islands is tattooed in red with the word *equus* inked beneath it. Latin for *horse*."

"Horses were extremely prized by the Mongols," Josip said. "They were literally the life's blood of their riders. Warriors would often drink their mounts' blood while on long journeys or ferment mare's milk to produce *araq,* a potent alcoholic drink. Without horses—"

A noise at the door drew all their attentions around.

Josip visibly tensed, but when the tall figure bowed into the room, he relaxed, breaking into a broad smile of greeting. "You're back! And what timing. We have fantastic news!"

The priest hurried over and hugged the young man, who could be Sanjar's brother, what with his similar taste in sheepskin and loose pants. Only this one must have left his falcon at home.

Josip led the stranger back to the table. "Everyone, this is my good friend and the leader of my excavation crew." He clapped him on the shoulder. "His name is Arslan."

13

Batukhan stood in the middle of his gallery, wearing a thick robe and slippers. He had spent the past quarter hour pacing through his collection, something he did often when in a contemplative mood.

He had treasures from across the golden ages of Mongolia: jewelry, funerary masks, musical instruments, pottery. One wall displayed an assortment of antique bows, once carried by Mongol warriors—from short, sinuously curved weapons meant for horseback, made of sinew and horn, to the oversized triple crossbows used to capture walled cities. He had other tools of war, too, including battle-axes, scimitars, and lances.

Still, such a collection was not just for show.

He spent many hours training in the old ways with his fellow brothers of the Blue Wolf, on the steppes surrounding the city, on horseback, in traditional silk garments, overlaid with lacquer-impregnated leather and iron-crowned helmets. He, like all his men, was skilled with both light and heavy Mongol bows.

He stared across the breadth of his collection. To accommodate its growth, he had turned the upper loft of his penthouse into his personal museum. A bank of windows overlooked the brightly lit parliament square and offered a spectacular view of the stars and the shining comet in the night sky.

But at the moment, he returned his full attention to a small case holding a gold wrist piece. The cuff was hinged on one side, featuring a phoenix being beset by demons. He had purchased the exquisite work from Father Josip Tarasco, back when Batukhan had considered the priest nothing more than a trafficker in antiquities, a crackpot in the desert.

In the end, the man had proved much more than he seemed.

Still, like the rest of his collection, the gold cuff was not just for show. He sometimes wore it proudly when among his brothers, knowing it had once adorned the wrist of Genghis himself.

For that privilege, Batukhan had paid dearly for the golden relic—only to have that money squandered by the priest, turned into hundreds of holes in sand and salt.

What a waste.

At last, the phone in his pocket chimed. He removed it and spoke, not bothering with greetings.

"Have you reached Father Josip? Are the Italians there?"

The caller was accustomed to his brusque manner and responded just as tersely. He pictured the young man huddled out of sight with his satellite phone. "They are here, along with a trio of Americans."

"More archaeologists?"

"I don't believe so. They look military, at least the men."

"Is that going to be a problem?"

"No, I have my crew taking them into consideration. We're almost set. But I wanted you to know that Father Josip believes he has a lead on a significant clue that could point to the great khan's tomb. They are all very excited and determined to set out this night to investigate."

A significant clue . . .

Batukhan stared across the breadth of his museum. It was a pale mirror of the true wealth and wonders that might be found in Genghis's lost tomb.

"Discover what that clue is," Batukhan decided. "And let them go search. If anything is discovered, make sure you secure it. After that—or if they don't find anything—proceed as planned. Bury them all under that rusted ship."

"It will be done."

Batukhan did not doubt it.

Arslan had never failed him.

14

Gray raced along the river road with his bike's headlamp off, trailed by the other two motorcycles, running equally dark. Tall marsh grasses and stands of willow trees further hid their race from Pyongyang to the Yellow Sea to the west. With the moon down and only starlight and the glow of the comet to light their way, their progress was agonizingly slow.

It didn't help matters that his shoulder burned. Half an hour ago, Seichan had halted their flight for a brief pit stop, removing the med kit from the bike's pack. As the others guarded from a distance ahead and behind, she had cleaned his wound, bandaged his shoulder, and popped him with an injectible analgesic and antibiotic.

It was the least she could do since she had shot him.

Luckily the bullet wound was only a deep graze. With the pain meds dulling the worst of the fire, he took the last shift on the bike, wanting to keep his arm from stiffening up in the cold. He didn't know what they would face once they reached the coast.

To their left, the expanse of the Taedong River reflected the starlight, winding from its source high in the mountains to the north, through its capital city, until it drained into the sea. They did their best to avoid the few industrial plants along the way, sticking to the smaller roads.

The city of Nampho glowed in the distance, marking the mouth of the river basin. Gray used that marker to gain his bearings. A rutted track, an agricultural road, split off and headed away from the river.

He slowed to check the GPS reader on his wrist. Though the distance from Pyongyang to the coast was only thirty miles as a crow flies—on a motorcycle in the dark, winding through mud or gravel tracks, it seemed ten times that.

Still, they were close to the end, but they dared not miss their midnight rendezvous at the beach. Their window of opportunity was very narrow. They would only have this one chance.

Gray pointed down the side road, wincing with the motion, and called to the others. "This is it! Should take us straight to the sea."

With a growl of his engine, he turned his bike and headed in that direction. It was less a road than a series of potholes and boulders strung together. They set off, moving as swiftly as possible. Gray found firmer terrain by running his motorcycle along the very edge of the road, where it wasn't as churned by tractors and other agricultural equipment.

The fields around them were fallow with the start of the winter season, rolling away in frost-crusted furrows. Closer at hand, tangles of barbed-wire fencing ran to either side.

Gray felt exposed out in the open like this.

Even the rumble of their motorcycles seemed to grow louder, echoing over the empty farmlands. But they only had a couple of miles or so to go.

Then a new noise intruded, an ominous *thump-thumping.*

Gray slowed enough to crane around, searching the skies.

Seichan clutched his good shoulder and pointed to the southeast. A dark shadow swept low over the barren fields, slightly silhouetted against the glow of Nampho.

A helicopter, running without lights.

It wouldn't be doing so unless it had already acquired its target. It flew in the dark, attempting to close as much distance on them as possible before being detected.

From this, Gray knew they had been found.

Someone in Pyongyang must have given up this escape route, or maybe some rural farmer reported the passage of the three dark motorcycles in the night. Either way, there was no hiding from here.

Knowing the helicopter was likely equipped with night-vision equipment anyway, Gray stabbed on his headlamp to better illuminate the road. They needed as much speed as possible from here.

"Keep with me!" he yelled to the others, gunning his engine.

Lights flared behind him, coming from the other bikes.

Off to the southeast, the sky ignited with the chopper's navigation lights. A spotlight beamed down upon the farmlands, sweeping toward them.

Gray raced his motorcycle along the edge of the rutted road. Kowalski took the other side, trailed close by Zhuang and Guan-yin. They had no means to take out the helicopter. Back at the prison, they had used up all their rockets. Any additional heavy equipment had gone with the truck, a defensive necessity. The vehicle was meant to be the larger target, intended to lure the hunt away from the bikes.

Seated behind him, Seichan swung around and raised her assault rifle. Clinging to the bike with her thighs, she aimed across the field and fired a short burst.

The chopper's course wobbled, but only from surprise.

Still, the distraction allowed them to stretch their lead.

Kowalski pointed to the right, toward a large farmstead. Pinned between the rows of barbed wire, their bikes had no room to maneuver, no way to avoid the coming onslaught. Their best recourse was to reach open country.

Gray agreed. "Go!"

The three bikes cut into the farm. Trundling over a cattle guard, they entered a wide gravel expanse. Rows of milking barns lined one side. On the other, a series of bunkhouses and mechanics shops. Corrals and fields spread out from here. It looked like a major operation.

House lights clicked on, illuminating faces at several windows, likely drawn by the noise. But upon seeing what was coming, they quickly ducked away and pulled their shades.

In his rearview mirror, Gray spotted the lights of the attack helicopter. The chopper dove toward them. It would be on top of them in the next few seconds.

"This way!" he yelled and swerved his bike to the left.

He raced for the open doors to one of the milking barns. They needed cover. Emphasizing this necessity, the rattling roar of a chain-gun erupted, ripping toward them. The pilot must have recognized that his prey was trying to dive into a hole.

Seichan fired back at them, and so did Guan-yin from the back of Zhuang's bike. Mother and daughter faced the coming barrage without flinching, doing their best to match it, their rifles blazing on full automatic fire.

Then Gray's bike flew through the barn doors and into its shadowy depths. To his right and left, the other two bikes followed.

The chopper brushed higher, thumping over the top of the barn, sweeping for the other side, where another set of doors stood open.

The barn was long and wide. It had a Soviet industrial feel to it, built for mass production. A long line of automatic milking machines and stations rose to the left. On the other side stretched a long line of pens, each holding four or five cows, their large eyes shining back at them, mooing a complaint at the intrusion.

Gray figured over a hundred head of cattle were housed inside. Beyond the far door, massive corrals flanked to either side, packed nose to tail with more cows. The smell was likely to kill them long before any gunfire.

He doused his headlamps and slowed to a stop halfway down the length of the barn; the others followed his example. The helicopter circled overhead, thumping ominously, knowing its targets were pinned down, waiting to see which end they might run out.

Unfortunately, Gray knew they would have to make the attempt. They could not stay here. Ground forces were surely en route.

But that was the least of his worries.

He checked his watch. It was almost midnight. If they didn't reach the coast in the next few minutes, none of this would matter.

"What's the play here?" Kowalski asked.

Gray explained.

Kowalski went pale.

11:41 P.M.

It's not like we have much choice, Gray thought as he got everyone ready.

Using a set of binoculars, he searched beyond the empty fields of the farm. A tree line beckoned a quarter mile away. If they could get there, the coastal forest should offer them enough coverage to reach the beach and make their rendezvous.

But that meant abandoning the shelter of the milk barn.

"Let's do this," Gray ordered.

He and the others dismounted their bikes and swiftly went about opening the pens, starting from the middle and working their way to either end. With pats on rumps, they got the cows moving into the alleyway in the center. It didn't take much effort as the cattle were clearly conditioned by their regular milking schedule.

With the central corridor crowded now with large milling bodies, Gray waved everyone back onto their bikes. From the middle of the barn, they kicked their engines into a roar, which got the cows moving away in either direction. To get them going faster, Seichan raised her rifle and fired a spat of rounds into the metal roof. The deafening noise did the job.

Bellowing loudly, the cows fled for both exits, bumping into one another, spreading and heightening the panic.

Gray followed the herd streaming out the back. The other two bikes did the same. They ran dark, headlamps off, tucked amid the stampeding bodies.

Caught off guard by the thundering forms bursting out both ends of the barn, the helicopter buzzed from one side to the other, plainly unsure what was happening.

Lost amid the chaos, the three bikes shot out into the night. For the moment, the helicopter hovered on the far side of the barn. But it was already heading back, its searchlight sweeping toward them.

Once in the open, Gray cut off in one direction, Zhuang the other. In tandem, barely slowing, mother and daughter hopped off the bikes and slid open the gates to the larger corrals on either side.

The panic of the neighboring stampede had already set the crowded pens to mooing, shifting nervously, and stamping their hooves. Growing alarm spread like a match in dry grass through the packed cows.

As the gates opened, the pressure inside released. The closest beasts burst free, drawn in the wake of the others. More followed, slaves to herd mentality.

In seconds, the trickling stampede became a flood.

Kowalski sat on his idling motorcycle to one side, while the women rushed back to their respective bikes. He had his rifle pointed up, steadied on his shoulder.

The thumping of the helicopter became a roar. The rotor wash and noise further panicked the animals—not to mention the blinding glare of its searchlight as it swept over the barn.

Kowalski fired from his position.

Glass exploded above and darkness returned.

The chopper, caught by surprise, shied away.

With Seichan and Guan-yin back on their bikes, the trio set off with the cattle. Staying low, lights off, they raced amid the thundering herd as it stampeded out into the open fields, away from the barns and toward the distant trees.

Gray tried his best to avoid colliding into any of his beefy companions, but the courtesy wasn't returned. Several times, he got sideswiped or smacked with a tail, but he managed to keep them racing across the cold fields.

The other two bikes kept up.

Behind them, the helicopter still circled near the barn, baffled as to where its quarry had gone. With clear hesitation, the chopper slowly swept out into the fields. By now, the herd had spread out and ran in all directions.

Still, the helicopter refused to admit defeat. Its chain-gun rattled to roaring life as the chopper began sweeping back and forth in a deadly arc, ripping through cattle in its path.

Gray's heart went out to the poor beasts, but considering the cruel housing, the poor conditions, the signs of neglect and abuse, maybe this was a kindness. At least the beasts had a momentary taste of freedom.

Kowalski had his own assessment as they reached the forest and slowed. He looked back at the slaughter. "Fucking assholes."

It was a costly escape, but Gray intended not to waste it.

They fled through the shadowy coastal forest until they reached a road. Using GPS, Gray sped them to the coordinates at a breakneck clip. A minute later, they roared out of the trees and onto a wide stretch of rocky beach.

Gray searched the curving banks of the cove, as waves lapped against its flat stones. Starlight shone coldly down upon them.

It all appeared empty.

"Is this the place?" Kowalski asked.

Gray nodded, but he feared they were too late. From the storage pouch of his bike, he slipped out a flare, ignited it, and tossed it to the beach.

Green fire sparked to life, reflecting off the water.

He prayed someone would see it.

Someone did.

To the right, the North Korean helicopter burst out of the forest. Thumping loudly, it swung out over the water and sped back toward them, drawn by the sputtering flare.

Its guns chugged to life.

Then a flash of fire winked out in the darkness beyond the cove, accompanied by a furious whistling. A hellfire missile slammed into the side of the helicopter and exploded, shattering the chopper into fiery ruin.

Ducking from the deafening *boom,* Gray watched flaming debris rain into the forest, while the scorched bulk of the aircraft fell heavily into the sea.

Even before the blast echoed away, a small aircraft sped through the smoke and drew to a hover over the beach. It was a new design of stealth aircraft, a miniature version of a U.S. Blackhawk helicopter, with harsh angles and flat surfaces meant to confound radar.

But the fiery blast would not go unnoticed for long.

With its missile pod still smoking, the helicopter lowered to the beach and the doors opened to receive them.

Gray had arranged this extraction with Kat earlier. As planned, the stealth aircraft had taken off from a U.S. ship parked in South Korean territorial waters and flown low over the waves to the beach. Kat had warned that this was a onetime deal, requiring perfect timing. The North Koreans wouldn't fall for it twice.

As his team clambered into the chopper, a crew member slammed the door shut behind them. The helicopter immediately turned its back on the Korean peninsula and sped away, whisking over the water, its blades whispering through the night.

Strapping in, Gray looked toward the shore, weighing all the risk and bloodshed. As he settled back, he saw Guan-yin reach from her seat toward Seichan.

For the first time in decades, a mother gently touched her fingertips to her daughter's cheek.

Gray turned around, staring forward now.

It had been worth it.

15

As the Eurocopter lifted in a swirl of salt and sand, Rachel worried about her uncle. He was deep in conversation with Josip, their heads bent together, seated next to each other, like excited schoolboys about to head out on a field trip. But neither of them were *boys*.

Especially Vigor.

Though he put on a strong façade, age was beginning to crack through that veneer. She saw it as he climbed into the helicopter a moment ago, needing an extra hand, when in the past he could have vaulted inside. She had noted it in a thousand different ways before this trip, even commented upon it a couple of months ago, but he had dismissed her concerns, blaming it on the time he spent now at a desk versus out in the field. She suggested he lighten his schedule, take on fewer responsibilities at the Vatican, but that was like asking a freight train with a full head of steam to slow down.

During this trip, she had grown even more concerned. Prior to this mission, she hadn't seen as much of her uncle as she would have liked, just the occasional family dinner or holiday. But now, spending the past twenty-four hours with him, she feared it was *more* than age. She had noted the dark circles under his eyes back at his university office. She now saw how he breathed heavier, how he sometimes clutched his left side. But whenever he caught her looking, he dropped his hand.

He was not telling her something.

And it terrified her, even more than the end of the world.

After her father had died in a bus crash, Vigor had filled that void. Under his care, knowing she was hurting, he had taken her by the hand and kept her moving, exploring Rome's museums, going on outings to Florence, diving at Capri. He taught her to pursue her passion, never to settle for less as a woman. He had also instilled in her the respect for and love of history and art, where the greatest expressions of humankind were cemented in marble and granite, oil and canvas, glass and bronze.

So how could she not want to protect him? Back in Rome, fear had made her want to bottle him up, to shelter him from harm, even against his will. But as she watched him now, smiling and excited, she knew she had been wrong. She didn't know how many years she had with him, but she recognized it was time now for her to take *his* hand, to be the one to offer him strength when he needed it, to keep him moving.

He had given her the world—she could never take it from him.

Knowing that, she turned her attention to the blasted landscape below. The helicopter banked away from the rusted ship and turned to the north, headed for a region even more desolate and barren. Moonlight turned the baked salt flats into an endless silver expanse, broken by boulders, the decaying hulks of other ships, and the occasional chalky hill.

She pictured the seas refilling the basin below, swamping over the flatlands until the hills became islands again. They were headed to such a spot about forty kilometers to the northeast, a lone atoll in this ocean of dry salt and dust—all based on a map inked on the tongue of a dead conqueror.

She could not help but feel some of her uncle's excitement spark inside her. What might they find? The others looked equally enthused, even the reluctant Jada Shaw. She shared a window with Duncan, a new Sigma operative, both equally young. Their eagerness shone from their skin.

Monk caught her staring and smiled, as if to say, *remember when we were so young*. He now had two girls at home and a wife who loved him, and he wore his scars proudly. Even his prosthetic hand was a badge of honor.

She sank back into her seat, happy for the company around her, even the young Sanjar, who carried his falcon on his wrist, held close to his body. Its plumage was a striking silvery white, accented with stripes of black and slate gray.

He noted her attention and nodded.

"What type of bird is he?" she asked.

Sanjar's back straightened, happy for her interest. "He is a gyrfalcon. *Falco rusticolus*. One of the largest falcon breeds."

"He's beautiful."

He grinned, showing a flash of white teeth. "Best he not hear that. Heru is already quite full of himself."

"But he sits so still."

He ran a finger over the top of a tufted bonnet. "Without sight, a bird knows not to move. A hooded falcon will remain motionless, trusting his handler. In the past aristocrats used to carry them to court, to banquets, even on horseback."

"And apparently now on helicopters."

"We must all adjust to the modern world. But falconry goes back to the time of Genghis Khan. Mongol warriors used to hunt foxes, even sometimes wolves, with falcons."

"Wolves? Truly? Something so large."

He nodded. "Not just *wolves*. But humans, too. In fact, Genghis's personal bodyguards were falconers."

"Then you are keeping up a proud tradition, Sanjar, continuing to look after Genghis even today."

"Yes, my cousin and I"—he nodded to Arslan in the next row of seats—"we are very proud of our great ancestor."

The pilot interrupted. "Folks, we're a minute or so out from the designated spot. Do you want me to land or circle for an aerial view?"

Vigor answered, leaning forward. "From the air, please, that might prove useful."

They all turned their attention to the windows as the helicopter swept over the Aralkum Desert, the salt marsh glistening even brighter here.

Ahead, a gloomy peak broke through the dried crust. It was steep sided and wind carved, slightly concave on the top, looking not unlike a boat riding a wave of rock.

The helicopter circled it twice, but nothing of note struck anyone.

"We'll have to land to continue our search from here," Josip decided.

Monk yelled forward. "Put us down! As close to that hill as you can!"

The pilot expertly maneuvered the aircraft and landed within ten yards of the leeward side of the rock. But it had clearly been a struggle.

"Wind's kicking up out there," the pilot warned. "Pressure front must be moving in."

As the doors were swung open, his weather report proved true. The temperature had dropped several degrees. Even sheltered by the bulk of the hill, Rachel felt an icy wind cut through her jacket.

They all hopped out.

Salt crunched underfoot. Around them spread a strange sight. It looked like someone had spread a thick layer of french fries over the hardpan. Bending down, she realized they were geometric straws of salt, each crystal a finger wide and pointy ended. It cast a prickly, otherworldly appearance to the place.

Standing beside her, Josip ignored the geological feature and stared up at the hill. Steep cliffs faced them, though some sections had crumbled down into flows of sand and boulders.

"We should circle around it on foot first," he suggested, as flashlights were passed out.

Vigor nodded—though he held a hand pressed to his side.

Rachel crossed to her uncle and offered him the use of her shoulder for support. "Come on, old man, you dragged me out here . . ."

He scowled good-naturedly and took her up on her offer. Together, they headed out across the field of ice crystals. He leaned on her for the first ten minutes, then eventually felt strong enough to continue on his own. She wanted to question him about it, but she gave him the space to come to her when he was ready.

Monk came over, likely noting the same debilitation, his brow creased with concern. Still, with his usual infallible ability to sense a mood, he stayed silent. Or at least about her uncle.

He stared around the crust of sharp crystals. "Looks like no one has set foot around here in ages."

She realized he was right. "No footprints."

The crystals looked fragile and likely took years to form. If anyone had traipsed through here, there would have been a record of it in crushed salt.

Eventually they circled out of the shelter of the hill and into the wind's teeth. It blew hard and steady, stinging of sand and tasting bitter on the tongue.

Sanjar had trouble controlling the falcon perched on his gloved hand. He slipped off the hood and cast the bird into the wind, letting it stretch its wings and work off its anxiety. It screamed into the night, its silvery wings flashing in the moonlight.

The young man's cousin pointed to the horizon. The crisp line between salt flats and starry sky blurred out there.

"Storm coming," Arslan warned.

"A black blizzard," Sanjar clarified.

Shielding her eyes against the wind, Rachel stared out at the churning wall of sand, salt, and dust, remembering her uncle's warning of the toxicity of such clouds.

"We don't want to be here when it arrives," Arslan warned.

No one argued, so they set a faster pace.

Within yards, they were soon covering the lower halves of their faces with handkerchiefs passed out by Sanjar. Clearly such a precaution was commonplace here, where winds regularly whipped over this ancient dead seabed. Still, between the burn of the stinging dust and the cold bite of the wind, any exposed skin felt flayed and raw.

The winds forced them to stay close to the hill. Moving single file, flashlights bobbling, they crossed into a narrow cut between the cliff face and a line of fanged rocks, perhaps the remains of an old reef. Any shelter from the wind was a welcome respite.

A shout rose from ahead.

Rachel hurried forward with the others, bunching together around Josip. He shone his flashlight at his feet, to the bottom of the cliff, where a large crack broke into the rock face. Rachel failed to understand what had the priest so riled up.

"Does that look like a horse's head?" He pointed out the features with the beam of his light. "Nose high, ears pulled back, neck stretched."

Stepping back, she realized he was right. It looked like the silhouette of a horse, drowning in billowing sand, trying to thrust its head up for air.

"*Equus*," Vigor gasped out. "Like what was written on the tattoo."

Josip nodded, his eyes feverishly bright.

Monk knelt at the entrance and shone his light inside. "Looks like there's enough room to climb into it."

"Is it a tunnel?" Jada asked.

Duncan searched up the cliff. "If so, it would've once been a *sea* tunnel," he clarified. "When this lake was full, this entrance would have been underwater."

Josip stared over to Vigor. "Just like the Tisza River in Hungary. It was only during the *drought* that the secret entrance to the river vault revealed itself."

"Then what are we waiting for?" Monk asked.

He ducked inside, taking the lead in case there was any danger. The others quickly followed.

Vigor glanced over to Rachel, grinning ear to ear, ready to follow, barely able to contain himself.

This is what he lived for.

She prayed that it didn't also kill him.

10:37 P.M.

Vigor followed on hands and knees behind Josip.

The tunnel had more headroom than he had expected, but it helped that Monk used his industrial-strength prosthetic hand to clear any blockages out of the way: tumbles of rocks, berms of sand, crusts of salt. He was a living drill bit, tunneling deeper into the former island.

"Looks like it opens a few yards ahead!" Monk called back.

A minute later, he was proven right.

Monk's light vanished from view, leaving its glow behind. Then Josip followed him out, climbing free of the tunnel. Once on his feet, his friend froze, then stumbled weakly to the side, clearly in shock.

With his heart thudding harder, Vigor clambered to the tunnel's end and pushed into the cave beyond.

Stunned, he lifted his light higher as he stood up, adding his illumination to the others.

A large cavern stretched before them—caked entirely in salt. The domed white roof dripped with glistening stalactites of crystalline salt. Stalagmites rose like opalescent fangs. Elsewhere full columns of salt connected floor to ceiling. Silvery-white crystals coated every surface.

The others joined them, voicing various levels of astonishment as they entered.

Duncan came last, adding, "Holy Mother of—"

Josip cut him off, gaping around. "This cave must have been underwater, too. When the waters receded, seeping slowly away, it left only the sea's salt behind."

"And hopefully something else," Vigor added and pointed across the chamber. "We need to search for more of Genghis's relics."

The group spread out, working gingerly across the floor. It was a difficult task as the stone underfoot was piled thickly with the same fingerlike crystals seen outside, only some here were as thick around as a man's thigh, leaning drunkenly upon one another, like a felled forest of salt.

The crunch of crystals echoed off the walls as they labored. The air smelled of the sea and burned the eyes.

Jada whispered with Duncan, but her voice reached everyone due to the cavern's acoustics. "Water levels must have risen and fallen in here over the centuries to create this accumulation."

"And rainfall added to it each year," Duncan said. "Leaching more salt from the ground above."

Jada stared up to the roof. "I'm guessing during Genghis's time this cavern was not entirely flooded. But only accessible by swimming underwater."

They were probably right.

Suddenly tired, recognizing that perhaps archaeology was a young man's sport, Vigor leaned on a salt column as wide as a telephone pole to rest, believing it sturdy enough to hold his weight. Instead, it cracked under his hand, breaking in half, proving its fragility.

Luckily Monk and Rachel were there to pull him back and shield his body as a shower of crystal shards and larger chunks rained down.

"Take care, Uncle," Rachel warned, helping him straighten and brushing sparkling dust from his shoulders.

"Look here," Monk said, pointing to the flared base of the broken column.

Vigor turned, bringing up his flashlight. He shone its brightness into the core of the translucent pillar. Something buried there reflected his light even brighter.

"Over here!" he called to the group.

Others gathered and added their own beams, helping to reveal what was preserved in the salt.

Josip dropped to one knee. "It appears to be a pedestal of stone, holding up a box of some sort."

His friend stared up at him, wonder shining in his face.

"Like the Hungarian bishop described in Attila's tomb!" Vigor exclaimed. "This must be it."

Josip stood. "We must break it free of the salt!"

Arslan appeared, bringing up a small satchel of tools. Using hammers, chisels, and brushes, Josip worked with Arslan to chip away at the thick base of the column.

As it was slowly revealed, the box proved to be large, a foot or so tall and twice as long.

Josip swept crystals off its black surface. The chisel had nicked it in a few places. Vigor's friend used a fingernail to dig more vigorously at one of the scratches. "It looks to be silver under the tarnish."

Vigor leaned closer as Arslan freed the lower half of the chest. "I think you're right. And it's hinged at the back here."

In short order, the remainder of the box was broken free of the crust. It shifted on its pedestal with a final strike of a hammer.

Arslan stepped back, his work done.

Vigor waved to Josip. "You open it. You've earned the right."

His friend gripped his arm in gratitude, speechless with anticipation, his fingers shaking slightly on Vigor's arm.

With both hands, Josip lifted the lid and cracked it open with a salty grate of its hinges. As he raised it, the front panel fell open, apparently hinged on its bottom edge.

Rachel stepped away, covering her mouth. "My God . . ."

11:02 P.M.

As Vigor's niece moved back, Duncan had a clear view of what the box held.

It looked like a miniature sculpture of a boat, with a prominent keel that swooped into a knobbed bowsprit at the front, its sides made of artfully curved planks. A pair of masts supported square sails, both slightly ribbed like a closed set of blinds.

"Looks like a Song dynasty junk," Vigor said. "During the Middle Ages such ships plied the seas and rivers of China."

Rachel shook her head. "But this one is constructed out of rib bones and vertebrae. The sails are made of dried human skin."

Duncan stepped closer and saw she was right. The curved planks of the boat's side were *ribs*. The knob of the bowsprit was a spinal *vertebra*. He would take her word that the sails were made of human skin.

"More of Genghis," Monk said.

"Can we be sure?" Rachel asked.

"I can send a sample to the same genetics lab in Rome," Vigor offered. "We could have confirmation in a day or so."

Jada nudged Duncan and stated, "Or we find out right now."

All eyes turned to him.

He understood. "She's right." He lifted his hands and wiggled his fingers. "If this tissue is from the same body, I'll know."

The others cleared out of his way. Stepping forward, he reached out and moved his fingertips to the curved sides of the boat. Immediately he registered the same pressure, the same unique energy field as in the earlier relics. He swore now he could almost sense the *color* of the field. It was a term people like him used to describe the minute variations of electrical fields that defied adequate description.

Like trying to describe *blue* to a blind person.

Only, in this case, if he had to pick a color for this field, it would be *black*.

He stepped away and shook the tingle from his fingertips, shivering all over for a breath.

"Definitely the same," he concluded.

Before anyone could comment, a piercing screech made them all jump. Sanjar's falcon flew effortlessly through the tunnel and swept high into the room. Sanjar lifted his arm and the bird dove to a fluttering landing, panting through its open beak.

"Storm must be here," Sanjar said, brushing dust from the falcon's feathers. "We should be going."

Another squawk erupted. This time it was from the team's radio. Monk spoke with the pilot and got confirmation.

"He says we must get going now." Monk pointed Duncan toward the box. "Close that up and let's get moving."

With Josip's and Vigor's help, Duncan secured the tarnished chest and hauled it up. It was damned heavy. If it was indeed silver, it was likely worth a small fortune.

Monk assisted him in getting the chest through the tunnel. Once back outside, Duncan understood the falcon's sudden desire to rejoin its master. The starry night of earlier was gone. Black clouds roiled over-head. Sand blasted against the cliff. To the west, conditions looked even worse.

The group hurried across the flatlands, following their crushed path back. They all shuttled sideways, putting their backs to the wind. Visibility was crap. Duncan carried the box under one arm and had a hold of Jada's hand in the other. Ahead of him, Monk and Rachel helped Vigor, while Sanjar and Arslan supported Josip.

Finally they circled to the far side of the hill, out of direct assault by the storm. The pilot spotted them. He hopped out, opened the side door to the helicopter, and waved them to hurry.

Not that any of them needed the encouragement.

As a group, they ran for the shelter of the chopper's cabin and clambered inside. Even before they had strapped in, the pilot had the bird lifting off.

Once the wheels were off the ground, the helicopter swung around and flew low across the salt flats, keeping to the shelter of the tall hill for as long as possible, putting as much distance as possible between them and the storm.

Everyone found seats, and harnesses clicked into place.

Finally, the helicopter shot higher, buffeted by the storm's leading edge, and fled under full power. The bouncing and rattling jarred teeth and challenged the strength of their seat belts.

For a few more long minutes, no one spoke, and hardly anyone breathed.

Then the flight of the helicopter evened out as it escaped the teeth of the storm.

"Should be smooth sailing from here," the pilot said, though his voice had a shaky edge that suggested their escape was closer than Duncan cared to think about.

They rushed through the night, the stars shining overhead again.

Duncan finally let out a long shuddering breath. "Well, that was fun."

Jada looked at him aghast.

11:33 P.M.

As they flew back toward their base of operations, Vigor studied the tarnished silver box. It rested on the seat next to Duncan, who kept a palm atop it.

Vigor pictured what it held, but he wasn't the only one wondering.

"There must be a clue contained within that boat," Josip said. "Some indication where we must go next."

Vigor pictured the eye sewn shut on the cover of the book—and the secrets it had hidden. "You are probably right. Once at your library, we'll see what we can discover."

Josip must have noted the lack of enthusiasm in his voice. "What's wrong?"

He waved a hand dismissively. "Just tired," he lied.

"I wonder how many more caches of Genghis's relics are out there," Josip said. "Into how many pieces had the great khan been divvied?"

Vigor shifted in his seat, surprised that Josip was so dense. "There is only *one* more spot to go."

Josip frowned at him. "How do you know—?"

Then understanding dawned in his eyes. He patted Vigor on the knee. "Your body may be tired, my friend, but not your mind."

Monk stirred across the way, having eavesdropped on the conversation. "How about you explaining it to those who are tired in both body and mind?"

Vigor smiled with warm affection at him. "The box we found is *silver*." He nodded to the chest at Duncan's side. "But according to the Hungarian bishop's account, the box at Attila's tomb was *iron*."

Josip sat straighter, thrilled. "Which means the final box, the one holding the greatest treasure of this hunt, will be *gold*."

Monk got it. "Like the three original boxes of St. Thomas's reliquary. Iron, silver, gold."

Vigor nodded. "We are one step away from the lost tomb of Genghis Khan."

Duncan patted the box with his palm. "That is, if you can solve the riddle of that boat made of bone."

Vigor sighed, praying that God would keep him strong enough for this challenge.

If only for a little longer . . .

The pilot reported good news. "We're back to where we started, folks. But we may need to batten down the hatches for the night. The weather coming is not going to be fit for man or beast."

Vigor looked out toward the storm on the horizon. It seemed that the black blizzard hadn't given up its chase and bore down on them with all its fury.

Knowing what was coming, the helicopter dropped quickly toward the rusted bulk of the ship, seeking its shelter. The giant vessel had clearly weathered such gales in the past and would do so again.

Vigor settled back, relieved.

Once we get underground, we should be safe.

16

Seichan stood at the rail of the USS *Benfold*, a United States guided missile destroyer. She wore a borrowed parka, its fur-edged hood tossed back. She could not stand the confinement below any longer, with its cramped hallways, the press of bodies, the windowless chambers all painted the same drab colors.

She needed air, so she climbed topside.

The night was bitterly cold, the stars hard as diamonds; even the comet looked like a lump of ice dragged across the sky.

The ship cruised south through the territorial waters of South Korea. So far no alarm had been raised by Pyongyang. Likely those in power up north were too embarrassed to admit their failure. Still, it had been a very close call. Gray was with the medics getting properly attended.

She flashed back to firing her pistol, acting on instinct, blind to anything but survival. She had only meant to knock the rider off his bike. Still . . .

I almost killed him.

A deck hatch clanged open behind her. She closed her eyes, not wanting any intrusion. Footsteps approached, and a form stepped to the rail next to her. She smelled jasmine. The scent threatened to cast her deeper into the past if she let it. Even now, an image of a flowering vine in sunlight appeared in her mind's eye, with purple flowers, the bobble of fat-bellied bees.

She pushed it down.

"Chi," her mother said, using her old name, a single note from the lips that carried too much weight for that short exhalation of breath.

"I prefer Seichan," she said, opening her eyes. "I've been that far longer than the other."

Small hands gripped the rail beside hers, not touching hers, yet close enough for Seichan to feel the warmth from them on this cold night. Still, the distance between them remained a vast gulf.

Seichan had imagined this reunion a thousand ways, but none of them as such profound strangers. She had studied her mother's features during the trip back here. She could touch and point to those that were achingly familiar: the arch of an eyebrow, the curve of her lower lip, the shape of her eyes. But at the same time, it was the face of a stranger. Not because of the purplish scar or the tattoo, but something deeper.

When last she looked upon her mother, she had been a child of nine. She looked upon her now as a woman two decades older. She was not that child any longer. Her mother was not that young woman.

"I must leave soon," her mother warned.

Seichan took a deep breath, testing how that made her feel. Tears threatened—but only because she felt *nothing* at those words, and it devastated her.

"I have obligations," her mother explained. "Men and women who are still in jeopardy and need my help. I cannot abandon them."

Seichan held back a bitter laugh at the irony of those words.

Her mother must have still sensed it.

"I looked for you," she said softly after a long pause.

"I know." Seichan had heard the same from Gray.

"They told me you were dead, yet still I searched until it hurt too much to do so anymore."

Seichan stared down at her own hands, surprised to find them so white knuckled as they gripped the rail.

"Come with me now," her mother asked.

Seichan remained silent for too long.

"You can't, can you?" her mother whispered.

"I also have obligations."

Another silence stretched, filled with far more import than their words.

"I heard he is leaving again. So you will go with him?"

Seichan didn't bother answering.

They stood together for a long time, both with so much to say, and so little to talk about. What else could they do? Compare scars, swap tales of horror and bloodshed, of what one did to survive? In the end, they said nothing.

Finally, her mother unclasped her hands and faded back, turning away, leaving only a whisper behind. "Have I lost you forever, my little Chi? Did I never really find you again?"

And then she was gone, leaving behind only the scent of jasmine.

3:14 A.M.

Gray leaned against the conference table, too tired to trust his legs. He and Kowalski had the officers' wardroom all to themselves, courtesy of the ship's captain. The crew had brewed coffee and laid out a spread of scrambled eggs and bacon.

It wasn't every day a couple of U.S. operatives escaped North Korea.

With his wounded shoulder scrubbed, sprayed with a liquid bandage, and wrapped, he felt worlds better. The muddy coffee certainly helped, too.

Kowalski sat in a neighboring chair, his feet propped up on the table, a plate of bacon resting on his stomach. He yawned with a jaw-cracking pop.

The large LCD monitor before Gray finally flickered to life. The feed was being dispatched through high-security channels to this private room. He found himself staring into the communications nest at Sigma command in D.C.

The director faced him, with Kat seated to the side, tapping furiously at a computer console. She had set up this private videoconference call.

Painter nodded to him. "Commander Pierce, how are you holding up?"

"I've had better days."

And worse.

Despite all that had happened, they had succeeded in rescuing Seichan and made it out alive with their skin intact—okay, not entirely *intact,* but close enough.

"I know you've been through hell and back," Painter said, "but we need you up and running for another mission, if you're able."

"In Mongolia," Gray said.

He had already debriefed with Kat and was relatively up to speed in regard to events surrounding the crashed satellite.

"I need an honest assessment," Painter said. "Are you and Kowalski fit enough to continue?"

Gray glanced over at Kowalski, who merely shrugged and picked up another slice of bacon.

"I think *fit enough* pretty much describes us," Gray answered. "But a little more sleep en route, and we'll be even better."

"Good, then I wanted to show you this." Painter turned to Kat.

She shifted into view, still tapping at the keyboard with one hand while staring at him. "I'm going to patch you in with Lieutenant Josh Leblang, out of McMurdo Station."

"In Antarctica?"

"That's correct. He's with a recon crew about a hundred klicks out from the base, on the Ross Ice Shelf." Kat punched a few more keys and spoke into a microphone by her chair. "Lieutenant Leblang, can you show us again what you found? Walk us through what you saw?"

A sputtering response reached Gray that sounded vaguely affirmative.

Then the screen cleared and was replaced with the face of a young man in a military parka. He had his hood thrown back, apparently enjoying the bright morning of an Antarctic summer. He wore a woolen cap over his short dark hair, his cheeks reddened from the cold, or maybe flushed from excitement.

From the shaky image, someone was filming him with a handheld camcorder. He spoke while walking backward up a ridge.

"About two hours ago, we saw five huge fireballs shoot over McMurdo. Thought it was a missile attack. The sonic booms—one after the other—had the entire base scrambling. My team was sent out to investigate. This is what we found."

He reached the top of the ridge and stepped aside. The cameraman moved forward, the image jangling wildly. Once he stopped and steadied his hand, a hellish landscape came into clear focus.

Across the expanse ahead, massive craters pocked the blue ice, roiling with steam, blackened at the edges. Gray pictured the five meteorites punching through the ice and melting in the sea three hundred meters below. He spotted men, small black ants, moving on the ice, likely a part of Leblang's crew. They offered perspective as to the huge size of those smoking pits.

Thunder rumbled over the speakers.

Gray didn't understand the source of the noise—until a resounding series of thunderclaps followed. On the screens, cracks exploded across the snowy field, shattering ice high into the air. Fault lines burst jaggedly from crater to crater and splintered outward across the shelf.

Out of view, Leblang swore loudly. Then he appeared, running down the slope toward his endangered crew. The videographer dropped his camcorder and followed, too. The camera landed askew in the snow, still shooting, offering a crooked view of the chaos.

Fissures in the ice split wider, tearing apart the terrain below.

Men fled the destruction in all directions. Faint screams reached the camera's microphone.

Gray spotted a pair of sailors falling away as the ice opened under them. An entire continent of ice slowly split away from the main shelf. Another crack skittered toward the camera and exploded before its lens, then the screen went black.

Kowalski, a former navy man himself, was on his feet, his fists clenched in frustration, unable to do anything.

Then Painter was back, red-faced and shocked, bent beside Kat, passing on orders. "—McMurdo Station. Raise the alarm. Tell them to get birds in the air ASAP."

Gray waited silently as Painter and Kat sounded the alarm.

Once done, Painter finally returned his attention to Gray. "Now you understand what we might be facing."

"What do you mean?"

"Shortly before Leblang reported from Antarctica, technicians and engineers over at the SMC in Los Angeles had confirmed their initial speculation that the destruction caught digitally by the crashing satellite was secondary to a cluster of meteor strikes along the East Coast."

Gray pictured the devastation from a moment ago, imagining what would happen if those five meteors had hit a population center.

"The techs estimate that what impacted Antarctica were superbolide meteors, averaging seventeen to twenty meters across. They each struck with the energy equivalent of eight atomic bombs."

Gray swallowed.

No wonder that shelf shattered into pieces.

Painter continued, "From analyzing the satellite image in great detail—taking into account the blast patterns, the depth of the impact craters, the degree of catastrophic destruction—they estimate that it would take meteors threefold larger than in Antarctica to cause that much damage."

Gray went cold, picturing all his friends and family out there, including everyone at Sigma command.

"And it might not just be the East Coast," Painter warned. "We have only this *one* snapshot. There is no way of telling if the destruction is more widespread, even global."

"Or if it will happen at all," Gray added, still skeptical. But after what he'd just witnessed, he was willing to err on the side of caution.

"That's why we need that satellite recovered," Painter said. "We have every eye looking skyward at the moment—Hubble, NASA's Swift satellite, the UK Space Agency. We're tracking a slew of rocks dragging in the wake of that comet, some as large as two hundred meters across. So far, according to all estimates, none of them are at risk of hitting the earth."

"But what about the ones that just struck Antarctica?"

"That's the problem. We can't catch everything. It's taken NASA fifteen years to track fewer than ten thousand asteroids in near-Earth orbit, meaning the vast majority go undetected. Take the Chelyabinsk meteor that exploded over Russia last year. It came as a total shocker. And if that meteor hadn't exploded in the upper atmosphere, releasing a lot of its energy, it would have hit Russia with the force of twenty Hiroshima bombs."

"So we can't be sure of anything."

Painter glanced to Kat, as if reluctant to say something.

"What?" Gray asked.

Kat nodded to Painter, who sighed loudly.

"There's one last bit of disturbing news coming out of the SMC. It's too early to draw any firm conclusions. But one of the physicists who was working closely with Dr. Jada Shaw has been analyzing her data on the initial gravitational anomalies in the comet, those same inconsistencies that Dr. Shaw believed proved the presence of dark energy."

"And?"

"And the physicist at the SMC has been continuing to track those anomalies, as the comet comes closer to Earth. He's convinced they're growing *larger*."

"What does that mean?"

Painter shot a glance toward Kat. "We're still waiting for an answer to that very question. It could be significant . . . or it could be meaningless. We won't know until more data is collected and analyzed."

"How long will that take?"

"Half a day at the least, maybe longer."

"So in the meantime, we find that satellite."

"It may hold the answers to everything." Painter stared hard at him. "How soon can you leave?"

"Now. If Kat can arrange the logistics—"

She shifted back in her seat. "I can get Commander Pierce's team on the ground in Mongolia by daybreak."

"What about Monk's team?" Gray asked.

"I just heard word out of Kazakhstan," Kat said. "A storm front will have them pinned down for a short time. But barring any other problems, they should be able to join you in Ulan Bator by midmorning."

"Then let's make that happen," Painter said. "We need as many eyes on the ground out there as possible. Is Seichan willing to join you?"

On the way to this meeting, Gray had spotted Guan-yin heading down the hall, hiding the tears in her eyes. She was flying back to Hong Kong to assist those of her Triad who were still in harm's way. From those tears, Gray could guess the answer to Painter's question.

"I believe Seichan will be coming."

"Good."

Painter quickly signed off, plainly busy on multiple fronts.

Gray stared at the black screen, again picturing the destruction in Antarctica, appreciating the urgency.

Monk had better not be late.

17

Rachel and the others hurried below, returning to the clutter of Father Josip's inner sanctum. Deep in the warren of tunnels and rooms, the howl of the wind reached them as the storm bore down upon the derelict ship above their heads. It whistled through the rusted hull, shook loose tin, rattled broken rails.

Up above, the pilot was securing the chopper against the storm, positioning the craft on the leeward side of that mountain of corroded steel, and doing his best to seal and cover the engine and moving parts from the blowing salt and sand.

More of Josip's crew occupied the lowermost levels, seemingly oblivious to the racket and danger, plainly used to retreating below when Nature grew too violent above. They lounged, or played cards, or did simple chores to occupy their time.

Rachel took some small comfort in their ease.

"Let's get this box on the table," Monk ordered Duncan.

As the two hauled the tarnished silver chest across the room, Jada shook sand from her hair and patted dust and salt off her clothes. But she wasn't the only one with her feathers ruffled.

Sanjar coaxed his hooded falcon to a wooden perch. Heru flapped his wings several times, irritated, but his sharp claws clung to the roost; he knew better than to fly blind. His handler whispered soothingly, calming the bird with a preening scratch behind its neck.

Rachel stood next to him, appreciating his skill.

Her uncle had other interests. He waved Josip toward the table. "We should study this as thoroughly as we can, discern any clues about where to go next."

Josip nodded, but again he wore that distracted look, as if his mind were elsewhere. He stood staring at a tall bookcase, his back to the table as Monk and Duncan placed the box next to the other relics.

Arslan moved to the priest's side, as if to consult him.

Instead, he placed the muzzle of a black pistol into Josip's side and barked loudly, "Everyone away from the table! Hands up and high!"

Caught off guard, no one moved for a breath—then men poured into the room through the open door, carrying rifles or curved swords. They appeared to be members of the excavation crew hired by Josip.

Gunfire echoed out in the hallway.

Rachel could guess the fate of the remainder of that crew. She pictured the explosion at the university, the bombing in Aktau. It seemed the enemy had been closer than anyone suspected all along.

Josip turned to his foreman, wearing a confused expression. "What is this about, Arslan?"

As answer, Arslan cuffed him hard across the mouth, splitting his lip. He then roughly grabbed Josip's arm, spun him about, and moved the pistol to the middle of his back.

Sanjar stepped forward. "Cousin, what are you doing?"

"I do what the Master of the Blue Wolf commands," Arslan said. "And you will obey. You swore allegiance, same as I."

Josip turned to Sanjar with a wounded expression.

Arslan motioned with his head toward the door, bitter command in his voice. "Go now, Cousin. Or be buried here with them."

Sanjar took a step back. "I agreed to watch, to report on Father Josip's actions . . . but not this, never this. He is a good man. These others have done no harm."

"Then die with them," he said with ringing disdain. "You were always too weak, Sanjar, your head in the winds with your bird, pampered by your rich parents who looked down upon their poorer cousins. Never a true warrior of the khan."

Turning aside, Arslan shouted to his crew in Mongolian. Four immediately ran up, scooped the relics from the table, and retreated to the door.

Rachel watched their hard-won treasures vanish.

Arslan followed in their wake, with Josip clutched in front of him, using the priest as a hostage and a shield. He called to his men, who began closing the door to the chamber. It was heavy steel. From the rivets and rust, it was probably a hatch salvaged from the ship above.

From the doorway, Arslan shared a final threat for his cousin, for them all. "While you were all gone, my warriors placed explosive charges throughout this hollowed-out rat's nest. Rock will turn to dust, collapsing all. And as the heavy ship above sinks atop you, it will be your gravestone. None will ever know what happened here."

A few men laughed harshly.

The crew kept their guns trained, especially on Monk and Duncan, wise enough to recognize the biggest danger to their plans.

"Kill them," Arslan ordered his men in the room. "Then join us up top."

Sanjar cast a glance toward Rachel, rolling his eyes up, then over to the falcon.

It took her a heartbeat, then she understood.

With the crew ignoring her, Rachel reached over and plucked the bonnet from Heru's feathered head.

Sanjar yelled a command in his native tongue and pointed at Arslan. The falcon exploded off the perch, sweeping up to the wooden rafters that bolstered the sandstone roof.

Weapons shifted, shooting at the bird, the blasts stinging Rachel's ears.

Untouched, Heru dove down, a feathered arrow shot from Sanjar's bow. Claws raked Arslan, splitting cheek and scalp. Wings beat at his face, driving the man to his knees, screaming in pain.

Then gunfire erupted in the middle of the room.

12:38 A.M.

As soon as the nearest weapon swung toward the roof, Duncan moved. He bowled into the nearest guard, taking him down. The gunman's head hit the corner of the table, hard enough to crack bone. The man fell limp under him.

He grabbed the loose rifle and rolled away. Still, on his back, Duncan took out a second assassin with a burst of rounds to the chest. Then gunfire chewed into the stone between his legs, chasing him backward, until he was under the table.

From his sheltered vantage, he took out the shooter's left kneecap—as the man toppled, Duncan placed a round between his eyes.

Another attacker slid into view on his knees, strafing under the table.

Then the neighboring bookcase fell on top of him, crushing him. Monk clambered over the top and punched a stunned gunman in the throat with his prosthetic hand. With his larynx crushed, the man fell to his side, writhing, choking on blood.

At the exit, one of Arslan's crew clubbed the bird away from their leader's face.

Josip used the chaos to break free and run deeper into the room.

Two shots cracked loudly.

The priest's chest blew out. He collided with Monk, who caught him in his arms.

Behind them, Arslan's pistol still smoked as his men dragged his bloody form through the door. Duncan fired after them, but the hatch swung closed with a clang of steel.

Climbing back to his feet, Duncan rushed the door and shouldered into it. It refused to budge, likely braced on the other side. They were locked in.

He surveyed the room, taking swift inventory.

Jada rose from a crouch behind another bookcase, shoved there by Monk as the first shots rang out.

Sanjar knelt by Heru, as his stunned bird flopped dazedly on the stone.

Rachel hurried alongside her uncle to Josip's gasping form.

Seeing the blood pooling beneath the priest, she knew the man did not have long to live—which was probably true for all of them.

12:40 A.M.

No, no, no . . .

Vigor knelt beside his friend, who had come back from the dead only to die again, a man whom the Fates had already afflicted so cruelly, gifting him with both brilliance and madness. He did not deserve this end.

He took Josip's hand and began last rites.

Josip stared up at him, disbelief in his eyes, blood on his lips, unable to speak, his lungs collapsed and shredded by the bullets of a traitor.

"Lie still, my dear friend."

Monk cradled his thin form in his lap, supporting him.

Vigor took Josip's hand, squeezing all his love for the man between his palms. He could do no more. He had seen that truth in Monk's eyes.

Stripped of his voice, Josip found the strength to take Vigor's hand and bring his palm to his bloody chest. Vigor felt the beat of his friend's heart.

"I will miss you, too."

In his eyes, he read the man's struggle, his regret. Josip knew the danger the world faced and could do nothing more to help.

"You've shouldered this burden long enough, my friend. Let me carry it from here."

Josip kept staring at Vigor as he gently anointed a cross on Josip's forehead.

"Go rest," Vigor whispered.

And he did.

12:42 A.M.

Duncan helped Monk place Father Josip atop the table.

"I'm sorry," Duncan said. "I wish we had the time to bury him properly."

Vigor fought tears but nodded, staring around the chaotic library. "This is a good spot for him."

Monk got them all moving. "Let's not make it our burial spot, too."

Duncan turned to Sanjar. "Is there another way out?"

Sanjar had his falcon wrapped in a blanket. "I'm sorry, no. The other tunnels just lead to more rooms. Dead ends. The only way up is through this sealed door."

Duncan knew they had at best another few minutes or so to break free. Once Arslan and his crew evacuated the ship, they'd blow the lower levels. His only hope was that the assassins would drag their feet long enough to scavenge anything of value on their way out, but he couldn't count on that.

Jada stood, wide-eyed, hugging herself with her arms. "They meant to kill us," she said, shivering, near shock.

"And they may still succeed," Duncan conceded, figuring there was no reason to sugarcoat their situation.

She scowled at him. "That's not what I meant. Think about it. If we hadn't gotten the upper hand, we'd be dead. The explosions were meant to bury our *bodies* in this unmarked grave."

Duncan still didn't get it.

"We're not supposed to be alive right now," she said, her voice growing heated. She waved a hand around the room. "That jackass said he planted bombs throughout this place. So why not here, too? It's the lowest level. He thought we'd be dead already."

Of course . . .

Monk swore and set off looking along the walls.

Cursing his stupidity, Duncan canvassed the other side. It took him less than thirty seconds to find one of the charges. It was hidden at the base of a thick wooden brace that helped support the roof to this large room.

"Got one!" Duncan called out.

"Found another over here!" Monk yelled from across the room.

"Remove that one's transceiver!" he shouted back. "And be careful!"

Rachel had followed him over. "Do you think you can defuse them all in time?"

"Not the plan," he said as he worked. "They're likely planted all over the place."

With great care, he freed the wad of plastic explosive, being careful of the blasting cap and transceiver. He rushed with it over to the steel hatch.

Monk met him there, another transceiver in hand.

Duncan slapped the chunk of explosive to the thick hinges of the hatch. He popped open the transceiver, a device that contained both a radio *transmitter* and a *receiver*. Using a fingernail, he changed the receiver to a different setting, one unique from the other charges planted throughout this maze.

Don't want to bring this whole place down.

He then took the transceiver out of Monk's hand.

"Do you know what you're doing?" his partner asked.

"I didn't take all those electrical engineering courses to work at Radio-Shack." Working quickly, he adjusted the transmitter to the new frequency, then waved everyone back. "Find shelter and cover your ears!"

He retreated with the group and hid behind a sturdy bookcase. Once in position, he brought his thumb to the tiny red button on the transceiver. His jury-rigged charge should be the only one that responded to this new frequency—but when it came to explosives and radios, bad things sometimes happened to good engineers.

He pressed the button.

From the skull-crushing explosion that followed, Duncan believed he had failed, that he'd blown everything. Smoke and dust rolled through the space. Standing up, he waved and coughed.

Across the way, the hatch was gone, along with a fair amount of the wall around it.

Monk joined him, sounding as if he were speaking underwater. "Bastard probably heard that!"

Duncan nodded.

In other words, *run!*

12:46 A.M.

Jada sprinted up the steps behind Duncan, who led the charge topside with their only flashlight. Behind them, Monk and Rachel helped Vigor with the steep stairs, half carrying him between them. Sanjar brought up the rear.

At any moment, Jada expected the world to explode around her, crushing her under tons of stone, burying her in sand and salt.

The exit that led into the ship's rusty hold seemed an impossible distance away. The size of this labyrinth swelled around her, stretching higher and wider, expanding in proportion to her terror. Above her, the winds whistled and howled through the corroded bulk of the ship, taunting her to run faster.

"Not much farther!" Duncan gasped, taking two steps at a time, his rifle in hand.

She craned up, but his bulk blocked her view.

In another five yards, he was proven right. Rock turned to steel treads under her boots. The group clanked the last of the way up—

—then the ground bucked violently under them, accompanied by the sound of the earth cracking beneath their feet.

They all went crashing to their knees on the salt-corroded stairs. A flume of sand, dust, and smoke blasted up from below, choking them, blinding them.

Jada climbed the remainder of the stairs on her hands and knees, drawn by the glow of Duncan's flashlight. A hand grabbed hers and hauled her up and out of the stairwell, lifting her as if she were weightless.

Placed back on her feet, she stumbled to the side as Duncan drew the others into the hold with her.

"Make for the exit!" he hollered and pointed to the hole cut into the port side of the ship's hull.

She turned, but her footing slipped as her world tilted under her. The stern of the ship dropped precipitously behind her with a groan of steel, while the bow rose up. She pictured the back half of the thousand-ton vessel collapsing and crushing into the sinkhole created as the labyrinth below imploded.

Across the length of the hull, a half century of windblown sand suddenly shifted en masse, flowing toward the stern.

Jada could not hold her place any longer, dragged by the tide of sand. She fell to her knees and started sliding down the steep slant. The others fared no better, unable to gain any traction as the sands turned into a streaming cataract, growing deeper, pouring faster, trapping limbs, tumbling them all back toward the sinking stern.

Jada fought, flailing, feeling like a swimmer about to drown.

And maybe she was.

A sandstorm swirled treacherously below, waiting to swallow her up—behind her, the other half of the ship's sand flowed after her, ready to swamp her once she was trapped.

Then Duncan appeared and sped past her, half skating, half body surfing, not resisting the tidal pull like the others.

He quickly vanished into the dusty cloud ahead.

Has he simply given up?

12:50 A.M.

Racing atop the sand, Duncan aimed for their only hope of survival.

He recalled their arrival earlier in the day, when the Land Rover came wheeling out from a makeshift garage in the ship's stern, sweeping out to confront the newcomers.

As the world upended a moment ago, he had spotted the Rover still parked back there. He aimed for its bulk, already axle-deep in sand and being buried rapidly. He hit the bumper hard and flung himself onto the hood. Once at the windshield, he squirmed sideways through the open side window and dropped into the driver's seat.

He checked and found the keys still in the ignition.

Thank God . . .

With a twist of his wrist and a pound on the gas, he felt the paddle-treaded tires churn, kicking up a rooster tail of sand behind him. Then he was moving, tires digging back up the slope.

Monk had already noted Duncan's goal and swept fast down the slanted hull, no longer resisting the pull of the sand. Reaching the Rover, Monk leaped over the front grill and rolled up onto the hood, landing belly down, passing Duncan a prosthetic thumbs-up.

"Keep going!" Monk yelled.

Duncan slowly ground his way upslope as Monk fished the others out of the churning flow of sand. Vigor slid across the hood until his back rested against the windshield; Rachel soon joined him. At the right fender, Jada helped Monk grab Sanjar, who still clung to his blanket-wrapped falcon.

With everyone on board, Duncan gave the engine more gas. Staying in a low gear, he climbed up the steepening slope, picturing the massive weight of the ship shifting to the stern, driving it deeper into the collapsing subterranean complex.

Even with sand tires and four-wheel drive, the Rover fishtailed in the flow. He held his breath each time the vehicle slipped, knowing if they fell back to the stern, they might never get out. If that happened, they'd be quickly buried alive as the ship's five decades' worth of sand, silt, and salt filled the stern.

As he labored, the rusted vessel groaned, echoing with the strain of stressed steel. Hull plates popped like gunshots and tumbled into the stern. It was all coming apart.

Angling to the port side, he finally reached the hole cut through the hull. With the ship tilted, the opening was several feet off the ground, but they would have to risk the jump.

Duncan fought the tide to hold them steady, as Monk shuttled everyone through the hole, half tossing them into the teeth of the storm out there.

"You next!" Monk screamed into the wind blowing through the opening.

Duncan waved to him. "Go! I'll follow!"

It was a lie. There was no way Duncan could move. Once he let up on the gas, the Rover would immediately roll backward.

Monk stared through the windshield, read Duncan's determination—then with a scowl, the man turned and jumped toward the hole. But rather than leaping through the opening, he hung from its lower edge by his prosthetic hand and reached out with his other arm.

"Pull even with me!" he yelled. "Then grab my hand!"

Duncan balked, knowing such a maneuver would likely end with both of them dead.

"Don't make me jump down after you!" Monk bellowed.

Guy probably would, too.

Knowing that, Duncan gunned the engine and gained a couple of yards, his tires spinning on the sliding sand as he fought to hold his place. With one hand on the wheel, he stretched his arm out the window.

Monk caught his fingers, then his palm, gripping tightly.

With a silent prayer, Duncan let go of the steering wheel, took his foot off the gas, and shoved out the window. As he had suspected, the Rover immediately plummeted backward, shedding from around his body as it fell away, leaving Duncan hanging from Monk's arm.

He gasped in relief.

But it was premature.

As he hung there, the ship broke in half.

1:04 A.M.

From only yards away, huddled low against the storm, Jada watched the middle section of the rusted vessel fracture, splitting in half with a scream of rent steel. The entire bow came crashing down, blasting up more sand into the storm.

They all fled backward as debris rained down around them, whipped viciously by the wind. Sand swirled everywhere, obscuring anything beyond their noses.

Duncan . . . Monk . . .

The constant gale of the wind quickly cleared the worst of the dust, blowing it across the salt flats.

She searched the ruins of the ship.

Movement along the hull revealed two small forms climbing free of the hold and falling to the sands. Luckily, the ship had fractured *above* the exit, sparing their lives.

On the ground, Monk helped Duncan through the reefs of sharp steel littering the vessel's skirts. He held the younger man under one arm as Duncan limped alongside him.

Jada hurried forward, shielding her face against the wind. Her heart quailed at the sight of Duncan's blood-soaked pant leg.

The others gathered with her.

"What happened?" Jada asked.

"I tried to go down with the sinking ship," Duncan said. "But Monk convinced me otherwise."

"Let's keep moving," Monk warned, squinting through the storm. He noted someone was missing. "Where's Sanjar?"

Jada searched around. She had failed to notice that he had slipped away.

Vigor answered, "He went to check on our pilot."

Jada felt a flare of guilt, glancing toward the shadowy bulk of the helicopter. She had not even considered the man's fate. Somewhere at the back of her mind, she must have assumed him dead, murdered like the rest of Josip's crew at the onset of this assault.

Monk headed toward the helicopter with Duncan. Along the way, they found three bodies, sprawled in cooling pools of blood.

All shot.

Duncan limped through them. "Seems like our flyboy put up quite the fight."

"And saved our lives at the same time," Monk said. "His showdown likely delayed Arslan from blowing up the ship long enough for us to make our escape."

Jada felt doubly guilty now. She had never even learned the pilot's name.

They crossed to the helicopter and found its flank peppered with bullet holes, its canopy chipped and splintered. The tarps around it flapped and twisted in the wind.

A fast search found no sign of Sanjar.

Then from out of the dark storm, a pair of shadowy shapes appeared, leaning against each other, huddled against the fierce winds and the sting of blowing salt.

Sanjar and the pilot.

Monk left Duncan with Jada and helped the other pair back to the helicopter.

"I followed his blood trail," Sanjar said, as he rejoined them. "From the helicopter out into the storm . . ."

"Got shot in the upper thigh," the pilot said. "Pinned under the helicopter, I thought I was a goner, but then there was a big blast from the ship. Used the distraction to limp off into the storm, hoping to get lost. Which apparently worked."

Jada pictured the shattered hatch down below.

So in the end, it sounds like we both saved each other.

"Can the bird still fly?" Monk asked.

The pilot frowned, eyeing the damage. "Not in this weather. But with a little bit of spackle and glue, I can probably get her flying after that."

"Good man," Monk said.

They all retreated into the helicopter's cabin as the winds howled. But the storm was the least of their problems.

Monk turned to Sanjar, who had recovered his falcon from a seat, still covered in a blanket. He must have secured the bird inside the cabin before searching for the pilot.

"Do you know where Arslan was taking the relics?" Monk asked.

"I can't say with certainty. But most likely back to Ulan Bator."

Vigor pressed him. "Once there, what then? Who is he going to give them to?"

"Now *that* I can state with certainty. He'll hand them over to head of my clan. A man who goes by the title *Borjigin,* meaning the Master of the Blue Wolf."

"That was Genghis Khan's old title, too," Vigor said.

Sanjar nodded.

"What's his real name?" Monk asked.

"I do not know. He came to us always wearing the mask of a wolf. Only Arslan knows his true identity."

"Fat lot of good that does us," Duncan said as he bandaged a deep gash on his leg.

"Without that last relic," Vigor said, "we are doomed."

Jada stared out the window as the storm began shredding apart, revealing the glow of the comet in the night sky. As a scientist, she put her faith in numbers and facts, in solid proofs and indisputable calculations. She had scoffed at the superstitions that led to this side excursion to the Aral Sea, dismissing it as irrelevant.

But as she looked skyward, she simply despaired, knowing the truth with all her heart.

The monsignor was right.

We are doomed.

THIRD

HIDE & SEEK

18

"And you all believe this cross is important," Gray said.

He sat with everyone in a suite of rooms at the Hotel Ulaanbaatar in the center of the capital city's downtown. The façade of the building looked Soviet industrial, a holdover from the country's oppressed past, but the interior was a display of European modernity and elegance, representing the *new* Mongolia, a country looking to an independent future.

Their suite even featured a meeting room with a long conference table. Everyone was seated, with Monk's team on one side, Gray's on the other.

Only an hour ago, a knock at Gray's door revealed a familiar bald and smiling face. Monk had grabbed him in a bear hug, almost ripping his shoulder back open. Behind him, his new partner, Duncan Wren, bowed his tall physique inside. He was accompanied by a young Mongolian man wearing a midthigh sheepskin coat. He had a pet carrier in hand and something stirring inside.

But it was the pair who came last who triggered his strongest reaction, a mix of joy, warm memories, and deep affection.

Gray had grabbed Vigor with as much enthusiasm as Monk had him a moment ago. He found the monsignor his same self: tough, resolute, yet gentle of spirit. Only now Gray saw the man's age physically, how his frame seemed thinner, wasted. Even his face looked more gaunt.

Then there was Rachel.

Gray had greeted her just as warmly as the others, memories blurring as he held her in his arms. She clung to him an extra moment longer than ordinary friendship warranted. The two had been close for some time, intimate even, beginning to talk of something long term, until the shine of new romance waned into the practical realities of a long-distance relationship. The romance settled instead into a deep friendship, not that it didn't occasionally well up into something more physical whenever they still happened to cross paths.

But circumstances had since changed . . .

Gray looked at the woman seated across from Rachel.

Seichan also knew of their past history and had her own complicated relationship with Rachel, but the two had come to terms, respecting each other, but were still cautious.

Once Monk's team had time to settle in, Gray had ushered them into the meeting room, needing to decide how to proceed from here. They all placed their figurative cards on the table.

After receiving permission from Painter, Monk had shared the details of the crashed satellite with Vigor and Rachel, even with the Mongolian named Sanjar. The young man had offered his services as a guide into the Khan Khentii Strictly Protected Area, the mountainous region northwest of the city.

The story of the destruction captured by the falling spacecraft and the recent events in Antarctica had sobered the jubilance of their reunion. They now all understood the stakes at hand.

But Gray still remained doubtful about one detail. Monk's group had filled him in on what had transpired in Kazakhstan. They all seemed convinced that this cross, one carried by St. Thomas in the past, bore some significance to the potential disaster to come.

Even Dr. Jada Shaw believed it was vital to find.

She explained that now. "I know from my observations and calculations that Comet IKON is shedding an unusual energy signature, one triggering gravitational abnormalities."

"That you believe is caused by *dark energy*," Gray said.

"All I can say is that those anomalies exactly match my theoretical calculations."

"And the cross?"

"According to Duncan, the ancient relics are also giving off some form of energy. We believe it was because Genghis was exposed to, and contaminated by, that same energy while carrying the cross for many years on his person."

She ticked off additional points on her fingers, her dark eyes flashing with certainty. "*First,* the cross's history is tied to a meteor strike. *Second,* it's connected physically to a prophecy of a disaster set to play out in roughly two and a half days, matching the same time frame as the satellite image. *Third,* it's giving off a strange energy signature that left its trace on these relics. I say it's worth investigating. Or at least somebody should check into it."

"But not you," Gray said, challenging that certainty.

She sighed. "I'll be more useful going after the wreck of the crashed satellite. My expertise is astrophysics. I know that spacecraft inside out. My knowledge of history, on the other hand, barely extends beyond the last presidential election."

It had already been decided that Jada, Duncan, and Monk would head straight for the crash site deep in the remote mountains. Sanjar would act as their local guide and interpreter. Gray wanted to go with them, but Monk and his team were unanimous in their belief that somebody had to find that cross, one prophesied by a dead saint to be vital to surviving the coming fiery apocalypse.

Vigor was adamant about continuing on this path. If so, he would need logistical support and protection. Everyone faced Gray waiting for a final decision.

He still balked, and for good reason. "But you've *lost* that last relic, which held the only possible clue to the location of the cross."

"Then we find it again," Vigor said.

"How? You don't know where it was taken or the identity of this mysterious clan leader. With the timer counting down, it seems a better plan to pool our resources and go after that satellite together. At the moment, the wreckage of the spacecraft is our best chance of learning more about this pending disaster. And that knowledge could be our best *weapon* to avert it, not this cross."

Even Jada sank back in her seat, clearly accepting the wisdom of his plan. But then she was a scientist, accustomed to following the dictates of logic.

Vigor, on the other hand, was a man of faith and heart. He simply crossed his arms, unconvinced. "I am no use to anyone on this search, Commander Pierce. And I made a promise to Father Josip that I won't break. I will still pursue the cross with every effort. Even on my own."

Rachel caught Gray's eye, clearly worried about her uncle. They both knew how stubborn Vigor could be, and she did not want Vigor pursuing this alone. The danger of that path was evident enough in all their bruises, scrapes, and cuts.

She looked to him to sway her uncle against this course.

To that end, Gray turned to Sanjar. This local man could better express the futility of that path.

"Sanjar, you've already stated that you have no clue as to the identity of this clan leader named Borjigin—the Master of the Blue Wolf—but you know how resourceful and ruthless he can be."

"That is true," the man said solemnly. "His core followers, like my cousin Arslan, will do anything to serve him. To them, Genghis Khan is a god, and the clan leader Borjigin is their pope, a conduit to the glories of the past and a promise of an even brighter future."

Gray heard the echo of that same nationalistic passion in the man, but Sanjar had failed to drink all of that madman's Kool-Aid.

"Borjigin claims to be a direct descendant of the great khan. I remember once, he even wore—"

Sanjar's words abruptly stopped. He sat straighter, his eyes wide. He pressed a palm to his forehead. "I am a fool."

Vigor turned to him. "What is it, Sanjar?"

"I only just remembered it now."

He bowed his head toward Gray as if thanking him—but thanking him for what?

"As proof of his claim," Sanjar said, "Borjigin once displayed a gold wrist cuff, a treasure he said once belonged to Genghis himself. I doubted it at the time, thought it was mere boasting. So I never gave it much thought." He turned to Vigor. "But then I overheard what Father Josip confessed in Kazakhstan yesterday. I knew Josip sold a treasure to finance his search, but I never knew *what* it was until that moment."

Vigor's voice grew sharper. "You're talking about the gold cuff found in Attila's grave, the one with Genghis's name on it. Could it be the same one?" He reached and clasped Sanjar's forearm. "Did the cuff you saw Borjigin wearing have images of a phoenix and demons on it?"

Sanjar cast the monsignor an apologetic look. "I did not get a close look at it. Only from a distance and only that one time. That's why I failed to connect the two until now."

He slipped his arm from Vigor's.

"And I may still be wrong," Sanjar admitted. "Antiquity dealers across Ulan Bator have shelves of items said to be tied to Genghis. And wrist cuffs are nothing unusual. The tradition of falconry is still prized here. Many wear such cuffs as a token of our illustrious past. From something simple, like the leather one I wear." He bared his wrist, exposing a thick piece of scarred leather. "Or something ornate, worn as jewelry."

"But how does this revelation help us?" Gray pressed. "If what Josip sold to finance his dig is the same cuff worn by the Master of the Blue Wolf, how does that bring us closer to identifying the man?"

Sanjar ran fingers through his hair. "Because, though I didn't know what Father Josip had sold until last night, I knew *who* he sold it to."

Rachel stirred. "I asked that very question of Josip."

Vigor looked stricken. "And I dismissed it as unimportant."

"Uncle, you were just trying to protect Josip's feelings. We could not know the importance of such information."

Gray stared hard at Sanjar. "Who bought the priest's treasure, this gold cuff?"

"Workers talk, tell stories, so even this might not be true. But everyone seemed convinced it was sold to someone important in the Mongolian government."

"Who?"

"Our minister of justice. A man named Batukhan."

Gray considered this new information, recognizing the thin nature of this line of conjecture. Maybe it wasn't the same gold cuff. Maybe Batukhan wasn't the one who bought it. And even if both were true, the minister could have sold it to someone else long ago.

All eyes were upon him.

"It's worth checking out," Gray finally admitted. "At least we should pay this guy a visit. But if this minister is Borjigin, he'll likely know all your faces." He nodded to Monk's side of the table. "But he won't know mine. Nor Seichan's."

Excitement drove Vigor to his feet. "If we can recover that last relic—"

Gray held up a hand. "That's a big *if*. And I'm not willing to delay the hunt for the wreckage of the satellite on this long shot alone." He pointed across the table. "Monk, you take Duncan and Jada and head into the mountains with Sanjar. You've got the latest GPS waypoints from Painter that mark off the search grid, right?"

The team at the SMC had further refined the trajectory estimates of the crashing satellite, narrowing the parameters to as small a region as possible.

"It's still a lot of terrain to cover," Monk conceded.

"So we'll get started immediately. In the meantime, I'll investigate this minister with Seichan and leave Kowalski to guard Vigor and Rachel here at the hotel. If nothing pans out, we'll join you in the mountains as soon as possible."

With a nod, Monk stood, ready to go.

Kowalski stretched and mumbled, "Yeah, it's always a good idea to split up. That's worked so well for us in the past."

12:02 P.M.

Seichan paced her room. She had come in here to take a fast nap after Monk and his group headed out to begin their trip into the mountains.

In the next room, Gray worked with Kat back at Sigma command.

They were putting together a profile on the Mongolian minister of justice, including where he worked and lived and the schematics of both places. They also gathered financial records and a list of known associates, business partners, anything that might prove useful before approaching the enemy.

If he was the enemy . . .

No one was ever who they seemed to be. It was something she had learned long ago, thrust as a child into the realities of the harsh world, where everyone had a price, and faces were as much of a façade as the clan leader's wolf mask. She had learned to trust only herself.

Even around Gray, she could not totally let her guard down.

She wasn't afraid of him seeing her true face. Instead, she feared she had *no* face. After so many years, playing so many different roles to survive, she feared nothing was left. If she dropped her guard, would anything be there at all?

Am I just scar tissue and instinct?

A knock at the door drew her from her thoughts. Glad for the interruption, she called out, "Yes?"

The door opened and Rachel poked her head inside. "I didn't know if you'd fallen asleep yet."

"What do you want?"

It came out more brusquely than she intended, revealing some of that scar tissue. She felt no animosity toward Rachel. While they could never be friends, she respected the woman's abilities, her sharp intelligence. But she could not discount the spark of jealousy when she first saw Rachel today. It was mindless, a feral instinct to protect her territory.

"I'm sorry," she tried again. "Come on in."

Rachel took a tentative step inside, as if entering a lion's cage. "I wanted to thank you for agreeing to help my uncle. If he had gone out on his own . . ."

Seichan shrugged. "It was Gray's decision."

"Still . . ."

"And I like your uncle." Seichan was momentarily surprised how true those words were. Upon entering the hotel room earlier, Vigor had touched her arm with affection, knowing full well her dark past. That simple gesture meant a great deal to her. "How long has he been sick?"

Rachel blinked a few times at her question and swallowed.

Seichan realized Rachel hadn't fully accepted that reality. From the pending tears, Rachel must know it down deep, but she hadn't truly faced it.

At least not out loud.

Seichan waved her farther inside and closed the door.

"He won't speak about it," Rachel said stiffly and moved to a chair and sat on the cushion's edge. "I think he believes he's protecting us, sheltering me."

"But this is worse."

Rachel nodded and wiped a tear. "I'm sorry."

"It's okay."

"He's been going downhill for a while. But it's been so gradual, each small decline easy to dismiss and excuse. Then suddenly you truly see him. Like on this trip. And you can no longer deny the truth."

Rachel covered her face with her hands for a long breath, then lowered them again, struggling to keep her composure.

"I don't know why I'm burdening you with this," she said.

Seichan knew but remained silent. Sometimes it was easier to open one's heart to a stranger, to test emotions upon someone who means little to you.

"I . . . I appreciate you helping to watch over him." Rachel reached out and took her fingers. "I don't think I could have done this alone."

Seichan involuntarily stiffened, wanted to yank her hand back, but fought against it. Instead, she whispered, "We'll do it together then."

Rachel squeezed her fingers. "Thank you."

Seichan slipped her hand away, awkward at the intimacy. She knew Rachel wasn't only thanking her for shouldering the burden of her uncle, but also for allowing her to share her fears. Silence fueled anxieties, gave them their true power. Expressing them aloud was a way of releasing that tension, of letting go, if only for a brief time.

"I should get back to my uncle." Rachel stood up. As she headed out, she paused at the door. "Gray said you found your mother. How wonderful that must be for you."

Seichan froze, weighing how to respond. She considered taking Rachel's example, of telling the truth, of attempting to share her own fears and trepidations with another, a near stranger to whom she could test what it would feel like to open up.

But she had been silent all her life.

It was a pattern hard to break—especially now.

"Thank you," Seichan said, hiding behind a lie. "It is truly wonderful."

Rachel smiled at her and left.

As the door closed, Seichan turned to the bright windows, ready to face what lay ahead, glad to put thoughts of warring Triads, her mother, and all of North Korea behind her.

Still, she felt an ache deep in her stomach.

Knowing her silence was wrong.

1:15 P.M. KST
Pyongyang, North Korea

"What is she doing in Mongolia?" Hwan Pak asked.

Ju-long followed the North Korean scientist out of one of the administration buildings of the prison. Ju-long was still at the camp, not as an inmate, but for his own protection.

Or so he had been informed.

Once he'd been freed from the interrogation room in the middle of the night, it had taken hours to settle matters, to discover their captive had escaped out of North Korea, whisked away by American forces, not that this event would ever be officially acknowledged.

It had put Ju-long in a precarious situation. The North Koreans, especially Hwan Pak, needed someone to bully, someone to blame. Ju-long was a convenient target.

Still, from long experience, he never entered hostile territory without a secondary plan in place. Years ago, as a precaution, he had taken to tagging his merchandise, including sales like this. It was only sound business practice to keep track of your inventory.

While the pretty assassin had been in his custody and drugged, Ju-long had planted a micro-GPS tracking device on her. She had been significantly abraded and lacerated following the ambush in the streets of Macau, when he'd slammed his Cadillac into the bike she had been driving. He had the microtracker—a postage-stamp-sized wafer of electronics—sutured beneath one of her wounds. Eventually it would be found or the battery would die, but in the short term, it worked wonders at keeping tabs on his merchandise.

Earlier this morning, he had played this card, informing Pak about this ace up his sleeve. Ju-long suspected it was the only reason he had been treated so well after last night's events. They had even offered him a bed in the officers' quarters, where he caught a couple of hours of fitful rest. Before retiring to bed, he had placed a call to Macau and had the tracker activated. It had taken longer than he would have liked to discover the escaped prisoner's whereabouts, mostly because no one expected to search so far afield.

"I don't know *why* she's in Mongolia," Ju-long admitted as they reached the same building where all this had started, the prison's interrogation center.

Pak had said he left something important here, something to help them capture the woman. Ju-long followed the man through the building to the back. They entered the same room where he and Pak had been trapped last night.

A new prisoner sat strapped to the chair, his head hanging listless, blood pooled beneath him. Cigarette burns blistered his arms. His face was so badly bruised and swollen that it took Ju-long a moment to recognize him.

He rushed forward. "Tomaz!"

It was his second-in-command.

Hearing his name, Tomaz groaned weakly.

Ju-long swung to Pak, who stepped forward with a smile. It seemed the North Korean had been denied his pain last night and took it out on another this morning.

"Why?" Ju-long asked, furious.

As if taking cruel joy in punctuating his point, Pak lit a cigarette, drawing deeply until the tip glowed a fiery red.

"As a lesson," Pak puffed out. "We don't tolerate failure."

"And this loss of the prisoner was my fault?" He pointed to Tomaz. "His fault? How?"

"No, you misunderstand me. We don't blame you for her escape. But we will hold you accountable for her capture. You will continue to track her and accompany an elite Spec Ops team to retrieve her. The Americans rescued her for some reason. My government wants to know why."

"I don't handle lost merchandise," Ju-long said. "In good faith, I delivered her to you. She was in your custody when she escaped. I don't see how this is my responsibility."

"Because you did not screen your merchandise as thoroughly as you should have, Delgado-*ssi*. You delivered what my government considers to be a bomb onto our soil, one that was still armed. If we had known this woman was so important to American forces, we would have handled this differently. So you must make amends for this grievous error and embarrassment to our country."

"And if I refuse?"

Pak removed his pistol, set it to the side of Tomaz's head, and pulled the trigger. The shock as much as the noise made Ju-long jump. Tomaz fell limp within his restraints.

"Like I said, this is a lesson."

Pak reached for his phone and held it out to Ju-long.

"And this is your incentive to succeed."

Stunned, he took the phone and raised it to his ear. A voice came immediately on the line, trembling with fear.

"Ju-long?"

His heart clenched with recognition, and all it implied. "Natalia?"

"Help me. I don't know who these—"

Pak snatched the phone back, keeping his pistol pointed at Ju-long's chest. A wise precaution, as it took all of Ju-long's control not to break the North Korean's neck. But he knew it would do his wife no good.

"We are holding her . . . and I suppose your son, too . . . in a location in Hong Kong. Neither will be harmed as long as you cooperate. At the first sign of insubordination, we will have a doctor remove your son and mail his body to your home. We'll keep your wife alive, of course."

If that happened, Ju-long knew his son's death would be a kindness compared to what they'd do to Natalia.

Pak smiled. "So do we have a deal?"

19

Duncan crossed a span of centuries in a matter of hours.

After he and the others had left Ulan Bator in an older-model Toyota Land Cruiser, they passed through a small mining town to the east, a postapocalyptic landscape of coal pits, heavy machinery, and soot-coated Soviet-era buildings—but then a sharp turn to the north cast them into a valley thick with poplars, elms, and willows.

Farther ahead, a silvery river split the rolling grasslands of the higher steppes, all colored in shades of winter amber. Tiny white yurts—which Sanjar called *gers*—dotted those brittle waves, looking like boats in a storm-swept sea.

As he stared out at the spread of nomadic tent-homes, Duncan imagined the countryside had changed little since the time of Genghis Khan. As they climbed out of the valley, though, he saw evidence of the modern world encroaching upon this ancient way of living. A satellite dish sprouted from a yurt. Next to it, a small Chinese-made motorbike had been secured to an oxcart.

Winding their way slowly higher, they aimed for the mountains rising ahead, the most distant to the north capped with snow. Under them, the road changed from asphalt, to gravel, eventually to dirt. The *gers* grew less frequent, more authentic, with goats in pens and small horses tethered outside. As their SUV trundled past, a few short-framed, sun-wizened folk in sheepskin jackets and fur-flapped hats came out to watch.

At the wheel, Duncan offered them a curt wave, which was returned with genuine enthusiasm. According to Sanjar, hospitality was a highly esteemed virtue among the Mongols.

In the front passenger seat, Monk played copilot and navigator. He had a map unfolded on his lap and a portable GPS in hand. "Looks like you should take the next left turn. That road should take us into the search zone."

The word *zone* was rather generous. The search parameters placed the debris field in a box one hundred miles on each side. Still, that was down from five hundred miles yesterday.

Duncan made the next left turn and headed at a grinding pace into the mountains. The terrain challenged the SUV's four-wheel drive. It was mostly broken rock and patches of grassland, crisscrossed by forests of larches and pines. Rains had washed out parts of the road, requiring a careful traverse.

"I'm not sure this region needs special protection by the government," Duncan said. "I think Nature is doing a pretty good job of it herself."

Sanjar leaned forward from the backseat, which he shared with Jada. "It is why our ancestors chose these mountains for our grave sites. You'll find them throughout this area. With tombs often stacked atop other tombs. And, unfortunately, grave robbing is a real problem. Locals will often search these old sites, then middlemen from the city drive through and purchase anything scavenged from these tombs to resell in China."

He pointed ahead to a rounded peak higher than the others. "That is Burkhan Khaldun, our most sacred mountain. It is rumored to be the birthplace of Genghis, and where most people believe he is buried. Some say he is entombed in a large necropolis under the mountain, believed to hold not only his body and treasures, but also that of his descendants, including his most famous grandson, Kublai Khan."

"That's a mighty big prize for whoever finds it," Duncan said.

"People have hunted for his tomb for centuries. Which has led to much looting and vandalism. To protect the environment and our heritage, the government restricts access here, even by air."

That was one of the reasons their team was driving. But they had another motive, too. Satellite imaging of the region had failed to pick up any trace of the crashed spacecraft, so it was unlikely that a search by helicopter or airplane would have fared any better.

It was even possible the satellite had entirely burned up during reentry. All this might be a wild-goose chase. But they had to make the attempt.

"I should warn you that there is another reason for these restrictions, too," Sanjar said.

Jada turned to him. "What reason?"

"It is said that Genghis himself declared this area sacred. Many locals believe that if his tomb is ever found and opened, the world will end."

Duncan groaned. "Great. If we find his tomb, the world will end. If we don't find his tomb, the world is doomed."

"Damned if we do, damned if we don't," Jada mumbled.

Duncan caught her eye in the rearview mirror, and she offered a small smile.

"Something Director Crowe said before I set off on this trip," she explained. "Seems he was right."

Monk stirred, his nose still in his map. "Never bet against Painter."

2:44 P.M.

An hour later, Jada half drowsed in the backseat when Duncan loudly declared, "End of the road, folks!"

Jada sat straighter, rubbing her eyes, realizing he wasn't speaking metaphorically. The dirt track ended at a cluster of five *gers*. Free-ranging goats ran from their path as the SUV rolled toward the tents. Farther back, a group of horses roamed a large paddock.

After reaching the perimeter of the search zone, Sanjar had recommended this detour off the main road. It wasn't on any map. But he said that the best bet to find the satellite was to question the locals.

They know every movement of twig and shift of breeze up here, he had declared. *If something large crashed in the area, they would know.*

As the Land Cruiser drew to a stop, Sanjar hopped out. "Follow me."

They all clambered free of the vehicle into the chilly day. Jada stretched circulation back into her stiff limbs. Once they were all moving, Sanjar headed straight for the closest *ger*.

"Do you know these people?" Monk asked.

"No, not personally. But this is a fairly established encampment."

Sanjar strode up to the stout wood door and pulled it open without knocking. He had warned them that this was tradition, another hallmark of Mongol hospitality. It would be considered an insult to the family inside if you knocked, as if you doubted their good manners and generous disposition.

So in he strode, as if he owned the place.

They had no choice but to follow him. Jada obeyed his prior instructions, careful not to step on the threshold and to turn right as was traditional as she entered the circular tent.

She found the place surprisingly spacious and warm. The roof was supported by ribs of wood; the walls were framed by lattice. It was all sealed against the winds and cold by thick layers of sheepskin and felt.

Faces greeted them with smiles, as if expecting them. It was a family of four, with two children under five. The husband formally buttoned the collar of his *del* robe and waved them to stools.

Before she knew it, she had a cup of hot tea warming her hands. Apparently an early dinner had been under way, judging from the boiling pots on a central hearth. She smelled curry and steaming mutton. A bowl and plate landed in front of her. The wife encouraged her to eat, smiling broadly, pantomiming with her hands.

"It's boortz soup," Sanjar said. "Very good. And those bits on the plate that look like broken pottery are *aruul* cheese. Very healthy."

Not wanting to be rude, Jada tried a chunk of the cheese and found it to be as hard as pottery, too. She ended up sucking on it like candy, which the locals also seemed to be doing.

When in Rome . . .

Sanjar spoke with their host in a native dialect. It involved much gesturing, some corrections. But the husband began nodding vigorously, pointing northeast.

Jada hoped it was a positive sign.

The talk continued for some time after that. She could only watch and eat. To the side, the children found Monk's prosthesis fascinating. He had one boy on his lap, showing the child how the hand could be detached from his wrist, yet the fingers still wiggled.

Jada found it actually disconcerting.

The children were enthralled.

Finally, Sanjar grabbed his own bowl of soup and tucked in with a spoon. He explained while eating. "Our host, Chuluun, says he heard stories from someone passing through yesterday, coming from the north. The man spoke of a fireball in the sky. It supposedly crashed into a small lake at the snow line of the neighboring mountain and set the water to boiling."

Monk frowned. "If the wreckage is underwater, no wonder it was never picked up by satellite."

"Then how are we going to get to it?" Jada said.

They hadn't thought to bring diving equipment, let alone a wet suit.

"We'll have to cross that bridge when we get to it," Monk said. "Let's find this place, confirm the location, and we'll ship in what we need from there."

Sanjar had an additional precaution. "Be warned. It's a treacherous trail to reach that location. We'll never make it by car or truck. I've asked Chuluun if he would be willing to lend us four of his horses."

Jada balked at that idea. She could ride, just not well.

Still, it's not like I have much choice.

"Did he agree?" Monk asked.

"Yes, and he'll even send one of his cousins to guide us there. With luck, we should be able to reach the lake before the sun sets."

Monk stood up. "Then let's go."

Jada followed his example, bowing her thanks to their hosts. Chuluun led them outside and spoke to one of his children who ran off to a neighboring *ger,* likely to fetch the cousin.

Chuluun pointed past the neighboring sweep of meadows, patched with dense forests, to the next peak, its upper slopes white with snow.

That was clearly their destination. It looked no more than twenty miles away. With their goal so close, trepidation set in. Responsibility settled heavily on Jada's shoulders. The world was looking to her for answers, for a way to avert the coming doomsday.

As if reading her intimidation, Duncan stepped to her side, answering her silent question.

This is how.

By working together.

A commotion drew them to the next *ger.* A young woman, no older than eighteen, came charging out, snapping together the collar of her sheepskin jacket snugly. She had a flag of black hair, loose to her midback. With a leather tie in hand, she magically bound her hair into a fast braid. Once done, she snatched a curved bow from beside the tent and shouldered a quiver of arrows. She also carried a rifle over her other shoulder.

Was this their guide?

She approached them in knee-high Mongol boots that looked well worn. "I am Khaidu," she said in heavily accented English. "You wish to go to the Wolf Fang. I will take you. Good time to go."

She looked to be in as much of a hurry to leave as they were.

An older man appeared at the door, calling over to her.

She harrumphed and stalked away.

Sanjar explained. "A suitor for her hand. Likely an arranged marriage."

No wonder she wants to leave.

They all hurried to catch up as she headed for the paddock.

Monk smiled. "This trip just got a little brighter."

"You're married." Duncan nudged him. "With kids."

He scowled back. "You say that like I'm dead."

Jada sighed.

Maybe I'm better off going alone after all.

3:33 P.M.

Duncan stared up at the Wolf Fang as they set off on horseback across the highland valley toward the snowy peak. The mountain did indeed look like a hooked fang, pointed up at the sky.

With the sun overhead, the day's chill quickly warmed away. It was a pleasant afternoon for a ride, made more so by the rugged landscape they traversed. With a thunder of hooves, they raced across meadows of porcupine grass or skirted dense forests of white-barked birches, fringed with blueberry and blackberry bushes.

Jada clearly did not share his passion for this ride. He noticed how tentative she was with her horse, so he kept by her side.

Monk brought up the rear, while the fiery Khaidu rode ahead with Sanjar. But in the true lead was Heru.

It seemed the falcon had recovered from taking a hard knock yesterday. Set free, the bird soared high into a crisp blue sky, obeying the occasional whistled command from his handler.

Sanjar was plainly showing off for Khaidu, who kept close to his side. And it seemed to be working. She leaned over often to ask a question or point out some feature in the land.

Meanwhile, Jada's attention was not on the skies, but on the ground zipping under her mount's hooves.

Duncan tried to reassure her as they climbed a slippery slope of shale. He patted his stallion's spotted neck. "Just trust your mount! They know what they're doing. These are sturdy Mongol horses, descendants of those that Genghis himself once rode."

"So in other words, they're last year's model." She offered him a crooked smile, trying to put on a brave face.

A few minutes later, they reached a narrow path with a steep drop on one side. He drew abreast of her, putting himself between her and a long fall to the sharp rocks below. Now was not the time to panic. To distract her, he talked shop.

"What do you think really happened when that satellite crashed?" he asked. "About the image it shot?"

She glanced to him, clearly distracted but willing to talk. "Dark energy is the stuff of time and space. When we drew that much energy into the earth's gravity well, the smooth curve of space-time around the planet wrinkled along that path."

"And time skipped a beat," he said. "You also mentioned to Painter that you believed the *Eye of God* might have become entangled at the quantum level with the comet."

"If it absorbed enough dark energy, it's a possibility. I'll know better once we reach the wreck of the satellite."

"Then let's examine the converse."

She glanced at him.

"The cross," he explained. "Let's say it's a piece of the comet that fell to earth when it last appeared. Or maybe it's some asteroid that passed too near the comet at that time, absorbed its energy like Genghis's tissues did, and fell to earth as a meteor."

She nodded. "I hadn't even considered that second option, but you're right. That's a possibility, too."

"Either way, I'm not sure it matters. The bigger mystery is: *how* did the cross grant St. Thomas the ability to predict this doomsday?"

"Hmm. That's a good question."

"So I've stumped you, Dr. Shaw."

"Hardly," she said, clearly spurred by the challenge in his voice. "Three facts to consider. *One,* dark energy is the driving force behind quantum mechanics. They are one and the same. A universal constant."

"You mentioned that before."

"*Two,* some individuals are more sensitive to electromagnetic radiation. Even without magnets."

She looked pointedly at his fingertips.

He was actually familiar with the concept of *electromagnetic hypersensitivity.* Some people got sick if they were exposed too long to power lines or cellular towers, showing symptoms of headache, fatigue, tinnitus, even memory loss. While conversely, some individuals had a positive effect. It was believed that dowsers—those people wandering around with divining rods looking for water, buried metals, or gemstones—were uniquely attuned to the tiny gradient fluctuations in the ground's magnetic field.

"*Three*," she continued, "a common consensus among neuroscientists is that human consciousness lies within the quantum field generated by the vast neural network that is our brain."

"So consciousness is a quantum effect."

She smiled whimsically. "I've always found that last thought reassuring."

"Why?"

"If that's true, then by virtue of quantum mechanics, our consciousness is entangled across all the various multiverses. Perhaps when we die, it's just a collapse of that potential in this timeline and our consciousness shifts into one where we are still living."

From his doubtful expression, she delved deeper. "Take cancer. You have this cell in your body that divides wrong, a small mistake in a process that happens over and over again in a healthy body. If it divides correctly, no cancer. If it makes a mistake, you get cancer. A mere toss of the genetic dice. Heads or tails."

Duncan hid a wince from her. Her words struck too close to home. His hand rose to touch the palm print tattooed on his chest. He pictured his younger brother, wasted to bone in a hospital bed, leaving behind nothing but the ghost of his shit-eating grin. Billy had died of osteogenic sarcoma, losing that toss of the genetic dice.

Jada continued, oblivious to his reaction. "But what if we are all entangled across multiple universes? That opens up a unique possibility. In one universe, cancer may kill you, but because you're entangled, your consciousness shifts into that *other* universe where you *don't* get cancer."

"And you keep living?"

"Or at least your consciousness continues, merging with the other. This can happen over and over again, shifting each time to a timeline where you live . . . until you live your fullest life."

He pictured Billy's face, finding comfort in that possibility.

"But what happens after that?" he asked. "What happens when *all* those potentials collapse down to a single universe and you die there?"

"I don't know. That's the beauty of the universe. There's always a new mystery. Maybe all this is just a test, a grand experiment. Many physicists are now convinced our universe is just a hologram, a three-dimensional construct built upon equations written on the inside of the sphere of this universe."

"But who wrote those equations?"

She shrugged in her saddle. "Call it the hand of God, a higher power, a superintelligence, who knows?"

"I think we're getting off track," he said, returning to the subject of St. Thomas and his vision of doom. "To summarize your three points. The human brain functions quantumly, dark energy is a function of quantum mechanics, and some individuals are extrasensitive to EM fields."

She looked at him to see if he could put it all together.

He was up to the challenge and proved it.

"You think St. Thomas was a *sensitive*. Because of that, he was especially affected by the dark energy given off by the cross, an energy that warped the quantum field in his brain to bring him a vision of this time."

"Or there might be a simpler explanation."

"Like what."

"It was a miracle."

He sighed loudly. "Whether science or a miracle, it still strikes me as damned coincidental that both the *Eye of God* and inner eye of St. Thomas had a vision of the exact same moment in time?"

"And *God doesn't play dice with the world*," she said, quoting Einstein. *Nice.*

"I don't think it was a coincidence," she continued. "Remember, time is just a dimension. It has no inherent flow backward or forward."

"In other words, *the distinction between the past, present and future is only a stubbornly persistent illusion*?" He raised an eyebrow toward her. "See, I can quote Einstein, too."

She grinned, looking five years younger. "Then consider time like a point in space. Both the *Eye of God* and that inner eye of St. Thomas slipped to that same point in time, likely when the comet's corona of dark energy will come closest to Earth. There, like hitting a deep groove in a record, they both became stuck, trapped and playing the same bit of music over and over again."

"Or in this case *vision*, showing the ruin of Earth."

She nodded.

"But what do you think is going to happen then?"

"From what Director Crowe shared concerning Antarctica, I think when that dark energy corona reaches its maximum, it will bend space-time near the earth, just like gravity does normally."

"Because *dark energy and gravity are intimately entwined concepts*," he said, this time quoting her.

"Exactly. Only this time, instead of a *wrinkle* of space-time, it will create a *chute*, down which a rain of meteors will roll, like marbles along a slide."

"That's a cheery thought."

"It's only a theory."

But seeing her expression, Duncan could tell she believed it.

Afterward, she remained silent for too long, as if something was bothering her.

"What is it?" he asked.

"I don't know. Seems like I'm still missing something."

Before they could look deeper, a shout drew their attention forward. They had reached the end of the precarious ledge, and a wide plateau opened before them. Directly ahead rose a sharp mountain peak.

Sanjar thundered back to them, trailed high by his falcon. "We've reached the Wolf Fang!"

"See, the ride here wasn't so bad," Duncan reassured her. "The worst is over. It should be smooth sailing from here."

3:34 P.M.

"We found them," Arslan reported over the phone.

Batukhan sat in his office in the parliament building and waved his secretary out, a young thing in a tight dress and jacket. While her outfit was distinctly of the West, not traditional in the least, he appreciated its form-hugging cut. Some customs of the West would be welcome in the new Mongolia, an empire he planned to create with the treasures of Genghis Khan.

He already envisioned what he would do when that tomb was found. First, he would handpick and smuggle out the most valuable items, treasures that could be melted down or stripped of gems and sold on the open market. Then he would announce his discovery to the world, turning that fame into power. He wanted to be the wealthiest man not only in Mongolia, but in all Asia. He would conquer the world like his ancestor had in the past, creating an empire of wealth and power, with himself at the helm.

But there were a few loose ends to clean up first.

After the storm had blown over in Kazakhstan, a member of Arslan's crew had returned to the Aral Sea to confirm the deaths and salvage the abandoned helicopter—only to find the aircraft gone.

No one knew if the pilot had escaped alone or if anyone else had survived. Batukhan had no fear of repercussions personally—as only Arslan knew his identity. Still, as a precaution, he had planted spies throughout the lower steppes between Ulan Bator and the Khentii Mountains. He wanted all roads into the region watched, in case any survivors attempted to continue their search for Genghis's tomb by heading into those sacred mountains.

Truthfully, he had not expected to catch anything with this net. The spies were placed mostly to guard those mountains—where he still believed Genghis was buried—until such a time that he could study the stolen relics and discern the tomb's location.

It was a shame Father Josip had to die before Batukhan could question him. Genghis abhorred torture. Batukhan considered this to be the khan's biggest fault.

Now came this news.

"What do you wish me to do?" Arslan asked.

"How far ahead of you are they?"

"They have an hour's lead, but so far, they make no effort to hide their passage."

"Then another thirty minutes will make no difference. Gather your most loyal men, those who show the most skill with sword and arrow. Form a full mounted battle group. I will join and lead you."

"Very well, Borjigin."

Desire rang loudly in Arslan's voice.

It sang to Batukhan's own bloodlust. In the past, the clan's practice skirmishes out on the steppes had been with props and stand-ins. The worst injury sustained had been a broken arm when someone fell from a horse. Batukhan found it fitting that his ascendancy to the throne of the new Mongol Empire would require bloodshed.

But more important, he had also always wanted to put an arrow through someone's chest. Now was his chance.

"I should also inform you," Arslan said, "the traitor Sanjar is among them."

Ah, now I understand the fiery hatred in your tone.

Batukhan pictured Arslan's face after the man had returned from Kazakhstan. His scalp had been ripped down to bone, a cheek punctured clean through by a talon. The man clearly wanted revenge for his disfigurement.

And he would get it.

Traitors must be taught a lesson.

His intercom buzzed. "Minister Batukhan, I have the two representatives from the mining consortium here for their four o'clock appointment."

"Hold them there a moment."

He finished with Arslan and considered canceling this meeting, but this could be a very lucrative contract, one that could pay off handsomely and be yet another brick in his road to a new empire.

He buzzed back and said, "Send them in. And bring us tea."

These were Westerners, so they would probably prefer coffee, but he had never acquired a taste for that brew, preferring traditional tea.

It is high time Americans grew accustomed to our traditions.

The door opened and a tall man with storm-blue eyes and a hard face entered. Batukhan felt the twinge of a challenge, sensing a worthy adversary in this one. Behind him came his aide, a handsome Eurasian woman in a prim suit. Normally he felt no threat from the softer sex, but with her, his hackles rose even higher.

Interesting.

He waved them to a seat.

"How may I help you?"

20

Gray knew an enemy when he faced one.

On the far side of the desk, Batukhan put on a friendly face, showing all the common courtesies. He seemed a pleasant enough fellow, fit and hard for someone in his late fifties. But Gray caught peeks of someone else, cracks in his mask: a hungry glint in his eyes, an overlong and dismissive glance down Seichan's form, an unconscious clenching of a fist on his desk.

During their discussion of mineral rights, oil futures, and governmental restrictions, the man was on edge the entire time. Gray caught him glancing at his watch once too often.

Seichan had already planted a wireless bug on the underside of his desk, so they could track any conversations following this meeting. But for that bug to attract the spider, they needed to tweak its web.

Gray shifted in his seat, noting a cabinet of Mongolian artifacts to the left of Batukhan's desk. It held pottery, weapons, and a few small funerary statues. He also noted a pair of carved wooden wolves.

"Excuse me," Gray said, cutting the minister off in midsentence, irking him purposefully. He pointed to the cabinet. "May I take a closer look?"

"Certainly." His adversary puffed out his chest a bit with pride at his collection.

Gray stood and crossed to the glass case. He bent his nose close to the small carvings. "I see wolves all over the city. Lots of places carry the name Blue Wolf."

In the reflection in the glass, he saw a sly tightening of the corner of the man's lips, someone savoring a secret.

Hmm . . .

"What's the significance?" Gray asked, straightening and facing the man.

"It goes back to the creation mythology of our people, where the Mongol tribes are said to be descended from the mating of *Gua maral,* a wild doe, and *Boerte chino,* a blue wolf. Even Genghis Khan took the clan title of Master of the Blue Wolf."

He heard the telltale catch in the other's voice.

Gray had no doubt this was their man, the mysterious Borjigin.

"And why this continuing fascination with wolves?" Seichan asked, clearly noting the same. She stirred and stretched a long leg, baring her ankle.

"They are a good luck symbol here, especially for males." He had to clearly pull his gaze from her leg. "Wolves also represent a lusty overabundant appetite."

"How so?" Seichan asked, crossing her other leg, keeping the guy distracted.

"A wolf kills more than he can eat. According to our stories, God told the wolf that he could eat one out of every thousand sheep. The wolf misheard him. He ate one out of every thousand sheep he *killed.*"

Gray heard a hint of envy in his words, also maybe threat.

Batukhan made a show of checking his watch. "Perhaps we should finish our business, as the day grows late. And I have other matters needing my attention."

I'm sure you do.

Gray quickly concluded their business and made their good-byes. Once out of sight of the office door, he slipped a small earpiece into place.

Seichan mumbled next to him, "Do you think we got him suspicious enough with all that talk of wolves?"

Gray had his answer quickly enough. He heard Batukhan speaking to his secretary, canceling the rest of his day. Then he was on the phone again, his voice taking a harsher edge of command.

"I'm heading out of the city," he said. "While I'm gone, keep the packages under guard at the warehouse at all times. Around the clock."

He gave Seichan a thumbs-up.

Gray had thought they could unsettle the man enough to get him to lead them to the stolen relics, but this was good enough. From Kat's review of the Mongolian minister's holdings, he had only one warehouse in the city.

Back out on the street, Gray hailed a cab. They quickly crossed a city that was an odd mix of ornate Mongol palaces, blockish Soviet-era buildings, and serene Buddhist monasteries. Over it all hung a shadowy pall, courtesy of the city's pollution and smog.

He leaned next to Seichan, slipping his hand into hers, and whispered like a lover in her ear, "Feel like climbing through some sewers?"

She smiled. "You always know how to make a girl feel special."

4:28 P.M.

With the sun low on the horizon, Seichan stood next to Gray as he pried open a manhole cover, exposing the steam tunnels that crisscrossed beneath the world's coldest capital city. A waft of hot air blew up from the city's bowels.

Along with it came faint singing, like a distant children's choir.

It was disconcertingly sweet coming from this steamy netherworld.

"People make their homes down there," Gray said.

Seichan had spent her fair share of time in such hiding places, fleeing the cold, finding company with other children of the street. With the city's high level of unemployment, coupled with its struggle to make the transition from communism to democracy, people fell through the cracks, including lots of homeless children.

Gray headed down first. Their actions were hidden by the shadow of a neighboring apartment complex. It lay only a couple of blocks from their goal. Back in D.C., Kat had pulled blueprints for the warehouse from city records. They discovered this set of steam tunnels led directly under the building and offered access to it via heating ducts.

Seichan descended the ladder, quickly abandoning the bright, cold day for the warm, dark tunnels. With each rung, it got hotter, quickly becoming nearly unbearable. And then there was the overbearing stink of refuse and waste, some of it human.

Gray clicked on a flashlight and dropped to the tunnel floor below.

She joined him, hunched down, coming close to burning herself on a pipe overhead. She switched on her own flashlight and swept its beam down the tunnels that branched in four directions. Down one, she spotted a scurry of motion, a flash of a small, scared face.

Then nothing.

Even the singing had stopped.

She expected the tunnels were regularly raided, the children rounded up and likely sent to detention centers that were little better than the North Korean prison.

No wonder they ran.

"This way," Gray said and headed in the direction of the warehouse.

The path was not straight and required checking their map twice. Finally, Gray waved her low.

"That next ladder should lead up to the main warehouse floor. We'll only have the element of surprise for a short time, and we don't know how many guards we'll find up there."

"Got it."

In other words, move fast.

She adjusted the night-vision goggles atop her head. Gray wore a matching set, looking like he had the disarticulated eyes of an insect.

She waved him forward, having to go on hands and knees from here. As Gray departed, Seichan felt something grab her ankle.

She twisted around, a pistol in her hand, elongated with a silencer.

She found herself facing a small girl of nine or ten, with almond eyes and wide cheekbones, as if looking in a mirror of her own past. The child cowered from the weapon.

Seichan pulled the pistol away, freeing her leg from the girl's fingers.

"What do you want?" she whispered in Vietnamese, knowing it was close to Mongolian.

The girl looked after Gray, or at least in the direction he was headed. She shook her head and tugged the edge of her pant leg as if to pull her back.

It was a warning of danger.

The children living here must have surmised she and Gray were not with the police. Then, tracking the two of them, they must have realized their goal. Clearly the children down here must have had encounters with the warehouse guards—and not pleasant ones. The effort to warn them was likely less about concern for her and Gray than it was for themselves. Whatever transpired, it was likely to have dire repercussions for the street kids down here.

And they were probably right.

Retribution might be exacted upon those living down here after they left. But there was little Seichan could do about that. She couldn't change the harsh and unfair ways of the world. She'd had that beaten into her enough times to know.

I'm sorry, little one. Get as far from here as possible.

She tried to communicate that.

"Đi," she said in Vietnamese. *Go.*

With a final scared flash of her eyes, the child vanished into the darkness, a shadow of her former self.

Gray hissed for her from the foot of the ladder, oblivious to what had transpired. She hurried over to him. He silently climbed the rungs and secured tiny charges to the locked grate up top.

Dropping back down, they both ducked to the side as he hit the detonator.

A fast bang echoed. It was not much louder than a firecracker, but it would surely draw any guards in the warehouse.

Gray rushed up with Seichan behind him. He hit the smoking grate with the palm of his hand, knocking it open. With his other hand, he expertly tossed in two smoke grenades, rolling them in opposite directions. As the bombs blew with a flash of fire and a blast of smoke, Gray and Seichan rolled out onto the warehouse floor.

She already had her night-vision goggles in place. Lying on her back on the concrete floor, she targeted every light she could see through the smoke.

Firing rapidly she took them all out, sinking the warehouse into deeper darkness.

Gray was already moving, running for the office. It was the most likely place the relics would be secured. If they were wrong, they would force one of the guards to talk.

Muffled blasts of suppressed fire marked Gray's progress across the chasm of the warehouse. She stayed on her back, hidden by the smoke, holding their exit. She toggled her scope to infrared, picking out the heat signatures of guards rushing from the far side of the warehouse. She aimed her pistol.

Pop, pop, pop . . .

Bodies crumpled.

Others scattered, seeking cover, firing back blindly.

Seichan knew the smoke cover would only last a few more minutes, then she would be left exposed out here.

Don't take too long, Gray.

4:48 P.M.

Sweeping through the smoke, Gray fired upon anything that flared through his scopes. He took out two men on the floor and another on the open stairs leading to an office that overlooked the warehouse. He climbed two steps at a time, staying low.

A bullet pinged off the stair rail.

He swung toward the source, identified the heat signature, and fired.

The shooter fell.

Clambering to the top landing, he shot out the door lock, not even bothering to pause to check if it was unlocked. This high up, he was clear of the smoke.

Proving the danger, a burst of rounds peppered the front of the office.

Not slowing, he shouldered through the door and rolled low inside. He kept away from the windows and kicked the door closed while still on his back. At the same time, he swept his pistol across the small space. A door at the back led out to more administration spaces and a conference room.

Finding the room empty, he stayed crouched and checked that back door.

Locked.

Good.

He didn't want any surprises from that direction.

The desk was not in direct view of the windows so he stood up, noticing the boxes and cases stacked there. The largest was tied up in a blanket. It was the right size from Vigor's description. A peek through a fold revealed tarnished silver.

Gray pawed through the rest but failed to find the other relics. He tried the desk drawers. In the bottom one, he discovered a wolf mask staring back up at him.

So Borjigin had been here, likely savoring his new treasures.

While bent down, Gray spotted a small army duffel tucked into the knee well of the desk. He unzipped it and found the skull and the leather book inside. Relieved, he tossed the duffel over a shoulder and lifted the box under one arm. It was heavy and awkward, but it left one hand free to hold his pistol.

A quick glance out of the window showed the smoke beginning to clear.

His search had taken too long.

Using a toe, he nudged open the door. He spotted two men running up the steps toward him, both carrying submachine guns with flashlight undermounts. Beyond them, a firefight was under way in the fading smoke as Seichan kept the rest of the warehouse at bay.

Thinking quickly, Gray ripped off his night-vision gear, rushed back to the desk, and opened the bottom drawer. He grabbed the wolf mask and tugged it over his face. He snatched his pistol back off the desktop— just as the door was kicked open.

As he turned, two men burst inside, submachine guns at their shoulders. Their flashlights blinded him, but the sight of the wolf mask startled them. Fear of its mysterious owner made them pause for a fraction of a heartbeat.

Gray used it to place rounds in both of their heads.

As their bodies fell, he leaped past them, stopping only long enough to trade his pistol for one of their weapons. With the mask still over his face, he burst out the door and slid down the stair's railing to the main floor. Rounds ricocheted around him as he landed hard in the thinning pool of smoke.

He crouched low as he fled, coming upon a guard running at him.

The man's eyes widened as the apparition of a wolf's head appeared out of the pall before him. Gray cut him in half, firing at point-blank range.

Only afterward did Gray realize *why* he'd run into the man.

The firefight from a moment ago had gone silent.

The guard had clearly been trying to escape.

He found Seichan where he had left her. She was up on a knee, disheveled but unharmed. She swung toward him, and it took her a visible extra beat not to shoot him.

He tugged off the mask and threw it aside.

She scowled at him. "You truly have to stop wearing disguises, Gray. It's very unhealthy for you."

"Don't worry. I'll make sure you're unarmed next Halloween."

4:52 P.M.

Seichan assisted Gray in getting the blanket-wrapped box and satchel down into the steam tunnels. With the smoke down to a heavy haze, she kept watch, but it appeared any surviving guards had fled.

Searching around, she noted the warehouse was stacked with boxes of dry goods, electronics, car parts, even baby formula. It seemed Batukhan had his fingers into many different pies, including hoarding foodstuffs in a city where many starved.

She followed Gray below, back into the stink and the heat.

He managed the box, crawling ahead, while she shouldered the duffel.

Reaching a side tunnel, she spotted a familiar face shining back at her. Seichan paused, reached to her own head, and tossed over the night-vision goggles. They would be invaluable to a little girl trying to survive in this dark netherworld. But it wasn't only this one child.

Beyond the little one's shoulder stirred more shadows, likely representing hundreds of other kids.

Seichan pointed back to the ladder, to the wealth lying unguarded above.

"*Đ! Hãy! Nó là an toàn!*" she called to them all. *Go! Take! It is safe!*

With nothing more she could do, Seichan headed after Gray.

She might not be able to change the world, but she could at least make this small part of it momentarily a little better.

21

Jada and the others climbed out of the darkness and into the light.

With the sun less than an hour from going down, the group had set a hard pace up the forested flank of the mountain. The upper peak blazed with the day's last light, reflecting off snow and ice. The woods below—a mix of birch and pine—lay in deep shadows as night filled the lowlands.

Wolves howled out of that rising darkness, accompanied by yipping echoes, welcoming the coming sunset. It seemed the Wolf Fang had not earned its name from its shape alone, but also from what haunted its slopes.

Beyond the forest stretched the highland meadow they had crossed earlier. It seemed impossibly far below.

Hard to believe we gained this much elevation.

Jada thought she spotted movement down there, along the edge of a patch of dark woods, but as she strained to see what it was, it vanished.

Shadows playing tricks . . .

Duncan still had his ear cocked to the chorus of the neighboring woods. "The wolves. Will they attack people?"

"Not unless provoked," Sanjar said. "And seldom when faced by numbers such as ours. But it is the start of winter, and they are beginning to grow hungry."

Duncan plainly did not like that answer. "Then let's keep going before we lose any more light."

"Why?" Sanjar pointed ahead. "We're already here."

Jada swung in her saddle to return her attention forward, to this last island of daylight in the sea of night. They had reached a wide plateau, a giant's step in the side of the mountain. The snow line began another thirty or forty yards upslope, but she saw no lake.

"Where is it?" Duncan asked.

"Around that tumble of boulders to the west," Sanjar explained and trotted his horse in that direction, dragging them all with him.

They circled past the old rockslide. It was a narrow squeeze between the pile of boulders and the edge of a steep cliff. Jada eyed the precarious stacking. It looked like an avalanche that had frozen in place, but more likely it had been there for centuries.

Clearing the rockfall, they saw the plateau spread even wider on the far side. It dropped off to sheer cliffs to the left and rose into a snowy slope to the right. Filling most of the remainder of the space was a two-acre lake, a midnight blue to match the darkening skies, reflecting the few clouds. Its shoreline ran right up to the edge of the ice, suggesting the lake was fed by snowmelt, likely swelling in the spring to pour over that ledge into a glistening waterfall.

Monk drew alongside her. "If something crashed here, it sure doesn't look like it now."

He was right. It looked pristine, untouched.

Khaidu had ridden ahead to the lake's edge. She slid smoothly out of her saddle and walked her overheated horse to the water. Her mount dipped its nose as if to slake its thirst, but then tossed its head back and trotted back several steps. Khaidu steadied the mare with a firm hand on the lead, keeping it from retreating straight over the cliff.

With a furrowed brow, Sanjar hopped down and handed Khaidu the reins of his own horse. He crossed to the shore and dipped his hand in the lake. He turned and gave them a wide-eyed look.

"It's warm . . ."

Jada remembered the story from the eyewitness, the one who saw a fireball crash here. He had said it set the lake to boiling. It certainly wasn't now, but Jada pictured the overheated metal slowly cooling in its depths. The lake must not have had time to fully cool back down yet.

"It's in there," Duncan said, clearly coming to the same conclusion.

"But how can we be sure?" Jada asked.

Monk jumped off his horse and helped her down. "Looks like someone's going to have to dive in there and take a look."

5:12 P.M.

Duncan stood in his boxers at the edge of the lake. He shivered in the icy breeze sweeping down from the mountaintop. Having grown up mostly in the southern half of the United States, he was not a fan of cold weather.

His family had moved almost yearly, across a swath of states: Georgia, North Carolina, Mississippi, Florida. Regularly switching jobs, his father shed his skin like a snake, mostly leaving his two sons to fend for themselves. It was why Duncan and his younger brother had grown so close. After Billy died, with their mother already long out of the picture, Duncan and his father had found themselves with nothing to hold their tiny family together. Unfettered, they spun coldly out of each other's orbit. Estranged for years now, he didn't even know where his father lived.

"Can you hurry up?" Duncan asked, not wanting to dwell on that past.

Jada knelt by an open laptop. "I just need an extra moment to finish setting up the feed."

Besides his boxers, Duncan also wore a headband equipped with a waterproof camera, radio, and LED light. A trailing length of antenna wire attached to a float would wirelessly transmit video back to the laptop.

"Can you hear me?" she asked.

He adjusted the radio earpiece. "Loud and clear."

Jada knew more about the satellite than anyone. She would follow his progress topside and communicate to him in an effort to guide his salvage operation.

"Then we're all set here," Jada said.

Monk stood beside Duncan. "Don't do anything stupid."

"I think it's too late for that."

Duncan waded into the shallows, finding the water warm, welcomingly so. He leaped outward into a shallow dive. After the cold wind above, the water felt downright balmy. In the past, he had done some diving in Belize, where the sea was like bathwater. This was even warmer.

He set off, swimming with long strokes across the surface, kicking hard. With a lake this large, it could take hours to explore fully, going grid by grid. Duncan decided to narrow his search by playing a kid's game of hot and cold.

Or in this case, *warm and warmer.*

If the crashed satellite was down there, the waters closest to it were likely to be the hottest. So as he swam, he turned away whenever the water grew cooler and explored the warmest patches by diving deep, sweeping his light along the lake's rocky bottom. He spotted some plump trout, someone's lost boot, and lots of sweeping moss.

Reaching a particularly hot spot in the lake, he took a big breath and dove, kicking his legs high to drive him deep. After he had gone down three meters, with his ears complaining of the water pressure, he spotted a flash below, something reflecting his light.

"Turn more left," Jada directed him in his ear, excitement in her voice.

Following her order, he twisted and kicked himself farther in that direction. The beam lit the waters around him and speared deep to the bottom.

And there it was, resting in a crater of blasted river rock, surrounded by a halo of slag metal and charred debris.

The *Eye of God.*

It was in utter ruin.

5:34 P.M.

Jada felt like crying.

"There's nothing left," she mumbled to herself and to the others.

Even with the poor reception, which only grew worse the deeper Duncan dove, she could tell there would be nothing to salvage here. The original satellite had been the size of a hot dog vendor's cart, a beautiful synthesis of theory, engineering, and design.

She stared at the shaky image on her laptop screen.

All that was left was a scorched heap of wreckage the size of a mini-fridge. After the blazing heat of reentry, followed by the blast impact and water damage, all that remained was charred junk. She picked out a few details: a burned horizon sensor, a piece of the solar array melted into the outer casing, a shattered magnetometer. Any hope of recovering significant electronics or data was nil.

She had to admit that to herself—and to Duncan.

Needing air, he had resurfaced. He exploded from the lake, sluicing water from the hard planes of his body, his hair plastered to his head.

But he already knew the truth.

His face was a mask of defeat.

She imagined her own looked no better.

After coming so far, surviving so much . . .

She shook her head. Worst of all, the wreckage held no hope for answers, no solutions to the catastrophe looming on the horizon.

Duncan pointed his thumb down. "It's resting about fifteen feet under me. I'm going to see if I can at least haul it up. I may have to do it piecemeal."

She recognized that the guy needed to do something to keep busy, anything to stanch the sense of defeat.

"I'd better let Sigma command know," Monk said, removing his satellite phone and stepping away to keep his grim conversation private.

Sanjar and Khaidu hung near the cliff's edge, sensing their disappointment.

On the screen, Jada watched Duncan dive below again, kicking deep, reaching the satellite quickly. He tentatively reached his hands toward the wreckage, perhaps fearing it was still hot. As his fingers touched the outer casing, the image on the screen blacked out.

Lifting her head, Jada checked the lake. The antenna float bobbed like normal on the surface. She should still be getting feed from below.

"Duncan?" she radioed. "If you can hear me, I've lost the connection."

After another thirty seconds of silence, with the chop of the lake from his dive smoothing out, she grew concerned.

She stood up, half turning and calling to Monk.

"Something's wrong."

5:38 P.M.

As soon as Duncan's fingers touched the wreckage, he felt a familiar tingle in his fingertips, that sense of something pushing back, even through the pressure at this depth. The warm water went cold as he recognized that oily, black *feel* to the energy signature, the same field as he had sensed emanating from the relics.

If there was any question about the ancient cross being connected physically to the comet in some way, that was gone now. They clearly must share the same strange energy.

Dark energy . . .

He wanted to burst back up and tell Jada, but not without first recovering the remains of the satellite. He grabbed hold and tried to yank it up, but it wouldn't budge. It seemed to be stuck to the rock beneath. He pictured its metal shell, still molten from the heat of reentry, cooling and fusing to the blasted rock.

Frustrated, he passed his hands over the surface, noting a gradient to the energy field. It pushed stronger near one end than the other. Probing with his fingertips, he found a crack in the surface, the edge of a steel plate, curled and bent from the force of the impact.

Maybe I could crack it open.

He tried using his fingers, but he couldn't get good leverage. Recognizing the futility and running out of air, he pushed off the bottom of the lake and shot back up.

As he surfaced, taking in a big gulp of air, he saw Monk splashing into the water, fully clothed, a panic to his actions.

"What are you doing?" he called to shore, treading water.

Jada stood behind Monk. She lowered the hands that were at her throat. "We thought you were in trouble! We suddenly lost the feed and you were down there for so long—"

"I'm fine." He swam for shore. "Just need some tools!"

Reaching the others, he began to rise out of the water, but the first frigid breeze drove him back into the warmth.

"Pass me that small crowbar," he said. "I'm going to attempt to crack through that hard shell and search inside."

Jada passed the length of steel to Monk, still knee-deep in water, who handed it to him.

"Why?" she said. "Nothing significant could have survived."

"I'm feeling an electromagnetic signature off the wreckage. A strong one."

Her brow furrowed, her expression doubtful. "That's impossible."

"My fingertips don't lie. And I'm pretty sure I recognize the unique quality of this energy field."

He looked hard at her, lifting an eyebrow.

"Like the relics?" Her eyes widened. "The skull and the book . . . ?"

"Same damned signatures."

She took a step forward, looking ready to join him in the water. "Can you get the wreckage to shore?"

"Not all of it. The majority of its shell is melted into the rock. But I think I can break it open and gut out whatever is inside."

"Do it," she said.

He saluted her with the crowbar and dove back down.

5:42 P.M.

With the sun below the horizon but the skies still glowing to the west, Jada crouched by her laptop. For some reason, the feed had resumed after Duncan had surfaced. She again watched him descend toward the wreckage.

"Duncan, can you hear me?" she radioed, testing their connection.

He gave her a thumbs-up.

As he went deeper, the image on the screen grew sketchier, with pixel loss and cutouts.

Could it be the presence of the wreckage?

Urging caution, she told him, "I think the energy field off the wreck might be interfering with the feed."

Monk shivered next to her in his wet clothes. "Tell him not to touch it. His ungrounded body might have acted like a conduit before and temporarily fritzed his gear."

He was right.

"Duncan, keep back and let me see what you see. Show me where you feel the energy is the strongest, where you want to use the crowbar. We don't want to damage anything that might prove vital later."

Hearing her, he shifted to one end of the crashed satellite and pointed the tip of his crowbar.

"That end looks to be the main electronics module," she radioed. "And you're pointing to the thermal radiation door. If you can get it open, I can try to guide you from up here."

Duncan dug the end of the crowbar into a gap in the door.

"Careful . . ."

Using the steel bar as a fulcrum, he got his feet on the rock to either side of the wreckage—and heaved down. The thermal hatch resisted his efforts for a few seconds, then ripped away, flipping through the water.

It took Duncan a moment to swim into proper position to point his camera into the innards of the crashed satellite.

Again Jada felt a sink of defeat. All the electronics were charred, most of it melted into mounds of plastic, silicon, and fiber optics.

On the screen, Duncan moved one hand over the inside, still careful not to touch anything. His finger pointed at one square object, a block of steel with visible hinges on one side. Protected by the bulk of the craft, it looked relatively intact. From the urgency of Duncan's motion, it was clear he was trying to communicate.

"That must be where the energy is the strongest," Monk said, looking over her shoulder and apparently reading her mind.

"Duncan, that's the gyroscopic housing. If you can, try to keep it intact. It should only have a single fat cable running to it. If you can twist that off, it should lift free as a whole."

He gave her another thumbs-up and leaned the crowbar against the side of the satellite. He would need both hands free to pull this off.

Again, as his fingers touched the housing, the feed went dead.

Jada shared a look with Monk—then they both stared toward the lake. If Jada's theories of dark energy were correct, Duncan could be about to wrestle with the very fires that fueled the universe.

Be careful . . .

5:44 P.M.

Running out of air, Duncan fought both the satellite and his own revulsion. *Stubborn piece of—*

He wasn't prone to swearing, but between the melted slag that trapped the gyroscopic casing and the repellent touch to its energy field, it felt as if he were trying to unscrew a pickle jar while his fingers squirmed in electrified gel.

As soon as he had popped the hatch in the back of the satellite, the EM field had surged stronger, pushing like steam out of its scorched interior, rising from this steel heart. When he touched the housing, his fingertips felt as if they were pushing through mud. The energy field resisted him, or at least it registered as such to his magnetic sixth sense.

When his fingers finally made contact, it was indescribable. During his training as an electrical engineer, he'd brushed against a live wire or two. But this was no bite of copper. It was more like touching an electric eel. The energy had a distinct *living* feel to it.

It set his hairs on end.

Finally, with a savage twist of its half-melted cabling, he broke the housing free. He lifted it out, as if removing its power core, and kicked off for the surface, anxious to be rid of it.

Reaching the surface and fresh air, Duncan breathed heavily and kicked for shore. He carried the gyroscopic housing in one large hand, as if palming a basketball, a ball he was more than happy to pass off to a fellow player.

5:47 P.M.

Jada waited for Duncan at the edge of the lake, carrying a blanket in one hand. As he reached the shore, he shoved up, dripping wet, his tattoos bright against his chilled flesh, covering his shoulders and down his arms.

Clicking off his headlamp, he fell into shadows. Focused on the laptop, she hadn't realized it had already gotten so dark. Night did not waste any time falling at these elevations.

Duncan waded out of the lake. She traded her warm blanket for his steel prize.

"Why is this so important?" he asked, his teeth chattering a bit.

"I'll show you."

She moved to her makeshift desk, basically a flat boulder holding her laptop, and placed the housing down.

She explained, "If this is giving off the same electromagnetic signature as the relics, it must be tied to the comet's corona of dark energy. If I could get this to a lab and properly study it, I might be able to get some real answers."

She glanced significantly at Monk.

"On it," he said. "Kat will get us back to the States by the fastest route possible."

Jada spoke as he raised his satellite phone. "We're already this far east. It'll be quicker to reach my labs at the Space and Missile Systems Center in L.A. I've got everything I need to do a complete analysis there, plus access to engineers and techs familiar with my research. If there are any solutions to our problems, my best chance to discover them is there."

Monk frowned, as if disagreeing with her, but that was not the source of his consternation. It was his satellite phone. "Can't get any signal now . . ."

"Might be the energy given off by this thing," she realized aloud. She pointed him toward the neighboring rock pile. "Try farther away. I'll have to figure out a way to insulate this if we're going to travel by air."

Duncan crouched next to her, back in his clothes after drying off. "I ran a hand over the remainder of the wreckage after yanking that thing out. I couldn't feel any trace of the energy left in the satellite. It all seemed to be emanating from that housing."

"Makes sense."

"Why?"

"This is the heart of the *Eye of God,* its very namesake."

She shifted her attention back to the housing. She searched along its sides until she found a small latch and undid it. With great care, she broke the case open, the two halves hinging apart to reveal what it protected.

Duncan leaned closer.

Seated inside, reflecting the glow from the laptop, was a sphere of quartz about the size of a softball. Though you couldn't tell from looking at it, the sphere was virtually flawless.

"This is the gyroscope that spun in the heart of the satellite," she explained. "We used it to measure the curve of space-time around the earth during our experiment."

"But why is it charged with energy now?"

"I'll need to do a hundred tests to confirm it, but I have an idea. As it was spinning out there, measuring the curve of space-time, it monitored the *wrinkle* that formed. I believe the stream of dark energy that created that wrinkle flowed along that crease and poured into the eye of the only observer."

"The crystal sphere."

"Turning it into a true Eye of God."

"But how does that help us?"

"If we could—"

A strange whistling noise drew both their eyes—followed by a *thunk* of something striking flesh.

Khaidu sank to her knees, her back to the cliff.

Her hands found her belly.

And the steel arrowhead sticking out from there.

22

Vigor paced around the conference table in the hotel suite, his heart thudding tiredly, his eyes sore. For the past hour, he had been balanced between jubilation at Gray's recovery of the relics and frustration at his inability to solve the eight-hundred-year-old mystery.

The focus of everyone's attention rested in the middle of the table: the macabre sailing ship made of bones and tanned skin.

Vigor had spent a solid hour with magnifying loupe in hand, poring over the relic that they had recovered from the Aral Sea. He could still smell the salt off the tarnished silver box sitting next to it, a bitter reminder of the loss of his friend.

Josip had sacrificed everything to uncover this artifact.

And to what end?

After an hour of study, Vigor had come to no firm conclusions, except a deep respect for the artisan. The rib bones of the hull had been boiled and bleached to make them easier to carve. Intricate waves had been scrimshawed into them, along with a plethora of fish, birds, even seals, the latter of which frolicked in the sea and leaped high out of the water. The sails were rigged with twisted human hair and ribbed in the traditional manner of Chinese junks of the Song dynasty, an era that matched Genghis Khan's time period.

But what did it all mean? Where was this bread crumb supposed to lead them? To solve that, he had a laptop open on the table, where he had been researching anything and everything that might offer a clue. But he had hit dead end after dead end.

Everyone around the table looked to him to solve this mystery, but maybe it was beyond him. He wished for the hundredth time that Josip were here. He needed his friend's mad genius now more than ever.

Gray spoke up, seated beside Seichan. "Since it's a Chinese ship, it must be pointing to somewhere in China."

"Not necessarily. Genghis was a great admirer of the science and technology of the nations he conquered. He absorbed and incorporated whatever he found, from Chinese gunpowder to the compass and the abacus. He certainly would appreciate such boat-making skills."

"Still, it is a *fishing* boat," Gray continued, pointing out the details of the scrimshaw. "Doesn't that suggest the hiding place is somewhere along the Pacific Ocean or the Yellow Sea?"

"I agree. And that coast does mark the easternmost reach of Genghis's empire."

Josip's earlier words played again in his head.

I believe Genghis had instructed his son to turn the entire known world into his grave, to spread his spiritual reach from one end of the Mongol Empire to the other.

His friend was right. Genghis's head had been ceremonially buried in Hungary, representing the westernmost reach of his *son's* empire. Then the bone ship was hidden in the Aral Sea, marking the western edge of *Genghis's* conquered territory. So it only made sense that the next spot would be along that *eastern* edge.

There was only one problem, and Vigor voiced it aloud.

"If we're right, that's nearly a thousand miles of coastline. Where do we even begin to look?"

Rachel stirred on the opposite side of the table. "Maybe we need a break. To clear our heads and start again fresh."

"We don't have the time to spare," Vigor snapped back at her, but he regretted his tone immediately and patted her shoulder in apology as he passed by her while continuing to pace.

Something kept nagging at him and wouldn't let him sit still. Then contrarily, the stitch in his abdomen flared with every step, making it harder to think.

Maybe Rachel is right. A little rest might be a good idea.

Gray frowned and tried talking it out. "They buried his head in Hungary, and I guess, because the ship is made of rib bones and vertebrae, it represents his chest."

"Or more likely his heart," Vigor corrected, that nagging feeling flaring as he said that.

"Head and heart," Kowalski mumbled. He was sprawled on a neighboring couch, an arm over his eyes. "Guess that means all we have to do is find this guy's feet."

Vigor shrugged. That actually sounded right.

Head, heart, feet.

Josip's words repeated yet again.

. . . spread his spiritual reach from one end of the Mongol Empire to the other.

Vigor stopped so fast he had to steady himself on the back of an empty chair. He suddenly realized that it wasn't Josip's *words* that he should have been paying attention to.

"You smart, crazy man," he mumbled. "I've been such a fool."

No wonder Josip had looked so full of regret as he died. It wasn't because his friend couldn't finish this journey—though that was likely part of it—but because he had recognized the lack of understanding in Vigor's eyes.

"He figured it out!" Vigor exclaimed.

"What do you mean?" Rachel asked. "Are you talking about Father Josip?"

Vigor placed his palm over his heart, feeling it beat. Josip had taken that same hand and put it on his own bloody chest—not just to say goodbye, but to communicate in the only way he could at the end, to offer a clue before he died.

"Head, *heart,* feet," he repeated, patting his own chest as he emphasized the middle note of the chorus. "We've been looking at this *all* wrong."

Rachel shifted straighter. "How?"

"The head marked the boundary of his son's empire, representing the *future* of the Mongol Empire after his death. The heart embodied the empire of Genghis's own lifetime, of his *present*. What we need to be looking for next is a marker where Genghis first put his feet down and made a name for himself, symbolizing his *past*."

"Head, heart, feet," Gray said. "Future, present, past."

Vigor nodded, slipping back to his chair in front of the open laptop. "Genghis didn't instruct his son to spread his body from one end of the empire to the other *geographically*. He wanted it spread from his empire's past to its future."

Rachel reached over and squeezed his arm. "Brilliant."

"Don't use that word yet." He tapped at the computer. "Right now I'm feeling rather stupid since Josip all but told me this before he passed away. And we still have to use this knowledge to discover where to continue the search."

"You'll figure it out."

Vigor brought up a map that showed the spread of the Mongol Empire during Genghis Khan's reign.

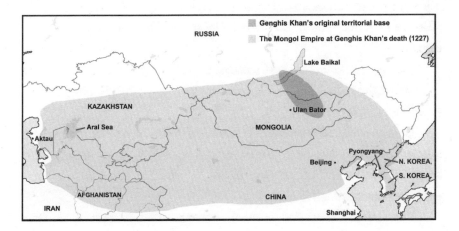

"Here you can see the extent of Genghis's empire," he said, "stretching from the Pacific to the Caspian Sea, but the darker oval in northern Mongolia represents the great khan's original territorial base."

He tapped that spot on the screen.

Gray looked over his shoulder. "That's still a lot of territory to cover."

"And it's landlocked," Vigor added. "As you can see, his original territory did not extend to the Yellow Sea or the Pacific."

Everyone stared over at the ship, while Vigor kept his nose close to his laptop's screen, bringing up more research files on the region.

"Then why leave a *ship* as a clue?" Gray asked, nodding to the relic.

Vigor zoomed in on the map and pointed to a large body of water at the northern edge of that darker oval.

"Because of that," he explained. "Lake Baikal."

"What's the significance of that particular lake?" Gray squinted at the crescent-shaped body of water. "Do you know anything about it?"

"Only what I'm looking at now," Vigor said and summarized aloud. "It's the *oldest* and *deepest* lake in all the world. It holds over twenty percent of the world's fresh water. To the ancient Mongol people, it was a major source of fishing . . . and still is today."

Gray stared closer at the scrimshaw. "Then I understand the *fish* carved on the boat's hull, but what about these frolicking—?"

"*Seals?*" Vigor asked, with a triumphant smile. He sat back and let them see the picture on his laptop, of a dark sleek shape sitting atop a rock. "Let me introduce you to the nerpa. The world's only breed of *freshwater* seal and—"

"Let me guess," Gray said, cutting him off this time. "They're only found in Lake Baikal."

Vigor's smile widened.

Gray's satellite phone rang. He glanced at the screen. "It's Sigma command." As he headed away to take the call in private, he pointed back to Vigor. "Learn everything you can about that lake."

"Already on it."

Vigor paused long enough to look heavenward.

Thank you, my friend.

6:18 P.M.

"And you've heard nothing from Monk?" Painter asked over the phone.

"Not a word." Gray had moved over to his bedroom for privacy, but also not to disturb Vigor's investigation into Lake Baikal.

"I've tried reaching him for the past ten minutes," Painter said. "But there's been no answer. The last update from his team was when they were heading out on horseback into the mountains."

"It's getting dark out here," Gray offered. "Maybe he's busy setting up camp."

Painter sighed in tired exasperation. "I had hoped to consult with Dr. Shaw before they settled in for the night."

"Why?"

"I just received a final assessment from the crew over at the SMC in L.A. I told you about the physicist who was monitoring the gravitational anomalies that Jada had first noted in the comet's path."

"Right. You mentioned something about them changing."

"Growing, in fact. They've confirmed that these tiny changes are incrementally increasing in direct proportion to the comet's approach toward Earth."

"You're not concerned about the comet hitting us, are you?"

It wasn't beyond the realm of possibility. In 1994, the Shoemaker-Levy comet collided into Jupiter, and sometime next year, a comet was likely to smash into Mars.

"No," Painter said, "the comet will pass close in astronomical terms, but it has no chance of striking us. But that doesn't mean we're out of danger. We've been tracking NEOs for the past day."

"NEOs?"

"Near-Earth objects. We've been monitoring any asteroids that might pose a risk of shifting earthward due to the stirring of the comet's energy through our neighborhood. Its trajectory has already shaken up the cosmic game of billiards out there, resulting in the recent meteor showers."

"Along with what happened in Antarctica."

"Exactly. That was why I wanted to consult with Dr. Shaw. She understands these gravitational anomalies better than anyone. The consensus out of the SMS is that the increasing flux could trigger the mother of all meteor showers as the comet reaches its closest pass by the earth. And NASA is monitoring some very large rocks beginning to respond to those deviations."

Gray heard the dread in the director's voice. "Is there anything we can do to stop this?"

"The physicist at the SMC believes that Dr. Shaw would be the best one to answer that question. He's growing to believe that there must be a reason these anomalies are growing larger in direct relation to its approach toward Earth. He thinks there must be something *here* on the planet that the comet's energy is responding to."

"Jada seemed convinced of the same," Gray conceded, suddenly glad he had agreed to search for the stolen relics. "She thinks this ancient cross we're hunting for might have been sculpted out of a piece of that comet when it last appeared. That it could still retain some of its dark energy, and that the two—the cross and the comet—are entangled at the quantum level."

"Then we need to find that artifact."

Gray offered a bit of hopeful news. "We may have a solid lead for once. Vigor is working on it right now. But as a precaution, can you get Kat started on arranging transportation for our group?"

"Where?"

"To Russia, to a lake near its southern border called Baikal. It's about three hundred miles north of where we are now."

"We'll get on it. That short a distance should only take a few hours of travel, but you'd better still hurry. We only have forty-eight hours remaining until the events pictured by the satellite come true."

Recognizing the urgency, Gray finished his call and returned to the others. As he stepped into the room, he found everyone gathered around Vigor and his laptop.

"What?" he asked.

Vigor swung to him. "The more I look into Lake Baikal, the more I'm convinced that's the correct spot."

Rachel smiled over, flushed with excitement. "We may even know *where* on Lake Baikal to look."

"Where?" He shifted to join them.

"First of all, legends say that Genghis Khan's mother was born on an island in that lake."

"Another island," Gray said.

That at least sounded right. The first relics were found hidden near *Boszorkánysziget,* the Island of the Witches, in Hungary, and the second beneath an island in the old Aral Sea.

"It's called Olkhon Island," Vigor explained. "Local rumors say that Genghis Khan's mother came from there. Which may very well be true."

Gray considered this. *If we're looking for where Genghis Khan came from, you can't get much earlier than his mother's womb.*

Vigor continued, "Other legends claim Genghis is indeed buried on that island. Not that we should put a whole lot of weight on that rumor. The same can be said of countless other places across Asia. But this particular story mentions that Genghis was buried with a *great weapon,* one that could destroy the world."

Rachel nodded. "This legend may be the source of the commonly held belief by the Mongols that if Genghis's tomb is ever found and opened, the world will end."

Gray felt their excitement seeping into his blood.

"From a real-world practicality," Vigor said, "archaeologists have found many Mongol weapons and relics on that island. There are even historical records of Mongol warriors of Genghis's time coming to that island. Though what they were doing there, no one knew."

"The island is also the center for a unique form of shamanism," Rachel said. "The local Buryat tribesmen, who descend from ancient Mongols, practice a religion that merges Buddhism with naturalistic animism. They believe a great conqueror of the universe resides on the island. Shamans still protect many of that ruler's sacred sites and believe trampling them would invite ruin upon the world."

Similar to the Genghis story . . .

"Last," Vigor said, "some travelers to that island report *fits of energy*. Those are their words."

Rachel nodded. "Maybe these folks are attuned or hypersensitive to whatever energy is emanating from St. Thomas's cross. Some even claim to have visited a cave that opened a door to other worlds."

Gray remembered Dr. Shaw's statements about dark energy and the multiverse. He also wondered if these *other worlds* could be related to the visions of St. Thomas.

"Then let's check it out," Gray said. "I already have Sigma command arranging our transportation."

"But what about Monk and the others?" Rachel asked.

Gray frowned. He doubted they could spare the time to wait for them. His group could easily lose half a day while Monk and the others returned from the mountains.

"We'll move on," Gray decided. "Update them when we can."

Still, worry nagged him.

What *was* going on with Monk's team?

23

Batukhan sat astride his horse, both mount and rider in traditional leather armor. He also wore a Mongol war helmet that was crowned with steel and draped with a mask made of real wolfskin to hide his features.

It was important to remain anonymous, especially now when murder was involved.

The bowstring near his ear still vibrated, singing a chorus of blood. He had watched his arrow pierce the back of the woman standing at the cliff's edge above, enjoyed seeing her sink to her knees in shock. He smiled under his mask, his heart thundering in his ears.

"Excellent shot," Arslan said, sitting on a stallion to the side. Similarly attired in leather, the man also wore a helmet, but the ruin of his face was bared for all to see. Sutures knit his skin together, laddering across his cheek and brow. It was a sight both gruesome and fearsome.

"I saved Sanjar for you," Batukhan said.

With only two targets visible along the cliff's edge, he had chosen the woman. He found the kill as exciting as sex, the penetration equally satisfying. He had left Sanjar standing, knowing Arslan would want that prize for himself later, to exact personal vengeance.

Now the cliff's edge was empty, their quarry likely terrified and hiding. But there was nowhere to go.

Batukhan cast his gaze across the dozen mounted men spread across the dark forested slope that led toward the shelf of rock above. They were the best and most loyal of the clan.

Twelve warriors against three men and two women.

Make that one woman now.

Ideally he would spare the last woman's life, so his men could celebrate afterward as the forces of Genghis Khan had in the past. It was their birthright and heritage, and a well-deserved reward after spilling blood this night.

They could always kill her afterward.

With a kick of his heels, he trotted his horse before his men, sitting tall in his saddle, knowing he cast a striking figure. He spoke a few words to each, showing respect, getting it back, like any good commander, readying his troops.

Once he'd made his rounds, he returned to Arslan's side and pointed up toward the plateau. Surrounded by ice-encrusted walls, his quarry was trapped. The only way down was through this forest—that, or leaping headlong off the cliff to the rocks below. There was nowhere else to go. It would be a slaughterhouse, with their victims' screams echoing across the mountaintops, possibly to Genghis Khan's own tomb, where he imagined the great man relishing the blood and horror to come.

Batukhan yelled, knowing there was no further need for stealth.

The first arrow had already flown, drawing blood.

"*Yavyaa!*" he bellowed, a traditional call to battle. "*Yavyaa!*"

6:33 P.M.

As the thunder of hooves echoed up from below, Duncan crouched with Sanjar. They hid in a cluster of boulders near the snow line.

Jada remained on the far side of the steep rockslide, near the shore of the lake, out of immediate harm's way. He had left her with his pistol and quickly showed her how to use it. She guarded over the injured Khaidu, who still lived but needed medical care soon.

After securing them, Duncan and Sanjar had joined Monk on the opposite side of the rock pile. They quickly prepared for battle, recognizing what was coming, knowing that the arrow had been sent to terrorize them, to draw first blood—a common tactic of Mongol fighters, or so Sanjar had informed them.

Sanjar urged Duncan to hurry once he heard the yell echo up from below, a battle cry to charge. "Tie it to Heru's jess. That piece of leather hanging from his claw."

Duncan held the damp headband in his hand and passed the dangling cord through it and secured it with a fast knot. Sanjar kept the hooded falcon close to his body, while Duncan finished.

"Let him go," Duncan said.

Sanjar tugged the hood off and sent the bird flying from his wrist. Duncan ducked from the initial heavy flaps and studied the laptop at his knees, the screen's glow lowered to its dimmest setting. On the monitor, he watched the falcon take flight, gaining a bird's-eye view of the forest below, the feed coming from the tiny video camera attached to the headband. It worked even better in the air than underwater.

The falcon soared high above the treetops, circling wide. Duncan did his best to count the number of horses pounding up from below. He saw at least a dozen, in full battle regalia, like their riders. He spotted no others on the ground.

He radioed Monk, who had left the shelter of their boulders to prepare a welcome for the coming forces.

"No more than a baker's dozen," Duncan reported in. "All on horseback. I spotted bows, swords, and several assault rifles."

Seems there was a limit when it came to sticking to the old ways.

"Understood," Monk transmitted back. "Just about ready here."

Duncan craned over the boulder to see his partner down on one knee by the rockslide. He had planted charges at its leading edge and was quickly securing them with wireless detonators. The explosives had been intended to destroy the wreck of the satellite in case it couldn't be moved or salvaged. They couldn't risk the Chinese or Russians getting hold of the classified advanced technology.

But matters had changed.

The plan was to hide here and lure the attackers toward the far side where Jada and Khaidu sheltered. Once within the narrow pass between the cliff and rockfall, they would blow the charges, trying to take out as many of the enemy as possible, while simultaneously closing off immediate access to the lake, keeping Jada and Khaidu safe for as long as possible.

Enemies left on this side would be for Duncan, Monk, and Sanjar to handle. Not great odds, but it wasn't like they had a whole lot of options.

And it would take perfect timing.

Hence, their eye in the sky.

As Monk came hightailing it back toward them, Duncan kept watch on the screen. He spotted a figure leading the charge through the woods wearing what looked like a wolf's head. It seemed like the Master of the Blue Wolves had decided to get his hands dirty this time.

"Here they come," Duncan hissed.

The three of them ducked lower, not wanting to be seen as the mounted battle group pounded up the last stretch and onto the plateau.

On the screen, they watched the horses and riders mill about momentarily. One had a rifle at his shoulder; others had bows drawn. Upon finding no one, their leader pointed toward the rockslide and the lake beyond.

"*Uragshaa!*" he ordered, which likely meant *go forward*.

Drawing a curved sword from a scabbard, the Master of the Blue Wolves led his men toward the hidden lake.

Good, Duncan thought.

Maybe if they could kill their leader, the rest would break ranks and flee.

Monk had his thumb on the detonator, his eyes fixed to the screen, waiting until the first few men had trotted their horses into the gap between the rocks and the cliff's edge.

Now, Duncan silently urged.

As if Monk had heard him, he pressed the detonator.

Nothing happened.

Or at least not much.

A blasting cap popped like a firecracker, flashing out in the darkness. The noise startled the nearest horse, sending it cantering forward, bumping and jostling the next in line. Other horses shied entirely away from the rockslide, keeping on this side.

"Cap must have fallen out of the first charge," Monk mumbled. "That's what I get for working in the damned dark."

He twisted the detonator to the next charge and pressed the button again. This time a major explosion rocked the plateau. Ice and snow showered over them, shaken loose from the cliffs above.

Monk didn't stop. In quick fashion, he blew the third and fourth charges in fast succession. Duncan's ears rang from the explosions. Horses reared and whinnied. Riders fell out of their saddles.

"Go!" Monk ordered.

The three of them burst out of hiding, guns blazing.

As he fired, Duncan prayed Jada and Khaidu were safe.

6:39 P.M.

From the far side of the lake, Jada had watched three riders barrel into view around the rocks, the first wearing a formidable wolf mask. She had heard the retort, like a gunshot, a second before.

Then a series of loud fiery blasts had her cringing, covering her face with an arm. Boulders shattered amid a roll of smoke and rock dust. More came tumbling down to close off the lake from the other side. Smaller rocks continued to rain down, splashing into the water or bouncing over the granite shelf.

Jada held her breath, hoping the explosions had dispatched the three riders—but out of the smoke, a trio of horses thundered back into view, the beasts in full panic.

Taking advantage, Jada fired. She squeezed her trigger over and over again. She had never shot a pistol before, or any gun for that matter. So she opted for quantity versus quality.

Still, she hit one horse. It reared, the rider clinging tightly. That was a mistake. As the panicked mount turned on a back hoof, it leaped blindly, tumbling over the cliff's edge, taking the rider, too. The man's scream of terror as he fell pierced through the echoing blasts of her pistol.

Jada kept firing wildly.

Another lucky round caught a second man in the throat as he tried to bring his bow up. He fell out of his saddle, landing facedown in the water, splashing feebly.

The third rider, unharmed, came charging for her, a curved sword raised high. His wolf mask hid his face, making him appear a merciless force of nature.

Jada squeezed the trigger again, but it wouldn't budge—the slide had locked back. Duncan had told her what that meant.

Out of bullets.

The rider swooped down upon her, his sword flashing in the moon-light.

Then an arrow zipped past her head, its feathers brushing her ear.

It flew and struck the horse in the neck.

The beast crashed, throwing the rider over its head toward Jada. She fled back on her knees, staring to the side as Khaidu struggled to notch another arrow to her bowstring, but the single pull had sapped the last of the young girl's strength. Her fingers shook, pained sweat shining on her face, then the bow tumbled from her weak grasp.

The rider climbed to his feet. Behind him, his horse had fallen to its side, the stone slick with arterial blood, struck through the carotid.

Khaidu stared toward the beast with pity; plainly the horse hadn't been her intended target. That was the man who picked up his sword and stalked toward them now. He had a palm resting on a holstered pistol.

Khaidu turned to her, the girl's expression no less pitying. "Run . . ."

Jada took the advice, leaped to her feet, and dove into the neighboring lake.

Cruel laughter followed her down into the depths.

They both knew the truth.

Where could she go?

6:43 P.M.

Duncan ran through the chaos of horseflesh and men. When the rock pile blew, a rough head count put eight men still on this side, armed with swords and rifles. Duncan, along with Monk and Sanjar, had dispatched half in the opening moments of their ambush.

Now it was a more dangerous game.

One of the combatants had dismounted near the edge of the plateau and set up a sniper's position, flat to the ground, taking potshots at them, keeping them on the defensive. Out in the open with little shelter, it would have been like shooting fish in a barrel—but with the mix of eight horses and the sniper's fellow men out here, Duncan and the others had some cover.

If only that damned cover would quit moving or trying to kill you . . .

Monk slammed into Duncan, dancing from a round that ricocheted at his toes. They both ducked behind a horse for a few breaths. Duncan kept hold of its lead to keep their stallion between them and the sniper.

Sanjar joined them a second later.

Monk gasped. "Dunk, go take out that shooter."

No argument here . . . that guy was really pissing him off.

"Sanjar and I'll try to make it over the wall," Monk said and pointed.

Moments ago, they had all heard the shooting on the far side, coming from the lake. A few of the enemy must have gotten through before the charges blew. Someone had to go help Jada and Khaidu.

Duncan understood. For that to happen, the sniper had to be taken out. Monk and Sanjar would never be able to scale that rubble and drop to the other side with the shooter having a clear shot at them.

"I got it," Duncan said, "but I'm going to have to borrow this horse . . . and this guy's helmet."

He tugged the headgear from a body underfoot and slammed it atop his head. Once ready, he hooked a boot in a stirrup, got a nod from Monk, then leaped into the saddle. Grabbing the reins, he turned his steed toward the sniper and goaded the beast into a full gallop, the leather armor flapping with each strike of a hoof.

Duncan kept low to his mount's neck, hoping the shooter only saw the horse and the helmet. The sniper fired—but he aimed into the chaos behind Duncan, likely spotting Monk and Sanjar striking for the wall.

Duncan centered on the muzzle flashes in the dark. He urged the horse faster in that direction, knowing he'd only have this one chance. Hooves pounded the granite; sweat flecked the stallion's neck.

Then he reached the sniper.

He caught a look on the man's face as the sniper realized the ruse too late. The horse tried to shy away at the last moment, but Duncan held him firm by the reins. Eight hundred pounds of Mongolian stallion trampled over the sniper's sprawled body, stamping bone and crushing flesh.

Then Duncan was past him, flying down the slope toward the forest's edge. It took several yards to slow and wheel the horse around and head back up. He slid from the saddle—not to check on the sniper, who was clearly dead, but to go for the man's gun, to turn the tables on the enemy.

Unfortunately, an unlucky hoof had struck the rifle, breaking the stock and bending the barrel. He lifted the weapon up anyway and looked through the night-vision scope for his friends.

A bobbling search across the killing floor revealed Monk standing over a limp form near the wall, his pistol smoking. Sanjar slit another man's throat, dropping his body. Then a horse moved, and Duncan spotted a final attacker, coming from behind them.

"MONK!" he yelled.

The whinnying and clattering of horses drowned his warning.

He could only watch as the man ran his sword through Sanjar's back, while raising a rifle with his other hand toward Monk. Duncan recognized the attacker, even with his face in ruins.

Arslan.

Duncan was already on his feet running, knowing he'd be too late.

6:47 P.M.

Victory must be savored.

Batukhan stood over the young Mongol woman, no more than a girl, her stomach soaked in blood. She had some skill with the bow, dropping his horse with a single arrow. He now had his sword pressed between her small breasts, pushing enough to pierce cloth and skin and touch its point against the bone of her sternum.

Pain etched her features, but she still stared stonily at him.

Tough, hardy stock.

A flicker of pride for his people flared through him, not that he wouldn't relish this kill. He remembered his favorite quote from Genghis Khan: *It is not sufficient that I succeed—all others must fail.*

He would grant this one a quick death.

The American would be slower.

He held his pistol in his other hand, pointed back toward the lake. He would stalk the defenseless woman at his leisure. There was nowhere for her to run, no weapon with which to defend herself.

Smiling behind his mask, he leaned forward, ready to plunge his sword to sweet satisfaction—then a loud splash erupted behind him.

A glance behind revealed a dark figure rising out of the lake, a Nubian goddess, rushing toward him, swinging a deadly length of steel in one hand toward his head.

6:49 P.M.

Jada swung the crowbar at the beast's head, ready to cleave it clean off the man's shoulders.

After diving into the lake, she remembered Duncan abandoning the tool below after cracking open the satellite's bulk. She might not be good with a pistol—but from years of racing triathlons, she had stamina and knew how to swim. While crossing the lake, she had taken a few breaths by surfacing on her back, bringing just her lips and nose up enough to get air. Once in position, she dove deep and used the moonlight through the clear water to find and seize her weapon.

Then she swam back, gliding through the shallows, trusting the reflection of starlight on the midnight lake to hide her.

She waited until the man was turned fully away to leap forth and attack. But alerted at the last minute, he shifted enough to take the blow to the crown of his helmet.

Steel rang against steel.

The shock ran up her arm to her shoulder, numbing her fingers enough to lose the crowbar. It clanked against the stone.

Still, the resounding strike dented the man's helmet and staggered him back. He dropped the sword, weaving on his legs—but unfortunately he kept hold of his pistol.

He raised it to point at her chest and swept his damaged helmet off with his other hand. He cursed at her in his native language, his face as much a mask as before, but now one of fury and vengeance.

He shoved the pistol at her—then winced in shock, dropping heavily and suddenly to his knees.

Behind him, Khaidu held his abandoned sword, bloody after slashing him across the back of the legs, where he had little armor, hamstringing and crippling him.

Jada kicked out with a waterlogged boot and struck the gun from his stunned fingers. The weapon flew and splashed into the water. She then retrieved the crowbar from the ground, and with an uppercut swing, cracked him in the chin. His head flew back—then the rest of his body followed.

He crashed to the stone, knocked cold, bleeding from his legs.

Jada hurried to Khaidu's side and helped her to her feet.

They weren't out of danger yet.

6:52 P.M.

As panic slowed time, Duncan ran through molasses. He staggered toward the tableau of Sanjar pierced clean through, of Monk turning too slowly, of Arslan aiming his rifle at his partner's back.

Underfoot, the rock ran slick with the blood of men and horses. Large panicked bodies shoved around him.

Never make it.

Sanjar slumped to his knees—then glanced up and yelled, "HERU!"

Arslan flinched from that name, dropping back and ducking, raising his rifle in defense against the falcon.

A bird that wasn't there.

Monk used the shock to swing around, shifting his pistol up.

But Sanjar surged to his feet, dagger in hand, and slammed it to the hilt into Arslan's neck. The falconer had used the phantom of his own bird to terrorize his cousin, knowing Arslan would react with panic and alarm after his recent mauling.

Sanjar dragged Arslan down, twisting his knife as he did so. Blood poured thickly from Arslan's mouth and nose, drowning him in racking quakes. As the man finally slumped, his eyes glassy, Sanjar shoved him away—then fell onto his back himself.

A shining dark pool quickly formed under him.

Duncan finally reached the others and slid on his knees to Sanjar's side. But someone beat him first to the young man.

A shadow of wings swept down, and a sleek form alighted onto his master's chest. The falcon fluttered and rustled, bending his head down, brushing Sanjar's chin and cheek.

Hands rose to cradle the bird. Fingers freed the leather jesses from around Heru's talons. He then brought the falcon to his lips, whispering something into the ruff of feathers.

Done saying good-bye, Sanjar let his head drop back, a shadow of a smile on his lips as he gazed up at the open starry sky. For several breaths, he lay there—then his hands went slack, slipping away, freeing his companion.

Heru leaped forth and sailed high into that same sky.

Sanjar stared upward, but he was already gone, too.

7:10 P.M.

Fear stoked them all to move faster.

Jada had changed into dry clothes and hurriedly secured her pack to her horse, patting the gyroscopic casing inside. So much blood had been lost to secure this piece of the wreckage. She refused to let those sacrifices be in vain.

Poor Sanjar . . .

As she worked, she kept her back to the carnage on the plateau, trying to hold it together. But she could not escape the stink of death. She kept her eyes averted from a body trampled into the rock nearby.

A few minutes ago, she had been relieved to see Duncan climbing over the rockslide, coming to their rescue. He was late, but at least he made up for it by helping her get Khaidu to the other side.

Monk still worked on the girl's injury. He was plainly a skilled medic, performing a swift triage using the team's emergency field kit. He had snapped off the steel arrowhead and did the same with the feathered end, leaving the wooden shaft pierced through her abdomen. He plainly feared to extract it. Instead, he had applied a tight belly wrap, working around the broken ends.

"Get ready to move!" Monk called out as he finished patching Khaidu for the ride back to civilization.

Duncan nodded and stepped to his own horse. He had been keeping tabs on the lower forests with a night-vision scope. Other combatants might still be out in the dark woods or reinforcements could be on their way.

But that wasn't the only fear driving them to hurry.

Howling rose like steam out of the dark woods, growing steadily louder, drawn by the scent of blood and meat.

They dared delay no longer.

Monk passed Khaidu up to Duncan, who cradled the girl across his lap as he sat astride his horse, prepared to carry her down the mountain.

Jada climbed into her saddle. She had her own reason for a hasty flight off this mountain. She rested a palm on the gyroscope's case. If this hard-won prize held any answers, she needed to get it to safety, back to the States, back to her lab.

And soon.

She would let nothing stop her.

Monk waved an arm and pointed below. "Go!"

7:25 P.M.

Batukhan woke to the sound of thunder.

Dazed, he rolled to a seated position beside the steam-shrouded lake. He frowned at the clear skies.

Not thunder . . .

As his head cleared, he recognized the fading echo of trampling hooves, heading away.

"Wait," he croaked out, fearing his men were abandoning him.

The single utterance flared pain in his jaw. His fingers rose and found his chin split and bloody. Memory filled in slowly.

Fucking bitch . . .

He rolled to his feet—or tried to. Agony lanced up his legs. He stared down at his blood-soaked limbs, confused by their lack of cooperation. His hands probed the fire behind his knees, discovering deep slashes, the tendons shredded, turning his legs into floundering appendages that refused to hold his weight.

No . . .

He needed to signal his men.

Fools must have left me for dead.

He hauled his leaden bulk toward his fallen horse, dragging his legs, pulling with his arms, each movement a new torment. Sweat pebbled his forehead. Blood dripped from his chin. It felt as if the lower half of his body had been set on fire.

Just need to reach my phone.

Then all would be fine. He could rest until rescue came.

Lifting his head, he spotted a shift of shadows on the far side of the lake, over the top of the rockslide.

Someone was still here.

He raised his arm—then heard the low growls.

More dark shapes flowed over the wall, leaping down.

Wolves.

Primitive terror keened through him.

Not like this.

He rolled toward the edge of the cliff. He would rather die a quick death by his own hand than be torn apart alive. His useless legs still fought his efforts, leaving a trail of blood. Shadows closed toward him, moving so silently for such large beasts.

But at last, he reached the edge and flung himself over, relieved in some small way. Then something snatched his trailing arm, latching hard onto his wrist, piercing flesh and locking onto bone.

Another jaw snatched the leather armor of his forearm, halting his fall. Strong legs and powerful hearts dragged him from the abyss.

More teeth found him, rolling him to his back.

He stared up as the pack leader loomed over his face, lips curled back into a growl, showing sharp teeth, long fangs.

This was no mask.

Here was the true face of Genghis Khan.

Merciless, relentless, indomitable.

Without warning, they tore into him.

24

On the other side of the globe, Painter stood in his office, staring into space. Literally. The large wall-mounted LCD screen on his back wall displayed a large dark rock against a backdrop of stars. Its surface was pitted and blasted, an old battle-scarred warrior.

"NASA's Infrared Telescope Facility in Hawaii sent us this picture a few minutes ago," Kat said behind him. "The asteroid's official designation is 99942, but it goes by the name Apophis. It's already been pegged as a troublemaker in the past, being the first asteroid to ever have been raised from a *one* on the Torino impact hazard scale to a *two.*"

"The Torino scale?"

"It's a way of categorizing the risk of a near-Earth object striking the planet. A *zero* meaning no chance. A *ten* meaning a certain hit."

"And Apophis was the first asteroid to get upgraded to a two?"

"For a brief time, it climbed all the way to number *four,* when it was believed it had a one in sixty-two chance of hitting the earth. Its risk factor got lowered after that—that is, until today."

"What are you hearing out of the SMC in Los Angeles?"

"They've been tracking the gravitational anomalies around the comet, extrapolating how it will affect local space, monitoring the largest of the NEOs in the path of the comet. Like Apophis. Right now, if the gravitational effects of the energy field around the comet remain static and don't change from here, Apophis is still a solid *five,* pushing it into the threatening level. But if the size of the anomaly continues to grow in proportion to the comet's approach, the asteroid's ranking will steadily climb up the Torino scale."

Painter stared over at her. "How high will it reach?"

"The SMC believes it will reach into the red zone. An eight, nine, or ten."

"And what's the difference between those upper levels?"

"The difference from a survivable impact—a number eight—and a planet destroyer."

"A number ten."

Kat nodded and pointed to the screen. "Apophis is over three hundred meters wide and lists a mass of forty megatons. That is what is headed toward the East Coast if our extrapolations hold true."

"But I thought it was determined that a *cluster* of meteors was destined to strike the Eastern Seaboard, not one big one."

"The SMC believes Apophis exploded in the upper atmosphere and the pieces peppered across the seaboard. What the satellite showed us was the aftermath of that barrage."

Painter read the lines in Kat's face like a map. Something else still had her worried. "What haven't you told me?"

"The timeline." Kat turned fully back to him. "The image from the satellite was dated about forty-six hours from now. But like I said, that's the *aftermath*. From burn rates, smoke density, and the level of destruction, an engineer at the SMC calculated that the actual time of impact was likely six to eight hours earlier."

"So we have even *less* time to stop what's coming."

"And not just six to eight hours less."

"What do you mean?"

"I told you that even if we could somehow switch off that comet, Apophis would still be a category five. The field has already shifted its trajectory that much."

"And turning it off won't reverse that new path."

"No."

Kat looked scared, as she struck for the heart of the matter. "I spoke to the physicist monitoring the gravitational anomalies. He has calculated how long it will take for Apophis to reach a Torino level of eight, passing into that set of rankings that guarantee a planetary collision. Once that point is reached, the asteroid will hit Earth. Whether we turn off that field or not after that, it won't matter."

"When will it reach that point of no return?"

Kat eyed him. "In sixteen hours from now."

Painter leaned back on his desk, finding it harder to breathe.

Sixteen hours . . .

He allowed himself a moment of horror—then forced it back. He had a job to do. He faced Kat, determined and resolute.

"We need Dr. Shaw."

8:14 P.M. ULAT
Khentii Mountains, Mongolia

After forty-five minutes of hard riding, Jada gladly slipped out of her saddle to the ground. Monk had called for a short rest stop in a small copse of trees in the dark meadow below the mountain. He helped get Khaidu down from Duncan's lap, where he had cradled her during the ride down the mountain's flank.

"Ten minutes," Monk said, moving off with Khaidu to a fallen log to check on her bandages.

Duncan headed back to Jada.

She knelt down and lowered her pack from her shoulders. Flipping back a flap and unzipping it, she reached inside and pulled out the gyroscopic housing unit. Undoing the latch, she opened it. She wanted to make sure her prize was intact after the rough handling of late.

The perfect sphere lay cradled in its housing, catching every bit of starlight, reflecting the sky along its curved surface.

It *appeared* to be fine, but looks could be deceiving.

She glanced over to Duncan. He must have read her concerned expression and moved his hand over the open casing.

"Don't worry," he said. "The energy signature is still strong."

She sighed in relief.

Monk called over to her, straightening up, apparently satisfied with Khaidu's wrap. He held up his satellite phone. "I've finally got a signal. I'm going to try to reach Sigma command."

Jada stood up. "I want to speak to Director Crowe, too!"

She needed to set things in motion over at her labs, so everything would be ready as soon as they touched down in California. Even a couple of hours could be the difference between success and failure.

Monk waved her over, but after she took a few steps in his direction, he held up his palm. "Stop! Signal just dropped off."

Jada glanced down at her hands. She was still holding the gyroscopic case. "Must be the energy field given off by the Eye," she yelled back to him.

"Leave it there then," Monk ordered.

Jada turned, searching around. She didn't want to abandon it on the ground.

Duncan came over, wearing a hangdog look, and held out his hands. "I'll take it and move off. I suspect the farther away I am, the stronger your reception will be."

"You're probably right."

Duncan took the prize with his sensitive fingers as if accepting the gift of a cobra. "Find out what's going on," he urged her and strode off toward the open meadow.

Free of the burden, Jada hurried to Monk's side. He already had Painter on the line and spoke in a terse fashion, quickly and efficiently describing all that had happened. Monk had clearly done such a debriefing many times, turning bloodshed and mayhem into clean, precise facts.

Once done, Monk handed over the phone. "Seems someone is anxious to speak to you."

Jada raised it to her ear. "Director Crowe?"

"Monk told me you recovered the gyroscopic core of the satellite and that it's charged with a strange power source."

"I believe it's the same energy as the comet, but I can't say for certain without reaching my lab at the SMC."

"Monk informed me of your plans. I agree with you. Kat will expedite a fast evacuation and get you to California as quickly as possible. But I wanted to inform you about what has transpired during your absence."

He then told her everything, none of it good news.

"Sixteen hours?" she said with dismay as he finished. "It'll take us at least two hours just to get back to Ulan Bator."

"I'll tell Monk to head straight for the airport. There will be a jet fueled and waiting for you and that Eye."

"Could someone also transmit the latest data from the SMC to my laptop? I want to review everything en route to California. Also I'll need a secure channel to speak to personnel out there while I'm flying."

"It'll be done."

She detailed her final preparations and passed the phone back to Monk, leaving him to work out the logistics.

Jada stepped away, hugging her arms around herself, chilled and scared. She stared up at the blaze of the comet across the night sky.

Sixteen hours.

It was a frightening, impossible time frame.

Still, a deeper terror settled through her, born of a nagging sense that she was still missing something important.

8:44 P.M.

Duncan stood at the edge of the meadow, trying to hold the gyroscopic case between his palms, keeping his fingertips away from its surface. Still, that dark electric field pushed against him, pulsing very faintly with tiny waves, giving off that feeling of holding something with a beating heart.

He shivered—but not from the cold.

Gooseflesh covered his arms.

C'mon already, guys, he thought as he listened to Monk murmuring over the satellite phone, likely making plans to leave here.

He was more than happy about that.

And getting rid of this thing.

Trying to shake the nervous feeling, he paced along the edge of the forest. His toe hit a root poking out of the soil. He stumbled a few steps, feeling stupid—until something worse happened.

The bottom half of the gyroscopic case dropped open between his palms. Jada must have forgotten to latch it after closing it. He never thought to even check.

In slow motion, he watched that perfect sphere of crystal—holding the very fire of the universe—drop away. It fell out of the bottom of the open housing, hit the ground, and rolled into the porcupine grass of the meadow.

He chased after it.

If he lost this . . .

He snatched it one-handed, like nabbing a basketball before it bounced out of bounds. The shock of grasping the sphere bare-handed, without its case as insulation, felled him to his knees. The black energy lit his hand on fire, his fingers spastically clenched around the curved surface. He could no longer tell where the energy field ended and the crystal began. It felt as if his fingers were melting into the sphere.

Still kneeling, he lifted the object high, ready to cast it away in revulsion—but a spark of fire inside drew his eye. He stared through the sphere, seeing a view of the Wolf Fang through its crystal heart.

Only now the tip of the peak lay shattered, frosted with a haze of rock dust. The lower forest burned, smoking heavily, the edges still raging with flames.

He lowered the crystal—and all was fine.

Back up again—and the world burned.

That can't be good.

Standing up, he swiveled around. No matter where he cast the Eye, it opened a view into a fiery apocalypse. Facing north, he spotted the likely source of this destruction: a distant smoking crater.

"What are you doing?" Jada asked, startling him as she came up behind him.

Too shocked to speak, he shifted the sphere toward her. He pointed through it toward the Wolf Fang.

Frowning at his apparent foolishness, she leaned against his shoulder and peered through the crystal. She stood that way for several breaths, surely as shocked as he was.

"So?" she finally said, turning toward his face.

"Don't you see it?"

"See what?"

"The mountain, the forest. Everything destroyed."

She looked at him as if he were crazy. "I don't see anything like that."

What?

Duncan turned his attention back to the fiery destruction glowing in the heart of the crystal Eye, an apocalypse apparently only he could see.

Here was confirmation that it wasn't *only* the Eastern Seaboard at risk. The entire globe was threatened.

Realizing this, he came to only one firm conclusion.

We're screwed.

FOURTH

FIRE & ICE

25

Gray huddled with the others on the frozen ferry pier. It was pitch dark under a clear sky, the night bitterly cold compared to Ulan Bator some three hundred miles due south. They were all bundled in parkas with fur-fringed hoods, looking not much different from the sole native who was also crossing to Olkhon Island at this very late hour.

Normally a boat transported visitors to the island from this tiny lakeside village of Sakhyurta, crossing the mile-wide strait that separated Olkhon from the mainland. But in winter, the only way to reach the island oddly enough was by way of public bus.

Not that there was any man-made bridge.

The bus would cross directly over the ice. Apparently, in winter the deep strait froze solid enough to support vehicles. He could even make out the road along the black ice, frosted with a dusting of dry, windblown snow.

Rachel eyed their transportation with a skeptical eye. No one else looked any more confident. Even Kowalski was in a darker sulk than usual.

"I've had my fill of trips over ice," the big man grumbled. "Ever hear of Grendels."

Gray ignored him. After the team's gear was stored, he waved everyone aboard. With the passengers all seated, the driver closed the door, ground the gears, and set off over the ice. It was early enough in the season to make Gray polish his fogged window and watch their passage with a twinge of trepidation. By January, the massive lake would entirely freeze over, allowing hardy individuals to trek from one side of the lake to the other.

It hadn't reached that level of freeze yet. Farther out on the lake, he saw waves churning across its surface. He had read up enough on this body of water to know it was a geological marvel, the *deepest* lake on the planet, formed by filling a gap between tectonic plates that were slowly pulling apart, enlarging the lake until eventually it would be a new ocean.

That is, if the planet were still intact by then.

He checked his watch. He had spoken to Painter after landing in the nearby city of Irkutsk in Russia, where he learned of the new tighter timetable. Even now, they were down to roughly twelve hours. He imagined Monk was lifting off right about now from Ulan Bator, on his way to California with Dr. Shaw and Duncan.

The plan was for her to study the gyroscopic Eye out there, while he attempted to retrieve the cross here. Maybe she could figure out some solution on her own, but Gray was their fail-safe—assuming he could find that saintly artifact.

But both he and Dr. Shaw were severely constricted by time.

She had a seven- to eight-hour flight back to the States, eating up precious hours. He was in no better position.

He couldn't begin his search until sunrise. It was too dark to accomplish anything now, and worse, they had no concrete lead on where to even start. The island was forty-four miles long and thirteen wide. The eastern half was all steep mountains, fringed in fir forests, rising to its highest peak, Mount Zhima. The rest of the terrain was a mix of sand dunes, grassy steppes, and patches of larch woods.

Even in daylight, it would be a nearly impossible search, especially without some road map of where to begin looking.

So Vigor had suggested another route.

Why not ask somebody?

The island was populated by about fifteen hundred natives, an aboriginal people called the Buryats, descendants of the original Mongol settlers.

Vigor had used his connections at the Vatican to arrange a rare meeting with their highest shamans. If anyone knew the island's secrets, it would be the head of this enigmatic religion, an odd mix of Buddhism and natural worship. The Buryats were notoriously leery of foreigners. Women were forbidden from their most sacred places. It was a singular event even to meet a shaman.

But how to get the man to talk?

Gray had suggested laying all their cards on the table—or in this case, showing the shaman all their relics from Genghis Khan. Gray hoped they might act as a key to unlock any secrets his people had about the island.

In the end, the shaman had agreed to meet them, but only at dawn, requiring that they be cleansed in the day's first light before he would speak to them. No amount of persuading moved the man from this position.

So many hours lost . . .

But he had to admit, they were all bone-tired, needing sleep and recuperation. Plus, by the time they met with the shaman, Monk and the others would be touching down in California. That left both sides about four hours to work out some solution to the threat looming over their heads.

No pressure there.

Kowalski flinched as the bus hit a ridge of ice and bounced. He had a white-knuckled grip on the seat in front of him, his nose glued to the window. "What's that out there, near that hole in the ice?"

Gray searched and watched a dark mass slip off the ice and into the water, disturbed by the passage of the bus. "Calm down. It's just a seal."

"That's what they want you to believe," Kowalski mumbled. "You can't trust what's hiding under the ice."

Clearly the man had some prior trauma concerning ice and open water. Gray let it go. They were almost to land anyway.

Vigor crossed and slipped into Gray's seat. He pointed out the window toward the dark bulk of the island. "Look at that cape of rock jutting out. It's called *Khorin-Irgi* in the native tongue, meaning *Horse Head*. See how it resembles a horse drinking water from the lake. There are stories of Mongol warriors from Genghis Khan's time who came here and paid homage at this spot, believing the shape of the cape was some universal acknowledgment of their leader."

Gray stared harder at the shadowy bulk. He knew the Mongols held their horses in high esteem. He remembered Vigor describing the tunnel that led to the boat of bones in the Aral Sea. It had been shaped like a horse, too.

"Do you think that's a good place to start looking?" Gray asked.

"I doubt it," Vigor said. "The cape is one of the busier spots on the island. Someone would surely have found something hidden there by now. My point was that many locations on this island are tied to the mythos of Genghis Khan. We just have to find out which one holds his tomb."

"And maybe that shaman can tell us."

"If he knows something, then it's only professional courtesy that he shares it with another man of the cloth." Vigor gave him a tired grin. "Do not lose faith, Commander Pierce. If the cross is here, we'll find it."

"Yes, but will we find it in time?"

Vigor patted his knee in a fatherly fashion and returned to his own seat. He slipped his arm around his niece, who continued to keep a sharp, concerned eye on her uncle.

With a large bump, the bus climbed off the ice road and onto solid rock. It trundled up the sandy embankment and onto a narrow road that ran the long axis of the thin island. Gray's team was traveling half its length to reach the largest village on Olkhon. They were to meet the shaman at a sacred spot near there.

Forty-five minutes of rough terrain later, sweeping through the broken brown steppes along the western shore, the bus rumbled down into the sleepy, picturesque village of Khuzhir, a neat little town of timber-framed homes with mossy roofs and brightly painted picket fences marking off small yards or sheep pens. The village hugged a small bay on the western side of the island and had only a couple of places for lodging.

Gray had chosen the smaller of the two. As it was the off-season for tourists, he had rented out the entire place, which consisted of only a dozen bedrooms anyway.

The bus delivered them to its doorstep. It was a two-story log lodge with a nice view of the bay off in the distance. There was a horse barn in back and a line of all-terrain vehicles parked along one side, clearly meant as rentals for its guests to explore the island.

They offloaded and headed inside. The proprietors—an older Russian couple, who did a lot of bowing and gesturing to make up for their poor English—had been expecting them and had a fire roaring in a stone hearth in the small communal room, a welcoming space of plank floors, overstuffed chairs, and a long dining table on one side.

The heat of the fire felt stifling for the first few breaths after the long chilly ride, but as they checked in and settled their room arrangements, Gray found himself drawn to the flames, warming his hands.

Vigor sank into one of the chairs. "I think I'm fine right here."

"Bed" was all Kowalski said, tramping up the stairs, rubbing his eyes like a kid who had been up well past his bedtime.

Gray didn't disagree with Kowalski's plan, proving it by yawning loudly. "Sorry. I think we all should get as much shut-eye as we can. We'll need to be up an hour or two before sunrise if we're to meet the shaman for his cleansing ritual."

"At least you *guys* will," Seichan said sourly.

That was another concession that had to be made to accommodate the shaman's rules. *No girls allowed.* It was clearly a boys' club when it came to the Buryats' sacred sites.

"Seichan and I will have to make a spa day of it then," Rachel said, "while you all go traipsing out into the cold."

Still, she didn't truly look any happier, staring at the back of her uncle's head. She didn't want Vigor out of her sight. She even sank into a chair next to him by the fire.

With a final few words, they all settled in for the night.

As Gray climbed the stairs, the wood creaking underfoot, he could not escape the feeling of foreboding. A window at the landing above shone with the light of the comet. But he felt the danger was much closer, like someone stepping on his grave.

Or someone else's grave.

Seichan followed him up, never even creaking a stair.

3:03 A.M.

Rachel woke in a panic, hearing a gunshot.

She found herself slouched in a chair by a fire. Another loud *pop* of wood from the hearth calmed her initial fear. She quickly remembered where she was. She checked her watch, discerning *when*.

Shocked, she shifted in her seat.

"Uncle Vigor, what are you still doing up? It's past three in the morning, and you have to be awake in another few hours."

Across the hearth from her, he had a local travel book open on his lap, his reading glasses perched on his nose, reflecting the flames.

"I slept on the plane ride here, took a nap on the drive over." He shooed her concerns away with a flutter of fingers. "A couple hours of sleep and I'll be fine."

She knew every one of those statements was a lie. She had watched him the entire trip. He had never closed his eyes once. Even now, she noted the sheen of sweat on his brow that had nothing to do with the fire. His pallid expression confirmed it.

His insomnia wasn't from old age. It wasn't even from his interest in the research book on his lap. It was pain.

She pushed from her chair and slid next to him, kneeling at his feet, hugging close to his legs.

"Just tell me," she said, knowing she needed no more words to clarify what she meant.

He sighed heavily, his eyes wincing slightly at the corners. He placed his book aside and stared into the flame. "It's pancreatic cancer," he whispered, as if ashamed—not at being sick but keeping this secret.

"How long?"

"I was diagnosed three months ago."

She stared up at him, showing him that wasn't the question she was asking. "How long?" she repeated.

"I have another two, maybe three months."

Hearing the truth was both a relief and a terror. After so long of not knowing, she wanted the truth, *needed* the truth, to be able to put a name to her fear. But now that it was in the open, she could not shield herself with false hope.

Tears rose to her eyes.

He reached and wiped them away. "No tears. That's why I didn't want anyone to know. I've had a good run."

"You could have told me."

"I needed . . ." He sighed again. "I needed this to be my own for a while."

He shook his head, plainly disappointed he couldn't explain it better.

But Rachel understood, squeezing his knee. He had to come to terms with his own mortality, its inevitability, before sharing that truth with others.

He then went and gave her more details. Like most pancreatic cancers, his disease was silent, asymptomatic. By the time he felt ill, initially dismissing it as indigestion, it was too late. The cancer had metastasized throughout his abdomen and into his lungs. He opted for palliative treatment only, drugs to stave off the worst of the pain.

"The small blessing," he said, finding a silver lining amid the darkness, "is that I can still be vital until near the very end."

Rachel swallowed the lump in her throat, suddenly so very glad she had not restricted him from this trip, one that was likely to be his last.

"I'll be there for you," she promised.

"And that's fine, but don't forget to live yourself." He waved a hand along his body. "This is only temporary, a small gift that hopefully leads to a greater glory. But do not waste that gift, do not set it on a shelf for some future use; grab it with both hands and live it now, live it every day."

She rested her cheek on his lap, shoulders shaking, losing her struggle against her grief.

He allowed it now. He placed a hand atop her head and spoke softly.

"I love you, Rachel. You are my daughter. You've always been that to me. I cherish that I got to share my life with you."

She hugged his legs—not wanting to ever let go, but knowing she must soon.

I love you, too.

3:19 A.M.

Seichan had an arm over her eyes as she lay in bed, holding her own tears in check. She had heard everything below. Her room was directly above the communal space. Every whisper rose to her, amplified by the acoustics of the wooden echo chamber that was this inn.

She had not meant to eavesdrop, but their voices had woken her.

She heard the love in those few words of the priest.

You are my daughter.

The truth cut her to the core—that although Vigor certainly was not Rachel's father, the two had forged a family despite it.

As she had listened, she had pictured her mother's face, now that of a stranger, the two of them separated by a gulf of time and tragedy. Rather than trying to renew their roles as mother and daughter, could they forge something new, to begin again as two strangers who shared a lost dream of another time? Could they take those faded embers and stoke something anew?

Seichan felt a flicker of hope, of possibility.

She rolled to her feet, knowing she would not be able to sleep.

Vigor's advice also stayed with her.

. . . do not waste that gift, do not set it on a shelf for some future use; grab it with both hands and live it now . . .

She climbed to her feet and slipped a loose shirt over her naked body. On bare feet, she moved silently from her room and down the chilly hall. She found his door unlocked and slipped into the warmer darkness inside.

A few embers glowed in the room's tiny hearth.

She stepped to his bed, a single like in her room, covered with a thick quilt and soft down pillows. Pulling back a corner, she slipped inside, sliding along his naked hard body, only now waking him.

He reacted suddenly, startled, a hand grasping her forearm in iron fingers, squeezing hard enough to bruise. Recognition softened his grip, but he didn't let go. His eyes reflected the hearth's glow.

"Sei—?"

She cut him off with a finger to his lips. She was done with talking, with trying to put into words what she felt, what he felt.

"What are—?"

She replaced her finger with her lips and answered his question.

Living.

26

Jada jerked her head up as the jet hit an air pocket. Her chin had been resting on her chest, her laptop open before her. She had drifted off as she worked, waiting for some data to collate.

"Push your seat back and get some real sleep," Duncan recommended, sitting next to her. "Like Monk."

He thumbed back to the third occupant of the jet's leather-appointed cabin, who was snoring in a steady drone to match the plane's engine.

"I wasn't sleeping," she scolded, covering a yawn with a fist. "Just thinking."

"Really?" Duncan lifted his arm, revealing Jada's other hand clasped to his. "Then may I ask what you were *thinking* about?"

Her face flushed with heat as she jerked her hand back. "Sorry about that."

He smiled. "I didn't mind."

Embarrassed, she glanced out the window and saw a sweep of clouds and water under them. The clock on her laptop said they had been in flight for a little under three hours.

"We just passed Japan," Duncan said. "Another five hours should have us landing in California."

As she stared around the cabin, she remembered another plane, another luxury jet. She had begun this adventure in Los Angeles, flown to D.C., then off to Kazakhstan and Mongolia, and now she was headed back to where it all started.

A full circle of the globe.

All in an attempt to save it.

She hoped it wasn't her farewell tour. If what Duncan saw through the Eye was real, then the entire planet was at risk.

Her eyes drifted to the box on the table. Before departing Ulan Bator, she had sealed the Eye in a makeshift Faraday cage, a box wrapped in copper wiring, to insulate its electromagnetic radiation from interfering with the jet's electronics. Passing his hands over the box, Duncan had confirmed that her efforts had indeed bottled up the worst of the radiation. But such a cage would have no effect on the Eye's larger quantum effect.

That was beyond any prison of copper wire.

Noting her attention, Duncan asked, "So why am I the only one who could see the destruction through that Eye?"

Glad for the distraction, she shrugged. "You must be sensitive to whatever quantum effect the Eye manifests. That makes me believe that what happened to the Eye also affected the glass lens of the satellite's camera, allowing its digital image sensor to record that peek into the near future as light passed through that altered lens."

"And what about me?"

"As I mentioned before, human consciousness lies in the quantum field. For some reason, you're more attuned to the quantum changes in the Eye. Whether because you *made* yourself that way with those magnets in your fingertips . . . or because you're extrasensitive."

"Like St. Thomas with his cross."

"Possibly, but I'm not going to go around calling you St. Duncan."

"Are you sure? I sort of like the sound of that."

A small alarm chimed on her laptop, as a new folder popped onto her desktop screen. It was the latest update of data from the SMC, sent via satellite.

Finally . . .

"Back to work?" Duncan asked.

"There's something I want to check."

Tapping open the folder, she read through the documents. She planned on building a graph of the comet's path, tracking its corona of dark energy.

Something continued to nag at her, and she hoped more information would jar loose whatever was troubling her.

She began collating the pertinent information and plugging it into a graphing program. She also wanted to compare the latest statistics and numbers to her original equations explaining the nature of dark energy. Her equations beautifully married her theory concerning the source of dark energy—the collapse of virtual particles in the quantum foam of the universe—to the gravitational forces it created. She knew that was the crux of the problem at hand. She could summarize it in one word.

Attraction.

The virtual particles were drawn to each other, and the resulting energy of that annihilation was what imbued *mass* with the fundamental force of *gravity*. It was the fuel of weak and strong nuclear forces that drew together electrons, protons, and neutrons to form atoms. It was what made moons circle planets, solar systems churn, and galaxies spin.

As she worked, she began to note errors in the SMC's equations, assumptions the head physicist had made that were not supported by this latest set of data. She began to work faster, sleep shedding off her shoulders. With growing horror, the truth began to materialize before her mind's eye.

I have to be wrong . . . I must be.

Her fingers began furiously tapping, knowing a way to double-check.

"What's wrong?" Duncan asked.

She wanted to voice it aloud, to share it, but she feared doing so would somehow make it more real.

"Jada?"

She finally folded. "The physicist back at the SMC, the one who did the initial estimates determining when we'd cross the point of no return . . . he made a mistake."

"Are you sure?" Duncan looked at his watch. "He said we had sixteen hours. Which still leaves us about another nine hours."

"He was wrong. He was basing his extrapolations on the fact that the comet's gravitational anomalies were increasing in proportion to its approach toward the earth."

"And he was wrong about that?"

"No, that part was right." She tapped to bring up the graph she had been compiling earlier. "Here you can see the comet's corona of dark energy being pulled earthward as it swings nearer, growing an ever longer reach.

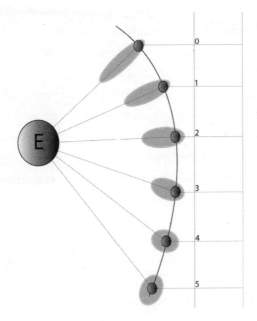

Jada continued, "Likewise, the curve of space-time around the earth is responding to that gravitational effect. That curvature is bending *outward*, the two drawing together, slowly creating that funnel down which that barrage of asteroids will tumble."

"So if the physicist is right, what's the problem?"

"He made an error, and I believe the new data supports it."

"What error?"

"He assumed the growth of the gravitational effect was *geometric*, growing at a set incremental rate. But I don't think it is. I think it's increasing at an *exponential* rate." She turned to him. "In other words, much faster."

"How much faster?"

"I want to run the data through my equations to be certain, but right now I would say we have only *five hours* until an asteroid strike is inevitable. Not nine."

"That's almost half our remaining time." Duncan leaned back into his seat, immediately understanding the problem. "We'll be lucky to be touching down in L.A. by then."

"And considering our past couple of days, I wouldn't count on luck."

4:14 A.M.

What the hell . . .

Duncan sat stunned.

Jada urged him to remain calm until she could confirm her estimates. To accomplish that, she was dumping data into an analysis program she had designed based on her equations.

As he waited, Duncan rubbed his temples with his fingers. "Why did that satellite have to crash in the middle of Mongolia of all places? Why not in freakin' Iowa? We're losing precious hours flying halfway around the globe."

Jada's fingers froze over the keyboard.

"What?" he asked.

"That's it . . . *that's* what was bugging me. I've been such a fool." She closed her eyes. "It's always been about *attraction*."

"What do you mean?"

She pointed again to the graph showing the comet's corona of energy being pulled toward the earth. "The physicist at the SMC theorized that there was something on the planet that the comet's energy was responding to. And I agree."

"You said before that you believed it might be the cross," Duncan said. "Because it was sculpted out of a piece of that comet when it last appeared."

"Exactly. The two—the comet and the cross—are most likely quantumly entangled and drawn to each other, at least energetically. I was hoping that if the cross was ever found, that by studying its energy—or even the energy of the Eye—I might find a way to *break* that entanglement."

He nodded. It made theoretical sense. "And if you did that, the comet's energy would no longer be attracted to the earth—and in turn, space-time around the planet would not warp toward it."

"And the funnel would never form triggering the massive asteroid strike."

Brilliant, Dr. Shaw.

"Two questions," Duncan said. "*How* can you be so sure of this attraction between the comet and the cross? And *what* can you do to break that entanglement?"

"The answer to both is the same. To quote Einstein again, *God does not play dice with the world.*"

Jada read his baffled expression. "A moment ago," she said, "you asked *why* did the satellite crash in Mongolia? That's the best question anyone could ask."

"Thanks . . . ?" he said tentatively.

"To answer it, I'll ask you another question. Where do we currently believe the cross is hidden?"

"An island in Lake Baikal, about three hundred miles north . . ." Then he understood, his eyes widened. "From a global standpoint, practically in the *backyard* of where the satellite crashed."

"And does that not strike you as wildly coincidental?"

He nodded.

And God does not play dice.

He stared at her, wanted to kiss her—more than he usually did. "The satellite fell in that general vicinity because it was *drawn* there, pulled by the energy of the cross."

"How could it not? It's charged with the same dark energy of the comet."

Duncan glanced again to that graph showing the nimbus of energy being sucked earthward. He pictured the satellite as a disembodied piece of that energy, imagining it being tugged out of orbit by the pull of the cross and dragged down to the planet's surface.

If true, that definitely supported Jada's theory of entanglement, but it didn't answer his other question.

He turned back to her. "You said this fact would also answer *how* to break this entanglement."

She smiled. "I thought it was obvious."

"Not to me."

"We have to finish what the satellite tried to do. We have to unite the energy of the Eye and the energy of the cross. Think of the pair as a positively charged particle and a negatively charged particle. While their opposite charges draw them together—"

"—when they unite, they cancel each other out."

"Precisely. The energy equivalent of joining matter and antimatter together. The explosive annihilation of the two opposites should break that entanglement."

It was beautifully theorized, but . . .

"Why are they *opposites*?" he asked. "What's the difference between them?"

"Remember, time is a dimension, too. While both the cross and the Eye are charged with the same quantum of dark energy, they hold two different and distinct flavors of *time*. Opposite ends of the same axis. One from the past, one from the present. Quantum entanglement means they both want to be one."

"Meaning they must annihilate each other."

She nodded. "I believe that will break the entanglement and release the pull on the comet's energies."

"Still, that raises the bigger question," Duncan said. "Where is the cross?"

"I don't know, but—"

The computer chimed again, interrupting her, announcing the completed run of Dr. Shaw's program. A number glowed within a blinking results box.

5.68 hrs

"But that's how long we have to find it." Jada turned to him. "You know what we have to do."

He did.

Duncan climbed out of his seat, crossed over to Monk, and shook his partner awake.

"What . . . ?" Monk asked blearily. "Are we there?"

Duncan leaned over. "We need to turn this plane around."

27

With the sun still down, Gray woke to his limbs tangled with another's, a warm cheek resting on his chest. The scent of their bodies, their passion, still hung in the air. His left hand clasped her shoulder, as if fearful she would slip between his fingers, turn into a ghost, a fevered dream.

She stretched, a languorous motion that was all soft skin and a hint of sinuous power stirring beneath. She made a contented noise that rumbled into his bones. Tilting her head, she opened her eyes, reflecting what little light there was in the room. She moved her leg lower, stirring him, waking him further.

He reached and touched a finger under her chin, drawing her up to him. Their lips brushed with a promise of—

His phone jangled loudly on the nightstand, breaking the spell, reminding them both of the world beyond this small knot of blankets and bed. He groaned between their lips, pulling her harder against him for a long moment, then let her go and rolled to the phone, keeping one hand on the curve of her hip.

"We've landed in Irkutsk," Monk updated him. "Caught a good tailwind. Got here faster than expected."

It was the second time his friend had interrupted them; the first time had been a couple of hours ago, informing Gray of his team's intent to join them out there.

"Understood," he said tersely. "That means you're still about two hours out from us."

The plan was for Seichan and Rachel to wait for Monk's group at the inn. Gray would take the others, learn what they could from the shaman, and rendezvous back here to regroup.

He checked his watch. They had to depart in forty-five minutes if they wanted to catch the sunrise ceremony at the grotto by eight.

Gray quickly finished his call and dropped the phone on the floor next to his bed. He moved his hand to the small of her back and rolled her under him.

"Now where were we . . ."

Half an hour later, Gray stepped from the room, followed by Seichan, both freshly showered. She wore only a long shirt. To him, there was no reason for her to wear any more clothing—but the chill of the hallway was a reminder of the subzero temperatures awaiting them both. With her hand in his, he swung her forward and kissed her deeply, sealing a promise of more to come.

As he let her go, a door opened down the hall and Rachel stepped out, catching them as they broke apart. She seemed momentarily flustered, then simply ducked her head, embarrassed, but Gray noted the small smile. She already knew of his tentative relationship with Seichan, but apparently now she knew it wasn't so *tentative*.

Rachel mumbled a good morning and headed downstairs, where the smell of cooking bacon and fresh-brewed coffee beckoned.

With a final peck, he sent Seichan back to her own room to change and headed below. In the communal space, the inn's proprietors took the *breakfast* part of B&B seriously. A lavish spread had been set out: soft cheeses, toasted breads, blackberries, hard-boiled eggs, thick slabs of bacon, fat sausages, along with an assortment of grilled and pickled fish from the lake.

Vigor sat at the table with a cup of tea warming in his hands. He looked tired, pallid in color, but there was an air of contentment about him this morning. Rachel passed behind her uncle, kissed him on top of his head, and grabbed a plate.

Gray headed over to join them, earning a raised eyebrow of amusement from Rachel, as if to say *about time*. Apparently her initial shock and embarrassment was settling into good-natured teasing. He also thought he noted perhaps a wistful hint of regret. But maybe that was his own ego reading too much into her look.

Changing the subject—though no one had spoken—Gray asked, "Where's Kowalski?"

"He's already eaten." Vigor nodded toward the door. "He went to check on our mode of transportation."

Through a side window, Gray spotted his partner's shaved head out in the dark, inspecting the ATVs parked next to the inn. They'd be taking the big-wheeled vehicles to a small grotto at the farthest point of the bay.

Gray tucked into a big plate of food, while Vigor checked on the duffel holding the cache of relics. Kowalski stamped back inside, bringing the cold with him. He looked anxious to get going.

"Are we ready?" Gray asked as he popped a final few blackberries into his mouth.

"Gassed up," Kowalski said. "Can go anytime."

By now, Seichan had returned. She touched Vigor on the shoulder as she slipped past him, her fingers squeezing with some unspoken understanding. The gesture seemed oddly intimate—not so much sympathy as silent support—as if she were acknowledging something that only she knew.

Gray glanced inquiringly at her as she sat down.

She gave a small shake of her head, indicating it was private.

Gray finally stood up, drawing Vigor to his feet, too. "We'll leave you both to hold down the fort," he told Seichan and Rachel. "Monk and the others should be here a little before nine, so be watching for them. We're not going to have a whole lot of time to coordinate. According to Dr. Shaw, it looks like our timetable has shrunk yet again."

He explained about the revised estimate, about the plan to unite the cross and the Eye.

"And all this must happen before *ten o'clock*?" Vigor asked, sounding outraged. "Sunrise is at eight. That gives us only a couple of hours to bring the Eye to the cross."

"Then we'd better get that witch doctor talking fast," Kowalski said.

"He's right," Gray conceded. "But the island isn't that large. As long as the location is not too remote, it might be doable."

It *must* be doable, he silently corrected.

7:44 A.M.

Buried in his parka against the frigid cold, Vigor rode the all-terrain vehicle down a sandy tract through a coastal forest of larch trees, the ground littered with fallen, brown needles, leaving the branches above bare against the brightening sky. Though the sun had not yet risen above the horizon, dawn glowed to the east.

Their path ended up at a curved stretch of beach, dusted with snow and fringed by ice that swept out a good ways into the bay. Sections had been shattered by past wave action, turning into knee-high shards of blue glass.

Beyond the frozen border, the early sheen of the day cast the waters an indigo blue. The water was so clear it could be drunk without fear of intestinal upset. In fact, if you swam in it, local legends claimed, it would add five years to your life.

If only that were true, Vigor thought, *I'd dive in despite the cold.*

Still, he was glad that he'd finally told Rachel the truth about his cancer. He had words that needed to be spoken, and he was glad that he had the time to share them. He did not fear death so much as he did the loss of the years he would have with Rachel: to see her grow, get married, have kids, to see them flourish.

So much he would miss.

But at least he got to tell her how much she meant to him.

Thank you, Lord, for that small blessing.

Ahead, Kowalski swerved and skidded his all-terrain vehicle, seemingly determined to test its limits against rolling over. Only the young were convinced of their own immortality, willing to challenge death with such abandon. Age eventually wore down that confidence, but the best of us still kept tilting at windmills despite that knowledge—or maybe even because of it, appreciating each day, living to the fullest, knowing one day there would be no more.

As they hit the beach, Gray slowed to ride alongside Vigor, drawing him out of his cold reverie. He pointed ahead toward a tall rock jutting out from the ice field and rising high and pointing at the sky.

"That's Burkhan Cape?" Gray asked.

It was also called Shaman's Rock, home to the gods of the Buryats, known as *tengrii*. The site was considered one of Asia's ten most sacred places.

Vigor nodded, shouting into the wind blowing off the lake. "The ceremonial grotto is on the far side, facing the water. That's where the shaman will meet us. At the end of this beach, there should be a narrow isthmus that runs out from the shore to the cape."

Gray nodded and sped up. He reined Kowalski in, and they swept around the curve and onto a thin strip of land that extended across the ice to a rise of craggy white cliffs, frosted with red moss.

A small figure stood at the end of the isthmus, guarding passage onto the promontory. He was a skinny young man in a long sheepskin jacket over a blue belted robe. He carried a hide drum slung over one shoulder. He waved for them to stop and turn off their engines, not looking happy about the racket. Vigor knew that in the past visitors used to cover the hooves of their horses with leather, so as not to disturb the gods of the cape.

"My name is Temur," he said in strained English, bowing slightly. "I am to take you to Elder Bayan. He is awaiting you."

Kowalski manhandled the duffel from the back of Vigor's bike and they set off after the young man along a narrow path through the broken rock and up some icy hand-hewn steps in the rock face. A large cave mouth opened above them, facing the lake.

Vigor found himself wheezing by the time they had scaled the cliff and entered the cavern grotto. Flanking the entrance were two stone cairns, wrapped in colorful scarves and flags that flapped in the steady wind off the water. Between them knelt a wizened old man of indeterminate age. He could be sixty or maybe a hundred. He was similarly attired as the younger man, only with the addition of a tall peaked hat. On his knees, he was attending a fire, tossing in dried juniper branches, casting forth an indolent smoke that swirled about the cavern.

Farther back, a tunnel led deeper into the promontory, but Vigor doubted even his Vatican credentials would gain them access back there.

"Elder Bayan wishes you to kneel to either side of him and turn your faces to the lake."

Gray waved them forward to obey.

Vigor took to one side, his friends the other. The smoke stung his nostrils and eyes, but it smelled oddly sweet. Temur began slowly beating his drum while the shaman recited prayers, wafting a burning juniper branch in his hand.

Beyond the mouth of the cave, the dark lake slowly brightened, turning the waters from a deep indigo to a sky blue. Ice glistened in a thousand hues of cobalt and sapphire. Then in a flash, fire spread across the water and ice, ignited by the first rays of the sun, flowing like molten gold.

Vigor let out a small gasp at the sight, feeling privileged to witness this. Even the wind died down for a breath, as if awed by the sight.

Then with a final loud bang on his drum, Temur turned to them. "It is done. You may now speak to Elder Bayan."

The shaman stood, motioning them to their feet.

Properly blessed, Vigor climbed up and bowed to Elder Bayan. "Thank you for meeting with us. We have a matter of urgency and seek someone who has great knowledge of Olkhon."

Temur translated their conversation, whispering in Bayan's ear.

"What do you wish to know?" the young man asked for the elder.

Vigor turned to Gray. "Show him the relics."

Taking the duffel from Kowalski, Gray unzipped the bag and carefully removed the objects, placing the skull and book down, alongside the tarnished silver box. Gray opened the lid and revealed the boat inside.

The only reaction from the elder was a slight widening of his eyes.

"What is all this?" Temur asked, but the question didn't come from the shaman, only from the young man's curiosity.

Instead, the shaman stepped forth and hovered his hands over each object, again whispering prayers.

Finally, he spoke again, and Temur translated. "The power is old, but not unknown."

Vigor stared at Bayan's wrinkled hands.

Did he feel the same energy as Duncan?

The shaman ended up with his palm resting above the skull.

"We know what you seek," Temur continued, speaking for Bayan. "But to trespass there is with great danger."

"We will be happy to face that danger," Vigor said.

Bayan frowned once this was whispered in his ear. "No, you will not." Temur turned specifically to face Vigor. "Elder Bayan says you are suffering much, but you will suffer more."

Misgiving rang through Vigor. He glanced at Gray.

Temur continued, "I am to take you to what you seek."

Vigor should have been overjoyed by this offer, but instead he found himself growing colder as the shaman continued to stare at him, his ancient face a mask of sorrow.

Vigor had accepted his death as inevitable. But for the first time in many months, he began to fear what was to come.

8:07 A.M.

Rachel walked through the horse barn at the back of the property. She tugged the zipper of her parka down. She had meant to take a walk after breakfast, needing to burn off nervous energy but also to think about her uncle.

She fought against wanting to control his disease, making lists in her head: which doctors to call, which clinics to consult, which new therapeutic trials to enroll in. But in the end, she knew she must simply let that go. Vigor had clearly made his peace. She must, too.

But she could not sit still in the quiet inn. She also didn't know what to say to Seichan after seeing her leave Gray's room. It was too awkward, so she went for a walk—until the cold drove her back to the inn, with her nose numb and her cheeks burning from the blustery weather.

Rather than immediately going back inside, she ended up in the barn, where she could escape the wind. Shadowy horses heated the space, nickering softly at her intrusion. The place smelled of hay, manure, and musty sweat. She walked the length, rubbing a velvet nose of a mare over a gate, offering a handful of grain to another.

Once warmed up, she headed back to the barn door and swung it open. The cold struck her with a gust of wind.

She bent against it and began trudging back to the inn.

A loud *crack* raised her head, echoing away. It sounded like a loose shutter banging in the wind. More blasts followed.

Gunfire.

She stopped, confused—when an arm closed around her neck from behind, clamping over her throat.

She felt the cold muzzle of a gun at her temple.

8:10 A.M.

Seichan only had a moment to react.

Attuned to her surroundings, she had felt something was *wrong*. Over the course of the morning, up in her room, she had learned the rhythms of the quiet inn: the murmur of the husband and wife below, the clank of pans, the whistle of wind through the eaves. She had heard the door open off and on, either one of the owners taking out the garbage, or the last time, Rachel leaving to explore the village.

When the door had opened a half minute ago, she had thought it was Rachel returning, but the noises below grew hushed, except for the clatter of a plate to the wooden floor.

She had tensed, muscles going hard, every sense straining. Even the dust in the air seemed to hold motionless in anticipation.

Then a creak on the stair—

She bolted, stopping only long enough to grab her SIG Sauer, still in its holster on her nightstand. She burst out the door, shaking the semi-automatic pistol free. She fled away from the stairs, toward the window at the end of the landing. With her weapon pointed behind her, she saw a shadow rise by the stairs, too furtive. Then a shape appeared, dressed all in winter camouflage.

She fired backward twice, while leaping and striking the window with her shoulder. A cry rose behind her. She had only winged the man, but it offered her enough of a delay to fly out the window in a shower of glass and splintered wood. She landed on the overhanging eave of the first-story roof below and rolled down its side and over the edge.

She fell through the air, twisting around to land on her legs, falling to one arm. She kept the other up, pointing the pistol all around. She had come out behind the house. A patch of forest beckoned across a small yard. She fled toward it—only to see a group of armed men, also in cam-ouflage, appear out of the tree line.

She veered to the right, where she knew a deep culvert ran along the neighboring road. She needed cover and a way to break through the cor-don that had clearly been set up around the inn.

She sprinted as gunfire tore the frozen turf around her, blindly firing back toward the woods. She might still be able to make it to safety.

Then a familiar voice rang out past the gunfire.

"STOP OR I WILL KILL HER!"

She didn't. She leaped the last distance and slid on her belly into the culvert. Ice cracked under her as she swung to face the man who had shouted. Keeping hidden in the deep gutter, she trained her pistol.

Across the yard, by the barn, she spotted a large, powerful-looking man gripping Rachel around the throat.

Ju-long Delgado stood to one side of her.

On the other, Hwan Pak.

The North Korean scientist held a pistol to Rachel's ear.

"Come out now! Or I will blow her head off!"

Seichan struggled to make sense of the situation. How could they be here? She noted the facial features of the team in camouflage, all North Korean, likely their country's elite special forces. But how had Pak found her?

Rachel yelled to her, "Run! Just run!"

Her captor cuffed her roughly in the head. Still, she struggled, strangling in his grip.

Knowing they would certainly kill Rachel if she attempted to flee— a course that looked less and less likely to succeed anyway—she finally raised her arms in the air, showing herself.

"Don't shoot!" she called back.

More soldiers came up from behind her, appearing like ghosts from hiding spots. She scanned their numbers. It seemed Pak had brought an entire assault team with him.

Why?

She was stripped of her weapon and marched over to Pak.

As Seichan approached, Rachel met her eyes. Rachel looked more angry than scared, apologetic for putting Seichan into this situation.

But Seichan could not hold the woman at fault. This was all her own responsibility, a danger she had dragged to this icy doorstep.

The brute holding Rachel must be the military team leader. He wore mirrored sunglasses with a hood pulled low, showing little of his face— what did show looked mean, displaying a cross-hatching of scars. She could smell the threat off the man. He was no new recruit, but a battle-hardened warrior.

Pak turned to her when she arrived. He smiled coldly, promising pain and sorrow.

"Now you will tell us where the Americans are."

28

Back on the ATVs, Gray led the way with the shaman's apprentice, Temur, riding behind him. They headed north from the crags of Burkhan Cape, driving atop the thick shore ice, following the coastline.

Kowalski and Vigor kept close behind on their own vehicles.

The morning brightened rapidly, turning the ice into glass, some places so clear it looked like open water. A dusting of dry snow and ice skirted in streams across the surface, pushed by the wind like the crowns of whitecaps.

"Around that tumble of rock ahead!" Temur called. "Another mile or so."

Using that landmark, they continued along a deserted section of the island, where sheer cliffs rose straight out of the water, topped by dense fir forests. Temur urged them closer to the shore, shadowing his eyes with his hand and studying the coastline.

"There!" he finally called. "That opening. We go in there!"

Gray spotted the mouth of a sea cave. It looked large enough to drive a minivan inside, except rows of massive icicles speared down from the upper edge, like a set of fanged jaws closing down to take a bite out of the ice shelf below. The remaining opening was only large enough to allow their ATVs to enter, if they went single file.

Gray angled toward it, slowing their speed to a crawl. He flicked his headlamp on and cast its light into the dark cave. White frost reflected off every surface, revealing a tunnel leading deeper. Stalactites of ice covered the arched ceiling in a solid mass. Streams of water froze in place on the walls, forming sheets of rippling crystal.

"We're not going in there, are we?" Kowalski asked, plainly leery. "Caves are one thing, but *ice* caves . . ."

As answer, Gray ducked his head below the first row of icicles and crawled his ATV inside, following the beam of his headlamp.

Inside, the space was even more wondrous. The ice under the tires was so clear he could see the mossy rocks far below, spot fish in the flowing water under the ice.

"Looks like it continues a ways!" Gray called back.

He headed deeper upon Temur's instructions. The tunnel grew larger, the walls sweeping to the sides, the ceiling rising higher. About thirty yards in, the sea tunnel ended at a large cavern, a cathedral of ice. Glistening blue-crystal chandeliers filled the domed roof, while diamond columns rose all around.

As they entered, the pressure of their passage made the ice beneath them groan and pop, the sound amplified and echoed by the sheltering walls. A few fragile branches of the chandeliers broke free and shattered to the ice, tinkling away with a dance of shards.

Across the room, a thick curtain of ice flowed in heavy ripples down the far wall, where a spring-fed waterfall had frozen over. A few trickles still ran down its surface, polishing the ice to a quartz shine, before freezing below.

Closer at hand, in the middle of the floor, a darker stain marred the pristine surface, marking a hole through the ice to the open water below. The steeply sloped sides were stained, worn in some places to form small chutes.

Gray had caught sight of a sleek brown body sliding down one of them as they had first entered. This must be a breathing hole for the most famous mammal of Baikal Lake, the nerpa seal.

With nowhere else to go, Gray stopped his ATV. Kowalski and Vigor joined him, flanking him on either side.

"Where are we?" Kowalski asked.

Temur answered, "This is a birthing chamber for our Baikal seals, where pups will be sheltered in deep winter. It is considered very special to our people. It is said we are descended from the spirit of such hardy, noble creatures."

"But why have you brought us *here*?" Gray asked, searching around. He wasn't in the mood for the full Baikal nature tour, not with the clock ticking down.

"Because Elder Bayan told me to bring you to this cave," Temur said. "That is all I know. I do not know *why* he asked me to do so."

Gray turned to Vigor, who looked equally baffled.

"Maybe the old guy just likes seals," Kowalski commented.

"Or it's a test," Vigor said. "All Genghis Khan's other sites were well hidden, often where land meets water, like this. But they were made somewhat easier to find because of the drought in Hungary or the ecological disaster of the dry Aral Sea."

"Well, nothing has changed in this region for millions of years," Gray said. "We're getting no free passes here."

"So it would seem."

Gray searched the ice-encrusted room, forcing himself to remain calm, realizing one fact. The shaman had not sent them here entirely without resources. Gray remembered Bayan instructing Temur where to take them. It was done with only a few words, yet Temur knew exactly where to go. That could only mean one thing.

"Temur, do your people have a *name* for this cavern?"

He nodded. "In our native language it is *Emegtei,* which means a woman's belly," he said, pantomiming a swelling on his own stomach.

"A *womb*," Gray said.

"Yes, that's right," Temur said. He then bowed and backed away. "I hope you find what you seek. But I must now go."

"My friend can drive you back to Burkhan Cape," Gray offered, motioning to Kowalski.

Temur shook his head. "Not necessary. I have family not far."

As the man departed, Vigor motioned to the breathing hole, drawing back Gray's attention. "A womb. That makes sense. This place is a birthing chamber for the island's spirit animal."

Gray shook his head, not disagreeing. In fact, he was sure the monsignor was right. Instead, he was taking a different tack. "Vigor, didn't you say that Olkhon Island is where Genghis Khan's own mother was from?"

His eyes widened upon him. "That's right!"

"So this sacred spot could have been chosen as some symbolic representation of where Genghis originated."

"His spiritual womb," Vigor conceded.

Kowalski frowned at the icy cavern. "If you're right, then his mom must have been one frigid—"

Gray cut him off. "This must be the right place."

"But how does that help us?" Vigor asked.

Gray closed his eyes, picturing this chamber as a womb, the tunnel to the sea a birth canal, flowing outward with life.

But life doesn't start in the womb . . .

It first needs a spark, a primal source.

According to Vigor, Genghis Khan was technologically ahead of his time, and while he might not have known about the fertilization of sperm and eggs, the scientists of his time surely knew about gross human anatomy.

Gray climbed from his ATV, grabbed his flashlight from his pack, and headed across the room, careful of the ice, giving the breathing hole a wide berth. He pointed his flashlight along the back wall, following that frozen flow upward, noting the rivulets of water still trickling across its surface.

Twenty-five feet above his head, he discovered the source of the spring. A black hole marked another tunnel, half full of ice where the spring-fed flow had frozen over.

Vigor understood. "Symbolic of a woman's fallopian tube."

Down which life flows to the womb.

"I've got pitons and climbing gear in my pack," Gray said. "I should be able to scale the fall and reach that tunnel."

As he turned back, he read the desire in Vigor's eyes and clapped his old friend on the shoulder. "Don't worry. Once up there, I can rig a line. We'll go together."

They rushed back to the ATV, and Gray began assembling what they would need.

Vigor shivered and stamped his feet against the cold, but excitement shone in his eyes as he stared at the tunnel. "That passage up there must be seasonally locked."

Gray frowned. "What do you mean?"

"In spring and summer, that hole is probably flooded, gushing with water, making it impossible to enter and traverse. Only in winter, when it's all frozen over, is the tunnel open and accessible."

Gray paused to consider this. "Could they have done that on purpose? The date on the skull marked the coming apocalypse as *November,* a winter month."

Vigor bobbed his head. "They might have been limiting access, preserving the treasure inside until the season when it was best needed."

After fitting his boots with spiked crampons, Gray straightened with a coil of climbing rope over his shoulder and a harness in hand, fitted with pitons and an ice ax.

Only one way to find out.

8:32 A.M.

Vigor watched Gray ascend the ice wall, holding his breath, a hand at his throat. *Be careful . . .*

Gray appeared to be taking no chances. They had no time for accidents or falls. He planted each piton with great care into cracks in the ice, drilling the eyebolts deep. He kept three limbs on the wall at all times, moving steadily, stringing a line as he went.

Three-quarters of the way up, Gray reached high and tested a split in the ripple of ice with his ax—only to have an entire section fall away from the wall. Like a glacier calving, it broke and plummeted below, crashing with a resounding boom. Ice boulders scattered all the way to the parked ATVs.

Gray lost his hold and fell to his last piton, swinging from the rope, but it held. He got his feet back to the ice and continued his ascent with even more care. Finally he reached the top and pulled himself up with the ice ax, digging in with his crampons, into the frozen tunnel.

A moment later, a light bloomed up there, turning the waterfall into rippling blue glass. His head popped back out, and Gray waved a flashlight.

"Passage goes on!" he called down. "Let me secure a line! Kowalski, help Vigor into a climbing harness!"

In short order, Gray had a rope running through an eyebolt screwed into the roof of the tunnel. Kowalski hooked Vigor to one line. By pulling on the other, the big man practically hauled him up the waterfall. Vigor did his best to help, pushing off pitons or grabbing the next.

With hardly any effort, he found himself on his belly next to Gray in the tunnel. Vigor looked down its throat. It looked like a chute drilled through the heart of a sapphire crystal.

"Let's go," Gray said, crawling on his hands and knees. "Stick behind me."

The passage rose at a slight angle upward, making the traverse across the ice flow treacherous. Its surface was slippery, trickling with cold water. One mistake and someone could go body-sledding back down the tunnel and shoot out into the open.

Another fifteen yards and the ice rose so high in the tunnel that Gray had to slide on his belly, squirming like a worm to continue on. Vigor waited at the bottleneck, suddenly feeling claustrophobic.

Gray's voice echoed back. "It opens past the squeeze! You need to see this!"

Spurred by the excitement in his voice, Vigor repeated Gray's action, wiggling his way through the pinch. Near the end, a hand clamped onto his wrist and pulled him the rest of the way out, like a cork out of a bottle.

Vigor found himself standing in another cavern, atop a frozen pond.

To his left, the shore of the pond rose in a sheer cliff of bedrock, maybe four meters high. Gray pointed his flashlight's beam to a set of stairs cut into it long ago. The way appeared to lead to a ledge up top.

"C'mon," Gray said.

They scaled with care. Gray used his ax to clear a few steps of thicker ice, until finally they reached the top.

Gray offered his arm to help Vigor to his feet, but he ignored Gray and stood up, staring at the far wall. Through a thin crust of blue ice, he saw an arched set of black doors.

Vigor gripped Gray's arm, needing his solidity to make sure what he was seeing was real. "It's the entrance to Genghis Khan's tomb."

8:48 A.M.

Gray didn't have time to stand on ceremony or savor the discovery. Using the butt of his steel ax, he cracked and scraped at the shell of ice covering the doorway. Huge sheets fell with every strike, the door ringing with each blow, indicating it was metal. In less than a minute, he had the doorway clear.

The archway was no taller than his head.

As Gray brushed the hinges clean, Vigor touched the surface reverentially. He had his own flashlight out and shone the beam at a spot where Gray's ax had pocked the metal door.

"It's silver under the layer of black tarnish!" Vigor said. "Like the box holding the bone boat. But look, where the door is gouged deep, I can see splintered wood under the metal. The silver is only plated on the surface. Still . . ."

Vigor's eyes glowed brightly.

With the crude hinges cleared, Gray swung a latch up that held the double doors closed. He offered Vigor the honor of pulling them open.

Plainly holding his breath, Vigor grasped the handle and yanked hard. With a grinding of ice crystals still in the hinges, the doors parted and opened wide.

Vigor fell back from the sight.

It wasn't what they had been expecting.

While nearly empty, it was no less astonishing.

A circular gold chamber glowed before them. Floor, roof, walls . . . all were covered in rosy-yellow metal. Even the inner surfaces of the doors were plated with gold, not silver.

Gray allowed Vigor to step inside first, then he followed.

Everywhere the gold had been sculpted and carved by skilled artisans. Across the roof, gold ribs led to a circular ring. The walls held posts of gold. The intent of the design was obvious.

"It's a golden yurt," Gray said. "A Mongolian *ger.*"

Vigor stared back at the archway. "And when the door is closed, it forms a solid vault. We're standing symbolically inside the third box of St. Thomas's reliquary."

Gray remembered the skull and book had been sealed in iron, the boat in silver, and now they were inside the final chest, one of gold.

Vigor moved to the right, as if nervous to enter any deeper. "Look at the walls."

Affixed to each sculpted gold post were what appeared to be jeweled torch holders. Gray reached for one, only to realize it was a crown. He searched the circular space. They were *all* crowns.

"From the kingdoms Genghis Khan conquered," Vigor said. "But this isn't Genghis Khan's tomb."

Gray had recognized the same as soon as the doors had opened. This was no sprawling necropolis, full of the riches and treasures of the ancient world. There were no jeweled sepulchers of Genghis and his descendants. That waited still to be found, possibly back in those Mongolian mountains.

Vigor spoke in hushed tones. "These crowns were left to honor the man whose crypt this is."

Vigor headed along the edge of the room, clearly still working up the courage to move deeper. His arm pointed to the walls between the posts, to the art depicted there. The bright surfaces had been hammered and worked into vast masterpieces. The style was clearly Chinese.

"It was typical for tombs during the Song dynasty to depict the life of the crypt's occupant," Vigor said. "This is no exception."

Gray noted the first panel to the right of the door showed a stylized mountain, surmounted by three crosses. Weeping figures trailed down the hillside, while an angry sky warred above.

The next showed a man on his knees, reaching toward the wounded flank of another floating over him.

Moving through the other panels, that same man made a great, terrifying journey, fraught with symbolic dragons and other monsters out of Chinese lore—until finally he reached the shore of a great sea, fraught with huge waves, where crowds welcomed him with flags and symbols of joy and enlightenment.

"It's the life of St. Thomas," Vigor said, as they finished the circuit. "Here is proof that he reached China and the Yellow Sea."

But that wasn't the end of the saint's story.

Vigor finally stopped at the last panel, having traversed the full circle.

The masterwork here showed a giant of a Chinese king handing the man a large cross. Over the king's shoulder, a comet blazed in a sky full of stars and a crescent moon.

It was the gift to St. Thomas.

Vigor finally turned to face the nearly empty room. The only object preserved in this golden *ger* was a cairn of stones in the center, not unlike the pillars seen flanking the entrance to the shaman's grotto.

Only this pedestal of rock supported a black box, simple and plain.

Vigor glanced to Gray, clearly asking permission.

Gray noted the yellowish pallor to the man's skin. Not all of it was a reflection of the gold, he realized. It was jaundice.

"Go," Gray said softly.

8:56 A.M.

Vigor crossed to the cairn, to the box it held. He moved on legs numb with awe, close to losing his balance.

Maybe it would be best to approach on my knees.

But he kept upright and reached the stone pillar. The box resting there appeared to be black iron, but it was likely some amalgam as it looked little rusted. On the surface, a Chinese character had been etched.

Two trees.

Just as Ildiko had described and copied.

With trembling fingers, he opened the lid with a small complaint from its hinges. Inside rested a second box. It looked as black as the first, but Vigor knew it was silver beneath that tarnish of age. Again a symbol had been inscribed there.

Command.

He obeyed that instruction and opened it—revealing a final chest of gold nestled within. It looked nearly pristine, shining bright, unadorned, except for the final mark found atop it.

Forbidden.

He held his breath. Using just the tips of his index fingers, he raised the final lid and pushed it back.

He said a silent prayer of thanks for this honor.

Resting inside, supported atop tiny pillars of gold, was a yellowish-brown skull. Empty sockets stared back up at him. Faintly visible, but still there, was an inscribed spiral of Jewish Aramaic.

The relic of St. Thomas.

Vigor came close to falling to his knees, but Gray must have noted him trembling. The man's arm propped him up, kept him standing for what he must do next.

With tears in his eyes, he reached to the relic. Vigor revered St. Thomas, placing him above all the other apostles of Christ. To Vigor, the saint's *doubt* made him all too human and relatable. It was an expression of the war between faith and reason. St. Thomas questioned, needed proof, a scientist of his time, a seeker of truth. Even his gospel dismissed organized religion, declaring that the path to salvation, to God, was open to anyone willing to do just that.

To seek and you shall find.

Had they not done that these past days?

"We found St. Thomas's tomb," Vigor said softly, stifled by awe and tears. "The Nestorians, along with Ildiko's last testament, must have convinced Genghis to build this shrine to the saint. That's why his gospel was crafted and left in Hungary. It was a written invitation to find this crypt. The first site preserved Thomas's words—and this last, his very body and legacy."

Vigor allowed his fingers to touch that sacred bone, to lift the skull from the golden reliquary.

Gray stayed at his shoulder. As Vigor cradled the relic of St. Thomas in his palms, his friend shone his flashlight to the bottom of the chest.

In a sculpted gold bed rested a simple black cross.

It looked heavy, metallic, as long as an outstretched hand.

"The cross of St. Thomas," Gray mumbled. "But can we be sure?"

Despite the gravity of the moment, Vigor smiled.

While Vigor had no *doubt,* Gray needed *proof.*

"Duncan will know," Vigor said.

Gray checked his watch. "We only have an hour left. I'll go check on their status."

"Go," Vigor said. "I'll wait here."

Gray squeezed his shoulder and quickly departed.

Only then did Vigor sink to his knees, cradling the relic of St. Thomas in his lap.

Thank you, Lord, for allowing me this moment.

Still, despite his reverential awe, a flicker of fear remained. He was still haunted by the eyes of the shaman—and his warning.

You are suffering much, but you will suffer more.

9:04 A.M.

Gray skidded his ATV out of the tunnel's mouth and into the bright morning sunshine. The vehicle spun a full three-sixty on the ice before coming to a stop. He had dared not waste a minute and needed to be outside the cave for his satellite phone to work.

He punched Monk's number. It was immediately picked up.

"Where are you?" Gray asked.

"On a bus. Driving across the ice. We're just about to the island."

Gray bit back a groan. The others were running behind schedule. "I need you to come straight here. I'll call Seichan in a moment and have her do the same. I'm three miles north of Burkhan Cape, along the coast, out on the ice at the entrance to a sea tunnel. I'll leave my ATV in the sunshine as a marker."

"Did you find the cross?" Monk asked.

Flustered, Gray realized he hadn't even mentioned that. "Yes. But we need Duncan to confirm it."

And the Eye brought here.

In the background, he heard Jada call to Monk, "*Tell him not to move the cross.*"

"What's that about?" Gray asked.

"I'll let her tell you. I'm going to see about a shorter route to your coordinates."

"What are you—?"

But Monk was gone and Jada came on the line. "You haven't moved the cross since you found it, have you?" she asked, sounding scared.

"No."

He hadn't even wanted to touch it without corroboration.

"Good. I think the best chance for us to break the quantum entanglement between the cross and the comet is to keep the cross at its current spatial coordinates."

"Why?"

"Because the cross is currently fixed to a *specific* point in the curve of the earth's space-time. I want *time* to remain the only variable. I can show you my calculations, but—"

"I'll take you at your word. Just get that Eye here in time."

"Monk is working on—"

In the background, Duncan could be heard yelling, "*That's your plan!*"

Gray heard a rising commotion, people yelling. "What's going on?"

Jada answered, flustered, but clarifying little, "We're on our way."

The connection abruptly ended.

Gray simply had to trust that they knew what they were doing. He called Seichan next. After a longer than expected delay, the connection was picked up.

"Where are you?" Seichan demanded, sounding angry.

Not having the time to analyze her curt response, he simply told her and ended with, "Come straight here."

She cut off the connection just as brusquely, not even bothering to acknowledge him.

Gray shook his head and headed on foot back inside.

He would have to trust she would do the right thing.

29

Seichan didn't know what to do.

Pak leaned close to her face. She smelled the tobacco on his breath from the cigarettes he had been chain-smoking since he got here.

"Tell me what they said! Where are they?"

He still held her phone in his hand. Behind Pak, the stone-faced North Korean unit leader—whose name she had learned was Ryung—continued to hold a pistol to Rachel's chest. Pak had forced Seichan to find out where Gray was, then ended the call before she could warn him in any way.

Both of the North Koreans were clearly losing patience.

Pak stalked across the common room of the inn, angrily puffing on a cigarette. Ju-long hung back by the fire, looking none too pleased about any of this. Seichan got the feeling he was under some coercion. He was a man driven by money and position in Macau. For him, there could be no profit in what was happening here.

Not that such sentiment would lead him to help them.

Rachel was bound to a chair across from her. Both of them had been expertly immobilized by Ryung's men. There was no magical way to free themselves from this situation. No secret knife, no way to break the chair or slip her bonds.

Seichan knew the reality of the situation. They were both at Pak's mercy—an emotion she doubted existed in the man.

Recognizing this, Seichan had told them earlier where Gray and the others had gone, to Burkhan Cape. If she had failed to do that, they would have shot Rachel. She had no doubt of that. She only had to stare over to the innkeeper's legs sticking out the kitchen door, one shoe fallen off, sprawled in a pool of blood, to be certain.

So she told them about Gray's sunrise meeting at the coast. She sought to buy time, hoping to create a long enough delay for Monk to arrive at the inn and possibly upset the scenario, maybe even rescue them, or at least allow Seichan a possible opportunity to free herself and Rachel during the chaos.

After her earlier confession, Ryung had dispatched a handful of men to Burkhan Cape. They returned thirty minutes later, getting confirmation that Seichan had spoken the truth. But while they were questioning the shaman, the man simply stepped out of the mouth of his cave and threw himself to the rocks below, never revealing *where* Gray had gone from there.

The North Koreans had to accept she didn't know either—not that they didn't use the time to rough the two women up. Rachel and Seichan had matching cigarette burns on the back of their hands as proof.

Then came the damned call.

Pak had used the opportunity to get an update.

"Don't tell them," Rachel said around a split lip. "You know what's at stake."

Clearly growing frustrated with Seichan's delaying tactics, Pak stubbed out his cigarette and returned from his angry stroll around the room. He came back rubbing his palms, a gleam of dark amusement in his eyes.

Seichan went cold.

"Let's make this interesting, shall we?" he said.

Parting his palms, Pak revealed a North Korean silver coin in his hand. On the surface was the smiling visage of the dictator Kim Jong-il.

"You know I am a betting man," Pak said. "So a game, a wager. *Heads.* We shoot your friend. *Tails.* She lives."

Seichan glared at the man's needless cruelty.

"I am going to keep flipping this coin until you tell me," Pak pressed. "The first *head* that comes up, she dies."

Ryung fixed his pistol more firmly to Rachel's chest.

Stepping back, Pak flipped the coin high into the air. It flashed silver in the lamplight.

Seichan relented, knowing she could delay no longer. "Fine! I'll tell you!"

"Don't!" Rachel warned.

The coin struck the floor and bounced until Pak trapped it under his boot, wearing a mean smile, enjoying this way too much.

"See, that wasn't so hard," he said. "Now tell me."

She did, telling him the truth, changing tactics. If stalling no longer worked, her best hope was to get them all moving. Once under way, she might find an opportunity to break free.

"Very good," Pak said, pleased with himself.

He lifted his shoe.

The fat-cheeked face of Kim Jong-il smiled up from the floor.

Heads.

"Looks like you lose," Pak said and signaled his man.

Ryung stepped back, aimed his gun, and shot Rachel in the chest.

Horror as much as the blast made Seichan jump, rocking her chair back, almost toppling over.

Equally stunned, Rachel stared down at the blood welling through her shirt—then back up at Seichan.

Seichan gaped at Pak, at his betrayal.

He shrugged, looking surprised at her response. "It's the usual house rules," Pak said. "Once the dice are in the air, all bets are final."

Across the way, Rachel's head slumped to her chest.

Seichan despaired.

What have I done?

9:20 A.M.

Cold darkness enfolded her.

All her strength and heat seeped out the single hole in her chest, taking at last the fiery pain with it. With each fading breath, she felt a small ache remaining, more spiritual than physical.

I don't want to go . . .

Rachel struggled to stay, but again it was not a fight of muscle and bone, but of will and purpose. She had heard the others leave the inn, abandoning her to her death.

But Monk would come . . .

She held on to that hope. She knew he could not save her, not even with his considerable medical skill. Instead, she clutched to that thinning silver strand of her existence for one purpose.

To tell him where the others had gone.

Hurry . . .

She drifted deeper into that darkness—when the creak of a door, a rush of footsteps, held her a moment longer from oblivion.

A hand touched her knee.

Down that dark well, faint words fell to her, nearly unintelligible, but still the desire rang through.

Where?

She took her last and deepest breath and told them, hope slipping from her lips—not for her, not for the world.

Instead, she pictured storm-blue eyes.

And was gone.

30

"This is nuts!" Duncan yelled.

"This is *faster*," Monk said.

Duncan could only watch as his partner hauled on the wheel of the bus, careening its long length around a point of the coastline. He fishtailed across the shore ice, coming close to clipping an ice-fishing hut. Then he was trundling onward.

After Gray's call, Monk had commandeered the bus, sending passengers and driver fleeing out the door. Monk then got behind the wheel and headed west from the southern tip of the island, blazing his own trail across the open ice. Monk must have anticipated this earlier, as he had spent much of the bus ride from Sakhyurta talking to their driver, asking about the thickness of the frozen shelf, how far it stretched from the coast this time of year.

Duncan somewhat understood his partner's reasoning. Both of them had plenty of time to study a map of Olkhon Island after landing in Irkutsk. A topographic chart showed that the road from the ferry station to the village inn was circuitous and winding. It would be a slow slog.

Additionally, the island was crescent shaped, bending toward the west at its northern end—where they needed to go.

So the most direct path, from point A to point B, was as a crow flies— or rather a seal swims. By traveling straight across the shore ice, they could halve their time in reaching Gray's team.

Still . . .

Jada clung to her seat, her eyes huge.

Ice boomed under them. Cracks skittered in the wake of their passage. People watched from the shoreline, pointing at them.

This far out, the thickness of the ice was questionable at best, so they dared not slow. Momentum was their best hope.

"That must be Burkhan Cape!" Jada yelled, pointing to a craggy promontory sticking out of a forested bay.

Duncan spotted the timbered houses of a small town hugging that same bay. *Must be Khuzhir.*

"Three more miles!" Monk called and pointed to the windows on the right side of the bus. "Gray said he'd left his ATV parked on the ice as a marker for the sea tunnel. Keep watch for it!"

Duncan moved to that side as Monk finally began angling closer to shore, where thankfully the ice should be thicker. After another long tense five minutes, Jada hollered, making him jump.

"There!" she called out and pointed. "By that big rock shaped like a bear!"

With rounded ears and stubby muzzle, the boulder did look like a grizzly's head. And past the granite beast's shoulders, a black dot marked the presence of a lone ATV, a small flag waving from its rear.

"That's gotta be it," Monk said.

As they drew nearer, the mouth of a tunnel appeared in the cliff, lined by massive icicles. Duncan thought he spotted movement in the woods at the top of the escarpment, but with the sun rising on the other side of the island, the forest was in deep shadow.

If anyone was up there, it was probably stunned onlookers come to watch the bus.

The brakes squealed as Monk slowed them—or at least, he tried to.

The bus spun sideways, skidding across the ice.

They broadsided the ATV and bulldozed it in front of them, pushing it back toward the mouth of the tunnel.

Duncan and Jada both retreated to the opposite side of the bus as the cliff wall came rushing toward them.

But the vehicle finally slowed to a shuddering stop, coming to rest ten yards from the mouth of the sea tunnel.

Monk rubbed his palms on his thigh. "Now that's what I call parallel parking."

Duncan scowled. "Is that what you call it?"

They all tumbled out the door, wanting to make sure they were at the right place before unloading their gear.

Gray came running from the shadows of the tunnel, drawn by the commotion, his eyes huge at their means of transportation. He clearly must have recognized the bus from his own icy sojourn from the mainland to the island.

"What?" he asked with a grin. "You couldn't find a cab?"

9:28 A.M.

Gray gave Monk a fast hug. It was good to see his best friend, even under the circumstances and his unusual means of transportation.

He quickly shook Jada's hand, but he pointed his finger at Duncan. "I need you to get that Eye up to that vault. Kowalski's back there and can show you. We found the cross, but we have no way of telling if it's energized in any way."

"I'll go with him," Jada said, offering her expertise.

Gray nodded his thanks, staring out across the ice, wondering what was taking Seichan and Rachel so long. He had expected them here before Monk and the others.

Jada stepped back toward the bus. "I left my pack—"

A sharp whistle pierced the morning, followed immediately by a massive blast of fire and ice. Jada got blown into Duncan, who caught her. The concussion knocked them all off their feet and down the tunnel, accompanied by a barrage of broken icicles.

Gray slid on his back, staring past his toes.

Outside, the bus upended, tipping up on its front grill, windows exploding. A fireball rolled from beneath it and into the sky, trailed by a cloud of smoke. The ice shelf shattered beneath its bulk, and the bus sank nose-first into the lake.

A rocket attack.

But who . . . and why?

Still, a greater question loomed. "Where is the Eye?" Gray asked, fearfully yelling, half deafened.

Duncan helped Jada to her feet. She pointed to the wreckage sinking into the lake.

"My pack . . ."

It was still on the bus.

"Everybody back!" Gray said, pointing deeper into the tunnel.

They fled away from the rage of fire and smoke—and into the cold darkness of ice and frost.

As they reached a bend in the tunnel, Gray glanced back. The rear of the bus stuck out crookedly from the ice, smoking and charred. Fire spread outward in streams of gasoline and oil. Shadows moved beyond those flames.

Who were they? Russian forces? Had someone in Moscow grown wise to their covert presence on the island?

"Monk, stay here," Gray ordered. "Alert us if anyone starts into the tunnel."

And they would, he knew.

Whoever had orchestrated this attack had purposefully targeted their only means of transportation, intending to trap Gray's group inside here. The reason *why* didn't matter. With time running out, only one objective remained: recovering the Eye and getting it to that vault.

Gray led Duncan and Jada back to the cavern. Kowalski anxiously awaited them.

"What the hell, man?" the big man asked. "What's going on out there?"

"Doesn't matter," he said and turned to Duncan. "We need to retrieve Dr. Shaw's pack from that burning bus."

"How?" Duncan asked.

Gray turned to Jada. "Do you think you can climb that rope by yourself when the time is right?"

She nodded. "What do you want us to do?"

Gray told them.

"You're nuts," Duncan said, looking around for support.

Kowalski just shrugged. "We've done stupider things."

9:34 A.M.

This is becoming a bad habit.

Duncan stood again in his boxers by a body of water—only this time, at the slippery lip to a breathing hole through the ice, its edges worn smooth by the bodies of mother seals sliding into and out of the water. He pictured those same seals dropping into the water here and swimming back through the tunnel, traveling under the ice all the while to reach the open lake.

Duncan wouldn't have to go that far, but where he was going was still a long distance in one breath. And he didn't have the fatty insulation of a winter seal.

Neither did his swimming companion.

Jada had stripped to shorts and a sports bra.

Beyond her, Gray and Kowalski readied the two ATVs parked in the cavern, checking weapons. The plan was for them to pick up Monk on the way out.

Duncan returned his attention to Jada, who shivered next to him, but little of her trembling had to do with the cold.

"Ready?" he asked.

She swallowed and nodded.

"Stick to my heels," he said with a smile. "You'll be fine."

"Let's get this over with," she said. "Thinking about it is only making it worse."

She was right.

Duncan cinched the shoulder holster tighter around his bare chest and gave her arm a squeeze. Lowering to his rear, he slid down one of the worn chutes in the lip of the breathing hole. With a short drop, he plunged into the pool of water beneath the thick sheet of ice covering the floor of the cave.

The cold immediately cut through him, worse than he had mentally prepared for. His lungs screamed, wanting to gasp and choke. He forced his legs to kick, his arms to pull, and swam away from the hole. Staying under the ceiling of ice, he headed toward the tunnel leading out. The plan was to swim beneath the ice of the tunnel and get to the outside without being seen.

He twisted back to see Jada splash into the depths. Her body visibly clenched, looking ready to go fetal from the shock, but she fought through it. With a savage kick of her legs, like a stallion striking out at a barn door, she came shooting toward him.

Damn, she was fast.

She had claimed as much when Gray had first proposed this plan.

Duncan kicked off a wall and headed down the tunnel. Diffuse light turned the ice above a deep azure blue, illuminating enough of the depths below to see. He stroked hard to keep ahead of Jada, flipper-kicking to go faster—but also to stay warm.

The tunnel was only thirty yards long, a swim he could normally make in one breath, but in this freeze, trapped under that thick ice, it was a deadly challenge.

He tracked their progress by monitoring the light. It grew brighter with every stroke and kick as he sought the morning sunlight beyond the tunnel.

Still, the cold quickly sapped his endurance. He found his lungs aching for air, his limbs starting to quake. As he neared the tunnel's end, pinpricks of darkness danced across his vision. He checked behind him, saw Jada struggling, too.

Keep going, he willed them both.

Ahead, he spotted their target. It spurred him into a frantic crawl.

Ten yards from them, the bus rested crookedly on its grill on the bottom of the lake. According to Gray, its rear end still stuck out of the ice above.

With a promise of fresh air, he swam over to its side. The windshield had been blown out by the concussive blast of the rocket. Reaching through, he grabbed the wheel and hauled himself into the shadowy interior of the vehicle. He shot upward past the seats and surfaced inside the pocket of air at the rear of the bus.

Jada appeared a second later.

They both gulped air as quietly as possible, appreciating not only the oxygen but also the warmth. The recent flames had heated the interior considerably. Neither of them complained.

Outside their hiding spot, Duncan heard voices, speaking what sounded like Korean, maybe Chinese. So far no alarm had been raised at their presence. The enemy had not expected its trapped quarry to pop up inside the submerged bus.

It was a small advantage.

He turned to Jada and pointed below. She nodded and they both submerged. Grabbing seatbacks, they pulled themselves back down the length of the bus, searching for Jada's pack.

Everything loose had fallen to the front of the bus or spilled out the missing windshield. Refreshed with oxygen, Jada swam like a seal herself, while he felt like a blundering whale. She found her pack quickly enough, and they returned to the surface.

Jada checked inside, the relief on her face expressed everything.

He offered her a thumbs-up, which she returned.

They had the Eye.

Impulsively, he reached over and kissed her. He didn't know if he'd ever get another chance. In that small gesture, he invested so much: a wish for her safety, a thanks for her efforts, but mostly a hope for more to come.

Surprise stiffened her—then her lips softened, warming and melting into his own.

Breaking apart, her eyes shone at him. She somehow looked both more determined and more scared. But she touched his cheek and slipped back underwater.

Duncan shifted to a shattered side window, staying out of direct view. He took in the lay of the land. Ropes draped from the cliffs above. A unit of armed men in military winter camouflage flanked the tunnel's mouth. He counted the number of enemy between the bus and the cliff.

Not good.

Freeing his SIG Sauer from its shoulder holster, he touched a throat mike and subvocalized to Gray. "The Eye is headed back," he said. "I've got twenty combatants. Ten to each side. I think they're Korean."

Gray swore. Apparently this made some sort of sense to the man. "Stick to the plan," the commander radioed back. "Count to thirty and begin firing."

Duncan swung back to the window.

Their team had no hope of victory against such odds.

Instead, the plan was a simple one.

Buy as much time with their lives as possible.

Duncan glanced to the dark waters. At this moment, the fate of the world depended on how fast Jada could swim.

31

Jada knew she would not make it.

Fear, cold, and exhaustion had taxed her to her limit. The drag of the pack across her shoulders further hindered her, feeling like a leaden weight, compromising the reach of each stroke. But that was not her worst problem.

A trail of blood wafted behind her, streaming with each pull. She had sliced her right arm to the bone on a jagged piece of blasted metal as she had exited the bus. Heat and strength sapped out of her body with every yard gained, flowing like a crimson flag behind her. She fought to keep going, as pain became numbness.

She had to kick harder as her right arm weakened.

Her lungs screamed for air.

The way became darker—but not because she fled the sunlight behind her for the tunnel. Instead, her vision squeezed, swimming with shadows.

Distantly ahead, she could make out a brighter pool of water, where a flashlight rested next to the hole in the ice, awaiting her arrival, along with warm clothes.

Never make it . . .

Proving this, her pace slowed, her right arm useless now, dragging alongside her. She flutter-kicked, desperate, but despairing.

A rumble shook through the water to her ears.

She glanced up to see a bright light sweep past her across the translucent ice, heading for the mouth of the tunnel behind her.

She reached and placed her palm against the ice.

Help me . . .

But they swept away, abandoning her.

Gray raced his ATV toward the morning sunlight. Monk rode shotgun behind him, while Kowalski trailed on the second vehicle. Ahead, the mouth of the tunnel grew larger. He spotted figures sheltering to the left and right.

Koreans, Duncan had said—but Gray knew they were, in fact, *North Koreans.*

How had they found them? Fear for Seichan, for Rachel, fired his blood. Was that why the women had not shown up by now? Had they been captured? He remembered the strained and brief conversation with Seichan.

They must have held her at gunpoint.

Still, that offered one hope.

The North Koreans clearly wanted to capture him and Kowalski and would likely try to take them alive.

At least, initially.

Gray was under no such compunction.

He heard the first pops from Duncan's SIG Sauer.

With the enemy's attention focused on the mouth of the tunnel and the approaching roar of the ATVs, Duncan fired at the Koreans' rear flank, catching them off guard.

Gray heard screams of shock and surprise at the sudden assault from an unexpected direction. Monk rose from behind and shot over Gray's shoulder, adding to the confusion.

With a final gun of his engine, he took advantage of the momentary chaos as the enemy was routed, perplexed and unsure how to respond to a battle on two fronts.

A soldier ran into view, framed in the tunnel opening, pointing a rifle.

Monk dropped him with a single shot.

Gray sped to the left of the body, Kowalski to the right.

They spun out into the sunlight, letting go of their handles, spinning their bikes, pistols up and firing in all directions. Duncan shoved open the rear door of the bus, popping into view, firing from on high.

Soldiers in winter camouflage dropped to the ice—either felled or seeking to make themselves less of a target for the barrage.

But Gray knew his team was outgunned and outnumbered. At any moment, the tide would turn against them. Rounds already began to chase their skidding bikes, splintering the ice around them.

They had only one goal here: buy time.

He had warned Vigor to stay in the vault, to await Jada's arrival, to help her with whatever she needed. The monsignor had agreed, not looking too well anyway.

With that goal in mind, Gray fired and fired, urging Jada to hurry.

9:46 A.M.

Jada struggled for that distant pool of light, kicking and clawing with her one good arm. She heard the gunshots behind her, as the others cast aside their lives for her goal. Such a sacrifice kept her throat tight, fighting the reflex to breathe, though her lungs burned. The rest of her body was ice, growing heavier, more leaden.

Then something bumped her body and swept past, startling a gasp of bubbles from her lips. It was a brown mother seal, sleek and supple in the water. With a twist and roll, it swung back to her and circled smoothly around her waist, brushing against her, then back forward, hovering with invitation.

Through the agony of ice and fire, she understood.

Reaching out with her good arm, she grabbed that tail. At her touch, the seal burst forward—whether startled or purposefully. It shot toward the hole inside the cavern, the closest breath of fresh air, dragging Jada along.

Willing all her strength into her fingertips, she held tight.

In seconds, they reached that bright pool of light and burst upward. Breaking the surface, Jada gasped, sucking air. The seal bobbed beside her, its brown eyes shining at her, as if to see if she were okay. Catching her breath, Jada took a moment to wonder at the sight. Was it just maternal instinct in the seal, seeking to aid an injured fellow mammal? Or was it truly the spirit of the island as Temur had said, coming to her rescue.

Either way, Jada silently thanked her. The seal nudged its nose a few times in the air, then dove away.

Jada swam to the edge, where Gray had left a rope hanging to help her pull out of the water and up the icy chute. Once up top, she crawled on her hands and knees, blood running down her arm and leaving crimson handprints.

She reached a set of blankets and rubbed herself dry. There were clothes there, too, but she ignored them, knowing she didn't have time to fully dress. Instead, she dropped her pack, pulled on the parka, and zipped it up.

Shaking all over, she slung her pack over her shoulder and stepped into a climbing harness. She pulled it up bare legs and secured it.

She stumbled toward the frozen waterfall, having a hard time controlling her limbs. Once at the base, she stared up the length of rope ascending the sheer cliff of ice.

Grabbing hold, she immediately recognized the futility. She could barely feel her fingers. Her strength continued to leave her with every quake of her limbs.

But gunfire echoed to her.

Her friends were not giving up.

I cannot give up.

Knowing she had only ten minutes left, she pulled herself up to the first piton, then the next. Renewed determination drove her upward, but strength of will was not the same as strength of limb.

She reached with her wounded arm, tried to hold—and slipped, falling back to the hard ice. She stared up, tears of frustration running hot down her cheeks, recognizing the truth.

I'll never make it.

9:48 A.M.

Gray knew the battle was lost.

The surprise of the initial assault faded as the enemy dug in. A round pinged off the side of the ATV, the ricochet striking Gray's thigh, burning a line across his hip.

He signaled Kowalski.

The big man dashed his ATV over toward the bus, while Gray and Monk covered him, sweeping across the ice and laying down a fierce barrage of gunfire.

Kowalski reached the broken ice around the bus and spun a one-eighty, skidding to a stop at the crumbling lip of the shattered hole.

Atop the bus, Duncan bounded out of its rear door, ran across its slanted back, and vaulted over the open water below, opalescent with leaking gasoline and oil. He landed hard on the seat behind Kowalski—and the pair immediately rocketed away from the bus in a fishtailing path toward Gray.

As they fled, rounds peppered the side of the bus and cracked shards from the ice.

Monk fired back toward the tunnel as Gray gripped the handlebars with one glove and blasted away with his pistol in the other.

They were all low on ammunition and needed to make a final stand.

He raced toward the tunnel, seeking its cover.

Kowalski barreled behind him.

Monk hit a soldier in the leg, sending him toppling. Others scattered as Gray's team concentrated their fire at the mouth of the tunnel. With the way clear, his group shot into the tunnel, raced ten yards in, then skidded sideways in unison.

Once stopped, they all fell to the far sides of the parked vehicles, using their bulk as a temporary shelter, setting up a roadblock between them and the enemy.

Gray took quick inventory. Kowalski bled from his shoulder and side. Duncan had an angry graze across his cheek. Monk held a hand to his thigh, blood welling through his fingers.

Still, they all looked fierce and ready to eke out every extra moment for Jada and Vigor to accomplish what they must. Unfortunately, they were down to a few shots each. They would have to make them count.

As if knowing this, the enemy regrouped for their final assault.

Gray braced for it, leveling his pistol.

Instead, a figure appeared, clutching another.

A large North Korean soldier in full body armor held Seichan, an arm across her throat, a pistol against her skull, using her as a human shield. Seichan looked defeated, the fire blown out of her.

"Throw your weapons to us!" a familiar voice called to them. "Come out with your hands on your heads or she will die before you. Just like we killed the other woman."

The plans that had been revising in Gray's head blew away at those last words.

. . . killed the other woman.

Monk clutched his arm, but he barely felt those fingers.

Rachel.

Frozen flashes popped through his head: the rich caramel of her eyes, the way she flipped her hair when angry, the softness of her lips, the stutter of her laughter when caught off guard.

How could that all be gone?

"Gray," Monk whispered to him, holding him to the present with his tone as much as his iron grip.

Fire welled up inside Gray, blinding him.

At the tunnel's end, Pak darted out, dashing into cover behind the tall Korean. "Come out now! And you will live!"

The triumphant whine of that insect's voice snapped Gray back to himself, to his duty. They still needed to buy time to save the world, but Gray had a new purpose: to avenge Rachel.

"What do you want us to do?" Duncan whispered, holding his SIG Sauer.

Gray considered sending the man back to help Jada, but Pak would know one of them was missing and go looking for Duncan, defeating their objective here.

"Do what he says," Gray said coldly, forcing his jaw to move. "It'll buy us more time."

With no other recourse, they threw out their weapons. Pistols skittered across the ice and into the sunshine beyond the tunnel.

Gray stood up, his hands on his head.

The others followed his example and climbed together over the blockage of vehicles.

Clearly knowing he had won, Pak finally stepped free as they approached. He felt at ease enough to light a victory cigarette and pointed its glowing tip at Gray.

"We will have fun, you and I."

Gray bit back a retort, constraining himself from reacting, trying to keep this guy talking versus entering the tunnel.

He had no idea if Jada had safely scaled the frozen waterfall at the back of the cavern, but the climbing ropes were still there. The enemy would know to follow that path up.

So he only glared.

Reaching the tunnel's end, Gray found rifles pointed at them, bodies strewn across the ice. At least they had taken out half of Pak's forces. Others bled from grazes and gunshots.

Gray would have to take satisfaction in that.

To the left, a familiar figure hung back from the others.

Ju-long Delgado.

He glanced at Gray, then at his toes, clearly ashamed of his role here.

It was unfortunate.

The man failed to see the thin shape sail down one of the Koreans' ropes, landing behind him without a sound—or the flash of silver as the sword pierced him from behind.

As Ju-long fell to his knees with a gasp of surprise, Guan-yin stood there, her dragon tattoo ablaze on her face, shining with fury. She raised her other hand, lifting a pistol into view, and began firing.

To both sides, figures flowed down the other ropes, shooting from above as they descended.

Her Triad.

Stunned, Gray could not fathom *how* Guan-yin had found them, but such questions would have to wait.

Taking advantage of her mother's distraction, Seichan stamped her captor's instep. While the hardened soldier was too professional to lose hold of her, it allowed Seichan to slip lower, her eyes fixed to Gray.

He was already moving, running toward her. The man fired at him, but Gray dropped and slid on the ice. As rounds blasted over the crown of his head, he grabbed the only weapon at hand.

Reaching the soldier's knees, Gray lunged up with a shattered length of icicle in hand. He drove it past Seichan's ear and through the man's exposed throat.

The soldier fell back, dropping his weapon and clutching his neck with both hands.

Gray turned to Duncan. "Go help Jada! Now!"

They were down to a handful of minutes.

9:53 A.M.

With a fire lit under him, Duncan sprinted, not bothering with the abandoned ATVs. He vaulted over them and ran, stretching his stride, trying to stick to the windblown dry snow versus the slick ice.

Gunfire continued behind him, but it was quickly sputtering away as the arriving forces overwhelmed the remaining North Koreans.

Reaching the cavern in seconds, he spotted Jada perched halfway up the ice wall, decidedly struggling. Vigor crouched in the tunnel above her, trying his best to pull her up, but the monsignor was plainly too weak.

As Duncan ran toward them, he noted the trail of blood leading from the breathing hole to the cliff. More icy blood trailed down the frozen waterfall, adding streaks of crimson to the blue.

"Hang on!" Duncan yelled.

"What do you think I'm trying to do!" she called back, both angry and relieved.

Duncan ran to the free line. "Hold tight. I'm going to haul you up."

He pulled hard, drawing the rope through the eyehole in the roof and towing Jada's body up to the tunnel. Once there, Vigor helped her clamber inside. Both looked clearly spent.

As Jada unclipped her harness, Duncan called up to them. "Keep going! I'm right behind you."

Jada waved her acknowledgment, having no breath left to speak.

The pair vanished as he mounted the line and scrambled up.

9:54 A.M.

Free at last, Seichan spun away from the guard who had held her. She heard Gray shout to Duncan and paused only long enough to grab Ryung's abandoned weapon, the same pistol he had used to shoot Rachel.

She stepped over his impaled body and went after the only target that mattered.

Pak fled across the ice at the first sign of trouble, running for cover behind the half-submerged bus. He had a pistol in hand and shot blindly behind him, panicked by the chaos and the sudden turn of fortune. But as a gambler, he should have known that luck always runs out.

She stalked deliberately after him.

He spotted her, swung his weapon at her, and fired.

She didn't even bother dodging.

Instead, she lifted her arm and squeezed the trigger.

She placed the round through his knee. He fell headlong with a scream, sliding on his belly, spinning. Reaching the broken ice around the blasted bus, he flew out over the open water and plunged into its depths.

She crossed to the edge and watched him come sputtering up from the cold. Compromised by his wrecked knee, she knew every kick that kept him afloat must be agony.

He struggled over to the edge, seeking a handhold, found one where a corner of the bus met the ice. Unfortunately, the bulk of the bus shifted slightly, settling further as its mass compressed the surrounding ice. The movement pinned his fingers in that crack. He cried out, struggling to free his four crushed fingers.

Seichan's mother had already taken the fifth one to repay a gambling debt. Pak owed Seichan much more.

"Help me!" Pak said, teeth chattering.

Seichan bent down, seeing hope flare in Pak's eyes.

Instead, she picked up the cigarette that had fallen from his lips as he spun into the water. She straightened and blew the tip to a glowing red.

Horror replaced hope. Like her, he must smell the leaked gasoline and oil, forming a thick layer on the water.

"Cold, isn't it?" she said. "Let me warm you up."

She flicked the bud below. A rain of fiery ash ignited the fumes first, then the pool of oil and gasoline. Flames chased across the blue water, reaching and swamping over Pak.

She turned from his screaming and headed back, leaving him to burn above and freeze below.

That's for Rachel.

32

Ju-long lay on the ice, his blood spreading in a warm pool under him. He had heard Pak begging for his life as the gunfire died down—followed by his screaming. He felt no pity for the man.

The bastard deserved a cruel end.

And maybe I do, too.

As if summoned by this thought, a face loomed into view, staring down at him, merciless despite her chosen name.

"Guan-yin," he mumbled. He lifted a hand toward her, but with a tremble, he dropped it, too weak. "Pak has my wife . . . my unborn son."

Her face remained impassive, as hard as the scales on her dragon, not accepting his excuse.

"I'm sorry," he gasped out, tasting blood on his lips. "I . . . I love them so much . . . please help them."

"Why should I help you? After what you've done?"

"I tried . . . how I could . . . to help."

A single line creased her brow.

"How did you think you found us?" he said, gasping around a twinge of pain. "Tracked Pak and me to this island?"

"Like you, I have ears everywhere. I heard you left North Korea for Mongolia. So I followed, trailed you. I knew you must still be going after—"

He cut her off. "Who do you think *spoke* to those many ears of yours? I told them to speak to you."

It was the truth. Ju-long had to be discreet while with Pak. Using the excuse of monitoring the assassin's tracker, he was able to regularly call Macau and manipulate matters from afar. While he could not raise his own army in Macau without alerting the North Koreans and risking his pregnant wife's life, he attempted to raise another, to stoke the hatred of Guan-yin to come to his aid.

He remembered the surprise of the sword piercing his chest.

Apparently he had stoked that hatred too well.

A small miscalculation.

"I drew you here to kill Pak, possibly to free me," he said with a small laugh full of blood. "To perhaps mend our fences in the end."

Now all that matters is my beautiful Natalia . . . and the son I will never see . . .

Guan-yin leaned back. He saw she believed him. Still, was that enough for her to help? She was not known for the quality of her mercy.

"I will find them," she finally promised. "I will free them."

A single tear of relief rolled down his cheek. He knew she would not fail him.

Thank you.

With this burden lifted from him, he allowed his eyes to close—but before they did, another face appeared next to Guan-yin, the pretty assassin who had caused so much trouble.

Only then did he see the resemblance.

One next to the other.

Mother and daughter.

He now understood the cause of his small miscalculation. In the end, it had never been about money or turf—only family.

No wonder you stabbed me.

Finally recognizing the error of his ways, his own silent laughter followed him into oblivion.

9:56 A.M.

"So that's how you knew how to find us," Gray said, standing behind Seichan and her mother, eavesdropping on the conversation.

He carried a pistol and guarded over them, as Monk and Kowalski helped the rest of the Triad mop up the situation on the ice.

Guan-yin stood. "Yes, it's how we knew you were on the island, but the last word to reach us claimed Ju-long would be at an inn at Khuzhir."

Gray understood. Ju-long must not have had time to call and update his spies before moving here. "Then how did you know to come out here?"

A sad look swept over her features. "We found a woman, shot, still alive. She told us."

Rachel . . .

Guan-yin read the rising hope in his face and quashed it. "She did not make it. But it was her dying words that brought us here."

And saved us all, Gray realized. *And maybe the world.*

Guan-yin touched his arm. "I think she was hanging on just to get that message out."

Grief ripped through him, but he held it in check until later.

They were not finished here.

He headed toward the tunnel.

Besides saving the world, he had another mission still to go, one even closer to his heart. As much as it would destroy the man, Vigor deserved to know the fate of his niece.

9:57 A.M.

"And Rachel?" the monsignor asked.

Duncan read the hope in the man's eyes as they crossed the threshold into the chamber of gold. Jada hobbled on the far side of Vigor, looking upon Duncan with an equal expectation of good news.

After climbing the frozen waterfall, he had caught up with Jada and Vigor on the small pond that served as an antechamber to the golden *ger.*

Duncan explained as best he could as they scaled the stairs. He had told them about Seichan being held at gunpoint, about the turning of the tides by the arrival of new allies—which still baffled him.

Still, he knew one truth.

"Rachel was killed," Duncan said, seeing no way to blunt the news.

Vigor stopped a few steps into the room, staring at him in disbelief, his face crashing into ruin. "No . . ."

Jada stayed next to Vigor as grief felled the old man to his knees. She pushed Duncan toward the rock pillar in the center of the room.

"Check the cross," she hissed, dropping her pack, going after the Eye inside. "But don't move it."

He understood. They needed confirmation that the artifact was what they all sought. He hurried to the nest of three boxes: iron, silver, and gold. A skull rested on the gold floor next to the cairn.

Keeping clear of the relic, he looked down into the innermost box. A heavy black cross rested inside, seated in a sculpted bed of gold that matched its shape.

He reached a hand inside, but even before passing through the outer box of iron, he felt the magnets in his fingertips respond. Again he sensed pressure, as if a force were resisting him. He pushed deeper into that field, drawing his fingers closer to its dark surface.

Again, he recognized the same oily, unnatural feel to the energy, but as his tips drew to within a hairbreadth of the cross, he noted a subtle difference. With this unadulterated power wafting off the meteoric metal, he recognized that this energy—while much the same—had a different flavor to it.

Or *color*.

It couldn't be described any other way.

While he had gripped the Eye, he sensed a *blackness* to it, like the darkness between stars, beautiful in its own right.

Here, he could only express this energy as *white*.

Jada had said the two items—the cross and the Eye—were opposites, different quantum spins from each other, separate poles on an axis of time.

But there was another fundamental difference.

With the Eye, he found its touch repellent.

Here, he had to restrain himself against grabbing that cross. It was nearly irresistible. Despite the warning from Jada, the tip of his index finger brushed the surface.

As contact was made, that whiteness enveloped him, blinding him.

From his background in physics, he knew *black* holes sucked all light into themselves, while theoretical *white* holes cast it all back out.

He felt that way now, *cast* out, thrust somewhere else, possibly sometime else. Through the brilliance, a figure approached, all in shadows. Like a dark mirror of himself, this shape reached to his outstretched hand, as if going for the cross, too.

As their fingertips touched, Duncan found himself blasted away.

The room returned, snapping so suddenly back he stumbled to the side, clenching and unclenching his hand.

"What's wrong?" Jada asked.

He shook his head.

"What about the cross?"

"It's . . . it's got energy."

He retreated from the pillar, but not before noting again the skull on the floor, picturing the shadowy figure in the light.

Could it be . . . ?

Not wanting to think about such a possibility, he reached Jada's side. "What do we have to do?"

"I think just touch the Eye to the cross. Bringing their opposite energies together should trigger an annihilation, thus breaking that quantum entanglement."

Duncan pictured that field snuffing out.

"Okay," he said, holding out his hand for the Eye. "Let's do this."

Jada lifted the sphere, but she pulled it away from him.

"What?"

She glanced around. "I think we need this room sealed when it happens. Gold is one of the most nonreactive metals. Pure gold won't even tarnish."

"Like silver and iron will," Duncan said.

"Maybe the ancients knew something. Felt such insulation was important." Jada stood up. "Either way, I feel it would be safer if everyone else was outside this vault after it's sealed. It could be dangerous to be in here when those two forces annihilate."

"Then you and Vigor head out and close the door."

"Maybe I'd better perform this," Jada argued. "I'm less sensitive to these energies than you."

Duncan could not let her risk it.

The stalemate was decided by another.

Vigor surged to his feet and snatched the Eye. He strode toward the ancient boxes. Duncan stepped after him, but the monsignor shoved an arm up, pointing a finger at him, his tone both commanding and grief-stricken.

"Go!"

Duncan recognized that Vigor would not relent.

Jada checked her watch and tugged Duncan's sleeve toward the door. "Someone has to do it. And we're out of time."

With a heavy heart, he fled with Jada for the threshold. As they stepped out and began closing the doors, he watched Vigor step before the pillar, his shoulders slumped, weighted down by grief.

No matter the outcome . . . thank you, old man.

Duncan closed the door and latched it tight.

9:59 A.M.

Vigor stood before the reliquary of St. Thomas, cradling in his palms a crystal sphere holding the very fires of the universe. Within the triple chests lay a cross forged among the stars and carried by a saint. He should have felt exultant, elated to be allowed this hallowed moment at the end of his life.

Instead, he felt only loss.

He had made accommodation for his death, happy that Rachel would live on in his stead. Maybe part of his inner peace was selfish pride, knowing he would be remembered, that she would tell her sons and daughters, even her grandchildren, about her uncle Vigor and the adventures they had shared together.

He wanted to curse God—but as he stared at the cross, he felt a measure of comfort. He knew he would see Rachel again. He was certain of it.

"I have no doubt," he whispered.

He followed it with a short, silent prayer.

He had time for no more.

But was that not the lament upon every deathbed? Regret about what could never be, the finality of death, the great destroyer of possibilities.

Sighing, he pictured all his friends, old and new.

Gray and Monk, Kat and Painter, Duncan and Jada.

Rachel had sacrificed everything to keep them safe, to allow them the fullness of their lives, though hers was cut short.

Could I do any less?

Vigor raised the Eye and placed it where the relic of St. Thomas had rested for millennia. It came to fit perfectly upon the small gold pillars that had supported the skull . . . as if the Eye were always meant to be there.

Only when the sphere touched the cross—

10:00 A.M.

Duncan gasped, stumbling back as if struck in the face by a fierce gust of wind—only he never really *stumbled*.

Instead, his consciousness blew out of the back of his skull. For a moment, he found himself staring at his body from behind, standing next to Jada, both of them facing the doors.

Then he snapped back, so hard he actually fell forward and hit the door. He caught himself with a palm on the jamb.

Jada stared at him. "Are you okay?"

"I'm suddenly glad I wasn't in there."

"What happened?"

He attempted to explain his out-of-body experience.

Instead of being incredulous, she nodded. "The blast from the annihilation of energies likely created a local quantum bubble, bursting outward. And for a sensitive like yourself, where your consciousness is highly attuned to quantum fields, it had a physical effect."

"And what about someone *in* that room? At ground zero?"

10:01 A.M.

It was a good question, Jada thought.

And one that frightened her.

Especially after hearing what Duncan had experienced.

"I don't know," she admitted in regard to Vigor's fate. "Nothing or everything. A flip of the coin."

She realized Vigor was like Schrödinger's cat. As long as the door remained closed, he was *both* alive and dead. Only once they opened it would his fate be decided one way or the other.

She pictured the universe splitting, depending on that answer.

Duncan reached for the door to collapse that potential, but before he could do so, a commotion drew their attention behind them. From the tunnel by the pond, Gray crawled into view, spotted them, and rushed up the stairs.

He quickly took in the situation and noted who was missing.

"Where's Vigor?" he asked.

Jada turned to the sealed door. "He agreed to take the Eye in there, to join it with the cross."

"Did he do it?"

"Yes," Jada said.

Gray frowned at the closed door. "How can you be certain?"

Duncan rubbed the back of his head, as if making sure it was still there. "We're sure."

Gray stepped to the door. "Then let's get in there."

Jada put her hand over the latch, suddenly feeling foolish, as if stopping Gray could truly leave Vigor's fate undecided.

"There's a good chance he didn't make it," Duncan warned, plainly trying to prepare Gray.

Jada nodded and dropped her hand.

Gray pulled the latch and swung the door open.

10:02 A.M.

Gray stepped into the golden chamber, finding it little changed. The vast murals depicting the life of St. Thomas remained. The cairn of stones stood in the middle of the room. The triple boxes sat on top of the pillar.

Only now Vigor lay crumpled on the floor, his head resting against the relic of St. Thomas.

Gray rushed to his side and rolled him over.

His chest didn't move.

Fingers at his throat found no heartbeat.

Oh, God, no . . .

Tears welled up.

He stared at his friend's face, noting the look of peace, of calm release.

"Did he know?" Gray said, not looking away. "About Rachel."

"He did," Duncan said hoarsely.

Gray closed his eyes, praying they were together again, finding a note of comfort in that thought, wanting it to be true, needing it to be so.

Be happy, my friends.

He kept bowed over Vigor for a long breath.

To the side, Duncan stepped to the boxes. He passed his hands over the sphere, picked it up, and examined the cross. He finally shook his head and passed his verdict.

"The energy is gone."

Did that mean they had succeeded?

Gray had a more important question. "Were we in time?"

Jada checked her watch. "I don't know. It all happened right at the cusp. It could go either way."

33

Painter waited with the others on the National Mall. The president and key members of the government had been evacuated. Coastal areas had been sandbagged and cleared. Even Monk and Kat had taken the girls for a short "vacation" in the Amish country of Pennsylvania, away from the potential blast zone.

Though that *potential* was not high, no one was taking chances.

Even his fiancée, Lisa, had suggested returning early from New Mexico to join him, but he discouraged her.

Washington, D.C., was under a voluntary evacuation order. But like Painter, not everyone had abandoned the nation's capital. A vast number of people crowded the Mall. Across the swaths of grass, tents had been pitched, candles lit, and much alcohol was drunk. Songs echoed to him, along with a few prayers and angry shouting matches.

From the steps outside the Smithsonian Castle, Painter stared across that great mass of humanity, with their faces raised to the skies—a few in fear, most with wonder. He never appreciated his fellow man more than at this moment. Here were curiosity, awe, and reverence, all the best traits of humankind squeezed down to this one moment, making each soul smaller against the grandeur of what was about to happen and far, far larger for being a part of it.

A scuffle of feet drew his attention behind him. Jada and Duncan came running across the street from the doors of the Castle. He noted their hands clasped together—though they broke apart once they drew closer.

He didn't say anything about that.

Painter faced Jada. "Don't tell me that the estimates from the SMC have suddenly changed?"

Jada smiled, carrying a cell phone in her other hand. "I keep checking in. So far it looks like Apophis is on track to hit the earth, but only a glancing blow at best. Still, it should be spectacular."

Good.

Painter pictured the destruction shown on the satellite image. By severing the quantum entanglement that was drawing Comet IKON's corona of dark energy toward the earth, they had stopped the potential warping of space-time around the planet, preventing a catastrophic bombardment of asteroids from pummeling a swath across the globe.

He remembered Antarctica, a sneak peek of what might have happened globally. That event had led to the death of eight navy men, and that number would have been much higher, if not for the brave efforts and ingenuity of Lieutenant Josh Leblang, who had heroically rallied his men to safety. Painter was considering recruiting the kid into Sigma. He had great potential.

Still, they were not entirely out of danger—what had already been set in motion by the comet's passing could not be stopped. A few meteors struck in the remote outback of Australia, more in the Pacific. A large rock hit outside of Johannesburg, but the impact did little more than frighten the animals in a nearby safari park.

The biggest danger was still posed by the asteroid Apophis. It had already been shifted from its regular path, and nothing could be done about that. While Sigma had succeeded in severing that quantum connection, it had done so too close to the point of no return. In the end, it proved too late to stop Apophis from striking the earth, but it was at least in time to keep the comet from pulling the asteroid into a direct path toward the Eastern Seaboard. Instead, the asteroid was destined to hit elsewhere.

Its current trajectory was now along a glancing course through the upper atmosphere, where that longer path should wear away much of its kinetic energy. There also remained a high probability it would explode, but rather than casting its stellar debris across the Eastern Seaboard, it would rain down upon the Atlantic Ocean.

Or so they all hoped.

Painter searched Jada's face for any sign of misgiving, any doubt in her calculations and projections, but all he read there was joy.

Then Jada turned away from the skies.

Another figure came running down the street, waving to them. She was a tall black woman in tennis shoes, jeans, and a heavy jacket, unzipped and flapping in her haste to join them.

Painter smiled, recognizing the appropriateness of this latecomer to the party. She truly should be here.

1:11 A.M.

"Momma!" Jada said, hugging her mother. "You made it!"

"Wouldn't miss it!" she said, huffing heavily, clearly having run most of the length of the Mall to make it in time.

Jada took her mother's hand, leaning against her.

They both stared up at the night sky, as they had so many times in the past, sprawled on a blanket watching the Perseid or Leonid meteor showers. It was those moments that had made her want to explore those stars, to be a part of them. Jada wouldn't be who she was without her mother's inspiration.

Fingers squeezed lovingly upon hers, full of pride and joy.

"Here it comes," Jada whispered.

Mother and daughter held tight.

From the east, a roar rose and a massive fireball streaked into view, burning across the world, trailing streams of light and energy, shedding the very forces of the universe. It ripped past overhead, hushing the crowd with its fiery course—then came the sonic boom of its passage, sounding like the earth cracking. People fell to the ground, windows shattered throughout the city, car alarms wailed.

Jada kept to her feet next to her mother, both smiling, watching the flaming star rush to the east—where at the horizon, it exploded in a blinding flash, casting fiery rockets farther out, vanishing into the distance.

A second boom echoed back to them.

Then the night returned to darkness, leaving the comet blazing in the skies. As they watched, a scatter of a hundred falling stars winked and zipped, the last hurrah from the heavens.

The crowed cheered and applauded.

Jada found herself doing the same, her mother cheering just as loudly, tears shining in her eyes at the wonder of it all.

A line from Carl Sagan struck Jada then.

We are star-stuff. We are a way for the cosmos to know itself.

It never felt truer than this moment.

34

Duncan sat on the stool with his shirt on his lap.

The tattoo needle blazed fire across the back of his arm, where his triceps formed a hard horseshoe. The fiery pain was appropriate considering the subject matter being inked upon his flesh.

It was a tiny comet, ablaze with fire and trailing a long curved tail. The design had a slightly Asian flare to it, not unlike what was sculpted in gold back at Lake Baikal, hanging above the Chinese king as he offered St. Thomas his cross.

A bevy of archaeologists and religious scholars were scouring that cave on Olkhon Island. Word was still being kept under wraps from the general public due to the sheer volume of gold inside, not to mention the twelve bejeweled crowns from Genghis Khan's conquests. Duncan expected the site would eventually become a new mecca for St. Thomas Christians— for all Christians, and likely those of Mongol descent, too.

Vigor would be proud, Duncan thought.

More than saving the world with his sacrifice, Vigor had likely renewed the faith and wonder of millions.

Clyde straightened from his work, wiping a bloody cloth across his latest addition to the tapestry that was Duncan's body. "Looks good."

Twisting to check in the mirror, Duncan examined the angry, colorful welting and passed his own judgment. "Looks *fantastic!*"

Clyde shrugged, humble. "I had practice with the first."

His friend waved to a neighboring stool, where Jada sat.

She shifted to bring her bare arm next to his, comparing her artwork to the fresh one on his arm. They looked an exact match, a shared mark of their adventure together.

Only this was her *first* tattoo, the first strokes on a blank canvas.

"What do you think?" he asked.

She smiled up at him. "I love it."

And from the look in her eye, maybe it wasn't just the tattoo.

Adorned with their new art, the two headed out of the warehouse and back into the midday sunshine. Out in the parking lot, his black Mustang Cobra R shone like a polished piece of shadow. His muscle car remained a symbol of his past, haunted by the memories of his younger brother, Billy, a blurry mix of sorrow and joy—and also of responsibility.

I lived, and he died.

Duncan had always felt he needed to live for the both of them, for all his friends whose lives had been cut short.

After opening the passenger door for Jada, Duncan slipped behind the wheel. He touched the knob of the gearshift—only to have soft fingers land lightly on the back of his hand. He glanced over to see Jada's eyes shining at him, full of unspoken possibilities.

He remembered her story in the mountains, of entangled fates, of the prospect that death is just the collapsing of a life's potential in this one time stream, and that another door could open, allowing consciousness to flow forward in a new direction.

If so, maybe I don't have to live all those lives . . .

He leaned over and kissed her, recognizing in the heat of that moment that by attempting to live so many lives, he was failing to live his own.

"How fast can this car go?" she mumbled as their lips parted. A mischievous eyebrow lifted.

He matched it with a smile, curved just as devilishly.

He shifted into gear, punched the accelerator, and rocketed away. The car roared down the bright streets, no longer chased by the ghosts of the past but drawn forward by the promise of the future.

For in this world, one life was enough for any man.

4:44 P.M.

"Thanks for the lift," Gray said, shouldering his overnight bag as he climbed out of the SUV.

Kowalski lifted an arm in acknowledgment. Puffing on a cigar, he leaned over. "She was a great gal," he said, unusually serious and sincere. "She won't be forgotten. Or her uncle."

"Thanks," Gray said and pushed the door closed.

Kowalski tapped his horn good-bye and jammed back into traffic, coming close to sideswiping a bus.

Gray crossed to his apartment complex and headed across its grounds, frosted with new snow, making everything look pristine, untouched, hiding the messiness of life beneath that white blanket.

He had flown back an hour ago from the funeral services in Italy, where Vigor's body had been given full honors at a ceremony in St. Peter's. Likewise, Rachel's services were attended by the uniformed and marshaled forces of the Carabinieri. Her casket had been covered in the flag of Italy. Blasts of rifles had saluted at her graveside.

Still, Gray found no joy, no peace.

They were his friends—and he would miss them dearly.

He climbed the steps up to his empty apartment. Seichan was still in Hong Kong, slowly building some kind of relationship with her mother. They had found Ju-long's pregnant wife imprisoned on an island off Hong Kong, safe and unharmed. They had freed her, and according to Seichan, the woman had returned to Portugal.

On Macau, Guan-yin had filled with brutal efficiency the power vacuum left behind by Ju-long's passing. She was well on her way to becoming the new Boss of Macau. Using that position, she and Seichan were already taking steps to better the lives of women on the peninsula and across Southeast Asia, starting with the prostitution rings, holding them to stricter, more humane standards.

He suspected these early efforts were a small means of repairing the fence between mother and daughter. By lifting the burdens of other women who shared their same hard plight, they were helping themselves, as if repairing the present could dull the pain of their brutal pasts, to allow room for them to find each other again.

But it wasn't the only way.

Seichan had taken it upon herself to help the lost children of Mongolia, those homeless boys and girls who had fallen through the steamy cracks of a city struggling into the new world. He knew by rescuing them, she was rescuing that child of the past who had no one.

While in Mongolia, she had also checked on Khaidu. The young Mongolian girl was out of the hospital, her belly healing from the arrow wound. Seichan found her at her family's yurt, training with a young falcon—a high-spirited bird with gold feathers and black eyes.

Khaidu had named the bird Sanjar.

We each mourn and honor in our own way, he thought.

Gray reached his apartment door and found it unlocked.

Tensing, he slowly turned the knob and edged the door open. The place was dark. Nothing seemed amiss. He stepped cautiously inside.

Did I forget to lock the door before I left?

As he rounded past the kitchen, he caught a whiff of jasmine in the air. He saw a flickering light from under his closed bedroom door. He crossed and pushed it open.

Seichan had set out candles. She must have returned early from Hong Kong, perhaps sensing he could use company.

She lay stretched on his bed, on her side, up on an elbow, her long naked legs dark against the white sheets. The silhouetted curves of her sleek body formed a sigil of invitation. But there was no accompanying sly smile, no tease to her manner, only a subtle reminder that they both lived and should never take that for granted.

Seichan had told him what she had overheard at the inn back at

Khuzhir, about Vigor's terminal cancer, of the final words an uncle and niece were able to share. In this moment, he remembered Vigor's most important lesson about life.

. . . do not waste that gift, do not set it on a shelf for some future use; grab it with both hands . . .

Gray stalked forward, shedding clothes with every step, ripping what resisted, until he stood equally naked before her.

In that moment, with every fiber of his being, he knew the fundamental truth about life.

Live it now . . . who knows what will come tomorrow?

TAILS

For now we see through a glass, darkly.

—CORINTHIANS 13:12

November 26, 10:17 A.M. CET
Rome, Italy

Rachel waited outside the exam room for her uncle to finish meeting with his physician. Vigor had only come to the hospital upon her firm insistence, especially as she had no sound basis for demanding this battery of tests.

The door finally cracked open. She heard her uncle laugh, shake the doctor's hand, and come out.

"Well, I hope that satisfies you," Vigor said to her. "Clean bill of health."

"And the full-body MRI results?"

"Besides some arthritis in my hips and lower back, nothing." Vigor scooped an arm around her waist and headed toward the exit. "For a man in such good health in his sixties, the doctor said I should expect to live to a hundred."

Rachel could tell he was joking, but she also noted a flicker at the edge of his eyes, like he was trying to remember something.

"What?" she asked.

"I know you insisted on this cancer screening—"

She sighed loudly enough to cut him off. "Sorry. Ever since coming back from Olkhon Island, I just had this bad feeling, like you were sick or something." She shook her head. "I'm just being silly."

"That's just it; as I was lying there with that machine clacking loudly around me, I was almost sure you were right, too."

"Only because of my insistence."

"Maybe . . ." He sounded unconvinced and stopped before they reached the hospital doors. "I have to tell you something, Rachel. Back when I placed that crystal Eye atop the cross of St. Thomas, I felt this tearing inside me, like my very being was being ripped out . . . or split apart. It felt like I was riding a fountain of white light. I was sure I was dead. Then in a blink I was back, and there were Gray, Duncan, and Jada bursting inside to check on me."

Rachel squeezed his hand. "And I'm glad you were safe."

He stared down at her. "For just a moment then, as I turned to face them, I was overwhelmed with grief, like I'd lost you."

"But I was fine," she said—*okay, just barely.*

She again pictured that silver coin flipping in the air, bouncing across the wood planks of the floor, of Pak placing his boot on it. She had been furious at Seichan for telling him where Gray and the others had gone.

Then Pak had lifted his boot, revealing the backside of the coin.

Tails.

Pak had such a disappointed look on his face. She was suddenly sure in that moment, if it had come up *heads,* he would have killed her.

"I survived," Rachel said.

"Well, I know that because you came running in after the others a minute or so later." He headed back with her toward the door. "But it makes me wonder why we both had premonitions of doom for the other. I mean, I could have had cancer, I suppose. If some cell in my body flipped the wrong switch—*up* instead of *down*—I could very well be riddled with tumors."

"Heads or tails," Rachel mumbled.

Vigor smiled at her. "So much of life and death is random chance."

"That's disheartening."

"Not if you trust who is flipping the coins."

She rolled her eyes at him.

He pressed his point. "There are a thousand paths into the future, forks after forks in the road ahead. Who knows, if one road closes, maybe another opens in another universe . . . and your soul, your consciousness, leaps over to continue that journey ever forward, always finding the right path."

Still, Rachel considered those paths left *behind,* of possibilities that would be gone forever. A flicker of sadness pierced through her, as though she had lost dear friends.

"You see," Vigor said, drawing her attention back. "There's always a path *forward*."

"To where?" she asked.

Vigor pushed open the door, blinding her with the brightness of the new day. "Everywhere."

AUTHOR'S NOTE TO READERS: TRUTH OR FICTION

Time to separate the wheat from the chaff. As in previous books, I thought I'd attempt to divide the book into its blacks and whites. Though, to be honest, there are many *gray* areas in this novel that tread the line so finely between fact and fiction, between reality and speculation, that you can safely argue both sides of that equation. So let's go walking that line and see where we end up.

First, history is already a pretty frayed tapestry of truths, but what do we know with relative certainty?

Attila the Hun. In AD 452, Attila was about to sack Rome when Pope Leo the Great rode out with a small entourage, met the leader of the Huns, and somehow dissuaded him from attacking. How? One speculation is that Attila's forces were already facing disease and threats from other fronts, so he opted to save face, decamp, and leave. Another is that the pontiff played off Attila's superstitious fears and stoked his concerns about *Alaric's Curse,* as described in this book. Yet, others believe the pope did indeed give Attila enough gold and treasure to buy him off.

No matter the reason, he called off his plan, Attila would die the next year, just as he was planning to return to Italy and attack Rome. His death was by nosebleed and did occur on his wedding night, after marrying a young princess named Ildiko. Some theories state Ildiko poisoned her new husband; others that he simply died of chronic alcoholism, exasperated by a night of carousing after his wedding. No one really knows what happened to Ildiko after she was discovered at her dead husband's bedside.

As to his lost grave, it is said he was buried in a triple coffin of iron, silver, and gold, along with most of his vast treasure. The entourage who buried Attila were all killed. Most believe a river (likely the Tizsa in Hungary) was diverted, his tomb buried in the mud, and the river returned to its normal course. Which brings us again back to the Tizsa River for the . . .

Hungarian Witch Trials. The story of *Boszorkánysziget,* or Witch Island, is true. The island is located near the town of Szeged, where in July of 1728, a dozen witches (men and women) were burned. Over four hundred people were condemned to this fate during the height of the hysteria. Drought—with resultant famine and disease—is considered to be a major instigator for this panic, although, as described in this book, some of those deaths were politically or personally motivated. Nothing like a scourge of witches to get rid of an enemy.

Genghis Khan. Most of the details in this book regarding the Mongolian overlord are true. He was born with the name Temujin (and probably the more accurate spelling of his title is *Chinggis Khaan,* but I chose to use the more common spelling of Genghis Khan for clarity). And his official clan title was indeed *Borjigin,* meaning the Master of the Blue Wolf. That name is now one of the most common names in Mongolia, as is Temujin.

On a genetic note, it's also amazingly true that one out of two hundred men in the world is related genetically to Genghis (and that rises to one out of ten in Mongolia), as defined by twenty-five unique markers making up Haplogroup C-M217. So it seems multiple wives and conquering countries does leave its mark—at least, genetically.

And speaking of his offspring: In the Vatican Archives, there truly is a letter from Genghis Khan's grandson (Grand Khan Guyuk) to Pope Innocent IV, dated back in 1246, warning the pontiff not to visit the capital of his empire or there would be dire consequences.

From the standpoint of advancements, the Mongol Empire was ahead of its time, by discouraging torture, advocating paper money, developing a postal system, and allowing an unprecedented religious tolerance. The Nestorians did have a church in the capital city, and these early Christians were said to have a significant influence on Genghis Khan.

As to his grave site, that remains one of the world's greatest mysteries. Most do believe the site is located somewhere in the Khan Khentii Mountains, which are under strict restrictions for environmental and historical reasons. Many other sites (like Olkhon Island) make a similar case. It is also believed that Genghis's tomb is likely a necropolis, containing not only his treasure, but that of his descendants, including his most famous grandson, Kublai Khan. I don't know about you, but I'm ready to take a shovel and go digging.

St. Thomas and China. The apostle known most famously as "Doubting Thomas" is traditionally believed to have traveled to the East, definitely as far as India, where St. Thomas Christians (the Nasrani) still thrive. It is also said he was martyred there, near the ancient town of Mylapore, where there is a basilica marking that site. As to his relics, they have an even shadier history.

A few historians also advocate that St. Thomas may have traveled as far as China, and possibly even Japan. There are some new archaeological discoveries that suggest Christianity arrived in the Far East much earlier than the eighth century, as is currently believed.

As to the possibility of Chinese characters pointing to knowledge of the Old Testament, the figures in this book are true, and there are many more like these that can be found on the Internet—whether all this is wishful speculation or some hint at a lost history, I'll let you be the judge.

Jewish Incantation Skulls . . . and Other Macabre Oddities. Archaeologists have uncovered more than two thousand Jewish incantation bowls, most dated between the third and seventh centuries. But they've also found a few such skulls used for the same purpose, as a ward against demons or for the casting of spells. Two can be seen at the Berlin museum. And yes, *anthropodermic bibliopegy,* the binding of books with human skin, is a real thing. Some rare books have been found to include nipples or people's faces. They range from astronomy treatises to anatomic texts, even including a few prayer books. But the strangeness doesn't stop there. French prisoners during the Napoleonic Wars used to craft boats out of human bones and sell them to the British. Then again, I guess everyone needs a hobby.

One of the joys of writing these books is that I get to explore fascinating parts of the world. How much of what I depict is real about these places? The quick answer is almost everything. But let me cover some highlights.

Macau/Hong Kong. If you like gambling, Macau is the place to visit, with its mix of Portuguese colonialism, Chinese culture, and Las Vegas glitz. In many ways, it's a gold rush city, where corruption and commerce run hand in hand, where Chinese Triads war with politicians and developers. The descriptions of the VIP rooms in this book are real, from the junket operators to the money laundering. And yes, there really is a "Hooker Mall" in the basement shopping center of Casino Lisboa.

The Hong Kong that I describe here is accurate, too. In fact, I based the architecture for the headquarters of the *Duàn zhī* Triad on the current Chungking Mansions.

Aral Sea. This is probably the worst man-made ecological disaster. The diversion of two rivers by the Soviets in the early sixties dried up a once-thriving inland sea, transforming it into the deadly salt flats of the Aralkum Desert, where *black blizzards* do indeed blow, and where life expectancy has dropped locally from sixty-five to fifty-one. And yes, the entire region is dotted with the graveyards of beached ships.

North Korea. Everything described in this book is sadly real. In a country run by a lineage of despots who believe themselves semidivine, stories of decadent excess coupled with extreme deprivation are commonplace—like building a billion-dollar mausoleum during a major famine. North Korea's prison system is still considered to be the harshest in the world, where prisoners fight for the right to bury the dead for extra food, where the average inmate does not live longer than five years, and where torture is a rule of life. In the cities like Pyongyang, it is little better. The populace is in constant fear of saying or doing the wrong thing, while enduring strict rations of electricity and food.

Mongolia. Ulan Bator is considered to be the coldest capital city in the world. Steam tunnels do run underground, where a growing population of homeless people now reside, many of them children, victims of the economy, alcoholism, or simply neglect. But it is also a city with a bright future, with one of the fastest-growing economies in the world. It is a country of vast natural resources and an untouched beauty. And yes, much of the population holds Genghis Khan as a demigod. As a consequence, massive statues dot the capital city, including a 250-ton shimmering steel figure of Genghis atop a horse. But then again, when one out of ten men is his descendant, I suppose that's a requirement.

Lake Baikal. First, yes, the nerpa is the world's only freshwater seal and is native to Baikal, but it is only *one* of many unique features of the planet's oldest and deepest lake. Scientists have even coined the term *baikalology,* for the study of the lake's unusual biosphere. In regard to some specifics featured in the novel, the lake does indeed freeze over solid. And in winter, one of the main ways of reaching Olkhon Island is by bus over an ice road. On the island itself, Burkhan Cape is real and considered to be one of Asia's most sacred places. The island also does have many ties to Genghis

Khan, including being the birthplace of his mother and where many still believe he might be buried.

The science in this novel is again mostly based on proven facts or accepted theories, with some speculation and extrapolation (but not as much as you might imagine). Welcome to the weird world of dark energy, quantum physics, and things that go bump in the night.

Comets. I based Comet IKON on a real-life ice boulder passing by the earth in November 2013 (named Comet ISON). That comet is set to blaze in our skies, hopefully without as much mishap and death. Similar to the comet in this book, ISON is expected to be one of the brightest comets in history, even visible during the day.

As to the study of comets, the *IoG* endeavor was based on the voyage of the *ICE* satellite that NASA sailed through the tail of Halley's Comet back in 1986. In regard to comets causing problems, a comet did indeed slam into Jupiter in 1994, and another is set to hit Mars in 2014.

Throughout history, comets have frequently been the harbingers of doom, said to predict the bubonic plague of Europe, the Battle of Hastings, even the death of Mark Twain. And it is believed the appearance of Halley's Comet in 1222 was a major inspiration for Genghis Khan's decision to head west and conquer much of the known world.

Asteroids. The explosion of the Chelyabinsk meteor over Russia in February 2013 can be seen on many news sites. It's a prime example of the unpredictability of near-Earth objects (or NEOs). NASA has currently identified over ten thousand NEOs, but that number is only the tiniest fraction of what's out there, including what exploded over Russia. That asteroid had the potential kinetic energy of about thirty atomic bombs, but as it exploded in the upper atmosphere, it lost most of that energy before the pieces struck the ground. Still, the shock wave from that midair blast blew out windows and injured over fifteen hundred people.

The asteroid Apophis (designated 99942) featured in this novel is real and does pose a significant risk of hitting the earth, but not until 2029 or later. Still, as seen in Russia, there are many other unclassified planet-killers lurking out there.

The Eye of God. It's real. Or rather *they* are real. Scientists have created four flawless spheres of fused quartz, each so perfect that any defects are no larger than forty atoms. They are the gyroscopic hearts of NASA's Gravity Probe B satellite, where they will be testing the curvature of space-time around the earth. And hopefully not to explore Comet ISON, because as we all now know, that's not a very good idea.

Dark Energy. I could spend pages writing about the speculations concerning an energy that makes up 70 percent of the universe—yet no one really knows what it is. So it's difficult to say anything about this subject that could be considered a hard fact. One of the greatest descriptions I read is included in this book as Dr. Shaw's theory: *Dark energy is the result of the annihilation of virtual particles in the quantum foam.* But there are many other theories, too.

In preparing for this book, I was able to visit the Fermi National Accelerator Lab (Fermilab) outside of Chicago where I was fortunate to view its scientists' work on the new Dark Energy Camera, a 570-megapixel array engineered there and installed on a mountaintop telescope in Chile. Dr. Shaw uses some of the data collected by the DECam for her research in this book. This camera is so strong that it can peer three-quarters of the way back to the big bang. I hope they include this camera with the next generation iPhone.

Quantum Entanglement. It's a real phenomenon where particles interact, then depart, each flying away with the same quantum signatures—where a change in one will result in an instantaneous change in the other. It was initially thought to be limited to subatomic particles, but it has now been shown to happen in larger objects, including a pair of diamonds, visible to the naked eye, created by scientists in 2011.

Holograms and the Multiverse. Again, courtesy of Fermilab, I learned that the entire universe might be a hologram, a three-dimensional construct based on equations written on the inner shell of the universe. Researchers at the lab are currently constructing a *holometer,* the world's most sensitive laser interferometer to prove this is true. I find that very disturbing (or at least the equation that defines my hologram is disturbed).

Likewise, theories of multiple universes abound, with many different conjectures about how those other universes function, interact, and relate to one another. But the most common consensus among theoretical physicists is that *they exist.*

And on a minor note, what about those . . .

Magnetic Fingertips. First, I want them. . . . And, second, they are real and just as strange as I describe. In the world of biohacking, there are thousands of people with rare-earth magnets implanted near the nerve endings of their fingertips. It allows them to experience electrical fields in amazing ways. Those I've interviewed describe these fields as having texture, shape, rhythms, and even colors. It opens up an entirely new way of experiencing the world. And once accustomed to them, it's apparently hard to go back. Many say they feel *blind* without them. It definitely is a new world.

Last, I posited a theory of my own in these pages. If human consciousness is indeed a quantum effect and could possibly be tangled across multiple universes, who is to say that when we die (say, *get hit by a bus*) our consciousness might not somehow survive, shifting into that timeline or universe where we looked both ways and didn't get hit? In a life full of chance—where the flip of a coin so often decides your fate—it's comforting to know that there are other paths possibly open to us.

So until next time, enjoy the journey—no matter which path you take.